D1138493

You ca; Pearce was born in 1976 and has two young children. She completed an English Literature degree at Corpus Christi College Cambridge in 1998 and was a winner of the SCBWI anthology *Undiscovered Voices* in 2008.

More information about Bryony can be found on her website: www.bryonypearce.co.uk and you can follow her on twitter @BryonyPearce.

The Girl on the Platform

BRYONY PEARCE

avon.

Published by AVON
A division of HarperCollins*Publishers* Ltd
1 London Bridge Street
London SE1 9GF

www.harpercollins.co.uk

HarperCollins*Publishers*
1st Floor, Watermarque Building, Ringsend Road
Dublin 4, Ireland

A Paperback Original 2021
2
First published in Great Britain by HarperCollins*Publishers* 2021

A catalogue copy of this book is available from the British Library.

ISBN: 978-0-00-844184-5

Typeset in Sabon LT Std by Palimpsest Book Production Limited,
Falkirk, Stirlingshire

Printed and bound in UK by CPI Group (UK) Ltd, Croydon CR0 4YY

MIX
Paper from
responsible sources
FSC C007454

To my husband, Andy,
and to my children, Maisie and Riley.

The girl is curled into such a tiny space that it seems she wants to disappear. Her feet are tucked so far up that her knees touch her narrow chin. Her trembling hands are wrapped around them. She's been shivering for a long time.

There is little light but, somehow, she has found it and it picks out her tear-stained face, cruelly highlighting the lines of her misery. One of her arms is hurt; she is wearing a bandage and cradling it carefully. The fingers of this hand do not hold her knee as tightly as those of the other. She has sock marks: ridged indents and a tan line that begins just above her ankle bone and vanishes under a pale yellow dress. She has old scabs on her knees and a fresh cut on one skinny elbow. There is a scar on her forehead, a faint smile of white skin, a little puckered. Her dark hair has been cut short but her eyes could be any colour. They are tightly closed, as if she is wishing herself away.

And she is crying. Her tears sparkle in the dusty glow and soak into the primrose material, darkening

1

her collar and sticking it to her skin. But she is crying silently. Sniffing into her elbow, desperately keeping quiet. She is not calling for her mother. She isn't calling for anyone.

Chapter 1

The District Line is closed, Euston impenetrable. Commuters, who know where they are going, are attempting to hustle around tourists, who don't. They crowd the centre of the concourse, forming an obstacle course of suitcases and swinging rucksacks.

The noise is making my already aching head pound: tinny announcements, parents shouting for their kids to *behave*, to *get back here*, the raucous laughter of a hen-party wearing sashes so pink they hurt my eyes. A row breaks out on my right; someone has trodden on someone else. It is all too much. I want to be home.

My belly wobbles as I up my pace, the jelly-like, post-baby jiggle unabated despite my vows to get back into pre-maternity clothes. I resolutely refuse to buy new work outfits and now my waistband is torturing me, cutting me in half, despite two unhooked buttons. With each step the yoke pulls tight over my wobbling backside.

I keep my head down, pushing towards the escalator, too-high shoes ticking on the floor, sweat tickling my body, exhaustion hanging off me like my unseasonal winter coat. My fingers keep loosening on my bag, as if my body has decided to just shut down and stop, regardless of my location. I lift the case higher and use it to batter my way towards the stair. If I miss this train, I'm facing a half-hour wait till the next one. Midnight before I can drop into bed and another day without feeling Grace's fingers around mine or looking into her eyes. I'll see her in the middle of the night when she wakes for a feed, and maybe in the morning, but she is like her mum; a grumpy waker, offended to have been dragged from her dreams by the demands of her stomach.

Just the thought of dreams makes my eyes shutter closed. I groan and start past a couple with a pram, my thoughts once again turning to my own baby and the Bugaboo I won't be using myself until the weekend.

'Excuse me, Miss? How do we get to the Underground?'

It hurts too much to look at them. I don't want to see their, no doubt sleeping, infant when I haven't seen Grace since the night before. I mutter something half-formed, refuse eye contact, point vaguely behind me and hurry on.

Finally, my feet hit metal and I sway to a stop, letting the moving step sweep me upward, my eyes on a pink chunk of bubble gum fingerprinted underneath the handrail, as if someone had wanted to leave evidence of themselves behind. The pressure of humanity eases slightly, and I relax, for a brief moment, just in time to be shoulder-barged by two teenage boys who yell as they race past, as though it is my fault, as though I too should be running full tilt. I stagger into the rail and a hand from behind steadies me.

'All right?' An impression of kind brown eyes, a turban. I nod and drop my head again, rubbing my shoulder with one hand, staring at my scuffed shoes. *God, what a day.*

I turn my thoughts once more towards home as I stumble through the ticket barrier and onto the platform, taking another breath as the queue is forced into single file by the machine that counts us through. The train is already here, and I adopt a shambling run, ignoring my aching feet. A wail of a siren from beyond the fence triggers the prickle of my let-down reflex. A whistle and the doors start to slide shut. 'No!' I wail, hurling myself faster, off-balance, tottering.

The guard sees me and sighs. He knows me. He should; I am here every day, Monday to Friday. I'd even introduced him to Grace when I brought her into work a few months ago, her tiny wriggling body still scrawny from the birth. He puts one hand out and holds the door beside him, waving me forward. I half sob my gratitude as I reach the step. He catches me with his other hand as I stumble. 'Careful.'

I nod, too tired to form words, my lips numb.

He tugs me on board and I almost sag into him, but he settles me on my feet and points. 'I saw an empty window seat two carriages down.' He winks.

I nod my thanks again, feeling a little like the Churchill dog. His eyes say he understands, and he lets me go. The train lurches and I grip the doorframe, then the top of seats as I pull myself along, fighting the sway, mumbling half-apologies as I touch greasy hair, or slip and grab a shoulder by mistake. Too much humanity. Too many people leaving bits of themselves all over the place.

Two carriages seem impossibly far. I hold my bag in one hand and try not to bump elbows with strangers as the aisle grows longer with every step. I force my way past a group who have chosen to stand in the gap between carriages, passing round a bottle of Schnapps. Someone offers it to me with a giggle, I shake my head and, eventually, I see it: the empty seat. Empty because the one beside it is occupied by a man two sizes too big for the space between the arm rests. He overflows. I don't even consider standing. My feet can't take it, but I *can* take being pressed against cool glass.

'Excuse me,' I have to think before verbalising; remember the shape my lips are supposed to make. I gesture towards the seat and the bristly velour that will itch even through my trousers.

The man raises his head and his brows, then sighs and makes a big deal of standing, forcing me backwards as he edges into the aisle, thick thighs making the table creak. Sweat stains the cotton of his shirt, as though even clothes cannot contain him. Opposite, a young woman looks up and then back down again, her expression unchanging. She is wearing head-phones and the light from her phone cools her face, brightening her chin and dulling her eyes. Beside her a kid, with a graphic novel and acne, sniggers as the fat man flushes.

I nod my thanks yet again and inhale as I squeeze into the seat, dump my bag on the table and sigh. For one moment my whole body relaxes into the welcome chair, then the man sits back down.

I can tell he is trying to make himself smaller; the boy opposite catches my eye with a smirk, but I ignore him. How awful to know what everyone around you must think. The man pulls his elbows into his sides; even his face is pinched, his features appearing squashed into the centre of a space too large for them. His forehead wrinkles, his eyes darting from side to side as if daring me to comment. I say nothing, only lean against the window as his forearms bulge into mine and his flesh presses against me, one hairy wrist tickling my own.

I pull into myself, turtle-like, curl my hands into my lap, and make myself as small as possible. His eyes go to my breasts, by now straining and pneumatic, and remain there.

The window is cool against my forehead. I turn towards the dark glass. My reflection stares back at me as if in shock. Dark hair, frizzing out of the ponytail I hurriedly constructed with an elastic band at lunchtime, skin white, eyeshadow smudged, so that, with the bags beneath my eyes, it seems as if I've recently lost a fight. My lips remain full and, so Tom says, kissable, but the lipstick has long since bled away, leaving patchy colour, like sickness.

The way I'm sitting emphasises the beginnings of

a double chin that I'll have to diet away as soon as I can face it. This is my post-baby face; the stranger's features which covered my own like a mask, after Grace. Gone the bright eyes, the healthy flush, the carefully applied make-up, the definition. Hello to a doughy, fleshy almost-me. A washed-out version of myself, like a watercolour dissolving in the rain.

I close my eyes, pushing the image away, trying to remember who I'm meant to be: Senior Manager in a London research agency, university graduate, party girl, fun wife, dutiful daughter, but my thoughts keep skittering away, to a sleeping Grace and to Tom, who'll be watching the telly with a beer and a bag of crisps by now.

My consciousness starts to slip, so I check my phone. Fifty minutes and we'll pull into my station. With fumbling fingers, I set an alarm: forty-five minutes. I can't risk sleeping through my stop, not again.

Last time Tom had been forced to wake Grace and they'd both come to collect me from the end of the line. Neither of them had been happy about it. I leave the phone on the table and lay one hand over the screen, as if I am protecting it, or it is protecting me. I'm not sure. I lean my head on the window.

'Good idea.' The fat man meets my eyes in the black glass, and I blink at him. Is he really trying to start a conversation? My fingers twitch on my phone. I close my eyes again, but sleep doesn't come. This has been happening more and more often. My body is so tired that I feel as if I don't hold on tightly enough, I might float away. But I can't stop thinking.

Always there is guilt over leaving Grace for so long, even though she is with Tom and we'd agreed that it made the most sense, financially, that I be the one to go back to work. There is the worry that she'll always love him best, and then remorse at such a selfish thought. Why shouldn't she? Just because I carried her, suffered unbearable backache, nausea and heartburn, endured contractions for two days, transition for over an hour, eighteen stiches, mastitis when she was first feeding, did Tom deserve her love any less?

Concerns about my most recent client bob to the surface. They keep moving the goalposts, requiring changes to the project and that will mean more late nights in my future.

I remember that I promised to have Mum over for dinner and worry about the hours I'll have to spend tidying up before she arrives.

My mental screen flicks to an argument I had with a girl at university, who has almost certainly never thought of me again. She makes a comment about me stealing Tom from her friend Trish. The things I said and the things I should have said.

That is crowded out by memories of the mess the baker made of our wedding cake and how I should never have paid her the full amount.

And I desperately need my roots done.

And I wonder whether Tom has done the washing up or if it'll be waiting for me again.

Then, over it all, an old Taylor Swift song which winds around and around my brain, digging its claws in until I want to *scream*.

My eyes flinch open, but my body remains heavy, immovable.

We are rushing by a station. One of those unidentifiable places with nothing but a platform and a dirt carpark, an unmanned ticket machine and a bench. The sign is black lettering on a dirty background, too fast to read. A sound like rushing water as the train hurtles past the platform. Opposite me, the girl opens a packet of biscuits and the fat man's eyes tear from my breasts.

Where are we? I force a glance at my phone: twenty-five minutes in. I fire off a text to Tom: *On the train. Back soon. Hope she went down okay.*

The phone beeps at me. *Unable to send message.* No signal.

I sigh and press my forehead against the window once more. This time I gaze beyond my reflection, peering into the murk at flashing streetlights and glowing cars. Another platform is coming up. I strain my eyes, trying not to think about lyrics and seeking to banish the bouncy tune that rattles around my brain: *Everything will be all right, if we just keep dancing like we're twenty-two . . .*

My eyes blur.

A white van is parked by the platform, no markings, the paintwork a flag against the darkness. From a weathered concrete post, a single light glows, illuminating a little girl. She sits on a case outside the shuttered coffee booth, kicking her heels against the leather. She can't be more than six. Where's her mum?

The train doesn't slow. We aren't stopping. We are going to burn past, leaving her behind in a swirl of leaves and dust.

I blink. And men are there, two of them. They lift the squirming girl to her feet, haul her towards the van . . . and then we are past.

I bang my palms on the window.

'Did you see that?' I strain to look back, but trees are flashing by and now a row of houses, long gardens backing onto the rails. 'Did you see?' I turn to the young woman sitting opposite.

She barely glances up from her phone. 'See what?'

'The girl. You must have seen her!' I look at the boy. He doesn't even acknowledge that I've spoken, but they are both facing the wrong way anyway. I grab the fat man's arm. 'You saw, didn't you? You saw the girl . . . and the men?'

He blinks at my hand and then lifts his eyes to my face. 'Huh?'

'The girl at the last platform, you saw her?'

He shakes his head. 'It's dark out there.'

'I know, I—' I grab my phone. 'I have to call the police.' I stare at the screen. No signal.

The train clatters on.

I drop the phone back on the table and leap to my feet, wobbling with the movement on the rails. 'Did anyone else see? Did anyone see the girl? The van?'

People glare at me.

'There was a girl.' I am screaming, my voice hoarse and cracked. 'At that last station, a kid. Come on, one of you must have seen her!'

The fat man puts his hand on my arm. 'Are you all right?'

The young woman opposite is gaping with wide-eyed alarm.

'We've got to do something. One of you must have seen her too.' I pinpoint the woman sitting in the same seat as me, a table behind, a blonde I occasionally see doing the same morning journey. '*You* saw her, didn't you?' My finger lifts, trembling. 'You must have.'

She slides slightly sideways, as if my finger is a loaded weapon, and shakes her head.

'You then?' I turn to the student sitting next to her. He shrugs and looks uncomfortable. He whispers something to the girl sitting opposite. She giggles.

I want to shake shoulders until someone says yes, they saw her. I am trapped in my seat.

'Please, just speak up. We can call the police together.'

Sniggers. Mutterings. A rustle of papers as commuters tuck their eyes back into their *Metros* or bury their faces in books. A couple of kids lift their phones, videoing me. The lights from their cameras gleam.

'Wasn't *anyone* looking out the window?' I plead.

'It's dark out,' someone yells.

'Sit down, you crazy cow.' An older teen, gel in his hair, leather jacket, laughing with his mates.

'You're embarrassing yourself.' The fat man's eyes are filled with sympathy. 'I don't know what you saw, but no-one else was looking. *Sit down.*'

'There was a little girl.' I thump back into my seat, pulling my coat around me. 'I–I think she was being kidnapped.'

The man shifts awkwardly in his seat. 'Are you *sure*?' he whispers.

I nod, then jump as my phone beeps: *Message sent.* For a long second I am unable to work out what it means. Then I grab for the slick handset, fumbling so it skids away from me.

The man stops it sliding and pushes it back towards me. 'You're really going to call the police?'

'I have to.' I clutch the phone like Grace gripping Frankie-Lion.

'They'll want to question the whole carriage,' he hisses. 'Maybe the whole train. People won't be able to get home.'

For a shameful second, I hesitate. How awful it would be to draw all this attention, to cause all this trouble, to make all this *noise*. Not something that nice girls do.

I bite my lip. 'It was a *little girl*,' I murmur. 'They'll understand.'

Chapter 2

I stumble up the steps on trembling legs and try three times to get my key into the lock. When it finally slides in, I lean my head on the paintwork, trying to muster the energy to force the door open. The door creaks, letting out a sliver of light as I sprawl inside. Tom catches me.

'Are you drunk?' He glares at me with narrowed, bloodshot eyes. 'Because if you are, you're not going in to see Grace. She's been up for the last fifty minutes and I've only just got her back to sleep.' He scrubs at his chin, three days' worth of stubble, and holds me at arm's length. 'You sent me a text *three hours ago* saying you were on the train. What happened?'

'Please, Tom,' I murmur. 'Let me sit down.'

He sighs and helps me over the stoop. 'Seriously, Bridge, you look awful. Are you all right? I tried calling, but your phone must have died . . . I even rang your mum.'

'You *didn't*!' The expression on his face stops me from saying more. But now I have another concern: Mum will be up worrying until she hears from me. 'I'm sorry.' I drop my bag in the hall and wrap my arms around my chest. 'I couldn't call. I wanted to . . .' I tail off.

His expression shifts from annoyance to concern, his blue eyes darkening. 'What would stop you from letting us know where you were?' His voice lowers. 'We can't go through this again. I mean I thought the anti-depressants were working. I mean when Doctor Lewis prescribed them, she said they would help.'

I nod. 'It's not that.' I clutch at his arm, wondering how much to tell Mum. 'I have to get off my feet – *please*.'

He guides me into the living room and, despite exhaustion that makes me lean my whole weight on his shoulder, I track the mess: his laptop and script-writing course books, two empty beer bottles, an empty packet of Tyrells crisps, a crumpled blanket, a cushion on the floor, Grace's baby bouncer, her playmat speckled with crumbs, and a dirty nappy thrown into a corner, the smell a ripe blend of shit and spilled milk.

I close my eyes, but not before Tom has traced them to the nappy. 'I had to change her before I put her back down.' Defensive. 'It's not been there that long.'

I nod and kick off my shoes with a groan. 'It doesn't matter.'

'*Obviously* it does.'

I force my eyes open, make myself look at him. 'Don't. Please. I've been with the police.'

'The police?' Tom pales. 'What happened? Are you hurt?' His face hardens. 'Has someone hurt you, Bridge?'

'No, it isn't that.' I grip his hands. 'It was horrible. And no-one else saw. Only me. But the police made everyone stay on the train until they'd taken their details. They were furious. The people on the train, I mean.' My words stumble over one another, as clumsy as my feet. I lean over to pick up Frankie-Lion. His beanbag body sags over my palm and he smiles up at me. I put him to my cheek. He smells of Grace: baby smell and milk, and a little bit of Tom's aftershave. Frankie must have been crushed between them at nap time.

'What happened?' he asks again, this time rubbing my back in small circles. 'Can you tell me?'

'There was a little girl.' I look at Frankie again and choke on a sob. Did the girl have a Frankie too? Was she terrified and alone and desperate for comfort? 'Oh, God!'

Tom looks stricken. 'What happened, Bridge?'

I peer at him through tear-blurred eyes. 'We went past a station – I don't know which one. The police kept asking but we went by so fast – you know what it's like – you can't read the signs . . . but I saw a little girl.'

'By herself?' Tom frowns. 'At that time of night?'

'That's what the police said too.' I swallow. 'She was sitting on a suitcase. I saw that much. I don't know why, or where she was going or . . . or where her mum was. Maybe getting a ticket, I don't know. She was about six I think, just sitting there on the suitcase.' I frown. 'She was wearing a school uniform, a blazer like your niece's. It was almost like she was looking right at me, but she couldn't have been.' I look at my hands. Frankie's arms and legs dangle on either side of my palm. 'These two people grabbed her.'

'Are you sure?' Tom murmurs.

I nod.

'It couldn't have been her dad, or . . .?'

'She struggled.' I blink away tears. They had a white van. I saw her being taken, Tom, and I couldn't even tell the police where she was taken *from*. It was just a platform and by the time I had a signal we'd gone by at least three more. They could be anywhere now. And they've got her and she's *just a little girl.*'

'Sssh.' Tom glances at the baby monitor blinking at me from the side table and I realise I am wailing.

I drop Frankie. 'There's a little girl out there and someone's hurting her.' My cheeks are wet now, salty dampness on my lips. 'What was the point in seeing her if I can't tell the police anything useful?'

Tom presses my hands between his. 'You're freezing.' He rubs his palms against the backs of mine. 'Come and look in on Grace. You'll feel better.'

I shake my head. 'What good am I?'

'Bridge.' Tom puts his forehead against mine. 'You won't be the only one to have called the police about this. Her *mum* will have reported her missing. They'll be able to work out where she was taken from. They might even have found her already. You've done more than most people would have. Come on. You need to get warm. Take your tablets and come to bed.'

'I can't,' I groan. 'I have to call Mum. You know she'll be awake until I do.'

'I'll do it.' Tom pulls me to my feet. 'I'll tell her the train was stuck; signal problems. I know you don't like to lie but . . .'

I nod, my eyelids like shutters, my head heavy. 'She'd rush over here if you told her the truth. Do you really think they've found her already?'

'All the platforms have CCTV. You told them about the van, about the two men. They're probably knocking on doors right now. It'll be in the news tomorrow or later in the week, I guarantee it.' Tom pulls me to my feet. 'Come on, it's late and you're done. I'm switching your alarm off. I'll get up with Grace in the morning.'

'But it's your turn for a lie-in,' I groan, sagging against him as if I have beans in my own torso, but I'm already thinking about the latest train that will get me into work on time.

Tom snorts. 'You can pay me back at the weekend.' He guides me to the stairs. My feet are like wood and I am barely able to bend my knees. 'Or on Neil's stag do. I'm planning to drink like a Viking and will be mightily hungover.'

I stumble upwards and into the dark hallway. Grace's door is a little ajar. It took us months to realise that she hated the full dark and needed a sliver of light to sleep. Like her mother.

I hesitate at the doorway and Tom pushes it further open. Inside I can hear Grace's soft breathing: a gentle snore on every other breath. She lies on her back, one fist curled next to her cheek. Her knees are splayed outwards, frog-like in her sleeping bag. Wispy

18

blonde hair is glued to her forehead, stuck there with tearstains and sleep-sweat.

She twitches in her sleep and, as I watch, her fists open and close, and her legs scythe back and forth. 'It's too hot for her pink pyjamas,' I mutter.

Tom shrugs. 'We spilled milk on the yellow ones. She'll be all right. I used the lighter sleeping bag.'

I nod.

He frowns. 'I do know what I'm doing.'

I lean against the doorframe for one more minute, counting her breaths, wishing I could hold her. 'I should have brought Frankie up.'

'And risk waking her?' Tom shakes his head. 'She's got Dobbie, look.'

Sure enough, the little, once-white bunny is crushed beneath her armpit.

'Come on.' He nudges me and I nod again. 'Don't bother cleaning your teeth.' Tom steers me into our bedroom and sits me on the mattress. I sink into it, already, in my mind, fast asleep.

He helps me out of my coat and jacket, undoes my blouse and trousers.

'I'm checking you out, just so you know, sexy thing.' He makes me lie down. 'Hang on, I'm going to call your mum quickly, then I'll bring you your medication.'

I pull myself up on the pillow, drag my arms out of my blouse, leave my underwear on and crawl under the duvet. I hear Tom's voice, then the sound of running water. After a moment he appears with two pills in one hand and a glass in the other.

19

I struggle to focus. 'Was she all right?'

Tom nods. 'You'll have to call her tomorrow.'

'I feel gross,' I murmur. 'My teeth are furry.'

'Brush them twice in the morning.' Tom strokes my hair back from my face. 'Take these.'

I lift my head just enough to gulp down water and the green and yellow bullets. Then I let my head fall back. Tom puts the glass on the side table next to my breast pump.

'I thought you might need it,' he says, nodding towards it.

'I do.' I roll away. 'I can't.'

'Okay.' He clambers onto the bed, lies beside me and pulls his legs up so that they cup mine.

'Will you stroke my head?' I whisper. 'My brain won't shut off.'

'Yes, it will.' Tom's cool fingers find my eyebrows and begin to stroke up and down, softly, distractingly. 'Go to sleep.'

'I ca . . .'

I wake way too early because I roll onto my left breast. It's a rock. I gasp myself into alertness as pain, like a poked bruise, shivers down my side.

'Don't wake Grace!' Tom is sitting up beside me. Our daughter is lying on his chest, arms and legs dangling on either side of his ribcage, her face crumpled against his t-shirt.

'I've got to express.' I struggle to sit, trying not to rock the bed. 'What time is it?'

'Six-thirty,' Tom whispers. 'Can't it wait?'

'Are you joking?' I point.

Tom goggles. 'I guess it can't.'

'I'm in agony.' I slide my legs out of the bed, watch them pimple in the autumn chill and grab the pump. 'I'll do it in the bathroom.'

'Are you sure?' Tom sits unmoving, his hands flat on the covers.

'Do you want anything?' I mouth. 'A book, your phone, a bit of coursework?'

He shakes his head. 'It'll only wake her.'

I stagger into the bathroom, pee and set up the breast pump. I shouldn't really be breastfeeding, not anymore, not on top of work, and maybe not while I'm on the Fluoxetine, although the doctor said it would be okay. But Grace has some kind of dairy allergy or maybe an intolerance, I'm still not clear on the difference. She hates the Nutramigen prescribed by the hospital, just spits it at us. My breast milk is at least free and, as long as I don't eat any dairy myself, it doesn't upset her stomach. I start to hand pump, my eyes half-closed, almost dozing, but nothing happens, my breasts are too hard. It had been stupid to risk mastitis again for the sake of a bit of sleep.

I sigh, run the hot tap, wet a face cloth and start stroking by hand. Eventually liquid dribbles down my stomach. I refit the pump and, finally, milk hisses into the plastic bottle. I close my eyes again, knowing I'll hear when it is almost full.

As soon as my eyes drift shut, I see the little girl, as clearly as if she is sat in front of me. She has brown hair, shoulder length and a little curly. Her eyes are hooded by a thick fringe but I think perhaps they're dark, like mine. Her face is narrow, her chin a little pointed, her nose straight and long.

She is wearing a blazer, almost as if she is going off to boarding school. Very *Malory Towers*. The suitcase she is sitting on is old-fashioned, leather, you don't see those around much. Perhaps her family is poor. But then, what about the blazer? I'll know who she is soon. Tom's right, she'll be on the news and I'll get a name to go with that face.

I open my eyes and check the bottle: eight ounces in less than five minutes. It has to be a record and the breast isn't even empty. I swap the bottle over, cap the full one and change sides.

Despite my greying maternity knickers, my flabby stomach sticks to my upper legs. 'Sexy thing' Tom called me. I know he loves me and he wants to help, but I'm not sexy, not anymore, so how can I trust anything he says when he lies like that to my face?

He's a good liar too. I'd have told Mum the truth last night and been up for an hour talking her off a ledge. Tom came up with a comforting and plausible story and was off the phone in minutes. I'd never mastered the skill.

When I have two full bottles and my discomfort has eased, I face myself in the mirror. Stretch marks, cellulite, sagging where I'd once had taut skin. My muscles are knitting back together, but slowly. I run my fingers over my waistline. Seven and a half months ago I made a human, squeezed her out of me, now

I am feeding that human. I'm not meant to be a stick figure right now. And yet.

'Sexy thing,' I mock in a whisper and then I turn my face away.

I put the bottles of milk on the bedside table and crawl back into bed, trying to be soundless, hoping the mattress won't rock and roll with me. I turn so I am facing Tom and put a hand on his shoulder, close enough that it's almost as though I am touching Grace. Then I let my eyes fall on my daughter's sleeping face.

'Are you all right?' Tom asks.

I nod. 'Just happy to be home.' Then I close my eyes and drift back to sleep.

When I wake again, Tom and Grace are gone and so are the bottles. I touch my breast. I'd been hoping to hear her cry when she woke, planning to feed her myself, desperate for a moment of closeness before I went into work. The pump makes me feel like a cow hooked to a machine, wondering where its calf has gone. Breastfeeding is comfort and love and I'd needed that this morning. Anger squirms in my belly and I clench my fists.

'Will it matter in six weeks?' I mutter. 'Am I being unreasonable?' I exhale. Of course I am. Tom is letting me sleep in, knowing it means I'll have to work late, leaving him to do bedtime alone again. He doesn't know I'm still full after producing sixteen ounces. 'He was being a good guy.' I sit up. 'And *you're* being ungrateful.'

I spot my dressing gown on the back of the door and smile. I'd left it on the kitchen chair the day before so Tom must have brought it up. I check the time: it's nine. Tom's been looking after Grace for at least three hours. I should get up. If I hustle, I can catch the half-past train, but I crave Grace like a junkie. If I spend half an hour with her now, I can still get into work before the 11 a.m. meeting.

I slip my arms into my robe, tie it closed and find my slippers. I hesitate for a moment, wanting to go and find my baby, but my mouth tastes like yesterday's McDonald's and I need to clean my teeth. I do as Tom suggested and clean them twice. Then I pad downstairs.

I find Tom and Grace in the living room. Grace is in her baby bouncer and Tom is on the sofa with one arm over his face.

'Hi,' I whisper, suddenly hoarse, and Grace catches sight of me. Her eyes shine and she babbles wildly, lifting her arms and clutching her hands as if she can grasp me from the doorway and carry me to her.

Instantly, I'm on my knees beside her, barely aware of moving across the room. I scoop her up and hold her tightly, putting my nose against the patch of warm skin behind her ear and inhaling: Johnson & Johnson baby cream, sleep sweat and something indefinably baby, uniquely Grace. One day I'll reach for that smell and it'll be gone. I want to cry at the thought.

I teeter on the precipice of the anxiety that's gripped me for months. The feeling that every moment with Grace is rushing away from me and the terror that

24

any second, she'll be taken: first by Sudden Infant Death Syndrome, then by other illnesses, accidents, some grasping stranger, time itself. It is all going too fast; she is changing too fast. She'll be at preschool before I know it. I gasp.

Her hair is soft against my forehead, her skin like cream.

Grace wriggles, pushing against my chin, gurgling and babbling as she berates me for being so late, and regales me with incomprehensible tales of all the things I've missed.

I peer past her to see Tom grinning at me. He's missed my moment of vertiginous terror, thank goodness. 'She's missed you.'

I smile.

'She's been annoyed all morning, desperate to go upstairs and find you. Maybe she'll forgive me now.' He sits up. 'I called your office and told them you wouldn't be in today. Is that okay?'

I nod, relief unwinding in my gut.

'Do you want a coffee?'

I nod again. 'Almond milk, remember.'

'I know.' He rolls his eyes. 'I'm not a complete idiot.'

'Sorry.' I stroke Grace's back, letting my fingers linger on her warm neck. 'Coffee would be great.'

Tom leaves us alone together. There had been a time a few months back when he'd watched me like a spy in a Bond film, driving me crazy . . . crazier I suppose. But now he trusts that I won't break; even after last night, he trusts it. Or rather he believes in the drugs. I glance at the kitchen. He isn't peering around the door at us while the kettle boils. In fact, I can see him looking at his phone, probably checking the football scores. Trusting me.

I smile into Grace's hair and she grabs mine and yanks it hard enough to make me wince. I detangle it from her fist.

'Mummy's fault. I should have tied it back.' I push it behind one shoulder. 'What did you tell the office?' I call as I tickle her tummy and she squeals out a giggle.

Tom sticks his head around the door. 'Migraine.' He gestures. 'Gives you a day off with no awkward questions.'

Another smooth lie told for my benefit. I can hardly object. 'Thank you.' I tilt my chin towards the clock. 'I *could* have gone in. I was thinking about the ten o'clock train.'

He shakes his head. 'Not today.' He vanishes for a moment and returns with a coffee cup. 'I'll put it up here, so she can't get hold of it.'

'How would she get hold of it?' I frown.

'She's starting to pull herself up.' As if she has heard him, Grace wriggles out of my grip, reaches for the coffee table and hauls herself, wobbling, onto her pudgy little feet.

I watch, open-mouthed. 'Is that normal? Should she be doing that already?'

Tom looks like he's won the lottery. 'She's going to be a runner, like her dad.'

'I missed the first time. Did you video it?'

Tom bites his lip. 'Sorry.'

'It's okay.' I focus on Grace. She is grinning at me. Showing two front teeth and a reddened gum; teething again. I smile. 'Yes, you're *very* clever, baby.'

She thumps back onto her padded bottom and reaches for Frankie-Lion.

'I . . .' I look up at Tom and take a deep breath. 'I know we said it made most sense for me to be the one to go back to work. I know we said you should stay at home with her and that you could do that course . . . but . . .'

'But it's killing you.' Tom kneels beside me and the scent of his shower gel tickles my shrivelled libido. 'I can see that.'

'What can we do?' I laugh bitterly. 'We can barely afford the bills on *my* salary. Move into an even smaller place?'

Grace smacks a button on her bouncer and *Twinkle, Twinkle, Little Star* twangs into the air.

Tom touches my shoulder. 'Your health's the most important thing. I'll sign up with a recruitment agent on Monday, see what's out there. I can do coursework in the evenings.' He looks at Grace, his expression regretful. He doesn't want to leave her any more than I do, and he doesn't want to go back to office work, but one of us has to. I rest my cheek on his hand. He touches my hair. 'I still think it's crazy you won't ask your mum for help. Wouldn't she loan us enough so you can have a breather? Just a few months of mortgage payments would ease the burden. You could go back to work when you're ready.'

I flinch. 'She *does* help. She takes Grace one day a week so you can write. That saves us a fortune in nursery fees. And she's already given us—'

'It doesn't have to be a gift. We could make it a loan, draw up a repayment plan. Neil will spunk legalese all over it, if we ask him.'

'So, *Neil* would know we need a loan from Mum.' I stiffen and he pulls away.

'Just think about it?' He focuses on me with that look, the one that says I'm his whole world. The one I'd do anything for. His eyelids crinkle. 'Even if I go back to work tomorrow, I wouldn't be earning as much as you.'

'And it would be another job you hate.' I sigh. 'What about your parents? Wouldn't Charlie and June—'

Tom squeezes my shoulder. 'They would if they could. If they had any money at all, they'd give it to us.'

'So why won't my mum?' I add the unspoken sentence. 'I just don't like to ask. She's been on her own since Dad . . . you know. She *needs* financial security. That cushion helps her feel safe. I can't take that away, even if it's only borrowing it for a while.'

'I do get it, Bridge. But at some point, you have to ask yourself which is worse: asking your mum for a loan, which she honestly can afford to give us, or going to work when all you want is to be home with Grace?'

I wipe my face, I'm leaking like a tap, more tears. 'If she offered, I'd take it, but *asking* her for money . . . it feels wrong.'

'Just think about it.' Tom hands another block to

Grace who bangs it on the first one and grins up at him. They're so alike.

Tom reaches over my head and picks the remote off the table. 'I know we don't usually, but would it kill her to have a bit of *Paw Patrol*?'

Grace has already seen the remote and she knows what it means. She yells excitedly at the television until Tom pushes the button and the screen lights up.

'I thought we'd agreed the TV doesn't work in the mornings,' I say, and he shrugs.

'It doesn't . . . usually.'

'Tom . . .'

'Look how happy she is.'

And she is. She crawls into Tom's lap as she watches, mesmerised, one fist in her mouth, the other clutching Frankie. I roll my eyes and focus on the mantra Aunt Gillian gave me to help me through my teenage years. 'Will it matter –'

'– in six weeks' time?' Tom finishes and I laugh. 'It *might*.'

'It won't, honestly. A couple of episodes of *Paw Patrol* won't send her square-eyed.'

I sigh and watch for a moment, the bright colours on the screen an incomprehensible blur. My thoughts return to the night before and I pull my phone from my dressing gown pocket.

Tom frowns, 'What are you doing?'

'I just want to check the news.' I look at him. 'Is that okay?'

His face tightens. 'Are you sure? Now? In front of Grace?'

'I need to know.'

'Fair enough, but it's still early, don't be surprised if there's nothing.'

I lean against his shoulder and scroll through the BBC website.

Politics, which I have to avoid unless I want to spiral into further depression. An over-tired lorry driver has caused a pile-up on the M5, two dead. Another stabbing. A celebrity I've barely heard of has got engaged. Yet another store I like is going into administration. That footballer is being arraigned. I keep scrolling down past more celebrity news and into sport.

I frown. Tom glances at me. 'Nothing? Told you it was too early.'

I ignore him, my fingers tapping: *kidnapping, train station.*

The most recent article that pops up is about a three-year-old boy taken from a platform in India in 2017. Kept for four days by a drug addict. No-one was caught. Nothing about last night.

Although my fingers itch to hit refresh and keep hitting it until I get answers, I lay the phone on the table and reach for my coffee.

The doorbell rings.

Tom looks at his watch. 'Who could that be?'

'Stay there.' I struggle to my feet, leaving Tom with Grace. 'It'll be the postman or something. I'll deal with it.'

I pull my dressing gown tighter as I reach the door and open it. Then I stand with my mouth slightly ajar. Tired, cold, exposed.

Chapter 3

The police are on the steps. There's a man who is examining me with mild disdain and a woman wearing a much kinder expression. I quickly run my fingers through the hair I haven't brushed and focus on the woman.

'Mrs Carlson?' She takes the last step upward so that we are on the same level. She has a trim figure, slightly wide at the hips, flat at the front, flattened further by her belt and uniform shirt. Her eyes are grey-blue, peering at my face with sharp intelligence, unlike her colleague who is examining my ratty gown and slippers. She's a little older than me, but it is hard to tell exactly, because her hair is pulled into a severe bun which drags her skin back from her nose and smooths out her forehead. She has a scattering of freckles and skin that would likely burn on a warm May afternoon. She is waiting for my answer.

'Yes, I'm Bridget . . . Bridge.' I wrap my arms around my waist. 'Are you here because you found the . . .'

'Could we possibly speak indoors?' The woman smiles and I find myself smiling back. I step nervously to one side. They walk past me, into the hallway.

'Thank you,' the woman says as I close the door. We crowd into the narrow corridor which suddenly feels crushingly small.

Tom appears in the living room doorway, Grace on his hip. 'Who is . . .' He stops. 'Oh . . . right.' He lifts a staring Grace onto his shoulder. 'Shall I make tea?'

Grace's eyes are wide and a little frightened. She buries her head in Tom's shoulder.

'Look at the police, Grace.' Tom points. 'Look at their uniforms. Just like on *Paw Patrol*.'

Grace refuses to lift her head.

'Cute kid,' the man says.

'May we?' The woman points and I let Tom take Grace into the kitchen before I lead them into the living room.

'Sorry about the mess.' I look helplessly at Grace's toys.

'That's fine.' The woman smiles again. 'You should see my house, it's like a tornado blew through after an earthquake. I never have time to clean.'

I brush some crumbs off the sofa in a mild panic. 'You can sit here . . . if that's okay?'

They sit, seeming expectant.

'Oh, right.' I collapse onto the chair opposite and press my hands between my knees. 'This is about last night?'

The woman nods and takes out a notebook. The man appears to be taking a mental inventory of the room. I follow his gaze: one baby bouncer, one plate with a toast crust on it, two coffee cups, a bottle with milk dregs clinging to the plastic sides, a dummy, Tom's laptop.

'I'm Sergeant Shaw,' the woman says. 'You can call me Naomi.' She gestures to her partner. 'This is Sergeant Ward.'

Ward nods.

Tom comes and stands in the doorway but Grace isn't with him. 'I've left her in her Bumbo,' he says in answer to my unspoken question. 'She's got a rice cake, she's fine.'

Naomi smiles. 'Sorry to bother you this early, but we have some follow-up questions for your wife.'

Ward leans forward, speaking to me. 'You may not know this, but you were the only passenger on the train who admitted to seeing anything.' He has a clean-shaven face with two razor nicks on the left side of his shallow jaw. His eyes are deep-set, his sockets dark as if he is wearing Halloween make-up. He looks ghoulish. I wipe my hands on my knees.

'Was I?' No-one else in my carriage had seen the girl, but on the whole train? 'There must have been *someone* else looking out the window.'

'No-one who's saying so.' Naomi glances at her partner. 'But don't worry, it just means that you're the only one willing to put yourself out. This is a kid we're talking about. You're a good person, Mrs Carlson.'

I look at Tom again. 'The kettle's boiling,' he says, returning to the kitchen.

'Did you . . . did you find her? Or find out who she is?' My fingers ache and I realise that I'm digging them into my thighs so hard that the knuckles are showing white through my chapped skin. I try to relax.

Naomi sighs. 'Not at this time. That's why we need your help. No-one has reported a child missing.'

I jerk. 'But that's not possible! Why wouldn't—'

Ward answers. 'Sadly, there're a number of reasons a parent might not report a child missing. The family could be in the country illegally.' He holds up a finger. 'Perhaps each parent thinks she is with the other.' He shows me another finger as I gasp. 'Some communities like to try and resolve things without getting the police involved. She could be escaping abuse—'

'But she's a little girl. It's not like she's a teenager.' I think of Grace. What possible scenario would have me unaware of her location even in six years, or ten, or fifteen?

'Maybe the person who left her at the platform has realised she hasn't reached her destination but is afraid of being blamed for leaving her unsupervised,' Naomi says gently. 'We'll probably get a call when they realise it isn't just a case of the little girl getting off at the wrong station or wandering off.'

A knot ties up my stomach. 'You think some mum somewhere let her little girl travel by train alone and she's only just realising she didn't get where she was meant to.'

'It's possible.'

'Christ.'

'So, as you're our only lead at the moment, we really need to get as much information as possible.'

I flush. 'I told you all I could.'

'Yes, but last night the team was pushed for time, trying to get through all the possible witnesses, hoping to build a bigger picture. Now we know it's just you we need to make sure we've got all the information. Things you might not even be aware you know.'

Tom walks back into the room. He has four cups on a tray, a bottle of milk, the sugar jar and two spoons. He puts the tray on the table and hands mine to me. It is already tan. I wrap my palms around the ceramic, grateful for the warmth. I hadn't realised how cold I was. He kneels on the floor beside me, one hand on my leg.

'Grace?' I ask.

'I'll stay here until she kicks off.' Tom squeezes my knee and I nod.

Naomi and Ward help themselves to coffee. Ward looks at the tray with a disappointed expression.

'You didn't bring biscuits,' I whisper.

'We're out,' Tom mutters. I look down at his crispy brown curls, starting to thin slightly at the top. He needs a haircut and a shave. My fault he hasn't had the chance.

'Mrs Carlson?' Naomi says gently. 'Can I just go over a few things?'

I pull the cup to my face, letting the steam form a kind of barrier between us.

'You called us at 22.20.'

'I guess so.' I look at my phone. 'I can check.'

'Go ahead.'

I pull up my recent calls and find the one to the police. I show them the screen and Naomi smiles.

35

'You said the abduction happened earlier, but your phone wasn't working?' She frowns at the phone.

'There wasn't any reception.' I swallow. 'It was in that bit, you know, between here and London?' I look at Tom. 'The reception is really spotty. I called as soon as I picked up a signal.'

'Of course you did,' Tom says gently.

'Who are you with?' Ward asks.

Tom answers for me. 'We're both on EE.'

Ward makes a note. 'I'll make a call. Get a map of the area where there's no signal, get an exact location.'

'You don't have a location?' Tom stiffens.

Naomi glances at her partner. 'To be honest, in the time between Bridget getting on the train and making the call, the train passed fourteen stations, not including South Hampstead, Kilburn High Road and Harlesden. There are seven which we think are possible and we're checking CCTV at five.'

'And the other two?' Tom's voice is a weirdly formal version of its usual self.

'At one the cameras weren't working. Some teenagers vandalised them the day before, and they hadn't been fixed.'

'And the other?'

'There's a blind spot on the platform, thanks to a new sign.'

A furious yell comes from the kitchen. Tom sighs and gets to his feet. 'My time's up. Will you be all right, Bridge? I shouldn't bring her in here.'

'It's fine. Take her to her room and read her some stories.'

Tom vanishes and Naomi looks at me. 'Last night you said you thought you'd already passed Kenton?'

'I thought so, but . . . they go by so fast. I couldn't swear to it.'

'All right.' She makes a note.

'And you said there was a single light at the station. Do you mean there were no other lights, no other lights working, or is it just that was the light which caught your attention, because it was shining on the girl?'

My eyes widen. 'Wow, I don't . . . I'm not sure.'

'Try and think,' Naomi puts her cup down. 'Every little detail can help us narrow the station down.'

I close my eyes. 'I only remember seeing one light. The others might have been broken . . . maybe?'

'And you said there was a coffee booth. Do you remember the franchise?'

'Pumpkin Café? I–I'm not sure.'

'Are you just saying that because it's most likely?' Ward tilts his head.

'Maybe.' My hands are shaking, my coffee in danger of spilling. I put my cup down. 'I think I saw the logo but it was all so fast, and it was the girl who caught my attention.'

'All right,' Naomi says. 'Don't worry. Can you remember hearing any announcements on the train, before or after the station?'

I shake my head. 'I was kind of dozing . . . in and out, you know.'

'Dozing?' Ward's voice is suddenly sharp.

'I *didn't* dream this.' I shift forward in my chair. 'I saw her.'

'No-one's saying you did.' Naomi shoots a warning look sideways, then returns her gaze to me. 'You said she was sitting on a case.'

'An old leather suitcase. And she had a blazer on, like a school blazer, you know. She had dark hair.'

'A school blazer.' Naomi's eyes narrow. 'No chance you saw the colour, or any other details?'

'It was all so *fast*.'

'I understand.'

'And it was *dark*.' I'm shivering now.

'What about the van you mentioned?' Ward leans forward, intense. 'You said it was white. Can you tell us anything else about it?'

'N-no.' I shake my head.

Naomi takes my hand; hers is warm and a little callused. 'Close your eyes. Think about the van you saw. Was it a big van or a small one? The size of, say, a post van, or was it something a workman might drive, or one you might use to move a sofa, or double bed?'

I hesitate. 'Bigger than a post van,' I say eventually. 'But too small for a house move.'

'All right. And you're sure it was plain white? Really *think*, no logos on the side or back, no markings?'

'I didn't see the side, just the back.'

'And the licence plate?'

I shake my head, feeling more and more useless by the second.

'And finally,' Naomi squeezes my hand, 'you saw *two* men.'

I nod.

'Can you tell me anything about them? Anything at all? For example, were they Caucasian?'

'One definitely was.' I picture his hand around the girl's arm. 'The other . . . I'm not sure.'

'Well done.' Naomi nods. 'What about build? Tall? Short? Fat? Thin?'

'I . . .' I hesitate. 'One was quite big, definitely. The other was smaller, slimmer.'

'Little and Large,' Ward says.

I don't smile. 'Yes, I suppose.'

Naomi glances at Ward and then back at me. 'You're sure both were men? I mean if one was so much smaller, could it have been a man and a woman?'

'I don't . . .' I hesitate. 'I hadn't thought. I just assumed . . . two men.'

'All right, don't worry.' Naomi pats my hand. 'Instincts are often right. Perhaps it was something in the way the smaller one moved that made you think male. The walk, or—'

'Yes.' I flush. 'That must be it.'

'Okay.' She looks at her notebook. 'What about hair colour?'

'It was—'

'Dark, I know. Don't worry. What about style – did you see? Short, long?'

'One was wearing a hat.' I sit up. 'The smaller one. *Little*. A woollen hat, like a beanie, pulled down low. The other had short hair.'

'And what were they wearing?'

'Jackets. Dark jackets.'

'Short or long? Formal? Casual? Leather? Denim?'

'Like bomber jackets. One of them might have been denim . . . I don't —'

Naomi looks at Ward. 'Anything else?'

Ward shakes his head.

'We're going to keep looking, Mrs Carlson.' Naomi stands up, putting her notebook away. She hands me a card. 'Call me if you think of anything else.'

'But what if it's the station with no CCTV, or the blind spot?'

'Then we'll have to investigate local businesses, see if their cameras caught the van. We'll canvas the local area, look for another witness.'

'And you'll find her?'

'That's our job.' Ward stalks into the corridor, looking as he does, into the kitchen, his eyes flickering over the table. 'Nice-looking family.' He points to the photo above the breakfast bar, taken at Grace's baptism: June and Charlie, Mum, the godparents Neil and Sam, Tom, Grace and myself, looking over-weight in my one stretchy dress and shocked, as if the camera had taken me by surprise. Mum had it framed for me.

'Thanks.'

As I see them out, Naomi hesitates, letting Ward start their car without her. 'Try not to worry,' she says. 'Ward works harder than anyone on this kind of case. There's a boy . . .' She shakes her head. 'I can't say any more, but just know that we'll be doing our utmost to find her.'

I shut the door behind her. Tom stands at the top of the stairs with Grace. 'Are you all right?'

I nod. Then, more honestly, I shake my head. 'No-one's reported her missing, Tom. No-one's even noticed that she's gone.'

'Here.' He brings Grace down and hands her to me. I bury my face in her hair and shudder. Tom puts his arms around us both and I melt into his warmth.

The girl is sitting at the back of the small room peering over the top of her knees. Her bruises have faded and her hair has grown so that it sticks out over her ears and curls into her pool-dark eyes. The tan line has faded too, yellowing like the awful itchy dress she's wearing, her skin sallow and pale. She hasn't been outside for a long time.

Footsteps. The woman is coming.

Whenever she sees her, the girl feels sick and shaky. She can't put a name to her emotion, she's never experienced such a huge thing. The closest she's ever felt is an aversion to snotty Martin Hyde who never has a hanky and always sits next to her at carpet time. She doesn't understand why her body is hot and red and her eyes are filling with tears. But she hates the woman. Hates her.

Hates her.

Hates her.

Chapter 4

I dream of the little girl, only this time, in the way you do in dreams, I *know* she is Grace. Grace is confused at first when the two men pick her up, but then she starts to struggle and when they smack her wrist into the sliding door, she screams. I am already running but too far away to stop them from bundling her into the back of the vehicle. Desperately, I race after the van, knowing that if I can just keep it in sight, I can save her. If I can get close enough I can at least read the number plate. But as I run after my baby, the road melts and each step is pulled through dripping cement, until I am barely moving. The van vanishes into the dark distance, Grace's shrieks ringing in my ears.

I wake, with a gasp, to Grace's hungry sobs. Almost eight months and still not sleeping through the night. I turn to Tom, who is sound asleep, snoring, with his arms thrown out as though he has hit the bed from a great height. I rise quickly and stumble from our room.

I put the hall light on and open Grace's door. She's standing in her cot, clinging to the bars, fat tears slipping down her cheeks, howling her hunger and loneliness. Navigating by the hall light, I sweep her up and into the chair under the windowsill. Then I pull up my t-shirt and she latches instantly onto my breast with a sigh.

As she feeds, I play with her fingers and stare out of the window at the streetlight opposite. How many other mums are awake, as I am, at . . . I check my watch . . . 2 a.m.? How many are staring out of their own windows?

My eyes are heavy, but I fight them open. Grace needs to learn to fall asleep in her cot, not in my arms.

How is it possible that no-one has reported the kidnapped girl missing? Is a stranger, speeding past in the leaves and dust, really her only hope?

Grace snuggles into me and her mouth falls open. I lay her back on her mattress and stroke her hair. She sniffs, shifts and I quickly shove Frankie under her questing hand. She cuddles back down, pulling him towards her chin.

I tiptoe out and hesitate at the top of the stairs. The iPad is in the study. I find it without turning on the light and search the news sites again. Surely someone has written about the missing girl by now.

Nothing.

I do a general Google search on 'missing girl' and my heart stutters.

Police launch urgent appeal to find 16-year-old girl missing in Cornwall

UPDATE: Latest on appeal to find missing 13-year-old girl from Cheltenham

Divers look for missing girl

Missing girl, 12, last seen leaving her home in school uniform

Police concerned over welfare of Burnley teenager

The list goes on. My chest tightens. How is it possible that all these girls are missing, are going missing, *all the time*? What is wrong in the world that these girls aren't safe at home? My fists are clenched, my nails digging into my palms.

Would they all be found?

I push the iPad away just as Tom staggers into the doorway. 'What are you doing?'

'I—'

'Come back to bed.'

He wobbles into the bathroom, I hear him pissing, then he weaves back, slapping the light off as he passes.

'Come on, Bridge. Leave it.' He looks at me and I rise.

'I had a bad dream,' I whisper.

'I'll protect you.' He puts an arm around me and tugs me in the direction of our bedroom. 'Cuddle in,' he says as he lies back down, his eyes already starting to close.

I put my head on his chest and listen to his gentle snoring.

How could so many girls be missing?

The next day is Saturday. There is still nothing on the news, nothing on the Internet. No mention of the kidnapping. How are the police going to find witnesses if they don't publicise the abduction?

'Should I speak to a reporter?' I sip my tea as I refresh and scroll through the news sites yet again.

There is a fresh appeal on the BBC website, a video of a press conference showing the parents of a five-year-old boy, Vihaan Sharma, who has been missing for a week. They sit behind microphones in their formal clothes, she in a frayed sari, he in a suit, their faces drawn, their eyes bleak, begging for his return.

So many missing children.

'Let the police do their job, Bridge.' Tom is putting Grace in her coat. 'Come for a walk with us.'

Feeling as if the iPad is stuck to my fingertips, I refresh once more and then, with difficulty, push it across the table. 'You're right. I should get some air.' I hesitate. 'Wait, it's almost twelve. Let me put the radio on.'

'If it's not online, it won't be on the radio.' Tom pulls Grace's hat over her ears. 'Come out with us.'

'Five minutes,' I snap.

Tom sighs. 'Fine, at least get ready while you listen.'

The news plays the Sharmas' appeal, but then, instead of talking about another missing child, the presenter segues into weather and sports. My heart thumps painfully. 'Why isn't anyone talking about her?' I look at Tom. 'It doesn't make sense.'

'Try and forget about it.' Tom puts a rice cake and a banana in one pocket and his wallet and phone in the other. He picks up the changing bag. 'Remember when we could go for a walk without packing like Sherpas?' He grins, slinging it over his shoulder.

I don't smile back. 'I wish I knew what was going on. Do you think they've looked at all the CCTV yet? Do you think they've found the van?'

'Bridge, *please*!' Tom is frowning now. 'There's no point in obsessing. There's nothing you can do, the police are doing their thing, now you need to do yours.'

'Mine?'

'You've hardly seen Grace all week.' Tom is heading for the cupboard by the door with Grace in his arms. 'Can you at least *try* to be present for the weekend?'

'That's not fair!' I lurch to my feet.

'I know.' Tom groans and stops. 'I'm sorry, just . . . let's have a nice walk. Find some flowers or something to show Grace. Forget about everything for half an hour or so.' He pulls the cupboard door open. 'Help me with the pram, will you?'

Although Tom offers, I want to push Grace. He walks beside us, feet crunching in the leaf-strewn verges, pointing out birds and handing her leaves or sticks when she points. I watch him, struck by how the last seven months have aged him. His hair is thinner on top, his face lined and tired, but his body is the same. Same flattish stomach, same tight rear, same runner's build, same bicep that bulges when he clenches a fist. I refuse to look down in case I catch sight of my tights cutting into my gut. With every step, my thighs wobble out of my skirt and my shirt pulls against my chest. Yes, Tom has changed, but barely. How long before he looks at me and sees, not the old me, but the new one? How long before he realises that he is now stuck with this frump for the rest of his life, and that this whole thing was a mistake?

Grace squeals and I look down; she is squirming,

yanking at the straps of her pram, trying to get to Tom who is jumping in a pile of leaves as if he's found a puddle.

Like an oncoming train, it strikes me that it won't be long before she is walking and then she'll want to walk without holding my hand. After that she'll be going to school, university, moving away.

'You're doing it again.' Tom has stopped kicking the autumnal debris. Now he is looking at me all concern, rubbing a hand through his dark hair, messing it up.

'She's going to leave us,' I sob, bent almost double, clinging to the pram. 'Look how fast these last few months have gone!'

'Bridge, we've got years yet. Years!'

I look at her, squirming to reach her dad and suddenly I can't breathe. 'What if she gets sick? It happens! What if someone takes her away, like that little girl? Or like the Sharmas' son, the one who was on the news?'

'Jesus, *Bridge*!' Tom tries to put his arm around me but I jerk my shoulders angrily.

'It could happen!' I'm shouting and Grace stares up at me, her eyes wide, lips trembling.

'You're scaring her.' Gently Tom pries my fingers from the pram and pushes Grace a little further away, towards the verge. I don't try to stop him.

A thick-set man in a Barbour jacket stops, his dark eyes flicking between us. He has a Cocker Spaniel on a lead. Grace is delighted.

'Is everything all right, mate?'

48

Grace reaches for the dog and Tom tears his eyes from me to deal with the newcomer. 'Yeah, man, we're fine. Just—'

The man looks at me. 'Are *you* all right, love?'

Tom touches his arm. 'She's a little upset, but we're fine. Thanks for stopping, honestly.'

The man clears his throat, hesitates, and then walks away. A younger couple are strolling towards us, arm in arm. He shakes his head at them, almost imperceptibly. They cross to the other side of the road.

Tom flushes. 'Bridge, you have to take a breath. Do you really want things to go back to . . . you know . . . before the medication?'

I shake my head but my heart is pounding. All I can think is that I'm going to lose Grace and there's nothing I can do. 'One day someone will take her away from us.' I look at Tom and he sighs.

'I'm investing in a shotgun and rocking chair as soon as she turns sixteen, remember.'

It's an old joke between us, started at the twenty-week scan.

'The birth is going to be quite enough of a shock for one day,' I laugh, when the technician asks if we want to know the gender. 'I don't need an added surprise on top of it. Plus, I want to decorate the nursery, buy baby clothes and pick names while I'm not high. I'm sure that's how babies end up being called Chardonnay or Estrella. New mums, nine months without drinking, high on exhaustion and diamorphine!'

'I can't guarantee anything,' the technician says

49

without cracking a smile. 'This is how it works: I look for a penis. If I find one, then it's likely you're having a boy.' He moves the stick around my slippery blue stomach, already swollen and bulging with a faint tracery of veins. He leans closer to the image. 'There doesn't *seem* to be a—'

'We're having a girl!' Tom gasps.

'Or I couldn't spot the penis,' he reminds us. 'Don't go mad buying pink nursery furniture. It does happen. We had a family last week—'

'A girl!' Tom grins at me, his whole face alight. 'It takes a *real man* to make a girl. I'll have to get a shotgun!'

I punch his shoulder. 'No boy will ever be good enough, right?'

'Are you kidding, I was a teenaged boy. No meaty-pawed, Jack-the-Lad is getting near *my* baby.'

It doesn't work today.

'I should go back to the house.' I glance over my shoulder. 'I'm ruining things. You and Grace go on without me, enjoy your walk.'

'No.' Tom shakes his head. 'Bridge, don't!' But I'm already striding away, head down, feeling the stretch between Grace and me, as if the cord still connects us, getting thinner as I walk away. Not snapping, not yet, but on the verge.

I glance back. Tom is getting his phone out. I check mine, thinking he might be wanting to talk, but it doesn't ring. Who is he calling?

I'm running by the time I get back to the house,

fumbling my key, suddenly desperate to be inside. I slam the door behind me and lean on it, as if someone is after me. My heart is racing and I'm sweating. Not because I ran; it's a cold sweat.

I hurl my coat into the cupboard, race into the kitchen and grab the iPad, already typing before I'm sitting down: *Child abductions UK*

There were 1.2 thousand child abduction offences recorded by the police in England and Wales in 2018/19, an increase of 61 when compared with the previous year. There were over twice the amount of child abduction offences when compared with 2012/13 when there were only 513 of these types of offences.

I grip the edges of my chair. Over a thousand just in the last year! How can these incidents be increasing? Surely, with modern technology and social media and advances in policing, you'd think things like this would be on the decrease. Even with only five hundred a year that's over five thousand children abducted in the last ten years, in the UK alone.

I sway. What is happening to these children?

I scroll down the list of links to find a report saying that 42 per cent of all abduction attempts are made by strangers. That means that most are undertaken by people the families knew: parents, relatives, friends. Surely some of these are divorce cases, child custody battles, kids who ran away by themselves. But not all.

I've always been good at maths. It was why I was nominated for Young Researcher of the Year before I had Grace. I can work through pages of numbers and find the real story they are telling. 'That's 504 children,'

I murmur, 'abducted by strangers. This year. And Shaw and Ward already have one case . . . at least one. No wonder I haven't heard anything from them.'

My fingers hover over the keypad again and I jump as the phone rings. Its shrill hum reverberates through the kitchen. *Pick me up. Pick me up.*

I do so without thinking. 'Hello?'

'Bridget, darling!' My mum's voice. 'How many times have I told you to answer the phone properly. You should say "Carlson residence".'

'Sorry, Mum.' I sit on the stool by the breakfast bar, tucking the phone under my ear, my heart slowing. I think of telling her that she is the only person we know who doesn't call our mobile phones. That I have no intention of being polite to people trying to get me to buy double glazing or sue someone for an accident I've never had. 'How are you?'

'Oh, you know me, can't complain! I'm calling because I'm hoping to take Grace this afternoon.'

'But . . . it's the weekend.'

'I know, darling, but I didn't see her this week. I've been very busy and Tom said he could manage without me.' She pauses. 'Gillian's back from France.' Her voice is excited and guilty relief ripples through me; Aunt Gillian is back! Mum doesn't have many people in her life. There was Dad, there is me and there is Aunt Gillian.

I don't remember much about Dad. But I often wish he was still around, mainly because some of Mum's attention would have gone to him, like a river being diverted. Sometimes her love seems to contain deep and dangerous currents, enough to wash us away.

'I'm really glad Aunt Gillian's home,' I say. 'How long has it been since you've seen her? Two years?'

'Almost exactly.' She sounds giddy and I'm delighted. 'And that's the other reason I want to take Grace.' Her voice fades and then comes back, as if she's taken the phone away from her ear. She's multi-tasking. Always busy, my mum.

'I don't under—'

'Gillian hasn't seen her. I've sent lots of photos and we've . . . face-timed . . . is that the word?'

'Yes, Mum, but —'

'And now she wants to meet her.'

'Does it have to be today? I've been working late a lot the last few days. I've hardly seen her either.' I look guiltily at the door, suddenly wishing for Tom to walk through it, but he said he wanted a half-hour walk and a half-hour walk is what he'll take.

He's probably gone to the park to show Grace the ducks. Or to the swings. Grace loves the swings. He takes his coat off and tucks it behind her, so she doesn't slip out.

I clench my fists on my lap. Why had I ruined things? Why wasn't I there, pretending to try and catch her feet as he pushed her? By the time they get back she'll need lunch, then a nap. I'll have missed her whole morning.

I realise that Mum has been quiet for almost a full minute. Then she speaks again.

'Tom called me the other night. I was very worried.'

'I'm sorry, Mum, I—'

'Luckily, I was still awake when he rang again to say you had come home. You aren't spending nearly enough time with him, darling. Normally I take Grace when you're at work, but if I took her for a couple of hours this afternoon, you could do something with Tom. Go out for a . . . a drink or something.' She talks as if she has no idea what couples do, but she was with Dad for twenty years. They ran a business together.

'I—'

'I'll understand if you don't want me to see her,' she says. 'I just thought . . . I missed her, and it would make Gillian so happy. If you haven't seen Grace much this week, I imagine you haven't seen Tom much either.' She hesitates. 'It's so important to make time for one another . . . while you have the chance.'

'Mum . . .' I swallow. 'Tom's not going to do what Dad did.'

'No, of course not.' I picture her looking down, plucking at her skirt. Her breath catches. 'He would never! Of course, I didn't expect your father to—'

'You can take her.'

'Really? Only if you're sure.'

'Yes. You're right. I should spend some time with Tom.'

'Wonderful. I'll be there at three.'

After she hangs up, I sit and stare at myself in the cupboard glass. Would it really be so bad to spend a couple of hours alone with Tom? If I hop in the shower now, while he's out, I can do my hair, put on

54

something nice and take him to The Queen's Head for a pint.

I look at the stairs. I can be in and out of the shower in five minutes. But then, before I know it, I'm pulling the iPad back toward me.

During 2013/14, 158 children were abducted by their parents, 401 children were abducted by people other than their parents and 321 children were kidnapped. Kidnappings, which are defined by the use of force or fraud to remove a child, include cases such as children taken in return for a ransom or young gang members held by rival factions.

The figures include both successful and attempted crime, however, PACT (Parents and Abducted Children Together) believes that many cases of attempted abduction and kidnapping involving children are never recorded by police and the true rate of offending may be four times higher than police figures suggest.

I'd always thought that kidnapping and abduction was the same. I type again.

Abduction is when someone uses deceit or force in order to take a person away from their home or relatives.

Kidnapping is taking away or forcefully transporting a person against their will and holding them in false imprisonment.

So, the little girl was kidnapped not abducted. Surely, I should have heard something by now. I look at the card pinned to the noticeboard with Naomi Shaw's contact details. But what if she's busy? What if she has a lead and taking time out to talk to me slows things down? Who am I anyway? Just a curious stranger.

I slide my finger over the iPad, switching the screen to black. I should get in the shower. Tom will be so pleased to see me making an effort. I touch my greasy hair.

The front door cracks open. 'We're home.'

Chapter 5

2:58 and Mum's footsteps are crunching on the gravel path. At one minute to three, the doorbell rings.

Tom watches from the living room with Grace in his arms. He's annoyed that I've agreed to let her go like this, without consulting him. And he's angry on my behalf. Our quiet afternoon of baby time is gone and on Monday I'll be back at work and complaining that I hardly see her. He shakes his head at me as I tuck Frankie into the pram and open the door.

Mum is a little taller than me and still battling the grey in her softly permed hair, which was once the exact colour of mine, but is now faded to steel. We have the same eye colour, but nothing else matches. Her nose is slightly hooked, mine turns up. Her skin is alabaster, mine is pale. She is curvy, I am fat. She is elegant, I am clumsy. She dresses well, I'm wearing jeans and a jumper.

I step backwards so that she can come in. 'Hello, darling.' She puts her arms around me. 'You look tired,' she murmurs. 'Are you getting enough sleep?' She pulls away and looks at me with concern. 'You

57

must look after yourself as well, you know. Mummy should come first.'

I nod.

'How is my Grace?' Her eyes dart past me, in search of her granddaughter.

'She's had a nap, so she'll be in a good mood.'

'That's nice.' She raises her voice. 'Grace, Grandma's here and I have Jelly Tots!'

Grace squeals and Tom struggles to hold onto her. 'Mum!' I lunge for the sweets but she's already dropping the packet in her handbag. 'If you want to treat her, give her rice cakes or a banana. She's only been on solids a couple of months. She shouldn't be eating sugar.'

'A little sugar won't hurt her.' Mum smiles. 'Anyway, I don't give her the whole packet, just one or two when she's being a good girl.' Mum turns to the hall cupboard. 'I'll need her car seat – we're going into town.'

I can feel Tom tensing behind me. 'If you're busy, we can keep Grace with us this afternoon.'

'Don't be silly, Tom. Gillian can't wait to meet her. We're going to Costa for a coffee.'

I reach for the car seat as Tom offers a warning. 'She'll be bored just sitting in her pram.'

Mum laughs. 'She'll be fine. There're always babies in Costa on a Saturday afternoon. She might make a friend.' She moves Frankie-Lion and fits the car seat onto the pram. Then she looks at me again and lowers her voice. 'Maybe pop a little bit of make-up on for Tom, Bridget.' She puts the bag over the back of the pram as my heart sinks. When I turn to get Grace from Tom, I avoid the sight of my reflection in the door pane.

Mum clips Grace neatly into her seat, crushing Frankie-Lion, and, as Grace starts to cry, whips out the bag of sweets and waves them in front of her.

'Alison—' Tom starts forwards, but she's already backing out of the door.

'Say bye-bye to Daddy,' she coos. 'Wave to Mummy.'

I clutch the doorframe as Grace bumps backwards down the steps, focused entirely on the unopened packet of Jelly Tots. At the last moment, she looks up and waves, her little fist opening and closing. She's just learned that. It hurts me every time I see her wave at me. She should be waving other people goodbye, not her mummy.

Tom takes my hand, as Mum walks Grace to her car. 'She'll be fine.'

'What if she takes her eyes off her?'

'Your mum?' He shakes his head. 'She wouldn't. She adores Grace.'

'True.' I lean my head against the side of his, neither of us willing to look away until Mum pulls away and Grace is out of sight.

'Who is Gillian anyway?' Tom looks at me, finally.

I frown. 'Aunt Gillian. I'm sure you've met her. She was at the wedding.'

Tom shrugs.

'They've known each other since Mum was at school. She's a therapist. She treated me after what happened with Dad, and then again when I was a

59

teenager. High school wasn't easy after being home schooled.' I smile at him. 'She's just back from France and Mum's giddy with excitement.' I hesitate. 'Do you want me to get dressed up? I can put on some make-up and we could go to the—'

Tom frowns. 'What makes you think you need to get dressed up to spend time with me?'

'I didn't mean—' I turn from the empty road. 'I just thought you might like to go out.'

Tom rubs his eyes. 'I've already been out, remember? Why don't you have a shower? *Not* because I think you need it, but because I think it'll make you feel more . . . human. Then we could have a bite to eat or a lie down.' He sounds almost as tired as I am. 'I wish you'd . . .' He lets the rest of the sentence hang and abandons me in the hallway. I hear the television go on in the living room, the muted hum of theme music and voices.

I stand for a moment, then close the front door. *I wish you'd stand up to your mum.* I think that's what he was going to say. But it's not a question of standing up to her. I wouldn't want Grace standing up to me. Or needing to. That's not what a good daughter does.

I walk heavily upstairs.

I let the shower run, but don't get into it, not immediately. Tom is watching television. The water is running. He can't hear me.

I pick up my mobile and dial, feeling uneasy, as if I'm sneaking around, having an affair. As soon as it rings, I regret making the call and start to take the phone from my ear to hang up.

60

'James Ward?' The voice comes through the speaker, distant and tinny. Quickly, guiltily, I put it back to my ear.

'H-hello?'

I was hoping for the other one, for Naomi Shaw. Are they partners? Is that why he's answering the number she gave me? I picture the police station, desks facing one another. Do Sergeants have desks? Or am I thinking of Detectives? But I suppose they must. They can't just drive around all day, going from door to door. They aren't itinerant.

'Um, Sergeant Ward? It's Bridget Carlson. I was just wondering . . . is there any news on the little girl who was kidnapped?'

There's a long pause.

'Sergeant Ward?'

'Yes.' Another pause. 'Look, Mrs Carlson, it's early days.' His voice is professional, sharp.

'I know, it's just . . .' I remember something I heard from a maternity leave spent in a fug in front of late-night television, a wakeful Grace clutching at my breast. 'I thought if the child isn't found in the first twenty-four hours – I mean, don't the chances of finding her go down and . . .?'

'Mrs Carlson, we're doing all we can. But . . .' Another pause. 'We've been looking at CCTV.'

'You found the station?' I'm delighted.

'Sergeant Shaw had the idea of looking at the camera on the train. She thought if we could spot the moment you saw the kidnapping, we'd be able to tell which station you were going past. But I'll be

61

honest, Mrs Carlson, it looks to me a lot like you get on, find your seat, then you lean your head on the window and go to sleep.'

'No.' My rising heart sinks. 'I mean I do rest my head on the window, but I'm not sleeping. Maybe I doze – a little – but I'm awake when—'

'Mrs Carlson,' and now his voice is low, sympathetic, 'I've been doing some digging. No more than I would into any other witness. You're on medication, right? Anti-depressants?'

'Y-yes, but . . .'

'Fluoxetine, is that the one?'

'Yes, but I don't underst—'

'The thing is, Mrs Carlson, among the many, *many* side-effects listed for Fluoxetine are tiredness, confusion, abnormal dreams and nightmares.'

'What are you saying? You think I *dreamed* this?'

Another heavy pause. I imagine him playing with a pencil, doodling on a notepad, his deep-set eyes hooded, perhaps a desk lamp casting shadows on his face.

'Listen, Mrs Carlson. You've just had a baby. You've been diagnosed with depression and I imagine that losing that child is the worst thing you can think of. It makes sense that you would have a nightmare about a child being kidnapped. And if not – I'll be honest here – you don't look that well. And I guess the baby gets a lot of attention. Maybe you wanted someone to look at *you* for once, huh?'

I gasp.

'We can't find any evidence of a kidnapping, no-one

has reported a child missing in this area and the only witness to the event looks as if she was asleep and is on medication that causes nightmares. What would you think if you were in my position?'

'You really think I dreamed it?'

'I'm sorry, Mrs Carlson. Listen, we aren't closing the case. But until we find some evidence that there really was a child . . . we're struggling under budget cuts, we have no time, no resources and no evidence.' He hesitates and then, finally, he answers my question. 'And yes, frankly, I think you dreamed the whole thing. Which is lucky for you because if we thought you were *deliberately* making this up, I'd be talking about charging you for wasting police time.'

I don't say goodbye, I don't say another word. I press the red button and drop the phone. It lands in the laundry basket.

The shower is still running. I can no longer see my face in the steamed-up mirror, only a ghost, haloed with a frizz of dark hair. I shed my clothes and step out of my knickers. I don't look at myself. I open the door and move into the shower. The hot water patters on my head, wetting my hair, dragging it over my face. It batters my shoulders, runs over my heavy breasts, makes rivers on my soft stomach, streams over the road map of my stretch-marked thighs. Was it possible that I did want to be noticed, to be seen? Did I dream the whole thing? I look at my reflection in the steamed-up glass and think again of the girl. Her terrified screams, her dark curls, the way she fought not to be taken.

The memory didn't have the quality of a dream.

But then, how would I know? My whole life had something of a dream-like feel. I'd always been a little confused about things, especially since Dad. Afterwards, I developed a kind of dissociative amnesia, my whole childhood lost in a kind of blur. Aunt Gillian told me it was grief and anger that made me block my memories of him. Then, when I left home and started university, I lost a whole month to anxiety and nausea before I dared venture out of my accommodation.

Since Grace there'd been adrenalin, then exhaustion and then depression, moving in like a cold front, taking me over as my life diminished to a bubble, dark around the edges.

So, maybe I was wrong. Maybe I did dream it.

I jump as the shower door slides open and Tom steps in behind me, pressing his long body against mine. My heart should rise but it sinks. I'm still going over Ward's words. *I'd be talking about charging you for wasting police time.*

'I thought of you in here all by yourself, you sexy thing.' There's a smile in his voice and his big hands slide around my waist, heading for my breasts. I block them.

'Not the—'

'I know, I know, sorry. I can't wait for her to stop breastfeeding!' He shifts direction, heading for my stomach and further down.

'I haven't washed my hair.'

He reaches around me for the shampoo. 'Let me.'

Plastic creaks as he squeezes the bottle into his hands. Yet another thing to feel guilty about, all the plastic in here. Then his fingers are on my scalp and I lean back into his grip, letting him massage my head, his chest against my back.

'You're so sexy,' he breathes and I stiffen. *I'm* not sexy, *he's* horny. Not the same.

'I wish you wouldn't say that,' I sigh.

'Why can't I say it? It's true. I wish you'd believe me.' He presses harder and I groan with pleasure, trying not to think about what comes next, how I dread his hands moving downwards, running over all the places I've gone soft and saggy.

How could he possibly find me sexy? He had to be comparing what I'd become with what I'd once been. How could he not?

'Tom. I know you're lying. I wish you wouldn't. It makes me feel . . . awkward.'

He freezes, then he pulls his hands out of my hair. 'I don't know what I can say to make you believe me.' Chill air hits my back. He's stepped away, opened the shower door and moved back into the bathroom. He grabs the towel from the radiator and leaves me alone.

Part of me wants to make him stay. I could invite him back in and give him a blow job, that way he wouldn't have to touch me. I'd be in control. He'd be happy with that, wouldn't he?

But another part of me is relieved. I let him go and stand in the shower as the bathroom door closes behind his bowed shoulders.

Chapter 6

The little girl is standing with her back to me and I know I have to get her to turn around, but she's behind glass. I bang on it until my fists bleed, but she makes no sign that she has heard. Her dark hair hangs down her back in two plaits tied with red ribbon. Her blazer is navy blue, her ankle socks are white. I know if I can make her turn around, I'll be able to save her. I hear the roar of a van's engine, the muffled voices of two men getting closer. I just need her to turn around. Finally, she does. She turns. Her face is blank, there is nothing there. That isn't when I start screaming. I scream when I realise that I'm not behind glass, I'm inside a mirror and she's looking right at me.

I look down. I'm wearing a blue blazer. My white ankle socks have a little lace trim and a tiny splash of mud on the edge. My Mary Jane shoes are a little scuffed on one side. There is an insignia on my blazer: a red rose. It matches the ribbons on my plaits. I reach up to touch my face.

It is a featureless blank.

*　*　*

66

I snap awake with a gasp at five minutes to five. Mum will be back with Grace any minute. I leap out of bed, stumble over my slippers and race to the bathroom.

My hair has dried into a bird's nest and I have deep creases on my cheeks. I drag a brush through the unruly curls and haul a patterned scarf over the top, then I look at my face. A frisson of relief when I see that it *is* my face; my features squashed with sleep, undefined by make-up, a little doughy with a layer of fat, but still *my* face.

Make-up: I have to put some on. I pat tinted moisturiser over the reddest spots and use my forefinger to blot brown shadow over my eyelids. It'll have to do. I grab the first lipstick I see, an old red-brown one that Tom likes. I slick it on swiftly and then use a bit of loo roll to blot away the bit where I've carelessly gone over the line of my lip.

The doorbell rings as I'm dragging a black t-shirt over my jeans.

I thunder down the stairs. Tom appears by the living room door, his own hair mussed, his jaw cracking in a yawn. He stretches and makes no further move towards the hallway.

'What time is it?' He frowns at his watch. 'Oh shit!'

'We fell asleep,' I agree and then I'm unlocking the door and taking Grace from her car seat. 'Hello, baby girl, I missed you.' She reaches for me and I hug her as I let out a huge breath.

Tom reaches past me to pull the pram in. 'Well, thanks, Alison.'

'I'm coming in.' Mum steps into the hallway and heads towards the kitchen.

Grace's eyes are rimmed with red and she has the thousand-mile stare, looking at Tom, but not seeing him. She's shattered.

Tom strokes her hair. 'Do you want me to take her?'

I shake my head. 'It's okay, let me have a cuddle before I make her tea.'

I follow Mum into the kitchen and find her rolling up her sleeves. 'Where are your tea towels?' she asks, frowning at the unwashed dishes, the pan on the hob crusted with beans and the frying pan gleaming with grease. Grace's bib, coated with mashed up carrot, is abandoned on the side, toast crumbs are scattered over the work surface.

'Don't, Mum, honestly. I'll do it. I just haven't had time.' I grab a sponge with one hand and use it to wipe the table, while balancing Grace on my left hip.

'Don't be silly, darling. You just sit down.' Mum starts to stack the washing up.

I give up after a moment, the cloth has just left more smears, and I sit awkwardly on the chrome bar stool which is even less comfortable than it looks, holding onto Grace as she lays her head on my shoulder and burps painfully. She gives a choking little sob. If I didn't know better, I'd think she'd had dairy.

Mum clatters the pans in the sink and starts to run the hot water. She doesn't look at me.

'Mum . . . is everything okay?'

'Not really, darling.' She starts to scrub the frying pan. 'I've been lied to.'

'L-lied to?'

She turns and sees Tom standing in the doorway. 'You told me it was signalling problems the other night. Is that what Bridget told you? Or did you know about the incident on the train?'

Tom sighs. 'We didn't want to worry you, Alison.' He steps into the kitchen and puts a hand on Grace's sweat-soaked curls.

Mum gives a little gasp. 'You know how I feel about lies. After Bridget's father . . .'

'I'm so sorry, Mum.' I hand Grace to Tom and jump to my feet. 'I didn't think.'

'You mean you didn't think I'd find out.' She wipes her eyes. 'Liars always get found out, Bridget, you should know that.' She sighs and then turns back to the washing up. 'Gillian's niece was trying to get home from work on the same train. She was delayed by three hours.' Mum puts the clean pans on the draining board and lets the water out. It gurgles away as she leans her hands flat on the worksurface. It's a familiar gesture and I tighten up. 'I had to hear about it from Gillian and she's only just back in the country.' She glances up at Tom again. 'You didn't think I should know that my own daughter was involved with the police?'

I press my nose against Grace's hair and inhale. She smells a little sicky. I wonder if Mum ordered her something in Costa and forgot to check the ingredients.

Tom folds his arms. 'Bridget saw a child being

kidnapped. She told the police. It's not as if she's been arrested.' He spreads his hands. 'You're making too big a deal out of this, Alison. Perhaps we should have told you, but it was late and Bridget was exhausted. I thought a white lie was for the best. Everyone needed to rest, not rehash what happened.'

I gasp. For a moment he's the young man I met at university. His hair long over his collar, his blue eyes gleaming as he watches me from across the bar.

The guy who kept telling everyone he went to Eton is putting his arm over my shoulder, informing me that he should have got into Cambridge; that his parents paid enough for his education that he should have had a guaranteed place there, but instead they're giving offers to girls and kids off council estates because of positive discrimination. And, by the way, did I enjoy the drink he bought me? His hand moving over my shoulder and towards my breast. Me trying to push him off and failing to shift his weight. His thick lips against my ear, his tongue on my neck. My squeal of protest.

Tom finally leaping over the table, dragging him off me and literally tossing him out of the bar by his neck, to the sound of applauding undergrads.

I can hear them now. A bar full of shouting students, as if they're in the kitchen, their cheers in my ear as Mum finally looks at me.

'You're happy for him to lie to me, Bridget?' She looks heartbroken. 'How does that affect the trust between us? How many other lies . . .?'

'None. I—'

Suddenly Tom seems less heroic. Mum turns back to him. 'Gillian says not one other person saw this kidnapping. Is she taking that medication I warned you against?'

Tom's own lips thin. 'Yes.'

'Well, apparently it's not working very well.' She gestures at the mess around us and I shrink in my seat.

I've failed. Failed as a daughter, as a wife *and* as a mum. Grace is living in squalor, I fell asleep instead of taking the chance to spend time with Tom and I let Tom lie to Mum, when I know how triggering that is for her. I turn my gaze to my knuckles, my whole world focused on how pale they look against Grace's pink cardigan.

'Darling!' Mum rushes over to me. 'I didn't mean to upset you. Listen – perhaps Grace should come and stay with me for a while. It would give the two of you a break. A chance to sort things out.'

'Sort what out?' Tom looks at us both.

Mum shakes her head, as if he's being deliberately obtuse. 'Bridget needs help, Tom. She's calling the police because she's *seeing things*.' Mum turns her smile back on me. 'Gillian's offered to work with you again, so that you can come off the drugs. I'll take Grace until you're feeling better.' She reaches for her.

Instinctively I turn slightly, blocking her. 'Thanks, Mum, honestly, but Grace has never spent a night away from us.' Grace clings to me, whimpering, her podgy little legs curled up.

'Oh.' Mum steps back, her face crumpling. 'I understand. You don't want your mum interfering. It's just . . . I didn't want to say . . . to remind you if you hadn't remembered, but . . . it's coming up to the anniversary of your father's death and . . . I thought spending some quality time with Grace would make me feel less . . . lonely.'

I lurch to my feet. 'Oh God, Mum. I'm so sorry, I *had* forgotten. It's all been a bit of a blur since Grace was born. I barely know what day of the week it is.'

I am the worst daughter.

'Your friend is back, isn't she, Alison?' Tom says. 'Couldn't you arrange to spend a few days with her instead? I'm sure she'd be better company than a baby. You should be focusing on yourself next week, not running about after Grace.'

Mum freezes. 'Yes,' she says. 'Of course, Gillian would be happy to . . . I mean she works, but in the evenings. Perhaps one day.'

Grace's sticky cheek is against my neck and, unbelievably her breath has started coming more evenly. I think that despite the atmosphere, and whatever is upsetting her stomach, she might have fallen asleep. I touch her soft head. 'If you really want to help . . .' I swallow. 'We were actually talking about Tom speaking to a recruitment agent, so I could stay at home with Grace.'

'Well, that's wonderful.' Mum's smile is back. 'You know I always said a baby needs her mum.'

Tom stiffens.

'But . . . we'd need a bit of money to tide us over.

Just enough to pay the mortgage for a couple of months.'

Mum's smile slides from her face. Her hands drop to her side. 'I offer to take Grace so you can address your health issues, and – and so I don't feel so lonely at a hard time of year . . . but instead you ask me for money?' She steps away from me. 'I'm going to go now.'

'You offered to *help*,' I say wretchedly as she passes. 'This is the help we need.'

'No,' Mum turns around. Her expression is devastated. 'What you *need* is to go and see Gillian about your mental health, because she actually knows what she's doing. What you *need* is a husband who is earning enough money to take care of his family.' She ignores Tom's intake of breath, fumbles in her purse and takes out a business card. She slides it onto the breakfast bar. 'I'm worried about you.' She frowns. 'Here's Gillian's number, for when you come to your senses.'

She sees herself out and I sit on the stool, balancing Grace in my arms and staring at the card.

Tom moves closer and silence hangs between us for a few seconds. Then he gestures towards a sleeping Grace. 'She won't eat her tea now. Do you want me to put her down?' I shake my head, so he takes the seat next to me. 'Don't beat yourself up. I'd forgotten about next week too.'

'That's not the same as *me* forgetting.'

He takes my hand. 'Are you all right? I mean about your dad and everything.'

I nod slowly. 'It's been fifteen years. I barely remember him.'

Tom frowns. 'Weren't you eleven though, when—'

'I know it seems weird. I should have all these happy memories.' I don't give in to the temptation to try and recall one. It's like picking at a scab; I know I'll end up scarred and regretting it, so I don't. 'I know how I'm meant to feel, and I know Mum will be upset, but it's like it happened to someone else.'

'Are you going to call her?' He points to the card.

'I don't know.' I shake my head. 'Aunt Gillian was great when I was eleven, and she helped me with some high school stuff too. But I wasn't *ashamed* of dad's death.'

Tom stiffens. 'And you're "ashamed" of having post-natal depression?'

'I'm a mum. It's supposed to be the most natural thing in the world, right? So, why can't I cope? It's humiliating.'

Tom lets go of my fingers. 'There's nothing humiliating about—'

'The medication *is* helping, isn't it? I mean—' I look at his anguished face.

'Yes, it's helping.' His blue eyes flash. 'Remember what you were like a few months ago? You couldn't sleep, you were roaming the house at night, screaming at me, just freaking out at every little thing. You couldn't work. You wouldn't let anyone else touch Grace. You carried her everywhere, terrified that if you put her down, she'd die, and you wouldn't notice. Don't you remember?'

'I-I remember.' I touch Grace's face with a finger.

'Then you remember what Dr Lewis said, it's not a crime to need medication.' He paces as he speaks. 'Your mum's got an odd view of drugs, but you don't get a medal for raising Grace without them, Bridge. If you had kidney stones or something, you'd take pain killers.' He stops and strokes my hair as if I'm Grace, dislodging my scarf. 'If you come off the Fluoxetine, you'll stop sleeping again.'

'But when I do sleep . . .' I tail off, suddenly afraid to tell him about the nightmares. About the girl in the mirror who is Grace and me and the kidnapped girl all at once.

'You've only been back at work a couple of months. It must be exhausting.' Tom keeps stroking my head. 'You're amazing.'

'I can't ask her for money again,' I whisper.

With sudden violence he reaches over me, crumples the card up and hurls it towards the sink. It skids over the draining board and bounces under the dripping tap where it sits like a dead white bird, absorbing water into its broken wings. The name, Gillian Thornhill, starts to blur and run.

The food comes three times a day.

The little girl has come to look forward to its arrival because it's a change, a break from staring at four boring walls.

Today it is pasta in tomato sauce. She's hungry but instead of eating she just stares at the plate until the food goes cold and the pasta sticks together. When the woman comes to take the plate away, she looks at the girl as though she's disappointed.

She feels proud of this tiny achievement.

The next day, breakfast is cold pasta with tomato sauce. The little girl doesn't eat it.

She's tired and she doesn't feel well. Her tummy rumbles. But it's easy not to eat it, it's cold pasta with tomato sauce.

The woman glares at her when she comes to take her plate away.

At lunchtime it is cold pasta with tomato sauce. The little girl thinks that she might fade away to nothing. Become so light that she can fly home. She feels sick and shaky. Her head is all muzzy.

At teatime it is cold pasta with tomato sauce. It

was a long day for a little girl. She's hungry. She feels sick. She eats it, gagging on every mouthful.

'You won't do that again, will you?' the woman says sternly, and the little girl shakes her head.

Chapter 7

I am in the same carriage, but on the other side. My bag is at my feet and the low morning sun hits my eyes intermittently as it shutters between houses, trees, telegraph poles.

The low hum as the train speeds through a tunnel reminds me of a van's engine. I tense and look at my phone. The signal goes, and I sit straighter, tug at my blouse, fix my eyes on the window. Maybe I dreamed the whole thing. Maybe . . . but maybe not. What if I can spot the right station myself?

Long back-gardens behind a tall embankment. How do the residents cope with the noise? Double glazing, low house prices?

Rubbish blows along the track as if racing the train: crisp bags, plastic bags, beer cans, a bright red scarf whirling among piles of leaves, a single shoe by a bridge. All of these pieces of people littered in their wake, stamping their presence in the world.

I press my hand against the window, then pull it off, staring at the print I've left, seeing it fade. The train clatters past a station. Last time I'd approached from the opposite direction. I go through a mental checklist of the things I need to find: a café, a single light, a parking spot for the van.

Another station, there and gone so fast I can barely read the sign. I have to remember to read the signs.

I lift my phone to the window. Perhaps if I record this ten minutes of the journey, I can play it back slowly and take in every detail. I hold the phone against the cold glass and watch as we pass a big storage warehouse, its yellow frontage glowing in the autumn light.

A woman's voice. 'Excuse me, is this seat taken?'

I don't answer.

'I said—'

'It's fine. Take it.' Distracting me as another station flies past. Where did she get on? Has she been searching for a seat since the last stop? Or has she moved, spotting a better option?

I don't take my eyes from the window, but feel her sit beside me, the dip in my seat as she takes hers. I smell her coffee and risk a glance over my shoulder. It's the blonde woman, the one I know vaguely by sight. She is tall, Scandinavian looking, but her voice is London all the way through.

A change in the timbre of the train as we pass another station. I whip around, miss it. My phone has slipped a little but is still recording.

I think of the little girl: her dark hair, her big eyes, her too-big blazer. I think of the conversation with Ward. Budget cuts and limited resources, he'd said. So many other kids to find. The Sharmas' little boy.

They aren't looking for her anymore, I'm the only

one, and now here I am, letting her down. Letting down a little girl just like Grace. My fingers tighten on the phone as it picks up a signal again. I haven't identified the spot. We'll be in London in ten minutes and then I'll have to go to work. But I am the *only one looking for her*.

The train draws into Euston and I follow the blonde woman off. She hesitates and casts back a smile as she heads for the platform steps, maybe wanting someone to walk with, but I shake my head a little guiltily and let her go.

My office is a fifteen-minute yomp up Eversholt Street, past Mornington Crescent tube station and the posh deli on the corner, where I usually buy a coffee and croissant. I have a lot of work to catch up on.

I don't move. With my gaze on the other side of the platform, I heft my bag and look at my phone.

'Come on, lady, out of the way!'

I retreat until my calves find a bench, then I open my camera, find the last recording and press play.

I should have put the video on slow motion. All I can see now is blurred grey as scenery flies past, and dribbles of water on the glass. The sound is a faint roaring clatter, like a van driving in the rain.

I press my lips together. Even with a good recording it would be difficult to spot the right platform. I need to be travelling in the correct direction.

I get to my feet and, with the phantom sound of a van growling in my ears, head after the final stragglers, down the steps, and into the main station. But, instead of leaving through the ticket barrier, I head for the platform facing the one I'd disembarked onto. The one that will take me home.

Feeling eyes on me, I glance up. The blonde woman is back. Now she is standing on the empty platform opposite, watching me.

My train pulls in and I get on. As I sit, I look out of the window to see her on the phone. She is frowning. Our eyes meet through the glass. As we pull away, she remains on the platform. I watch her recede and then vanish.

'Bridge, where are you? Diane rang, she wanted to know when you're coming back in, something about a report due to one of your clients and a problem with data collection in the phone centre. I told her you'd gone to work this morning. She said you aren't answering your phone and you never arrived! Call me, *please*.'

I click the voicemail off without bothering to call Tom back. I am still trying to record the journey. This is the third time I've gone around. I've *almost* got a clear image this time, by leaning the phone on the back of my bag, rather than trying to hold it still.

Suddenly I feel like a fool. What am I doing trying to record stations through a window? What I need to do is visit each one and look around.

If I get off at Apsley, I can catch the slow train. It stops everywhere, long enough for me to check out the stations properly. If one seems a possibility, I can disembark and examine it more carefully. It isn't a job for a workday. This Saturday perhaps.

But how much time does the little girl have? There is no-one filming an appeal for her, no-one offering a reward for information, or pleading for her return. There is only me.

I check my watch, blinking when I see the hands. No wonder Diane called. I should ring in and let them know I'm not going to make it. But then the train pulls into Apsley and I fly to my feet, grabbing my phone and bag and shouldering my way to the exit. I press the button, wait anxiously as the door slides open, and jump off. This is by far the better way to do things.

I stand on the platform, feet cold and aching in my high heels, a blister forming.

I've done nothing but jump from train to train all morning and my eyes are blurry from staring at platforms, seeking something familiar. My whole day has been a hazy impression of battered fences, ticket barriers, weathered concrete, yellow lines, sprawling bridges. Did this station tug at me because it was the right one or because they are all beginning to merge: the same *Metro* stands, the same benches, the same power lines, the same trees overlooking the car parks. Had I really seen the Pumpkin Café that night, or had I thought so only because it was such a common sight on train platforms that it had settled into assumption?

I turn from the wide window of the café and try to put the little girl into the picture before me. Had she been sat right here, in the dark, under the light, on her battered suitcase, with her back to the doorway? There *is* a light above me, but there are other lights along the platform too, leading to the little bridge. There *is* a car park by the tiny station, but is it close enough for me to have seen the van from my seat? The station is unmanned, except for one bored-looking girl in the café, who is looking at her phone.

This seems the best fit of the five I've explored so far. I blink up at the camera attached to a pillar between the carpark and the platform. Is this the station with the broken CCTV? Has Sergeant Shaw already ruled it out?

There is fresh graffiti on the bench outside the café, bright yellow on the pitted metal: *Go home, bitch*.

It seems directed at me. It can't be. And yet.

I shudder. Is it worth calling Naomi Shaw? My hand hovers over my phone, then drops. I need more evidence.

I crouch on the ground where I believe she was sitting. Perhaps the girl left something, or maybe there'll be scuff marks; some indication of the struggle I'd seen. Everyone left some sign of themselves on the world, an impression. So where was hers?

A sweet wrapper is trapped beneath the bench leg, blown there and secured. I am about to tug it free when I think of all the crime shows I've watched over the years. I open my bag, take out my sandwich, consider it for a moment and then remove it from the plastic wrapper. I use the baggie to pick up the trapped sweet wrapper. A Sherbet Dip Dab. A kid's sweet for sure. But hers? There is no way to know but, somehow, I feel it is. A tangible link between us.

I wrap the ripped and damp Dip Dab packet in the bag and drop it into my pocket. Then I stand, meeting the now curious eyes of the girl in the café. I look down at the sandwich still clutched in my hand: tuna mayonnaise. It's past lunchtime and suddenly I am hungry. I sit on the bench, feeling the ghost of the girl next to me and bite into my sandwich, wondering if they are feeding her, whoever has her. Immediately, the bread turns to dust in my mouth.

I don't know what to do with the sweet wrapper. The police can run fingerprints, but that will tell them nothing: she won't be in any files. I can call Sergeant Shaw, but I don't know what to say. I *might* have found the right station. Why? Because I found an old sweet wrapper trapped under a bench.

It can't help me. It isn't a real lead, but it proves, at least to me, that the girl existed. I am not going mad. It is *something*.

Over the muffled sound of music through the café door and the swish of wind through leaves, I hear the crunch of tyres on gravel. Someone is parking beside the small line of commuter vehicles, which will be sat there all day. I turn and stare: it is Tom's green Toyota Yaris. I toss my part-eaten sandwich into the cigarette bin beside the bench.

Tom leaps out. 'For fuck's sake, Bridget!' I can hear him over the fence and half the car park.

I can't seem to get up. I see the moment he realises

he will have to come for me. He marches to the other side of the car, unclips Grace from her car seat and heads with her towards the station entrance.

Suddenly I can move. I choke down the mouthful of tuna that has been clogging my mouth and pull out my phone. Then I snap a couple of photos of the station, the bench and the café. There is nothing else I can do. I rise and race for the turnstile, meeting Tom and Grace on the other side.

He glowers. 'You couldn't have called? I was worried sick. What the f—' He looks at Grace, grimaces. '*Fudge* are you doing anyway?'

I start to answer.

'No, don't tell me. I know what you're doing.' He hands Grace to me and drags his hands over his stubble and through his hair. 'I'm trying to understand, Bridge. I know you feel responsible, but this isn't on *you*. Let the police—'

'The police aren't looking for her anymore,' I whisper.

'How do you know?'

'They told me. They think . . .' I look back at the platform, unable to meet his angry blue eyes. 'They think I fell asleep and dreamed it. Or made it up for attention.' Tears well. 'I *didn't*!'

'I know. There's no way you would. They just don't know you.' He sighs. 'But that doesn't mean—'

'Yes, it does. It means *I'm* the only one looking for her. She's my responsibility.'

'*Grace* is your responsibility. *I'm* your responsibility. Your *job* is your responsibility. You've got clients. Aren't *they* your responsibility?'

We glare at each other as a fast train roars past, ignoring our little station, dragging our hair in its wind. Grace squeals and grips my shoulder. I shush her.

'It's a little girl,' I say towards the vanishing train. 'Grace has *you*, there are other people in my team at work. No-one even cared enough to report her missing.'

He examines my face as if he hasn't seen it before. I shrivel under his regard. I don't want him looking at me so clearly; I am afraid of what he'll see, the changes I've undergone.

'How did you find me?' I mutter.

'*Find my iPhone*,' he says, still with that odd, evaluating expression. 'I've got your number and your password is our wedding anniversary.'

'Right.' I look at my work bag. 'I'll call Diane, say I was sick on the train or something.'

'You'd better.' Wearily, Tom takes Grace back. 'I don't know how to help you with this, Bridge. Is this even the right station?'

Miserably, I shake my head. 'I don't know. I think . . . I mean I'm pretty sure, but . . . not enough to speak to the police.' I think of what Ward said: *wasting police time.*

Tom shifts Grace's weight in his arms. 'I think you need to take a couple of days off work. Go and talk to Dr Lewis, see if you need to up your dosage. I'm not saying . . .' He clears his throat, looks at the floor, then back at me. Restarts. 'You knew I was worried, and you didn't even call. I saw the search history on the iPad. What you're doing isn't healthy, you need to understand that.' He takes my bag from me. 'Are you ready to come home?'

I look back at the platform. For a moment I can see the little girl sitting there, her dark head bowed. Then she vanishes, just like the train, melting into the daylight. There is nothing more I can do.

'I'm ready.'

He leads me to the car park, as if I'll wander off and get lost, helps me into the back seat and shuts the door. Grace's car seat is on the passenger side, so she gets shotgun. I watch him strap her in, and then glance back to make sure I've put my own seatbelt on. I feel about twelve years old.

'I've been speaking to Neil,' he says before starting the engine. 'Sam would love to have you stay over while the lads go out drinking. She doesn't want us all back to the house while we're shit-faced, so we'll stay at the Premier Inn. You can have their spare room and we can put Grace down with India. Sam's excited to see you. You haven't seen each other since Grace's baptism.'

'India's older.' I stare out of the window. 'What if Grace keeps her awake?'

'Neil says India's been able to sleep through absolutely anything since she was four months old,' Tom says, with a trace of rancour, and I nod. 'So, what do you think? It'll be good for you to see Sam.' It's unspoken, but the other words are there.

I'll worry less if you come with me.

Or possibly:

She might be able to calm you down.

87

Or even:

I don't want to leave Grace alone with you . . .

I look out of the window without answering. There's a car parked over the road. The sun is reflecting from the windscreen, but I'm almost certain there's a familiar face behind the wheel: a blonde head.

Chapter 8

'Look at you! You can hardly tell you've had a baby!' Sam flings her arms around me, as I think: *Liar.* 'Not like me.' She pushes me back, long enough for me to see her round, grinning face, the flush in her cheeks, signs of a baby who sleeps through the night. Her natural afro is pinned up in a pineapple. 'The house is such a mess. You don't mind, do you?' She drags me in, and I search for the so-called mess, hoping to see the same litter of life with a child that perpetually covers our flat and, instead, finding an immaculate show home.

It's easy to forget that Sam has always been like this: seeking approbation through self-deprecation. I try not to resent it. Maybe she's not really showing off, perhaps she's just trying to make me feel better.

I put my hand inside my pocket and touch the plastic-covered sweet wrapper. It's a reminder that some things are more important. But it's also a reminder that there are better things I could be doing.

I grimace and follow her into the living room, letting Tom bring Grace in her car seat. The room is large and bright, the carpet cream, with a red rug. There's a huge Robert Aswani print on one wall and a professional portrait of the three of them, taken when India was only a few weeks old, on the other. Sam looks like a model, even then, when India *must* have been keeping her up. She's flashing her engagement ring in the picture. The coffee table has been pushed to one side and the leather sofas have African throws on them, making them look cosy. It's a lovely room.

As soon as we're all in, Sam takes the car seat from Tom and puts it on the rug like a centrepiece, kneeling in front of Grace, who glowers at her suspiciously.

That's my girl.

'Sorry, Sam. She's slept most of the way and woken up in a right grump, don't mind her.'

Sam tilts her head and sticks out her tongue. Grace smiles widely, reaching out with sticky fingers.

Okay then.

Tom bends over to give Sam an awkward one-armed hug. 'How's the fiancé?'

'Good, we're all good. Neil will be down in a bit.' She doesn't take her eyes from Grace. 'My goodness, Tom, she's even more gorgeous than she was last time we saw her. Facebook doesn't do her justice. She looks just like you. She's got your eyes though, hasn't she, Bridge? And the curl in her hair is yours.' She laughs. 'Not like India, you'll see her in a moment. She's practically the spit of her dad. Ungrateful brat.' She laughs again. 'Neil's just waking her from her nap. She'd sleep the clock round if we let her.' She has the grace to look sheepish.

I force a smile and release a squirming Grace from

her car seat. Sam looks at me for permission and takes her.

'Gosh, I'd forgotten how fast they grow. India's only ten months, but she's already so much bigger. It's lovely to hold a little one again. How is she sleeping?' She asks sympathetically, and I realise she is looking past Grace and at me with solicitous intensity.

After a bad morning with a fussy Grace I hadn't managed a shower, even though I'd meant to, so, my hair is tight to my skull with grease but frizzed at the ends, where I'd been leaning on the seat back. My jumper stretches tightly over my breasts and belly and I realise there's a stain on one arm. I thought I'd washed it but, apparently, I'd put it in the drawer dirty, confused one pile for another. My jeans, at least, fit me. 'My fat jeans' I'd always called them. Now they were my everyday jeans. I touch self-conscious fingers to my face. I'd put on make-up, but there wasn't enough blusher in the world to hide my exhausted pallor. Too much and I just looked feverish.

Tom quickly puts a hand on my shoulder. 'She's not eight months yet. I expect she'll be sleeping through in a few weeks.'

'Have you left her to cry?' Sam tickles Grace's chin. 'It doesn't do them any harm, does it, Gracie?'

'Left her to cry?' I almost snatch Grace from her. How could she suggest that I let my baby cry? Torture her with my disregard when I was absent from her for so long already? What kind of mum lets their baby cry? Probably the same kind who wouldn't report their little girl missing.

'My friend Angie did it with hers when he was six months. I promise you, Teddy cried for four minutes the first night, then three the next night, and by the third night he was self-settling and sleeping through. Yes, he was, wasn't he, Gracie?'

'It's Grace,' I mutter as Tom squeezes my shoulder.

'We talked about it with the health visitor, but we decided not to go down that route,' Tom says with a slightly strained smile. 'We're feeding on demand.'

Sam looks horrified. 'You're kidding? No routine at all?'

'She's getting into one, isn't she, Bridge? She usually gets up only once or twice in the night now and the afternoon nap is pretty much a given.'

Sam hands Grace to me and stands up. She looks at me for a moment and sighs. 'Listen to me! I'm such an arsehole. I've got this angel baby who sleeps fifteen hours out of twenty-four. What the hell do I know?' She leans closer to me. 'When she first started doing that, I was so worried, I made Neil take us to A&E.' She shakes her head. 'The doctor couldn't believe it. He's like, "You're complaining because your baby sleeps *too much*? Is that right?"'

Tom sputters a laugh. 'You're serious?'

'God yes. It was mortifying. The nurse was like, "Just go home and count your blessings."'

I can't help it, I laugh too. *This* is why I love Sam. She might come across as Little Miss Perfect, but she knows it, and she never quite crosses that line.

'You know, I was cleaning for hours before you

arrived.' She eyes me. 'I drove Neil nuts. He said you wouldn't care, but *you* have a job. What if you came here and were all like, "What does she do all day that her house isn't even tidy?"'

I gape. 'You think I'd judge you for a messy house.'

Tom throws back his head and snorts so loudly that Grace jumps and stares at him. 'If you saw *our* flat, Sam!' Then he stops and yells. '*Neil!*'

'Tommo!' Neil bursts into the room like a grenade, two beers in one hand and his daughter under the other arm like a rugby ball; a dark-haired miniature of him.

'Here, Sam, take your child.' He passes India to Sam, then throws both arms around Tom and claps him on the back. '*Mate!*'

'Mate!'

'Fatherhood, right?'

'Both with bloody daughters. What did we do to deserve that?'

'God's way of repaying us for being such players.' Neil winks at me as he gives Tom a beer. 'Bridget the Fidget, looking lovely as ever.'

But there's a fraction of hesitation, of surprise. I'm not what he was expecting. I touch my hair. 'It was a long journey.'

'But worth it, right? Moving to Clitheroe was the best thing we ever did. The great Northern escape!' He gestures at Sam. 'Get this woman some wine.'

I bite my lip. 'I'm not sure I—'

'We got in the one you like, New Zealand Sauvignon Blanc, right? Even shelled out for the good stuff. Sam said you liked Cloudy Bay? It was twenty-four-bloody-quid a bottle. Unbelievable. I told her you'd be fine with the six–quid stuff from Aldi, but you know what Sam's like. Don't tell me you aren't drinking?'

'It's not that. I—'

He turns back to Tom. 'We're heading into Blackburn and leaving Clitheroe to the ladies. Meeting the lads at The Drummer's for beers. Then we're booked into Achari for a curry, the comedy club at George's and we'll finish with a club. The Cellar probably. Ready to go in ten?'

'No problem.' Tom takes a drink, looking as if it's the water of life, and raises his eyebrows at me. 'You heard the plan, right?'

Sam answers him. 'Got it, don't actually need to know it.' She glowers at Tom. 'Just don't let him get tattooed, injured or picked up by some rando.' She points a finger at him. India copies her and adds a loud 'da-da-da' and a toss of her dark little head, for good measure. I realise that while India does look like Neil, there's a lot of Sam in there too. 'Tom, you're in charge.'

He holds up his hands. 'Don't put *me* in charge.'

'Too late.' Sam nods and so does India. 'I'm holding you responsible.'

'Why is that woman still without a glass of wine?' Neil looks at me again and Sam hands India to Tom on her way to the kitchen.

'Worship my princess while I pour.'

'She *is* a princess,' Tom says, instantly melting. He strokes her cheek and glances at Neil. 'How did *you* make that?'

'Could say the same about yours, mate,' Neil says, peering at Grace. 'In all seriousness, we came good in the end, didn't we?'

'Yeah we did.' Tom smiles at me, his blue eyes warmer than they have been in a while.

Sam comes back with two glasses in one hand and the bottle in the other. 'I thought, sod it,' she says. 'I've texted Mum. She's going to pop over from Whalley later in case we're incapacitated. She can bed in with me.'

'I'm still breastfeeding.' I fold my arms.

'That's okay, so am I.' Sam puts the wine on the coffee table. 'You can express in the kitchen if you like. Then you'll be good to go.'

'I–I don't know.' I look at Tom, then at Sam. 'Grace doesn't know your mum. I should stick to tea.'

Tom hands India to Sam, who takes her daughter without lifting her eyes from me. Then he puts an arm over my shoulders. 'Have a drink or three, Bridge. You deserve it. Grace will be *fine*. Sam's mum is lovely.'

'I know!'

'I've got two sisters and a brother,' Sam reminds me. 'There's *nothing* baby-related that Mum hasn't dealt with.'

'Grace has an allergy—'

'So do two of my nieces. You remember when they came for dinner, Neil? Total nightmare. Tomato, dairy, soya and *lentils*, would you believe? I mean, *lentils*. Mum knows all about it. She even did a special training thing so she can use the epi-pen properly.'

'Grace isn't that bad. She doesn't need an epi-pen, she just gets a really upset stomach.'

Tom gives me a gentle shake. 'See, Bridge, a couple of glasses won't hurt. Have fun with Sam. Grace will be fine.' I look down at her: she's already staring at India with complete adoration, mesmerised, as though she's never seen an older child before.

I pull Tom towards the door, and Neil realises I want some privacy. He draws Sam towards the coffee table.

'I just . . .' I think desperately. How can I put this? 'It feels as if I'm abandoning her, I mean if I drink and let some stranger look after her. Like I'm being a bad mum.' I clutch Grace more tightly at the thought and she squirms and wails, thinking she's being taken away from her new friend.

'Jesus, Bridge.' Tom rubs his eyes.

'It's not just that.' I swallow. 'I already feel like this weekend, not looking for the little girl, I'm being a bad person, abandoning *everyone who needs me*.' I choke on the last words, tearing up.

Tom takes Grace from my arms. 'I'm putting her on the rug,' he tells me. 'She's going to be all right with India for just a minute. Come with me into the kitchen.'

Sam nods but Neil stares as if he's never seen me before.

I don't think he ever saw me cry, not once in the six months we were going out. I was always together, always the fun one. I never stopped moving. He called me Bridget the Fidget, not just because it rhymed, but because I had so much energy. It was one of the reasons we split up. He said he needed someone he could relax around, someone whose drive was more in line with his own. I was amazing, he said, but in small doses. We were better as friends. I didn't even cry then.

I think of that old, university me and I wonder who she was. She's a total stranger, I can't even imagine not being tired and weighed down. Now I feel as if my body is anchored to the floor; it's an effort just to get up, to move forward, to lift an arm or a leg. Every day is just a non-stop effort to keep going.

Once I'd got over the terror of being alone in a new place, the old me fizzed. The new me is flat.

Tears drop onto my fingers like September apples, as Tom drags me into the kitchen. It's another beautiful room.

He sits me on a stool, kneels in front of me and takes my hands. 'You're not a bad mum, Bridge.'

'I *am*.'

I didn't want to do this now, in someone else's house. Not when he's meant to be going out and having fun. I didn't want to do this *ever*.

'You're *not*.' Tom starts to rub, as if my hands are cold and he's trying to warm them. 'Grace is happy. She loves you. You get up all hours with her in the night, even when you've been working all day. You won't let me do even one night feed.' There's a hint of accusation there. 'You don't eat dairy because it'll make her ill and you *love* Galaxy bars. I don't know how you're even surviving without them.'

I test out a smile. It doesn't feel natural.

'You keep the roof over our head,' he says. 'You're a maths genius, which is surprisingly sexy. You were cool when I said I wanted to give up my crappy office job and try to become a scriptwriter, even though we were trying to get pregnant. You're amazing, why can't you see that?'

'What about—'

'If you're going to talk about this kidnapping again, just don't.' Tom drops my hands. 'I know how you feel, honestly. But you aren't Nancy Drew or Miss bloody Marple. You wouldn't know the first place to start looking. What? Are you going to speak to your underworld contacts and track this girl down? The closest thing we have to an underworld contact is suspecting that the kid who hangs out behind the chippy sells weed.' He takes my hands again. 'You're a superhero to *us*. Can't that be enough? You can't do anything for this girl except be utterly miserable and that's not fair on me and Grace. You don't have enough of yourself to be sharing around with strangers.'

I don't say anything, he's right. It's the reason I agreed to come to Lancashire in the first place. I haven't the first clue what to do for the girl, no idea where to look, or even how to start. I'm hyperaware of the sweet wrapper in my pocket. It feels radioactive, as if it's emitting negative energy, draining me.

Finally, I hang my head. 'I just feel—'

'I know.' Tom sighs. 'It's totally shit that you were the one to see her. And it is crap that out of the antenatal group, *you're* the one who gets postnatal depression. *You*, Bridget the Fidget.' He lifts my face by the chin. 'It's shit that you're the one who has to go back to work because we have to pay that ridiculous mortgage. I should be the one working and I know it,' he growls. 'Everything is shit.' His shoulders sag and I see the top of his head; his hair is thinner there, his curls less bouncy than they once were, a little of his pink scalp shows between the coils.

'Not everything!' I'm totally ruining his night out. I've brought him down to my level. I'm the worst wife. 'Grace is amazing. You're fantastic with her.'

'Yeah?' He looks back up. 'Did you see how she charmed Neil? Had him wrapped round her finger with one look.'

'She's wonderful.' I sigh. 'Whatever happens, we made this fantastic little person, so we must be doing something right. And I know I won't feel this way forever.'

'It's still early days.' Tom nods.

'Maybe . . .' I glance away. 'Maybe I *should* be thinking about counselling.'

'If you think it'll help.' Tom gets to his feet. 'We can talk about it when we get home, yeah?'

I nod.

'Are you sure you'll be all right with Sam?'

I rise from the stool. I still feel shaky, but if I ruin his night out, what kind of person am I?

'We'll be fine.'

'And you'll have a couple of drinks? Try to have fun.'

'Yeah.'

'I'll call you from Blackburn.'

'Don't.' My lips tremble into a smile. 'The last thing I want is a drunk-dial from my own husband, waking the babies.'

'Hug?' He opens his arms and I step into them. He tightens his grip and I tighten mine. For a moment we're a solid unit like it was before we had Grace. Just him and me. I inhale his scent and smile. Then Grace cries out from the living room and we're separating and racing back, Tom just a little in front.

'What is it?' He hurtles into the room like gangbusters and I stumble to a stop as I see Grace and India entangled on the floor like a pushmi-pullyu. Grace is yelling blue murder and lying half over India, while India is waving her arms and legs as if confused why she can't move.

'They were both sitting on the rug.' Sam is laughing. 'Grace lost her balance and took India down with her.' She detangles them, her shoulders shaking. 'I shouldn't laugh but it was like a comedy sketch. Slow motion and everything.'

Tom sweeps Grace into his arms and tickles her until she stops yelling.

'Right, mate.' Neil stands, careful not to look at me, as if the sight of my tear-stained face is something he just isn't ready to deal with. 'Are you ready to head out?'

'Yeah.' Tom hands Grace over to me. 'You're sure you'll be okay?'

'She'll be *fine*.' Sam rolls her eyes. 'Go! Have fun. But not too much fun.'

'Yes.' I raise Grace's hand to help her wave. 'Enjoy yourselves, you deserve it.'

It takes them a few minutes to get out of the door. Lengthy goodbyes to their daughters, as if they're never going to see them again, kisses for each of us, a search for a mobile phone, a check for cash.

In the end Sam literally has to thrust Neil out and shut the door in his face.

'That's better,' she says and turns to me. 'Right, now explain to me why you missed my hen do!' I take a step backwards, but she grabs my hand. 'I'm kidding. We *are* going to have a drink later and I'm going to tell you all about the naked butler that Shehnaz got for us, but first we're going to walk the babies around the castle and you're going to tell me what's really going on. Don't take this the wrong way, Bridge, but it's obvious that you're not okay.'

Chapter 9

'It's beautiful here.' I look down from the walkway on the castle wall, hunch against the biting wind, and stare out over the Ribble Valley towards Pendle Hill. It is the shape of an axe head against the white sky, birds wheeling over the mottled darkness of its slopes.

'Better than London anyway.' Sam had seen the view 'a million times', so she was hiding from the wind behind a wall.

I rotate slowly. The town is mapped out in front of me, with its winding streets and old buildings incongruously splattered with modern shopfronts. Below us there is a park to walk through with the prams. Grace is silent in hers, perhaps shocked by the wind, but more likely exhausted by all the new things she's seen.

'This seemed a better idea when we were indoors,' Sam yells. 'Are you done yet?'

I wasn't. There was something about this place. Something that felt not *familiar* exactly; but looking at it made me feel the way I did when I'd heard Neil speak for the first time. I love the Lancashire accent; whatever is said in it sounds kind. And I think I am falling in love with this town, with its castle and park and even the new builds sprawling outwards from the older centre towards the endless fields and sky.

The castle itself isn't what I'd pictured when Sam said we were going to see it. It's just a cube on a hill, most of it long destroyed, but it was well-loved, that was clear. The residents were proud enough of their heritage to create a visitor centre filled with local artwork, and a surrounding garden, with hidden sculptures and a war memorial. The fort is under siege by local talent.

I wonder what it had been like when left wild, maybe twenty years earlier, before this obvious cash injection. I think perhaps I might have liked it even more.

'Come on, Bridge, I'm freezing. Let's take them round the park.'

'Okay.' I start down the walkway, bumping the pram from level to level. 'You're so lucky to live here.' I'm not just being polite.

Sam begins walking as soon as I reach her and I hurry to keep up. 'You don't know the half of it, you should hear about the schools.'

'They're good?' We turn and head downhill. A sculpture of a bird in flight rises in front of me and I pause to examine it.

'Excellent.' Sam stops to wait. 'There's a grammar school in town. It's marvellous. We'll be sending India there. If she's clever enough, that is. I mean, she does take after Neil so it might have to be the local comp.'

'Ha-ha.' I bend and adjust Grace's blanket over

her knees. 'A grammar school though, I thought that's the kind of thing Neil would be dead against.'

'Before we had kids, yeah. But then we thought back to our own schools, being picked on for working hard, and we thought, if she's clever enough why *not* send her somewhere she can learn without being bullied for being bright, or whatever . . . you know.'

I look at Grace. 'But you have to pay for it?'

'God no, it's free.'

'Free? You're kidding?'

'It's a *state* grammar school.'

'F-fudge!'

'And the house prices.' Sam is warming to her subject. 'I mean Clitheroe itself isn't cheap, but you can get a four-bed for under 300. It's less if you go out a bit. We paid 180 for our three-bed.'

'We paid 250 for our flat and it's still almost an hour into London'

Sam looks at me. 'Tom told Neil you were thinking of staying home with Grace, letting him go back to work.'

'You make it sound as if I'm stopping him.' My laugh is brittle.

'I didn't mean it like that.' Sam touches my arm. 'I mean, if you're leaving your job and Tom hasn't found one yet, why doesn't he look up here?'

I freeze. 'You're serious?'

'Why not?' Sam leans closer and I smell her perfume on the wind: peonies and bright pink berries. 'A change of scene might be good for what ails you. You'd get rid of that big mortgage, so there'd be less pressure on you both. You could have more room, a garden for Grace and then, later on, the school. And, of course, there's me and Neil. I can't believe we haven't seen you for so long. We miss you.'

'Us too.' But I've stopped listening to her, my mind is racing. Is it possible?

'Come on.' Sam turns the pram and heads in the other direction. 'Forget the park, let's go and look in the windows of some estate agents.'

I hang back. 'Not without discussing it with Tom.'

Sam snorts. 'It's not like you're buying today, Bridge. Think of it as window shopping. Recon. Information gathering.'

Suddenly my heart feels lighter. 'You make it sound like an army mission.'

'Exactly!' Sam takes my arm in one of hers, using the other to push her pram. 'We're the advance party. And the kids are too little for the park anyway.'

'Grace loves the swings,' I say, but I'm letting her lead me.

'And once we've done the estate agents, I'll take you to the chocolate shop. They've got some dairy-free in there,' she adds before I can say anything. 'And then,' she says, 'we'll go for a pint in The New Inn before we go home for that wine. The boys shouldn't be the only ones to get a decent beer today.'

Sam was right, looking in estate agent windows made me salivate. Now I had four bars of delicious-looking dairy-free in my handbag and we were sitting in a nook by a fire with two pints of what Sam called

'Moorhouse's' sitting in front of us. Sam was feeding India and Grace was spark out in her pram, the fresh air finally achieving what usually took a full feed or a long car journey.

'It's been hard,' I finally say, while tracing the condensation on my pint glass with the tip of a finger. 'It's like who I was has just been buried under this . . . avalanche and I can't dig myself out. I can't even work out which way is up.' As I speak, I watch India lying on Sam's lap, her lips working, her small arm waving wildly as if seeking something to hold onto. Sam takes hold of her fingers and tucks her arm down.

'You're on meds though? Tom said . . .'

'Fluoxetine. It's helped some.' I pick at my beer mat, fraying the edges, and my shoulders droop. 'I just feel like such a failure.'

'Because you need the drugs?' Sam frowns.

'*Everything*.' I can't meet her eye. 'No-one else seems to find motherhood this hard. I mean look at you.'

'Yes, look at me,' Sam says gently. 'India has the best grandparents in the world, right around the corner.'

'Mum lives near us. She takes Grace once a week so Tom can go to college or do his coursework. She's been great.'

Sam looks at me, saying nothing, then she carries on. 'Neil's parents are half an hour away, I can hardly get rid of them. I don't have to go back to work for at least another couple of months, *and* Mum's offered to take India when I do, so I don't even have to look for a nursery. Also, let's not forget that I was gifted this incredible sleeping baby, who is, no doubt, going to make me pay for it when she gets to school age. Plus, Neil.'

'Yes.'

'Did I thank you for introducing us?'

'Once or twice.' My smile is genuine.

'And even with all that, it's *still* hard. Motherhood is f—' She glances at India and grins. '*Fricking* hard, Bridge. If it was easy, men would be mums.'

I laugh awkwardly. 'But—'

'Betsie? Betsie Dobson! Bleeding hell.' It's an old man and he's drunk. He stumbles his way towards us, knocking over tables and causing a young couple to glare at him over their spilled drinks. 'Betsie Dobson! Where've you been? It's been, what, eight, nine, years?' He hiccoughs and some of his pint splashes on Grace's pram. He refocuses on Grace. 'Is that one yours?' His nose is mottled with veins and his cheeks are flushed. His grey hair is dragged over his balding head, needing a comb. There's a snowfall of dandruff on the tops of his shoulders.

'Sorry, ladies, sorry!' The barman has raced over. 'Come on now, Jack, this isn't Betsie. Look, this one's a youngster. Practically a baby herself.' He winks at me.

'Yes, it is, look at her.' Jack blinks at me, slowly, then at Sam, then back at me. 'Oh,' he says again, his voice quivering this time. 'I'm a stupid old man, ain't I?'

I shake my head, wordlessly.

'Betsie died a few years ago,' the barman murmurs as Jack stumbles away. 'She was a bit of a regular, Jack had a soft spot, especially after what happened to her . . . anyway.' He checks that Jack has returned to his friends and waves at the woman behind the bar to watch him. 'Enjoy your drinks. Apologies again.'

'Local colour!' Sam says. 'Hasn't put you off, has it?'

I frown. 'Betsie Dobson? What happened to her then?'

'Dunno.' Sam looks down at India, who has passed out. Her mouth has slipped from her nipple and she's starting to snore. Sam covers herself back up and shifts India into her pram. 'Do you want to stay and finish your pint, or would you rather head back to the house?'

'I'd like to go, actually.' The old man, Jack, is staring at us and muttering something. 'He's kind of creeping me out.'

Sam stands up. 'No problem.' She takes a quick last drink of her beer, puts on her coat and I follow.

We're on our way out when Jack runs after us. The barman is pulling a pint and the woman behind the bar is nowhere to be seen. He catches my arm and I flinch.

Sam starts to bristle.

'Wait,' he says. 'I didn't mean nothing. Here, this is for the little one. Buy her summat nice.' He presses a creased ten pound note into my hand.

'I can't!' I try to hand it back but he won't take it. He steps out of my reach.

'It's for the baby.' He's already backed right away. I can't give him the money back without chasing him.

Sam catches my eye and shakes her head. 'Let him give it you, it'll make him feel better.'

'But . . .'

'Don't worry,' Sam says. 'If you're that bothered, leave it with me and I'll pop into The New Inn later in the week, leave it behind the bar for him.'

'Okay.' We start walking but I look back. Jack is standing outside the pub, beside one of the benches, watching us go, wistfully.

Suddenly he calls out. 'Say a prayer for her, won't you?' he shouts. 'For the tenner. Say a prayer for Betsie Dobson!'

Chapter 10

The little girl is sitting on the train platform, her feet drumming on her leather suitcase. *Thud-thudthud-thud-thudthud*. Her tongue is pink from the lolly of the Dip Dab she has just finished. She hadn't intended to drop the wrapper, that was 'littering', but she had been told not to move from the suitcase, while her mum went to get tickets and drinks and to talk to the woman she'd spotted from the post office, so she can't really pick it up again.

Thud-thudthud-thud.

The light from the bulb above illuminates her dark hair and pale face, makes it seem as if she is sitting on stage, under a spotlight, waiting for the other actors to turn up so she can play her part. She fiddles with the bottom of her blazer and pokes at the pocket with its embroidered rose. She's excited to show her aunt her new uniform and to go to the bookshop with her voucher. She's bored though too, and she wants to go and look more closely at the tracks, see what they really look like. But she isn't supposed to move.

Thud-thudthud.

110

She looks up at the sound of an oncoming train and almost leaps from her suitcase to see it more clearly. But she remembers to stay still.

Thud.

There is a big man in front of her. He isn't her daddy. Someone else stands beside him. She doesn't know either of these people. They are wearing all black, like burglars. The first man leans over and grabs her arm. She opens her mouth and yells for her mummy. The other lifts her. They carry her together, away from the suitcase.

She'd been told not to move.

I wake with a small scream and clap my hands over my mouth, terrified that I'd woken Grace. For a moment I'm disoriented: this isn't my room, isn't my house. Then I remember where I am. Have Tom and Neil come back?

No, they are staying away tonight, and the house is quiet, save for a light regular thud-thud coming from the baby's room. Panic grips me and I fight my way free of sweaty, tangled bedding, gasping Grace's name as I race for the hallway.

I stumble to a halt at India's open door. There is a rocker by the window and Sam's mum, Althea, is sitting in the chair, tall and graceful, giving Grace her 2 a.m. feed by the light of the moon. As she moves gently back and forth, the chair thuds against the carpet. She looks up and catches sight of me. 'She's almost finished the bottle,' she whispers. 'Go and get the kettle on, I'll be there in a minute.'

I nod, knowing I won't be able to fall back to sleep, even if I try. I tiptoe past Sam's room and down the stairs. My head aches and my mouth is filled with cotton wool. Half a pint and two glasses of wine and I feel as if I've been on a three-day bender. That's what sixteen months of not drinking does for you. I fill the kettle and prepare two cups with decaf teabags, one with almond milk. Althea turns up as I am pouring the hot water.

'Thanks, honey.' She looks at me. 'Sit down, won't you. Grace is fine. Spark out. Sometimes it's easier when it's not their mum. They know there's no point in making a fuss.' She takes a sip of her tea and measures me solemnly. 'Samia tells me you're having a hard time. It's all right, don't answer.' She puts her tea down, rises and takes my own mug out of my hand. She places mine on the counter, then she puts her arms around me and hugs me tightly. She speaks again without letting me go. 'Samia doesn't know, but I had the baby blues, that's what they used to call it, you know, after her brother was born. She was only a little one at the time. I know what you're going through.'

A sob builds in my chest. Not just a sob, but a terrifying monster of a thing that wrenches its way from my gut and twists, rising past my heart and into my throat. I try to smother it but she hugs me more tightly, pulling my face to her shoulder, and her warmth squeezes the sound right out of my throat.

'Ah, sweetheart. . . honey . . .' She croons endearments as she rocks me and I cling to her, as the sound cracks my chest open and I bleed my pain all over her.

After a while, when the sound has vanished and my shoulders droop with exhaustion and a strange sort of relief, Althea pats my back and returns to her own chair. I hide my face in my cooling tea, unable to meet her gaze.

'It's all right,' she says. 'Nothing to be ashamed of. We all need a good cry now and again. You don't really know me, so who cares what I think? I just know that if you hold it together for too long, eventually you'll crack like an eggshell. It's not healthy.'

I lift my head. Althea looks like Sam, but an older, kindlier, more weathered version of her daughter. She has laughter lines around her eyes and mouth, and wears her hair short. She smells of talcum powder and Grace's Bepanthen cream.

I notice the nappy she has put by the bin.

'Oh, gosh, I'm sorry. You had to change Grace's nappy?'

'Of course I did.' She frowns gently. 'What are you sorry about?'

'I . . .' I paused. 'Nothing, I suppose.'

I duck my head and drink my tea. After a moment she puts her hand on my arm. 'What woke you? Grace?'

I shake my head. 'I had a nightmare.'

Althea says nothing and when I look up, she's still watching me. 'Want to tell me about it?'

I start to shake my head again, then I stop. Why

not tell her? 'When I was coming back from work I saw a girl being kidnapped. But no-one's reported her missing and there's no evidence she was ever there. The police think I'm making it up.' I frown. 'They say I might be in trouble for wasting their time. They think I want attention, or I dreamed it.'

'Do you? Did you?' Her voice remains calm, she isn't judging me. If I tell her I had made it up, or dreamed it, I think she'd give me another hug.

'No,' I say just as quietly. 'I didn't make it up and I was awake when it happened.'

Her face drops into lines of sadness. 'You mean there's a missing little girl out there and no-one cares except you? Well, no wonder you've the weight of the world on your shoulders.'

'There's nothing I can do to help find her,' I groan. 'I don't even know where to start.'

'And you dreamed about her?'

'I *keep* dreaming about her.' The tea is no longer warming me. I put it down and rub my eyes. 'I keep seeing her, sitting there, on the platform, on her little suitcase, wearing her uniform . . . it's like each time I notice more details. Tonight, I realised she had a rose on her blazer.'

'Blazer?' Althea mused. 'You mean like from a private school?'

'I suppose.'

Althea pursed her lips. 'You know, my other grand-daughter just had a policeman come to her school. She came home and told me I wasn't allowed to put any pictures of her in her uniform on my Instagram.

Would you believe it? Apparently, those paedophiles can track them down to their school if they work out which uniform it is that they're wearing. So, it shouldn't be impossible to find out which school has a rose on its blazer pocket.'

I stare at her. 'You mean, I could look it up?'

'Why not?' Althea leans forward. 'If you're the only one looking for the little angel, and you have a lead? The school won't be able to give you any personal information, but the police can make a call and find out if any of their kids have gone AWOL.'

'But . . . if the police think I'm wasting their time I could get charged.'

'I suppose,' Althea said thoughtfully. 'It all depends on how much you're willing to risk for this little girl.'

Sam appears in the kitchen doorway, her hair sticking up in all directions. Her eyes are bloodshot and she's cracking a huge yawn. 'What's going on? Is everything okay?' She stares at the teacups. 'Why are you drinking tea at 2 a.m., Mum?' She blinks at me, owlishly. 'And *you* were supposed to get a full night's sleep, that was the whole point of Mum being here. What are you doing up and gossiping?'

Althea rises and gives her daughter a squeeze. I look on a little jealously as Sam rolls her eyes. 'I'm off to bed now, honey,' Althea says, before looking back at me. 'Unless you still need me? I'm not as young as I used to be.'

I smile. 'No, thanks, Althea, go on up.'

'We should follow her.' Sam frowns. 'We only got to sleep a couple of hours ago.'

'I know.' I put the cups in the sink. 'Your mum's the best.'

'Told you.' It's Sam's turn to put an arm around me. 'Move up North, Bridget, and she'll let you be her sidekick in the WI.'

I laugh and follow her up the stairs.

Just as I'm leaving the bathroom, I hear the sound of a van on the road outside. I run to my room and pull back the curtains. A white van with no markings is idling on the road in front of the house. It stays there for a minute and then it drives away.

She's been in here so long that the woman has started to leave the door ajar when she comes in to bring her food, take her temperature, or measure her height and weight.

This time when the woman comes in with the thermometer, the little girl waits until she has turned around, then she bolts for the exit.

She's fast – her daddy always said she was like a greased weasel – and she thinks she'll run all the way home.

When she gets out of the room, there are stairs and another door but this one is locked. She fights with the knob, sobbing and shouting. She can feel the woman standing at the bottom of the steps, just watching her. After a while she gives up and turns around.

The woman points. 'Back to your room.'

The little girl shakes her head.

The woman sighs and climbs the stairs. 'I don't want to hurt you.' She catches the little girl by the fleshy part of her arm.

When she tosses her back in her room, the little girl has bruises in the shape of the woman's fingers.

Chapter 11

My coat is empty. I feel in both pockets, certain I put it in the right-hand side, but frantic enough to believe I made a mistake. There's no sign of the Dip Dab wrapper in its sandwich bag. I start looking around the floor in the hallway, unable to leave for my doctor's appointment until I've found it. Tom appears at the top of the stairs.

'What have you lost?'

'Something important.' I can't take my eyes from the floor. I'm digging behind the shoes now, fingertips dragging through the gritty traces of mud that we've tracked in and which have collected under the coat rack. It isn't there. It isn't anywhere. Maybe I took it out and tucked it in the hood of Grace's pram, where I sometimes keep things. I open the hall cupboard and yank the hood open, scattering crisp packets, pennies and hair bands on the floorboards. A piece of paper flutters past me, folded. Not mine. Automatically I lean to pick it up, but Tom is there first.

'Bridge, what are you looking for?' Tom retrieves the paper and slides it into his pocket. 'Let me help, or you'll be late.'

'It's . . .' I hesitate, reluctant to tell him that I'm losing my mind over a Dip Dab wrapper. 'You haven't seen a sweet wrapper, have you? It was in my pocket.'

'Why do you . . .?' he starts. Then he sighs, as if he dreads my answer. 'Well yeah. I wore your coat to take out the recycling yesterday evening after we got home. I emptied the rubbish out of your pocket. It was disgusting and you're welcome.'

'You put it in the bin?' I race for the kitchen.

'The wheelie bin outside.' Tom follows me. 'They took the rubbish this morning. It's gone, Bridge. I'm sorry, I didn't know it mattered.'

'It did.' I grab the kitchen counter. 'Oh God, it did.'

'Why?' Tom stares at me. 'What's so vital about an old sweet wrapper?'

'It was *hers*!' I shout, knowing I'm likely waking Grace from her nap. 'It was proof that she was there. A connection. Now it's gone and she'll never be found.'

'What the hell?' Tom doesn't move forwards, doesn't take me in his arms. 'This again? It's a *sweet wrapper*, Bridge. There's no possible way you could tell who it belong—'

'I just know, all right?' I'm yelling, top of my lungs, almost screaming. I hear Grace start to cry upstairs. 'I just *know*. It was hers and you *threw it away*.'

'Jesus, Bridge.' Tom starts to back off. 'I'm going to try and settle Grace back down. You have to go to the doctor. I mean you really need to. Talk to her about upping your dosage. Talk about counselling, call your mum's friend . . . whatever it takes. You have to get better. I don't know how long I . . .' He trails off, turns, strides towards the stairs. His feet are heavy on the treads, then they thud on the landing. I hear Grace's door open, the soft murmur of his voice against her hysterical sobs. I did that. I made her cry.

I open and close my fists. 'Crazy Mummy,' I murmur. 'Crazy Mummy.'

Dr Lewis is kind, but stern, and I can't imagine her having hysterics about anything, let alone a sweet wrapper.

'I–I'm not coping very well.' I keep my eyes on my fingers. 'I mean . . . the drugs have helped, but . . . is there anything stronger?'

She looks at me long and carefully. 'How much sleep are you getting?'

'Not much. I mean it takes me a while to get to sleep. And then I . . . I have nightmares. And Grace gets up at two for a feed, and then usually again at four.'

'Twice in the night still?'

'Yes.'

'Is there anything else going on I should know about?'

I shake my head, heavy with the lie.

'Here, fill this in for me. I'll wait.' She passes me an Edinburgh Scale; its questions are familiar to me now.

1. I have been able to laugh and see the funny side of things.

2. I have looked forward with enjoyment to things.

3. I have blamed myself unnecessarily when things went wrong.

4. I have been anxious or worried for no good reason.

5. I have felt scared or panicky for no good reason.

6. Things have been getting on top of me.

7. I have been so unhappy that I have had difficulty sleeping.

8. I have felt sad or miserable.

9. I have been so unhappy that I gave been crying.

10. The thought of harming myself has occurred to me.

I find it hard to fill in. I don't blame myself *unnecessarily*. When things go wrong, I blame myself *perfectly necessarily*. I'm the one who's meant to make sure things go right. I'm the mum. If things go wrong, it's my fault. And yes, I've been anxious and scared, but I've had every reason. Grace is a baby, she could die. Babies die. And they get stolen. Like the dark-haired little girl with the sweet wrapper and the blazer with the rose on it. Or like the Sharma boy, whose mum was crying on the Breakfast Show this morning. My breath starts coming in short gasps.

'You're having difficulty?' Dr Lewis takes the paper back off me. She looks at it. She consults my records. 'It's a better score than last time, which is good, but you've thought about harming yourself?'

I nod without looking at her.

'Often?'

'Not often.' I think of the drive over, how easy it would have been to have swerved in front of an oncoming lorry. How I barely kept my hands tight on the wheel, only by thinking of Grace and how hungry she would get if I wasn't there for her next feed.

'I'm going to up your dose of Fluoxetine.' She starts writing a prescription. 'You should still take two tablets at night, but they'll be stronger.' She glances at me. 'Have you thought any more about counselling? Last time we met you said you'd had therapy before, as a teenager, and you weren't keen to do it again. But I really think—'

'Yes.' The word stutters from me like a gunshot. 'I'll talk to someone.' At least that way I could tell Mum that I'd paid attention to her. And it might help. It might.

Dr Lewis actually smiles at me. 'Great. I'll put you on the waiting list.' She types something and looks apologetic. 'I'm afraid there *is* a waiting list. If you haven't heard anything in six weeks, let me know and I'll get my secretary to see what's happening with the referral.'

'Six weeks!' I gasp.

'I'm afraid so.' She looks as if she wants to pat my hand. 'Unless you or your husband have private health insurance?'

I shake my head.

'Well, see how you get on with the Fluoxetine and the six weeks will go by. They might even contact you sooner, you never know. Come back if you feel worse and I'll see if there's anything else I can do. Are you still in touch with your antenatal group?'

I lick my lips. I know she wants me to say yes but after I got sick, I lost contact with most of them.

Then I went back to work and the others drifted away. Or rather, I let them drift away. 'They meet up at lunchtimes, but I'm back at work.'

'I see.' She sighs. 'Having friends who are going through the same thing – well, it helps, I promise. Perhaps see if you can catch up again?'

I nod, knowing I won't. They aren't like me, those other mummies, with their Boden dresses, boots and leggings, their babies in Petit Bateau, or JoJo Maman Bébé, talking about their husband's jobs and how lucky they are to be able to stay at home and make organic baby food. Or the splinter group, with the teenaged mum who looked taut as an Olympic gymnast two weeks after giving birth, and the working mums who are so very smug about their career choices and how they are showing their sons and daughters 'a good example' and who always seem to be discussing which childminders are best. I was working, yes, but I didn't want to be, and we couldn't afford Boden or a childminder. I didn't seem to fit anywhere.

Dr Lewis tilts her head as she looks at me. Then she makes another note. 'I'm signing you off work for a week, Bridget. Try and get some rest, yes?'

'Thank you.'

'All right.' She stands up, my cue to do the same. 'I'm glad you came to me, Bridget. We'll get through this.'

I mutter a thanks and head for the door. Six weeks. Could I hang on for six weeks?

* * *

When I get back to my car I sit with my phone in my hand.

I think about calling Tom, then I consider Althea's words: how much would I risk for the missing girl?

I place the call.

This time Sergeant Shaw answers and, at the sound of her voice, my heart slows to a more regular beat. I hadn't realised how afraid I'd been of hearing Ward on the line.

'Shaw.'

'Sergeant Shaw . . . it's Bridget Carlson, from the train. . . . I saw the little girl being kidnapped.'

There's a pause on the other end of the line, a rustle of paper, then she speaks. 'Of course, Bridget. How are you? Are you calling for news?'

'There's news?' My heart starts to race.

'Not as such, I'm afraid. More of the same. How can I help you?'

'I . . .' I take a deep breath. 'I think I remembered something else, something about what she was wearing, and I was hoping . . .'

'Can you tell me what it was?'

'It was the blazer, the school blazer. It had a rose on the pocket, I'm sure of it.'

'A rose.' There's another rustle. 'That's very specific.' A pause. 'You went by very fast and you weren't that close to her. You're certain you saw a *rose*? Nothing else that could be similar in shape or colour?'

'A rose.' I clutch the phone tighter. 'I'm sure.'

'All right then, I'll look into it. Thank you.' She

doesn't hang up. 'How are *you* doing, Bridget? Something like this, it can be quite traumatic.'

'I'm okay.' I blink at the phone. 'I'm having nightmares.' I don't know why I told her that.

'Understandable.' Shaw's voice is gentle, kind. 'Let me know if you remember anything else, won't you?'

'I will. And there's a boy.' I speak in a rush. 'I keep seeing his family on the news. Vihaan Sharma, is he . . .?'

'I'm afraid I can't discuss other cases with you, Bridget.'

'Of course, sorry, I just . . . because he was kidnapped too, it feels . . . the same, I guess. It couldn't be the same people?'

'I don't believe so.' Now Naomi sounds impatient. 'I really have to get back to work.'

'Thank you for listening to me.'

'You're welcome. Take care, Bridget.' She hangs up and I relax a little. Naomi will find the uniform and the school, then the police will know that I'm not making all this up.

I start the car and head towards the main road but instead of turning towards home, I make a left past the shops on the corner and drive towards the library. I don't know why, it's only that the girl is on my mind now, and I can't go home and pretend to forget about her just to placate Tom. I want to do . . . something.

I pull into the car park and pick up my phone again. I shoot Tom a text. *Everything fine. Dr has upped dosage. Just need a couple of hours. OK?*

It's not a lie, not strictly. I wait for his answer and it soon arrives, bleeping into the car, a curt *OK*.

The library is quiet. A couple of mums with toddlers are in the children's section and an old man is using the computer in the far corner, grunting over the keys as he laboriously types an email. I imagine he has a son in another country, or maybe he's emailing a faceless department about benefits, a victim of the Government assumption that everyone is happy to communicate online. I prefer to think he is sending a message to a family member, that he's replying to a grandson who has been telling him about playing football and doing well in a test.

I'm not entirely sure what I'm doing here. I head to the desk where I buy an hour on the other computer for no real reason and then I go to sit there, with my back to the old man, and wonder what to do.

My fingers hover over the keys. I have an hour. Automatically I enter the search I've been putting in my own phone at home every night: *child kidnapping, UK*. I'm not expecting to find anything about the girl but something I said to Naomi sticks in my mind: *could it be the same people*? Have I unconsciously stumbled on something? The kidnappers seemed to know what they were doing and if this isn't their first time taking a child, there could be some kind of pattern.

And that's my job: looking for patterns in data. I'm good at it. Usually I'm looking for explanations such as why customer satisfaction in a particular company might be deteriorating, why a factory or department might be less productive, how a company could most effectively extend its reach. But there is no reason why my skills can't be applied to this. Tom is right, I'm a middle-class mother of one. I know nothing about criminals. I can't find kidnappers in the real world, that's Naomi's job, but I might be able to spot them hiding in the data.

An hour later I have bookmarked half a dozen stories from the past ten years. All children taken from a train station or near to one. Always in an area of lower affluence. The children all between the ages of four and seven years old. Have I found a pattern?

I use my work login to find Office for National Statistics data that isn't available to the general public, then I filter for cases with children between the ages of three and ten, who have vanished in the last ten years and who have never been found. There are so many.

So, perhaps I haven't found a pattern. Looking at the sheer number of missing children, it would be almost impossible not to find clusters with similarities.

But there are patterns, I'm sure of it. In that volume of data, there has to be. I buy another hour and extend my search to twenty years.

Some might think that more data would mean it would be more difficult to find one lost little girl, but more data means my findings will have more statistical validity. I can seek correlations, and differences will be more significant.

I need to graph the data and put things together: places, dates, numbers.

I glance at my watch. I'm running out of time. I really should go back to Tom and Grace. It's not fair on Tom otherwise. But I'm getting somewhere, finally achieving something. Raw data can't lie.

Dr Lewis has signed me off work for a week, but Tom doesn't have to know that. If I don't tell him, I can return tomorrow and keep working. If I don't tell him, it isn't exactly a lie.

I ask the librarian for some paper and make notes of the bookmarked pages, just in case. Unable to stop myself, I linger over a story about the tragic Sharma case: the boy, who was being watched by his older sister, Vamil, vanished from a park in Peterborough, when she left him for a few minutes to chat with a friend. Then I ask if I can do some printing, trying not to think about the fact that each of the lines of data represents a missing child.

As I am sweeping up the paperwork, the librarian arrives to switch off the printer and looks over my shoulder. 'Odd thing to be researching. For a dissertation, is it? You'd be amazed what we get people looking up nowadays for their courses.'

'Sure.' I nod. 'Something like that.'

'Well, if you're interested in this kind of thing, we've got a bookcase over in the far corner filled with True Crime. There're a few about child abductions: *Secret Slave, Girl in the Cellar*, that sort of thing. Those ones are autobiographical. One came in the other week about particularly tragic UK abductions actually, and that might suit you.

'Particularly tragic?' I must look taken aback.

'You know, where the child was never found, or found dead . . . or worse.'

'Worse?'

She lowers her voice. 'Worse. You know, abused or taken *to order*. Where the child has no idea who they once were. That's what I think happened to little Ben Needham. Remember him?'

I clutch the paperwork closer to my chest but the librarian doesn't notice my discomfort. 'Let me fetch it for you.' She bustles off and I exhale. I consider escaping, leaving the library before she can return with her book of horrors, but if I want to sit here all week, working, then I ought to remain on her good side. I wait patiently until she comes back. 'Have you got a library card, love?'

I shake my head.

'Let me sort that out for you first then. Have you got your driving licence?'

Fifteen minutes later I have a library card, a book of tragic child abductions titled *Kidnapped!* and a pile of paperwork, all of which I need to hide in my car. I battle the sick feeling in my stomach and stow it in the boot, under the crumpled picnic rug. Then I head for home via the chemist.

I do feel a little better, perhaps because I spoke to the doctor, but more likely because I feel as if I'm finally achieving something. I have a week, I think. A week to find them in the data. If they're in there, I can track them.

Chapter 12

I cradle a cup of tea and wait for Tom to finish his shower. Grace is finally asleep. It's dark outside and I'd like nothing more than to put my own head on my pillow, but we need to talk.

When I haven't been thinking about the kidnapping, my mind has been returning over and over to the market town in Lancashire with its castle and chocolate shop, where there is a house with three foot thick walls, a modern kitchen-diner twice the size of my own, a living room with wooden floors and a real fireplace, a claw-foot bath, two bedrooms, a small study and a garden, which costs *significantly* less than the poky flat I'm sitting in.

I pull the iPad towards me and this time, instead of typing in *kidnapping,* I put in the address for the Rightmove website and quickly locate the image of the house I fell in love with in the window of Honeywell Estate Agents. I flick through the photographs, daydreaming, letting my tea go cold. The house is a ten-minute walk from Sam and Neil in one direction and a nice little primary school with a preschool attached in the other.

When Grace is older, there's no reason I can't go freelance; work from home in the little study, tele-commuting for the research consultancy that currently employs me, or even work for myself. There must be companies in Lancashire that could use my skills. I think about putting a desk under the sash window, gazing at my own flowerbeds as I work.

Tom could use the study too, for his writing. He likes to work with his laptop on his knee so we can put the nursing chair in there for him. I feel a twinge of dismay at the idea I will eventually no longer need it for Grace but the image I've created draws me back in: Tom and I working quietly in the same room.

The shower goes off and the floorboards creak as Tom starts to dress. I flick onto the website of a recruitment agency. There actually are jobs there that Tom might like and which have flexible hours. There are a lot he won't: Machinist, Driver, Technician, Office Supplies, but two General Manager positions stand out. One is in a hotel and the other a bar; neither could be classified as 'boring office jobs'. I bookmark these for him to look at. There are also some Sales and Marketing positions, one of which has a particularly good salary and is based in Nelson. I look up the distance: easily commutable.

I hear Tom on the stairs and take a deep breath. Then I pull the Rightmove website back up and put the picture of the house on screen. As he strides into the kitchen, I wordlessly push the iPad towards him and bite my lip.

'What is it?' Tom glances down to see the house and

frowns. He uses one finger to flick through the images as I pass him a beer. 'Why am I looking at this?'

Again, wordlessly, I take the iPad back from him and open the Nelson job. Then I pass the screen back. He bends his head over the description. When he lifts his head, his eyes are shining with something that I think might be hope.

'Are you serious?'

'There's a good primary school nearby and it's not far from Neil and Sam.'

'But you always said you never wanted to be more than a stone's throw from London.'

'Things have changed. I mean, when did we last go to a show or out clubbing? Even before Grace it was too expensive.' I laugh. 'And . . . God, I know it's crazy, but I hadn't realised we could have a life away from the city, but you had a great night out in Blackburn, didn't you? And Clitheroe has some amazing pubs and bars. It's got its own cinema, theatre, and a train station so, if we get desperate, we can get to Manchester. Sam says the Lowry is great.' I swallow. 'I think . . . it could be really good for us. You miss Neil, don't you?'

'Of course I do.' He puts his hands flat on the table on either side of the iPad. 'You really want to do this?'

'I think so.' I lick my lips. 'It's not like we have a lot of friends around here anymore. A bunch of us started off in London, but we've scattered in the last few years. If I give up my job to stay at home with Grace we don't need to live in the commuter belt. What's keeping us here?'

'My parents wouldn't mind, it'd be easier for them from Chesterfield anyway,' Tom says. 'But your mum . . .'

My heart sinks. 'I hadn't thought about Mum.'

'We can't base our decision on your mum.' Tom takes my hand. 'And you never know, she might be okay with this.'

'She'll hate it. When I picked a university that wasn't close enough to home she was heartbroken. I didn't hear from her for a month.'

'It's not her decision, though, it's ours. You like this house? You think we should go and see it?'

My throat feels tight, but I nod. 'We can stay the night with Sam and Neil again, if they don't mind. It was Sam's idea anyway.'

Tom laughs and he sounds happier than he has in ages. 'This could be good, Bridge. So, what made you show me this, was it the doctor? Did she help?'

'She's upped my dose of Fluoxetine.' I bite my lip. 'But I think it gives me nightmares. I–I'm worried about going to sleep.'

'Did you tell her that?' Tom presses my fingers. 'There are other drugs, aren't there?'

'I guess. But you have to come off one, start the other, wait a couple of weeks to see if it works for you and then, if it doesn't, go through it all again. Really, I'm lucky with the side-effects of the Fluoxetine. I mean it's only nightmares. Another tablet could give me headaches, more weight gain, nausea.'

'You'd rather put up with disturbed sleep? That makes sense, I guess.'

'Dr Lewis suggested counselling and I thought it might help, with the nightmares at least.'

'You signed up for counselling?' Tom keeps his voice carefully steady, but I can sense his pleasure, his relief.

'She says there'll be a six-week wait before I even hear about an appointment.'

'Oh.' He sags. 'Well . . . that's not so bad.'

'It is though.'

He rubs his blue eyes. 'What about your mum's friend? It might be a *bit* weird speaking to someone you know so well, but if she can fit you in right away and if she helped when you went to her before . . .' His gaze flickers to the cork board by the fridge and for the first time I notice the tattered business card pinned up there: Gillian Thornhill, Therapist. He must have taken it out of the sink.

'I'm sure she'd see me.' I try not to shudder at the thought. What would I say? *Hi, Aunt Gillian, great to see you again. How was France? By the way I'm a complete failure of a mother.* And then there's the other issue. 'She's private, Tom. It could be £40 or £50 an hour.'

He looks crushed. 'Even for a family friend?'

'I don't know. I don't like to take advantage. If we decide I should see her, I'd at least want to offer to pay the full amount.' He grimaces and I force a smile. 'Let's see how it goes. If we arrange to look at the house, I think it could be good for me, for my mental health. If we decide we like it I can hand in my notice at work and we can get the flat on the market.'

Tom sidles to my part of the counter and puts his arm around me. 'You actually sound excited.' He puts his cheek on my head and inhales. 'You haven't sounded like this since . . .'

'Since Grace was born.'

'Almost.' He smiles against my hair and his hands start roving. 'It's a real turn on.'

'Yeah?'

'Yeah.' He shifts so that he's standing between my spread legs and strokes the sides of my neck. 'We could go upstairs.'

'Or stay here,' I whisper. 'Less chance of waking Grace.'

'Are you hungry?' I pick Tom's shirt off the floor and kick the rest of our discarded clothes towards the washing machine.

'I am now.'

'Why don't you look at Rightmove some more, see if there're any other houses you want to look at? I'll make us omelettes.'

'When do you want to go up?' Tom looks nervous, as if I'll snatch this away from him, but I put his shirt on over my bra and go to the fridge.

'How about Friday? I–I'll get the day off work and then we'll have the weekend if you want to look at the area some more.' I juggle butter, eggs and cheese in one hand as I shut the fridge. I'm standing with my back to him praying that Tom doesn't notice how I stumbled. That I lied. I'm already off work but he can't know that.

Guilt eats at me. I've never lied to Tom but I need this time.

'If we go up Thursday night, we'll have the whole day Friday and I can arrange a meeting with the recruitment agent as well.' Tom is making notes on the pad by the cork board while I beat the eggs.

'It's okay with me, if it's okay with Sam and Neil.' My voice sounds odd, even to me. I switch on the hob and focus on heating a knob of butter.

'I'll call them now.' Tom pulls his phone from his pocket as I spill the eggs into the pan, but I'm distracted and, as I pull back, I catch my wrist on the edge of the hot metal. I cry out and the mixing bowl clatters on the floor.

Tom drops the phone, un-dialled. 'Quick, put it under the tap.'

He grips my wrist like I'm a toddler, drags me over to the sink and holds the burn under the cold water. 'It's too cold,' I whimper.

'No, it isn't. You have to keep it there for at least five minutes.' Tom doesn't let me go.

'Your omelette!'

'I'll deal with it. Keep your hand right there.'

He releases me and goes to add grated cheese to the cooking eggs. I stand, shivering as cold eats into my skin, turning it white, then red. I look at my wrist where the blister is trying to form and watch as a crooked white line appears on my arm. It's a scar, one I haven't thought of in years, so old that it only emerges in the cold. I can't remember how I got it, I must have been really small. I touch my finger to the lace-like line and Tom comes up behind me.

'How's your hand, has it blistered?'

Silently I raise my wrist to show him. There's a red mark now, but no blister and the scar has faded away.

I pull into the library car park and check on my laptop, which almost flew off the seat at the round-about. There's a coffee in the holder beside me, and I lean back in the seat as I switch off the engine. I'd forgotten that the library didn't open till 9.30 but I'd had to leave the house at the usual time. Lies on top of lies. Now I have an hour of sitting in the car ahead of me.

I open the boot and fetch the book and paperwork from under the rug, putting them on top of the laptop. Then I pick up my coffee, settle back into my seat and open the book.

The contents page consists of a list of names, twenty of them: Madeleine McCann, James Bulger, Sarah Payne, Lesley Whittle, Frances Dobson, Shannon Matthews, Ben Needham, Mary Flanagan, Sasha McLeish, Sandy Davidson, Holly Wells and Jessica Chapman, Zhara Adbi, Lena Begum, Nial Mbarak, Lillian Lyustiger, Janique Irving, Daniel Entwistle, Aamina Khan, Yentl Baadjes.

Each name represents a chapter. Some of the names I know well, or think I do: Madeleine McCann, who had ensured my refusal, once I had Grace, to even consider Portugal as a holiday desti-nation. James Bulger; the CCTV image of the little blonde toddler seemed to be burned into the retinas of a generation. But others I haven't heard of: Frances Dobson, Nial Mbarak, Lillian Lyustiger, Janique Irving . . . all taken.

I start to read.

Half an hour later I turn the last page on Lesley Whittle and find myself looking at a little girl with curly brown hair and wide brown eyes. She is holding her mum's hand, one foot twisted behind the other. Her father is standing behind them, shading his eyes from the sun. Who is taking the picture? A family friend? I stare at the caption: *Betsie and Grant Dobson with daughter, Frances, five, outside their home in Sabden, Lancashire.*

It isn't the girl who grips my attention, but her mother: *Betsie Dobson.*

My heart is pounding as I lift the book and hold it to the light. Then I flip the page, hoping for another photo, a better one. There is only the one. I turn back to it. It's grainy, but even then, the resemblance is clear. I can see why the old guy, Jack, made his mistake. Betsie Dobson could be my older sister. We have the same build, the same hair colour, the same shape face and eyes. It's uncanny. I pull out my phone and snap a picture of the page, then I send it to Sam.

Found my double!

For a moment I'd forgotten that this picture was in a book about tragic kidnappings. I take a breath and start to read.

* * *

It was an overcast day in Lancashire the day that Betsie and Grant Dobson lost their daughter. Others have described it as grey, windy, gloomy even. Frances had gone to school as usual and, with her husband, a lorry driver, away overnight, Betsie had arranged to go and stay with her sister in Rochdale.

Locals describe Betsie as a dedicated mum, but Frances as a lively child: exhausting, a bit of a handful. Betsie didn't want to look after her alone that day.

A couple of months earlier, the family celebrated as Frances came second in her age group for a national poetry writing competition. You can still see her work printed in a little book titled 'I am the seed' by Faber and Faber. Now she had her prize, a twenty-pound book-voucher to spend.

Betsie picked Frances up from school and told her they were going for tea in a café and then by train to visit her aunt, where they would be able to spend her voucher on a book of her choice in Waterstones.

At the café, six-year-old Frances had sausage, egg and chips. Owner Ben Wright remembers her talking non-stop about the books she was going to buy as she cleared her plate. He gave Betsie a free cup of tea, 'as the poor woman looked frazzled by the end,' he says.

He recalled no sign that the small family were being watched but, in addition to his regulars, he had served several Travellers that day who had taken up residence in a field just outside the village.

Betsie had already packed an overnight bag for herself and Frances. When they got to the train station, she asked Frances to wait with the case. Then she went to use the ticket machine. While she was there, she encountered a friend, Angela Martin, and had a brief chat about a mutual acquaintance and his recent cancer diagnosis, keeping one eye on her daughter through the window. Then she went to get herself a coffee. She heard the 4.30 p.m. train to Clitheroe go past. Her friend, Angela, caught her again and asked about her husband. They talked for what Angela reported as another couple of minutes. When Betsie returned to the platform, she found the case but no sign of her daughter.

She searched the platform and enlisted Angela's help. Terrified that Frances might have fallen onto the tracks they sought any sign of her, but there was nothing. The girl had vanished.

Angela reported seeing a white van in the car park, but her sighting was never corroborated or confirmed.

Locals informed the police about the Traveller community who had been staying nearby but, despite prolonged investigation of the group, which caused one family to take out a harassment order, there was no indication that they had been involved in the kidnapping.

Police interviewed Grant Dobson but a receipt proved that he was in Exeter service station at the time of Frances' disappearance.

Other family friends were also interviewed but none of them raised suspicions and there was no sign of Frances.

A registered sex offender, Thomas Taylor, also lived

in Sabden and was the centre of the investigation for many months. The police used dogs to search his property and dug up his garden and allotment, but there was no evidence of wrongdoing. Thomas Taylor eventually moved to Leeds where he died six years later from heart disease, caused by type-2 diabetes. He always maintained his innocence with respect to the kidnapping of little Frances.

The search went on for weeks with volunteers combing the hillsides around Whalley station and throughout the Ribble Valley, where they lived.

To this day, her Reception teacher, Mary Wilson, who had entered Frances' work for the poetry competition, recalls her with great sadness: 'a lovely, bright child, endlessly curious and with a creative side to match.'

How could this little girl vanish, never to be seen again?

Was it the sex offender, Thomas Taylor, known for his proclivity for thirteen- to sixteen-year-olds, who turned his eyes to a younger girl and, either killed her in a sick game or, somehow, kept her secret from the police and all searchers? Did he perhaps have a property elsewhere that no-one was ever able to find? And, if he did, what happened to the youngster when he was under such scrutiny? Did he pass her on into a network? Or did she perhaps die of neglect? Does her body, to this day, lie in some unexplored shed or flat?

Was it a Traveller family, thinking they could sell her on, perhaps sending her quickly into some underground system that the police could not track?

Did she find her way onto the train tracks? And if so, why was there no evidence of her death?

Was it the father, as some have suggested, orchestrating her abduction from the other side of the country?

Or could the mother, unable to deal with her daughter's incessant demands, have masterminded the removal of her child, seeking an easy existence once again?

No-one knows. Perhaps we never will.

We do know that, for a long time, her parents refused to give up hope. Despite the painful scrutiny that descended upon them, they continued to look for Frances. Her father swept the country in his lorry, seeking his daughter at every stop, dropping off leaflets and posters of her face wherever he went. Meanwhile her mother became a recluse, terrified of leaving the house in case Frances should come home and find it empty.

As the years passed, however, the couple gave in to despair; regular faces in the public houses around Clitheroe, Sabden and Whalley, they sank into alcoholism and, on what would have been Frances' twentieth birthday, her mother, Betsie, killed herself after drinking a bottle of vodka, by cutting her wrists in the bath.

She is survived by her husband, who is now rarely seen outside the family home and who declined to give an interview for this book.

I realise that I have been engrossed by the pages for long enough that the library has opened. I put the book carefully on the seat beside me, as if it might break. There are obvious similarities between the story of Frances Dobson and the little girl I'd seen taken: the train station, the white van. There are differences though: Frances was taken at 4.30 p.m. in broad daylight.

I think of the pattern I've already spotted: children taken from or near to train stations. Frances was taken twenty years ago. Could she be part of the same puzzle?

Has someone been orchestrating the kidnapping of children for twenty years?

But why take them from train stations? I tap my wheel, deep in thought. Perhaps because people looking would waste time assuming a missing child had wandered onto the tracks? Or because parents are easily distracted in stations: a ticket check, a request for help with heavy luggage. Maybe because there are places to park a van close by or because stations are easier to surveil. You can loiter at a train station, sit and have a coffee and watch families with children, no questions asked.

If there is an organisation, there will be proof in the pile of data I've gathered. Leaving the book in the car, I sweep up the paperwork and the laptop. I have a long day ahead.

I stride past a white van to enter the library. Has it been parked opposite me all morning? Was it there when I first arrived? I can't remember. I try to see through the window, but it's dark: tinted glass. I can't see anyone in there. I shudder as I push through the revolving doors. Unmarked white vans seem to be everywhere.

*   *   *

I sit in a quiet corner and pile the printed papers next to me. First, I have to compile all the different sources and information into one table. I have SPSS, a statistical analysis software package, on my work laptop, so I use that. I give each case a unique number and add the date and time of the kidnapping, the child's gender, age, racial profile, postcode, the social demographic of the family, proximity to a train station, and whether or not they were found again.

It takes me all day. I get hungry and tired but I don't stop. In the end I look at my pile of papers. Tomorrow I'll finish getting all the data in one place and make it workable.

One more day and I can start hunting them.

Chapter 13

'Thank God you're home! Your mum rang, she's on her way over,' Tom calls as I open the front door.

'You didn't tell her our plans, did you?' Knowing Tom doesn't know my password, I lay my laptop on the table in the living room and head for the kitchen, stretching and wishing I didn't have to wear my work trousers to go to the library. Just one more consequence of lying.

'Do I look stupid to you?' Tom hands Grace to me and I wrap my arms around her with a moan of pleasure. She pulls my hair.

'No . . . and there's no reason to tell her anything until we've made a decision.' I tickle Grace's chin and she babbles at me. 'Hello to you, baby girl. I'm so glad you're up to see me.'

'She's wide awake.' Tom smiles at her. 'She had a nice long lunchtime nap for a change.'

'Good girl! So, did Mum say why she was coming over?'

'No. I think she's just feeling lonely.' Tom switches on the kettle. 'Tea?'

'I'd rather have wine.'

'You can if you want.' Tom tilts his head at me, and I shake mine.

'No, I'll stick to tea.'

'Coming up.'

The doorbell rings and Grace jerks in my arms, excitement lighting her face. 'She's here.' I carry Grace into the hallway. 'Let's go and see Grandma, shall we?'

'Hello darling.' Mum gives me a hug, squeezing me a little too tightly.

'Are you all right, Mum?'

'Yes, of course.' She doesn't step back. 'It's just . . . who knew a date could be so difficult?'

'The day after tomorrow.' I squeeze her in return, and she frowns a little.

'Would you like me to bring over some healthy meals next time I come, darling? You can put them in your freezer, it'll save you the hassle of cooking.' As I suck in my stomach, suddenly self-conscious, she takes Grace from me and lifts her to the light. 'Why is Grace dressed like a plumber? Why isn't she in one of the pretty dresses I bought her?'

I bite my lip. Grace is in a cute pair of cream dungarees. 'Tom dresses her, Mum.'

'And I think she looks lovely.' Tom is standing behind me now. 'Would you like a cup of tea, Alison?'

'Yes, please.' Mum carries Grace into the living room. 'I'll be in here with Grace.'

Tom strides back to the kitchen. 'Go and sit with your mum, I'll bring the tea through.'

Mum is on the sofa with Grace on the floor in

146

front of her, commando crawling after Frankie-Lion who appears to have fallen from the chair. It's a new thing she's started doing and it's adorable. I'm trying not to think about what it means for her next. Crawling, walking . . . leaving me.

'Where's Tom with the tea?' Mum raises her chin and I twist so that I can see into the kitchen. Tom grimaces over the counter at me, taking his time.

I raise my voice enough so that he can hear. 'He won't be long.' Then I turn back to Mum. 'I'm glad you came over, I was going to call. I know it's hard for you this week . . .'

'As a matter of fact, I came to see how *you* were doing.' Mum folds her hands. 'After all that business with the police, I wondered if you'd considered talking to Gillian?'

Tom comes in with two cups of tea, puts them on the coffee table, picks Grace up and puts her in the bouncer. She claps, then yells as Frankie drops to the floor. Tom hands him back and I sense immediately that she will love this new game. I'm proven right when Grace hurls Frankie back on the floor and looks at Tom with pleading eyes.

'Actually,' I look at Tom and then at Mum, 'I have spoken to the doctor about counselling, but there's a six-week waiting list.'

'I see.' Mum smiles at Grace, then turns to me. 'Well, Gillian's better than some NHS navel-gazer. You'll have to go and see her.'

Tom hands Frankie back to Grace then takes my hand. 'We really can't afford it, Alison.'

Mum almost smiles. 'I'll pay, of course. It was my suggestion. And I can come to the first session with you if that'll help. I know how you hate talking about things that bother you.'

'You'll pay?' Tom glances at me.

'I'm sure Gillian will give me a reasonable rate.'

I swallow. 'It's really kind, Mum. But, if you're willing to pay . . . maybe we could find our own therapist. One who specialises in post-natal—'

'Don't be ridiculous.' Mum claps her hands. 'I'll make an appointment for later in the week. How does Friday sound?'

Tom stiffens. 'Friday isn't good.' He catches my eye. 'I mean . . . shouldn't we be focusing on *you* this week, Alison?'

Mum shakes her head. 'Don't be silly, Tom, Bridget is my daughter and she needs this . . .'

I can't help glancing at the iPad. Behind its darkened screen the Rightmove website is right there, a silent accusation. 'It's just that we're going away on Friday. We're staying with Neil and Sam, in Clitheroe.'

Mum freezes and her knuckles whiten on her teacup. I'd forgotten her dislike of Neil. 'The one who dumped you.'

'That was years ago, Mum. He's Tom's best friend.'

Tom stands, one hand on my shoulder. 'And Grace's godfather. We've arranged to go and see them.'

'In *Lancashire*, I suppose.' Mum looks at me. 'Up *North*.' She rolls her eyes.

'We like it up there, don't we, Bridge?' Tom's look is icy. 'In fact—'

'*Tom, no!*' I try to speak over him, but he ignores me.

'We're going to look at houses while we're there.'

For a moment the room is silent and then Mum's cup crashes onto the floor, splashing tea in a brown arc which soaks my shoes and the carpet around us. She stands, like an old lady, levering herself up from the chair one joint at a time. 'You can't,' she says eventually. 'You can't leave me! This week of all weeks. How could you do this?'

'Mum, I'm sorry. Tom wasn't meant to—'

'So, you weren't even going to tell me?' Her brown eyes are wide and horrified. 'When was I going to find out? When the removal van arrived? When I received the change of address card? When I turned up to pick up Grace and some *stranger* answered the door?'

'Mum, it's not like that.' I reach for her and she steps back, as if I'll hurt her with my touch. Tears are gathering in her eyes. She's shaking. 'I didn't want to tell you until we'd made a decision. We haven't made any—'

'And I get no say in this?' She clenches trembling fists. Her rings stand out like knuckle dusters, diamonds glittering. 'I look after Grace once a week so Tom can go to "school" and I get *no say*!'

'We've only just started talking—' I gasp.

'And what *about* Tom's school? Suddenly he doesn't want to write anymore, is that it?'

'I can finish my course remotely,' Tom murmurs.

Mum staggers as if he's hit her. 'How convenient.'

149

Then she looks at me and her eyes are no longer tearing. 'I forbid it.'

Tom snorts a laugh. 'You what?'

'You heard me. I forbid it.' Sharp lines crack her face powder. 'How dare you even consider this? When will I see Grace? Do you expect *me* to move as well?'

'No, Mum.' I hang my head.

Mum looks at Tom. 'I assume this is all about you. I won't give you money, so you plan to take my daughter and granddaughter from me.'

'OK, that's enough.' Tom starts towards the door as Grace, who has been staring from one adult to another, begins to cry. 'I think we should cut today's visit short. Bridget's a grown-up. You can't forbid her to do anything and this is *nothing* to do with your money. It's about us and what's right for our family.' He's holding the living room door open, gesturing as if to send her through it by the force of his will.

'And moving to the middle of nowhere is good for Grace, is it? Being away from her family, from art and culture and—'

'Mum, *stop*.' I lift Grace into my arms. My own chest is heaving. 'Please. I can't bear this. Stop it, both of you!'

Mum looks at us and she looks suddenly very old. 'Do you want me to go, Bridget?' she asks, tremulous. 'Is that what you want?'

I hesitate, unable to answer.

She hangs her head. 'You want to take Grace away from me.'

'Mum, it's really not like that . . . I'm so sorry.'

She walks slowly towards the door. There she pauses and turns back to look at me. 'I'll book the appointment for Thursday then, if it's all right with your husband.' She says *husband* as if she'd much rather call him something else. 'I'll just have to get over the fact that it's your dad's anniversary.'

I nod wordlessly and Tom holds the front door open as she leaves.

He starts back into the living room, but I block the doorway. 'How could you? We agreed not to tell her until we'd actually decided something.'

'Bridge . . . I'm sorry. She wound me up.'

'Well, *you* don't have to see her on Thursday, and I do! You saw how upset she was, she's terrified of never seeing Grace again. I wanted to be sure before we told her. Now . . . I don't know if I can go through with it. She might never speak to me again.'

Grace squirms in my arms. She doesn't like my tone. Tom sighs. 'She wouldn't really not speak to you again, you know.'

I put Grace back in her bouncer carefully, as if she might break. 'You don't understand . . .' I speak without looking at him. 'You didn't meet me until spring term.'

He comes nearer. 'You were serious about her not speaking to you for a month? I thought you were joking. Exaggerating.'

'It's always been that way.' I stare at the floor. It needs hoovering, there are crumbs under my toes. 'She cares about me a lot. I used to think she might care too much. But if I did something wrong, she'd pretend I didn't exist until I fixed it.' I swallow. 'It sounds like I'm complaining. I'm not. She never hit me, not ever, and I learned to behave. But this might be unforgivable.'

Tom touches my shoulder. 'Bridge . . .'

I raise my eyes to Grace, who is absorbed by the mirror on her bouncer, and take a deep breath. 'It's . . . well, it's one reason I think I might be such a lunatic right now. I know about genetics, Tom.' Now I look at him. 'What if I kill myself, like Dad did?'

Tom freezes; not even his chest moves with his breath. It's as if he's paralysed. I plunge on.

'Or, if I don't, what if I end up getting so cross with Grace that she stops existing to me? I hated that so much when I was growing up but eventually Grace is going to talk back to me, or whatever, and then what do I do? I don't *know* anything else!'

'Shit, Bridge, I had no idea.' Tom puts his arms around me. 'You're not your mum. There're plenty of ways to teach Grace how to behave: positive reinforcement, time-outs, the naughty step, one-two-three, sticker charts. We'll buy some books and read up. Why didn't you tell me that's what was bothering you?'

I press my lips together. Finally, I answer. 'I didn't want you to think I'd be a bad mum. I was worried . . .' I clench my fists against his back. 'I was worried you might not want a baby with me.'

'Fuuuck.' He says it on an exhale. 'Have you . . . have you actually thought about killing yourself?'

I don't answer. I don't like lying to him.

'Jesus, Bridge.' He tightens his hold on me as if I'm flying away and he is the only thing keeping me on earth. 'The counselling will help, it has to. But not if your mum's in the room. How are you going to talk to her friend with Alison sitting right there?'

'Maybe she'll just get me settled in. You know, have a quick chat, pay, then leave.'

'Even if she thinks you're moving away? You don't think she'll want to talk about that?' I bite my lip and Tom stiffens. 'I really want this, Bridge. We need to get away from here.' He never spoke in that tone, almost pleading. Never.

I exhale shakily. 'I can't see a way of doing it without hurting Mum. But . . . I suppose we could still go on Friday if we make up a story.' I feel nauseous at the idea. Lying to Mum. What am I thinking?

Tom grins, surprised. 'You mean tell her we aren't going to Lancashire and go anyway?'

I bite my lip. 'We'll have to say we're going *somewhere* in case she wants to come over. Maybe you could tell her we're having a weekend away because I already got the day off work?'

'Sneaky!' Tom pulls me in for a kiss. 'I *am* sorry.' He hesitates.

At that moment Grace decides that she's had enough of being ignored, and starts a loud, demanding wail. Tom lets go of me to scoop her up. Then he hands Grace to me. 'Give her a cuddle while I make dinner.'

I stand in the middle of the living room, cuddling Grace and dreading Thursday. What can I say to Gillian? I need her to help me, but I don't want to say anything to upset Mum. And what if Mum finds out that we're lying to her?

'You can't go home, so stop asking. Your parents don't love you anymore.' The woman stands by her bed. 'They wanted me to take you away.'

'That's a lie!'

'Don't you remember when you made your mother really angry?'

The girl screws up her eyes, trying not to think of all the times she'd made her mummy start shouting. But there had been so many and how do you not think of something when it's right in front of you? She'd taken a biscuit when Mummy had said not to. She'd refused to eat her green beans. She'd dropped Daddy's remote control in the toilet when she was playing explorers. It had a light on the end and she'd needed a torch.

'M-maybe?' Her voice is hoarse with crying, faint with disuse.

'Well, there you go. You made *her* stop loving you. When a mummy and daddy stop loving their child, I take them away. I'm just doing my job.' She spreads her hands, looks sad. 'I wouldn't have had to do it if you hadn't been bad. Mummies only want perfect children. It's your own fault that yours doesn't love you anymore. All your own fault. Say it.'

The little girl chokes on a sob. 'I–It's my fault.' She looks up at the woman. 'If I promise to be good, can I go home?'

The woman shakes her head. 'It's far too late for that. But . . . I might be able to help you go somewhere even better.'

Chapter 14

I sit in the car park once more, staring at the white van parked two spaces to the left. It arrived shortly after me but there is no movement from inside. No-one has emerged. I wonder if, like me, they are waiting for the library to open.

I look at *Kidnapped!* and consider reading the next two chapters: Shannon Matthews and Ben Needham. I touch the book cover, but then pick up my phone instead and dial Naomi Shaw.

'Shaw.'

'Hi. It's Bridget . . . Bridget Carlson.'

'Hello, Bridget. How are you?'

'I'm okay. I was wondering . . . did you find the school?'

'You mean from the rose on the blazer?' There is a pause and then a sigh. 'Bridget, Ward and I have called every single local education authority and we can't pinpoint a single school with a uniform that matches the description you gave me. Not even one with a logo that looks like a rose or has a rose in it. Not for a child of that age.'

'Not one?' My voice is breathy.

'I'm sorry.'

'But . . . I saw it.'

'I know you think you did.' I hear the click of a keyboard and then quiet. 'Are you still having those nightmares?'

'I . . . yes.'

'It might be a good idea to see someone. What you went through . . . seeing what you did, it can be difficult to get past it.'

'You *do* believe I saw it though?' I grip the phone until it bites into my palm. If she says no, how can I call her again? Even if I find something in the data.

'I believe you saw *something*.'

I relax my grip. She doesn't think I'm making things up. She doesn't sound 100 per cent on my side but at least she's not threatening to charge me with wasting police time.

'*Ward* doesn't believe me.' I wince at the petulance in my tone.

'Ward has his opinion. It isn't mine. I know how genuine witnesses to a crime behave and you don't seem like someone who is making this up for attention.'

'Thank God.'

I can hear the gentle smile in Naomi's voice, and I picture her grey-blue eyes, warming as she speaks. 'There's nothing we can do to find this girl. It's easier for Ward to focus on other cases if he believes there's no girl to find.'

'I understand.'

'If you remember anything else, Bridget, call me.'

After she hangs up, I sit for a while, looking at my

blank phone. She believes I saw something. But it isn't enough. I have to come to her with more. I have to search the data.

By lunchtime I have a single file. I consider starting my analysis but my eyesight is blurring and I need to eat; I won't be able to think straight otherwise. I head to the front desk, leaving my laptop in place. 'Is there somewhere I can get a sandwich?'

The librarian smiles at me. 'There's a Tesco Express on the corner.'

I glance back at my laptop. 'Will it be all right if I leave it there?'

'Well, it's not really our policy. . . but it should be fine. We're quiet. I can keep an eye on it.' The librarian shoos me towards the door, and I leave, pocketing my phone and keys.

I walk past my car, past the white van, which still hasn't moved, and head towards the street. As I do, I hear the thud of a door closing and turn. I'm too late to see anything more than the back of a jacket and a bowed head but someone has just left the van and headed into the library. What have they been doing in there all morning?

I'm not sure if I'll be allowed to eat my salad in the library, but something nags at me and instead of sitting on a bench in the bright autumn sunshine, I race to get back, lengthening and quickening my strides, until sweat breaks out on my forehead and chest. My breath hitches and I'm suddenly feeling that I shouldn't have left the laptop sitting on my desk.

I locked the home screen but the papers I printed are all laid out beside the computer, covered in my little notes and ticks.

I don't know why it's a problem but I keep thinking of the person from the van. I keep watching them go into the library as if they'd planned to do it after I left.

If someone wanted to steal my laptop, who could stop them? The middle-aged librarian with her long skirt and neatly parted blonde hair? The geriatric on the other computer who had been reeking of cigarettes all morning, forcing me to work with my sleeve over my mouth?

If my laptop was stolen, that would be two days of work gone. I could replicate it, of course I could, but it was the *time* I couldn't get back: time the little girl might not have. Plus, it was a work laptop and SPSS licences cost a fortune.

I break into a run as I reach the car park and batter my way through the library doors, leaving them to swing wildly behind me. The librarian looks up with a frown as I race, gasping, towards my desk. There is nobody there.

My laptop is right where I left it.

I put my hand on the pile of papers with their little ticks. Has it been moved? I think perhaps the papers have shifted, as if someone has flicked through them, but how can I be sure?

I go to the librarian. 'Thanks for watching my stuff.'

'No problem.' She sounds colder. I've annoyed her, barging in like a war's started.

'I was just wondering . . . did anyone go over there? Did anyone look at my laptop?'

She raises an eyebrow. 'This is a library. People are free to roam. But no, I didn't spot anyone at your work station.'

'Okay. Thanks. Sorry.'

She sniffs and I head back. I sit and put my hand once more on the papers, as though I might be able to feel if someone has touched them; sense their residual heat, perhaps. The librarian would have said if someone had gone through my stuff. But had she really been sat there watching my things the whole time? My desk isn't in her line of sight. That's why I'd chosen it, because it gave me privacy. Had she in fact been shelving books, chatting with the three mums I now saw in the children's section, helping their children, taking a call?

I lift the top paper and freeze. Written in my own black marker, half covering my little ticks and the names and dates I've printed, are spiky letters spelling out the words: *LEAVE IT BITCH*.

Faster than thought, my phone is in my hand and I'm hovering my thumb over the redial button.

Then I hesitate. What if the library has a camera and there is a video of the incident? I should find out before I place the call. I could even watch the footage, see the person doing it. Then I really would have proof.

Pulse pounding, I replace the top paper and put my phone back in my pocket. Then I walk gingerly towards the librarian, as if the floor has become fragile and I'm too heavy for it. I stand in front of her desk and wait for her to look up.

'Someone has written something on my work,' I begin.

She frowns. 'Are you sure?'

'I'm certain.'

'I didn't see anyone over there but . . .' She gestures, almost helplessly.

'You were busy, I get it.'

She bristles at my tone. 'The laptop was left at your own risk, you know.'

'It's fine.' I put my hands on the desk and realise almost immediately that I'm unconsciously copying a gesture of Mum's: see, I'm angry but I'm controlling myself. 'I was wondering if you had security cameras, if the person who did it might have been caught on camera?'

'Only at the door.' She gestures. 'They'd have been recorded in and out, that's all.'

'Can I see?'

Her eyes widen. 'I . . . no, I don't think so. I mean I doubt that's allowed. I'd have to check. But, no.'

'But if the police wanted to look, they'd be able to?'

'Well yes, but do you really think this is a police matter? If all they did was write something?'

'Thanks.' I retreat from the desk. This has to be the girl's kidnapper and now they're on film. They might even have left fingerprints on the pen or sheet.

I sit back at the desk, shaking, excited, ready to

call Shaw. I pick up the top page again to look at the message, that angry, spiky handwriting. I'm planning to take a photo. I can send it to Naomi Shaw via iMessage. I freeze. I put the page down and pick it up again, then I look under the second page and then the third.

The page with the note on isn't there anymore. It's missing.

For a moment I wonder if I've dreamed the whole thing. Was there ever a message at all?

Then I realise that the printout goes from page one to page three. Page two isn't there. I spin in my chair and look around frantically. There is no-one nearby. Only the three mums and their children. Even the smoker has relocated to another part of the building.

As I watch, a man in a suit strides in with a handful of books. He greets the librarian cheerfully and goes to the automated machine, puts the books on the plate, taps the screen, shifts them to the shelf and leaves. She waves him out. I look again at the pile of papers. Someone was here. Someone had been here *all the time*, watching my reaction and waiting to take back the evidence. Surely, they'd have had to go past me to leave the building. Were they still here, hiding and waiting for their chance to go?

I stumble back to the front desk. 'Is this the only way out?' I demand. The librarian stares at me for a moment, not answering. I want to shake her. I settle for placing my hands flat on the desk. 'Is there another way out? Is there?'

She looks concerned. 'Are you all right?'

'*No!*' My voice cracks. '*Is there another exit?*'

'Yes. For staff only. Through the office.' She points between shelves of 'Large Text Novels' on one side and 'Science Fiction and Fantasy' on the other. There's a door at the far end. It's standing ajar. She frowns. 'That door shouldn't be open – it needs a swipe card. No-one should be back there.' She emerges from behind the desk and rushes down the aisle, her feet shushing on the carpet. She pulls the door shut.

'But someone *was* back there . . .'

She doesn't answer.

I'm onto something; I have to be, otherwise, why would they try to put me off? I can't call Shaw and tell her about the message. What evidence did I have that it was ever there – a missing A4 page? But what if I find whatever it is that they are trying to hide?

They want to frighten me away, but I won't be intimidated. A little girl needs help, and now I *know* I am close.

I unlock my laptop and stare at my table of data. The kidnappers are in here . . . somewhere.

In order to avoid confirmation bias, I have to resist running the correlation that I most desperately want to: proximity to a railway station. There might be other patterns, more significant ones, and I owe it to all the missing children in front of me to do this in a professional manner. I run the first set of correlations, then the second and the third.

To my surprise there is no correlation between

gender, age and racial profile, but something pings when I look at social demographic. Kids from poorer backgrounds are more commonly going missing and less likely to be found again.

But maybe that makes sense. I twiddle a pen between my fingers.

Were poorer kids more likely to run away or go with an abductor? Were they easier to take, less well-protected? Were they less likely to enter the news cycles and therefore a safer bet for kidnappers? Were the parents easier to dismiss? Did the police expend more resources looking for children from richer families?

I run another correlation: date against location. I quickly realise that I have far too many different postcodes for this to make any sense. An amateur mistake; I have to group them somehow.

I check my watch and go back to the data table. There I create another column and split the post codes in half. BB7 9DY becomes BB7 I then go one step further and create another column where I put it as just BB.

Then I re-run the numbers.

I clench my fists as the laptop whirrs and, finally, my answer comes. There *is* a connection between date and place. The numbers aren't world-shattering; I wouldn't have reported the finding to a client but it is enough to make me look closer at this particular set of data. And as I'm now looking at location, it's time to add in 'proximity to railway station'.

I glance at my watch again and wince. Then I

pick up the phone and call Tom. 'I have to work late, I'm sorry.'

'That's fine, I'm just giving Grace her tea.' There's a clatter and Grace babbles in the background.

My heart clenches but I just can't leave. 'Is she all right?'

'Enjoying her chicken and peas.' Tom hesitates. 'How's work?'

'Fine.'

'I called the estate agent and booked us in for two house viewings on Friday and one on Saturday morning, the one you like. I'm seeing the recruitment agent Friday afternoon.'

'That's great.' Deliberately, I turn my back on the screen of my laptop. 'Did you speak to Neil or Sam?'

'Sam, she's excited.'

'And she's okay with us staying two nights?'

'Couldn't be happier.'

'Great . . . well, I'll see you a bit later.'

'Any idea how much later?'

'Another hour or so, maybe.'

'Okay.' Tom sighs. 'Can't wait for you to hand in your notice. See you later.'

'Bye.' I hang up, ignoring a rush of guilt that makes me feel almost physically sick. I look back to my data. If there is a correlation between date and location, I need a map.

The librarian recoils when she sees me heading towards her again. She's clearly grateful when I simply ask her for a decent map of the UK, indicating

166

postcodes and including railway stations. Amazingly, she finds one within minutes. She hands it to me with a warning. 'We're closing in half an hour.'

'That's OK. Thanks.'

I blow the map up on the photocopier and borrow some coloured pencils from the arts and crafts box. Then I start drawing dots on it, to indicate abductions. Different colours for different years.

Within minutes my map is a senseless pointillism and I toss the green crayon I was using onto the table and stop.

I check the time: ten minutes before I have to leave. I print a fresh copy of the map and return to my data. I carefully remove all the outliers, focusing only on data points that corroborate my correlation. I am left with thirty-five dots. Carefully, using different colours for different years and using crosses for the twelve that are by railway stations, I put the points on the map, trying not to look too closely until I'm done, not wanting to prejudge. But, before I'm halfway through, I find the pattern. I'm going around similar postcodes in a circuit, in a roughly five- to seven-year cycle.

'Fuck.' I pick up the page. The pattern is focused on the north of England, as far south as Coventry and as far north as Carlisle.

Carefully, I put the map back on the table and add another data point. It's an outlier, just outside London, but I'm almost certain that it's connected. My missing girl.

I hesitate and then I add another, in Peterborough.

There's a train station not far from the park where the Sharma boy was taken.

There's a gang, I'm sure of it. But they've been careful not to hit the same area twice within a five- to seven-year span of time. They have a preference for railway stations but are careful not to limit themselves. Then they go back around, hitting roughly the same areas. They've been working for the last twenty years, maybe longer.

Maybe the North has become too hot for them. Perhaps communities are starting to notice. Now they're moving south, and they know I saw them. Was one of them on the train or do they have a contact in the police station?

They're watching me. Are they also watching Grace and Tom?

I slam the lid on my laptop and grab my map. I'm careful when picking up the pens: I do it with my sleeve over my hand. There might be a fingerprint and I don't want to lose it, but I don't have time to waste. I was looking at kids over the age of three. I don't know if they take babies, but what if they do?

What if they decide to take Grace?

I drive home as if I'm being chased by demons, ignoring speed limits. A speed camera flashes as I career along the high street; Tom will be livid, but I barely slow. I pull into the drive and leap from the car, grabbing the map but leaving the laptop and book where they are. I stand for a moment, looking up and down the street, searching for a white van.

When I don't see one, I run up the steps and into the flat, calling for Grace.

Tom appears at the living room door. He's frowning. 'I'm reading her a story, what's the matter?' He sees my pale face and the crumpled paper in my hand. 'What is it?'

I thrust the map into his hand and step past him, desperate to see her, needing to know she's safe. Grace is on the floor where Tom must have laid her when he heard me. She's wearing a onesie. Her hair is clean from a bath, fluffy around her ears. She's gripping Frankie-Lion in one hand and Dobbie in the other. Her skin is flushed with warmth. When she sees me she drops both toys and reaches upwards. I lift her into my arms and sink my nose into the sweet spot behind her ear, inhaling as if her smell is oxygen. Only then do I start to calm down.

Tom has opened the map and is staring at it without comprehension. 'What am I looking at?'

'It's kidnappings by location and date. Don't you see?' I take the map from him, one-handed, and lay it on the coffee table. 'Look.' I kneel beside it, balancing Grace between my legs. 'The different colours represent different years.' I point to Lancashire. 'See the area around Blackburn, the BB postcode. There've been *three* kidnappings. Two of them from railway stations: Whalley and Brierfield. The first one, from Whalley, was twenty years ago, then another, six years later, from Blackburn. And then Brierfield, seven years after that. One girl and two boys, all from poor families, they barely even hit the national news. These kids were never found.' I use my finger to trace a line. 'From Blackburn they go to Leeds, look! Then Middlesbrough, Newcastle. Then they go further south: Stoke, Sheffield. Always between six months and a year apart. But they have a circuit. Can you see?'

'Christ, Bridge!' I look up and catch sight of his face. Tom is staring, pale-faced, his eyes blazing. 'You did this at work?'

I freeze, bent over the table, one arm around Grace the other on the map. 'I–I've been at the library. Don't you see, I had to? I've found them. They're moving south now. *They* took the girl from the station.'

'I thought you were trying to forget about all this.' Tom takes Grace and holds her so that she can't see the table. 'You said you would. This isn't forgetting, this is *obsessing*. And these numbers could mean anything. It could all be coincidence. You don't think the police would have noticed a *kidnapping gang*? We don't live in some third world country. You're not *Hercule fucking Poirot*, Bridget.' He glances at Grace and winces but carries on. 'You *lied* to me. You said you were going to work this morning. Did you even call Diane to let her know you weren't coming in, again?'

'I . . .' I swallow. 'She knows. Dr Lewis . . . she signed me off for a week.'

Tom stands very still.

'It isn't a coincidence, Tom,' I say quietly. I put my hand on his arm. 'There was someone in the library, watching me. Someone wrote a message on my paper-work, warning me off.'

Tom steps away from me. 'You've been signed off work *all week*? But . . . you went off to work for the last two days.' He stares. 'You didn't just *lie* to me, you . . . you planned a whole deception.'

'That's not important, I—'

'Not important?' Tom steps further away. 'I thought we didn't lie to one another. You always said you hate lying. And now this! You know what . . . if you're off work for the rest of the week, *you* can look after Grace for a couple of days. I'm going to stay with Neil.'

'But we need to tell the police, about the map, about the library.'

'No,' Tom said. 'I need to pack and go and stay with Neil before I say something I'll regret, and you need to look after our daughter for a goddamn change. Two days you could have been at home, helping me out. Two fucking days!'

'But the police . . .'

'*No*, Bridget.' Tom drags his hand through his curls, making them stand up, reminding me that he needs a haircut. 'She's starting with a cold; did you know that? She's been fussy and difficult all day. Not that you care. You think it's easy to be the one who stays home. You want it so badly, but I'm *always* the one left looking after her when you've got something better to do.' His eyes skitter away from mine. 'I didn't want to tell you this, but Sergeant Ward came by the house this afternoon.'

'What?' I jerk, staring at him.

'He said you've been calling the station again. Something about a school uniform. He . . . he showed me a video. It's from the train. Bridge, you're asleep.'

'No! I-I'm dozing a little maybe, for a while, but I'm awake when I see the kidnapping.'

'I know what you look like when you're asleep, Bridge. You were asleep. Then suddenly you jump up and start yelling at everyone. You dreamed it. You dreamed the whole damn thing. And all of *this*,' he indicates the map, 'it's fantasy.' He pushes Grace into my arms. 'I'm going to call Neil and let him know I'm on the way.'

'Please don't. Stay!'

'I'm too angry, Bridget. I love you, but right now . . . I don't really like you very much.'

He stalks into the hall and I hear him climb the stairs, his tread heavy. There's thudding upstairs; he's getting the suitcase down from the top of the wardrobe. I hear him go into the bathroom and come back out, the slamming of drawers. Then the bang of our bedroom door and he comes back, suitcase in hand.

'I got your case down too. You'll need it for Friday. I left it by the bed.'

I don't say anything.

He takes Grace and kisses her all over the face. 'I'll see you at the weekend, baby girl.' She stares at him, looking as confused as I feel.

'Don't go.'

'I need some space.' He starts towards the door.

'When you come up on Friday . . . well, maybe I'll be feeling differently. We can have a nice weekend. But I can't look at you right now, not without wanting to . . .' He trails off.

I hang my head. 'I understand.'

'You have to let all this go.' He gestures towards the map. 'You *have to*, or I don't know what'll happen to us. You need help.' He groans and opens the front door. 'I'll send you a text when I get there, let you know I made it okay.'

I fight tears. 'All right.'

'I'm sorry, Bridget, but you treated me, and Grace, like . . . like we're nothing, like we're not important. *You lied to us.*' He's reached the driveway. He looks inside the window of my car, at my laptop and the book lying beside it. He shakes his head and walks into the street, to find his own Yaris. 'I'll see you Friday.'

'Be careful.' I don't know why I say it. I clutch Grace and watch his car pull out. Grace waves. He doesn't look back. He doesn't wave goodbye.

Across the street a woman is standing under a streetlight, watching us. She wears a hat pulled down over a scarf and a bulky coat but I still recognise her. I am sure I'm looking at the blonde woman from the train.

I take a tentative step forward and she retreats. Before I can say anything, she gets into her own car and drives away.

Chapter 15

The girl is in my head all night, crying for help, morphing into Grace and then into me, her face constantly changing. I see us on the train platform being bundled into a van, being bumped around inside the vehicle, in a dark room, a cell, alone and oh, so scared.

When Grace wakes crying at midnight, then at two, three, four-thirty and six, I'm almost grateful for the reprieve from my dreams. Tom's right, she has developed a cold and now she's struggling to breathe. Eventually we fall asleep together at six-thirty, with her drooping against my chest, snot smeared on my pyjama top and over her flushed cheek.

When we wake at nine, she wants to feed but she can't inhale through her blocked nostrils, so she's taking a few gulps then pulling off to sob and gasp for air. My nipples quickly grow sore. I try to blow her nose, but she writhes with rage until I give up and just wipe her face with my sleeve. Her eyes are red; she looks pitiful. Somehow, I manage to get her to feed by sitting her upright on my lap and angling myself backwards so that my nipple slides into her mouth. It helps.

At ten I give up, go downstairs, lie on the sofa and put CBeebies on. I wonder if I should take Grace for a walk, if fresh air would help or make things worse. I consider calling Tom to ask his opinion but I don't. All I have from him is one curt text. *Here safe.*

I'm meant to be looking after Grace. It isn't fair to ask him what I should do. I'm her mum, I should know.

The television distracts her for half an hour and then she's wailing and demanding attention. I'd drifted off during Teletubbies, dozing in and out as they waddled around. The Baby Club theme tune had woken me briefly, but now she's had enough. I groan and put her in her bouncer, which entertains her for ten minutes. Then we play the game where she throws Frankie-Lion and I hand him back. That takes five. I try the telly again, but she doesn't like Patchwork Pals or Mister Maker. I read her stories for what feels like forever but when I look at the clock, only forty minutes have passed. She wants to be held but when I hold her, she wants to be put down. She yells and sobs and snot emerges in great bubbles that burst, leaving slimy trails on her face.

Finally, I remember Calpol.

I race to the medicine cupboard feeling like an idiot. There I find an empty bottle, glued to its cardboard box with sticky pink residue. There isn't another one. If Tom knew she was coming down with a cold, why didn't he buy more?

Grace wails, I run back, pick her up and bounce her, then head into the kitchen. I put her on the floor with a bowl full of flour, not even caring about the mess it'll make and throw together some dairy-free biscuits, while she hurls handfuls of white powder over the tiles. While they're cooking, I manage to quiet her for a few minutes by standing in front of the mirror and holding her up to her reflection. Then I'm forced to sing songs for another ten minutes while the biscuits cool. A single biscuit keeps her happy for a little while. I can't bring myself to care that she isn't having a healthy lunch. I'll give her fruit later. We need to go to the chemist. Another night like the last one and I'll be a total basket-case; that'll give Gillian something to think about.

I look down at myself. I'm still in my pyjamas. 'Come on, baby.'

I carry her upstairs and try to get dressed, but she won't stop yelling. In the end I manage to swap out my pyjama bottoms and slip my feet into my trainers. I'm going to the chemist in Tom's tracksuit bottoms, a filthy pyjama top and an old beanie to hide my greasy hair. My face is unwashed, I'm wearing no make-up, I haven't cleaned my teeth and my baby is clinging to me like a limpet.

Even worse, *she* is going to the chemist in a filthy onesie, with her hair pasted into unruly spikes with help from a flour and snot concoction that has morphed into superglue. When I try to wipe her face, she screams as if I'm torturing her and I give up, wrestle her into her pram and cover her with a blanket that she almost immediately kicks off. She's red and I wonder if she has a temperature. I dither for a moment in the hallway, debating the merits of fetching the thermometer. But if she *has* got a temperature, I would only have to give her Calpol anyway, which I haven't got. So, either way, I'm going to the chemist.

I grab the pram and manhandle it out of the door. As soon as we start moving, Grace calms down and I realise I should have taken her outside all along. I start to walk along our street, and almost immediately her eyelids droop. She's going to fall asleep. I twitch the blanket back over her and as my shoulders relax along with her breathing, I risk a look up and around.

There's a white van parked on the road opposite, just one door down.

As I lengthen my stride, an engine turns over and the van starts to move. Slowly, it follows me down the street, at no more than walking pace. I speed up and look back: it's still there.

Grace's pram is bumping over the rough pavement now but I don't care. I want to turn us around and race back to the house but the van is behind me, between us and the front door. If I want help, I have to get to the high street. I lurch into a shambling run, pushing the pram faster so that Grace is woken, and she wails, balling her tiny fists and looking both furious and pitiful at the same time.

I look back. The van remains in my periphery, following slowly, its engine growling. It can't be in higher than first gear. Then the engine noise changes as the driver shifts up a gear and the van speeds up. I can't understand why, but then I hear laughter and turn to see a group of teenagers heading towards us, jostling and joking. The van passes me. As the teens amble cluelessly between us, I stand still, staring into the blacked-out windows. I can see no-one but I feel eyes on us.

The van takes the corner and is gone. I exhale, releasing a breath I hadn't realised I'd been holding. Grace is howling now and I consider racing us home, but she needs medicine. What kind of mum would I be if I didn't get it for her?

'Hey!' I call to one of the teenagers, a skinny black kid wearing baggy trousers and a grey hoodie. 'Hey, do you want to earn a tenner?'

They all turn. The one I was speaking to fiddles with his earbuds as if he was listening to music and has to switch it off. 'What's up?'

'It's just . . . my baby isn't well. I need to get her some Calpol from the chemist, but . . . I need to get her home. I was hoping you might go the chemist for me? And then deliver it to my house?'

The teens look at one another. I have no way of knowing what they're thinking or if they can be trusted. They'll probably take my money and run. I pull my purse from my pocket and fumble for a twenty. 'Here, look, you can keep the change. I live at—'

'We know where you live, we saw you come out.' One of the teenaged boys is a girl. She frowns and leans closer to me. 'That creeper in the van. Was he following you?'

I bite my lip and try not to cry. If someone else saw it then I'm not crazy, not paranoid. I nod.

'Do you know him?'

I shake my head, lower my voice to a whisper. 'I keep seeing him.'

One of the boys whistles. 'You've got a stalker, man. You should call the police! That shit can get out of hand.' He looks at me for a long moment as if trying to work out why someone who looks like me might attract a stalker.

I fight tears. I'm so tired. It would be easy to cry but I don't want to. I'm the grown-up here. 'I don't know who he is, I didn't get the number plate. What would I even say?'

'I hear you.' The girl reaches out for the twenty. 'We'll get the Calpol.' She looks sympathetically at Grace. 'She doesn't look very well. Do you want Nurofen too? You can use both to bring her temperature down.' At my shocked look she shrugs. 'I've got a little sister.'

'I . . . yes please.' I hand over the money.

'We'll knock on when we got it.' The girl folds the twenty and puts it in her pocket. 'Won't take long.'

The teens turn and head towards the shops while I push Grace back home, palming my phone as I go. The van could return at any moment but this time I'll be ready. Why hadn't I thought to take a picture of his number plate before?

I reach the front door and manhandle Grace awkwardly up the steps. She's starting to nod off again, thank goodness. I get the pram into the hallway, ignoring the marks the wheels leave on the floorboards, and stand on the step with the door open, looking out. Watching for the van, looking for the teenagers.

Just as I've given up hope and am preparing myself to take Grace back out, they come barrelling around the corner.

One of them breaks away; the one with the grey hoodie. He's carrying a small plastic bag. When he gets to me he hands me both the bag and a handful of money: a tenner and a few coins.

'I said you could keep the change.' I try to give it back, but the boy shakes his head.

'We talked about it. We decided we dint want your money. Ain't right, honestly. The chemist says give the baby the Calpol first, then give her a dose of Nurofen in two hours if she's still bad, then Calpol again two hours after that. If she's no better tomorrow, you could call 111, or make a doctor's appointment.' He's backing away down the path as if I might try to lure him inside. 'An' you should call the police about that creep in the van.' He reaches his friends and waves. 'See ya.'

'See ya.' I wave back, clutching the bag and staring at the money he'd returned.

There is no sign of the van.

'Hello, Bridget, it's lovely to see you again.' Aunt Gillian is just as I remember her, rail-thin, bird-like, shorter than me and older by about thirty years.

'Hello, Aunt Gillian, how was France?'

'Wonderful. I'll tell you all about it next time I see you at your mum's.' She gives me a hug that makes me think I've put my arms around a skeleton, and I try not to cough as I inhale a nostrilful of hairspray.

She wears her hair down, but it's so well-lacquered that it acts like a helmet, shifting in one gleaming mass whenever she moves her head. When I pull back, I spot a line of white in the centre of her parting: her roots need retouching. This sign of humanity is a relief. It makes me relax a little as she leads me to a seat. 'So, you're taking Fluoxetine. Is that right?'

She's wearing gold-rimmed glasses and she picks up a gold pen and notebook as she sits down.

Mum answers her before I can. 'That's right.' She is sitting beside me watching Grace who is lying in her pram, sleeping the sleep of a baby with a full dose of Nurofen and half a dose of Calpol still in her system. She is snoring gently.

'The doctor said—' I start.

Gillian huffs dismissively and I fall silent. 'Well, GPs are *General Practitioners*, of course,' she says. 'I'm sure your doctor . . .?'

'Lewis,' I supply.

'Lewis,' she agrees. 'I'm sure he's doing his best, but he isn't a specialist in *mental health*, is he?' She looks at me intensely. Her eyes are very light blue and they glisten fervently behind her glasses.

'She.'

'I'm sorry?' She blinks.

'Dr Lewis. She's a she.' I press my hands together.

'I see.' She gets back on her train of thought as though I hadn't derailed it. 'GPs prescribe pills left and right as if they're miracle drugs, these days. Did *she* talk to you about addiction and withdrawal? Did *she* talk about the problems people have coming off these antidepressants and all the side-effects that are ruining lives? Did *she* tell you how much the drug company is paying her to prescribe their pills?'

I think back to the appointment where I'd begged Doctor Lewis for help, practically on my knees. I was in a state, barely able to function. I didn't remember her talking about withdrawal but if someone is having an asthma attack, do you talk to them about the dangers of systemic steroids or do you give them an inhaler and make sure they aren't going to die?

'I . . . not really.'

'Did she even suggest therapy before she put you on these drugs?'

She had, but I'd needed an instant fix. I'd been going out of my mind. 'I . . . I wasn't comfortable talking with a stranger . . .' I tail off.

'It's lucky we know each other so well then.' Gillian reaches over and pats my clenched hands. 'The drugs have got you to this stage but now you're ready to take the next step towards *real* mental health.'

'I suppose.'

'Of course she is.' Mum leans forwards. 'So, what do you recommend, Gillian? About these drugs, I mean?'

'Are you having side-effects?' Gillian reaches over and taps on an iPad. She brings up a list of problems I could be having with the Fluoxetine.

Mum answers for me again. 'Well, there's obviously the weight gain.' She gestures and Gillian nods knowingly. I hunch over my stomach. I've made an effort today; I'm wearing my work trousers and a top I usually save for special occasions. My hair is freshly washed, my face made-up. But I can't disguise my failings, I shouldn't even bother. 'And she isn't acting like herself. You should have heard the way she spoke to me the other day.'

'Mum, I—'

'It's all right, Bridget.' She smiles at me. 'I know now that it was just your medication talking.' She looks back at Gillian. 'And, of course, she's *seeing things*.'

'Seeing things?' Gillian looks at me. 'What sort of things?'

I open my mouth but Mum speaks over me. 'As you know, she called the police because she thought she saw a kidnapping.'

'*Mum!*' Grace stirs and I lower my voice. 'I did see—'

'But you didn't.' Mum doesn't even look at me. 'She's having nightmares. She dreamed the whole thing.'

'No, I—'

Gillian hums thoughtfully. 'Yes, these are side-effects of the Fluoxetine: behavioural changes, vivid dreams, nightmares. Have *you* felt that your behaviour has changed recently, Bridget?'

I think of the lies I've been telling to Tom, to Mum. How easily they have come. I give a tiny nod.

'Then you could very well be seeing things. Have you been seeing anything else?'

There was the vanishing message in the library and there's the white van. But the teenagers saw it too, they told me to call the police. I'm not seeing things. I shake my head.

'Well . . .' Gillian taps the pen on her large front teeth. 'I'm sure it can't be nice for you to have nightmares.'

I shudder in agreement. Last night, about an hour after Grace had gone down, I'd woken with a scream and been too terrified to close my eyes again. I'd watched Friends re-runs until Grace was up for the day at six forty-five.

The girl was haunting me, her big dark eyes there whenever I closed mine, pleading, asking me why I hadn't found her yet.

'All right, Bridget. I can see that you're in a bit of a state.' Gillian pats my hands again; her skin is soft and papery. 'I recommend that you come off the Fluoxetine.' She ignores my gasp and the stiffening of my body. 'You'll have to do it fairly gradually. Halve your dosage this week, then take one every other day, then one every two days until you're off it completely. It's the best way to deal with the withdrawal. You've not been taking it too long, so it shouldn't be too difficult for your body to adjust.'

'But . . . the depression.'

'Of course, I won't leave you without an alternative.' She laughs, a short quick bark. 'Today I'd like to do some hypnotherapy. You might remember it from when you were younger. Let's see if you still react as well to it. If you do, I'd say twice a week for the next three months.' She looks at Mum. 'Is that acceptable?'

'Twice a week for three months, that's twenty-four sessions.' I stiffen. 'Assuming £50 an hour, that's—'

'That's enough, Bridget, thank you,' Mum snaps. 'I told you, I'd pay.'

'But . . . hypnotherapy? I thought I'd be mainly talking to Aunt Gillian.'

'What on earth about, Bridget?' Mum rolls her eyes.

Gillian looks past me and her eyes meet Mum's. I glance away and my gaze catches on a wall of certificates and photographs. There's one of Mum that I've never seen before; it must have been taken in the sixties. She's very young and her hair is long and swept over one shoulder. She is standing stiffly beside an equally young-looking Gillian who looks almost exactly the same as she does now, just less well-preserved. There's a third girl with them but I don't recognise her at all. Her hand is on Gillian's shoulder and she's laughing at the camera, her head thrown back. Her hair is short and Twiggy-ish and she's wearing trousers. I imagine that I'd have liked her.

'There's no need for traditional counselling,' Gillian is saying. 'Not for now at least. I think hypnotherapy would be best, to give you the tools you need to deal with your depression.'

'I thought hypnotherapy was for when you want to give up something?' I rip my eyes from the photograph; there's something mesmerising about the older girl's happiness and the way she has her hand on Gillian's shoulder, her fingers curled into her collar bone, like she has a claim on her.

'Yes, if you like,' Gillian says. 'But you're giving up . . . being sad.'

* * *

I'm lying on my back on a leather recliner and I have to strain to see Grace.

'Alison will keep an eye on the baby.' Gillian's voice is low and level. 'Keep your attention on me, please.'

Obediently, I shift so that Gillian fills my line of sight. This is all very familiar.

'All right.' She takes my wrist between her cool fingers. 'Your pulse is a little high, we need to bring it down. I want you to take deep calming breaths, in for a count of ten, out for a count of ten, keep doing that for me.'

I drag a breath in as she presses her fingers against my pulse. In. One-two-three-four-five-six-seven-eight-nine-ten. Out. One-two-three-four-five-six-seven-eight-nine-ten. In . . .

'You're doing very well.' Gillian's voice remains steady. 'Now keep breathing and I want you to picture a garden. You're standing in the centre of a green lawn, your feet bare on the grass, the feel of dew between your toes. You can smell only the fresh air and the scent of flowers. It is warm and sunny but not too hot.' Her finger is tapping my wrist, slowly, in time with my pulse. 'Can you see it? Are you there?'

I nod, not wanting to disappoint her. But actually I can see it, if I close my eyes. If I try. And again, it's familiar, a place I've been to before.

'What can you hear? Birdsong?'

I nod again.

'Good. Now walk forward. In front of you there's a gate. I want you to go through it. On the other side of the gate there is a smooth path, nothing litters the ground. You walk along it, feeling the warmth of the soil on the soles of your feet. There are trees on either side of you, casting a light shade. You can still hear the birdsong, but it is quieter here.' Her fingers keep tapping; the recliner feels more comfortable than my bed ever did. It feels as if I'm sinking into it. I sigh.

'Good. Now you come to a cliff edge. There is a beach below you. A sandy path leads down to a small blue boat that sits on the shore. I want you to walk down the path, down and down, the sand between your toes, the sunlight on your back. You can hear the call of gulls.' Tap-tap.

'When you reach the beach and the boat, I want you to take a deep breath. Can you taste the salty air?'

I take an even deeper breath.

'Good. Now I want you to get into the boat. Feel it rock slightly beneath you as you climb in. There is no seat, so you lie down on the smooth, warm wood. After a moment, the tide sweeps a wave beneath you and you find your little boat pulled away from the shore and into the sea. It rocks beneath you, the gulls' cries are far away, the sun warms your skin. The boat rocks and rocks.'

She has stopped tapping now, I think, but I'm not sure. I'm on the little boat, rocking on the sea. My eyes are closed. I couldn't open them if I tried. I don't want to. I'm completely at peace.

I think I hear her click her fingers above me but I'm unable to respond. It's not that I couldn't if I really wanted to, more that I want to stay in my little boat.

'Now, Bridget, I need you to listen to the sound of my voice, to my words. You are going to be happy, Bridget. You are no longer going to have nightmares. You are not going to think about kidnappings. You are going to accept that what you think you saw from the train was only a dream. There is no other little girl, only Grace. You are going to focus on your family: your husband, your daughter, your mum. You no longer need pills to be happy. Happy where you are. Happy with what you have. Happy . . .' She talks on and I'm vaguely listening. But mainly I'm on my little boat, feeling the depths of the sea vanishing below me.

The room is no longer dark; there's a film playing on one of the walls and its lights glimmer over her pale face. It is on day and night, its characters the only company she has. The sound is muted, and the figures move on and off the screen, as though they're walking through the walls of her small room, into the next one, and then back.

Although it is something to look at and she's bored, the little girl lies on the bed with her face in her pillow and squeezes her eyes closed. If the woman wants her to watch the film, then she won't.

But she can't lie face down on the bed all day. Eventually she has to get up, to pee or to stretch her legs and that is when she sees the film flickering around her. She begins to wonder who they are, these people, what they're saying, what they're going to do next.

Chapter 16

All through the drive north, I am riddled with guilt. Having told Mum that Tom and I are taking Grace to stay in a hotel, using a Groupon deal in case she thinks we're frittering away our money, I am feeling awful. I can hear her voice in my head: *No-one likes a liar, Bridget.* My fingers twitch on the wheel.

I'm pretty sure she'll ask to see photos, which also worries me.

Thankfully, a fractious Grace falls asleep in her car seat, with Frankie-Lion on her chest, just as I hit the motorway. A light drizzle mists the windscreen and I slow a little, moving into the middle lane and allowing the faster vehicles – the Audis and BMWs – to roar past without resentment. I'm nervous about seeing Tom. Other than a quick text to let him know what time I should be arriving, we haven't been in touch. He hasn't even called to check on Grace.

I'm wearing a dress today, one I know he likes, and I've showered. I had to have Grace in with me but I managed to do my hair and face. I'm scared that he's going to take one look at me and decide he wants the break to be permanent. I'm scared of what

I've done to our marriage. This is what happens to people who lie to one another.

Desperate to stop thinking, I put the radio on low; Classic FM, so that it won't wake up Grace. Then there's a flash of white to my right. A vehicle is sitting in my blind spot. I ignore it for a mile or so then I realise that it has no intention of overtaking me.

I indicate and pull into the left lane. The white vehicle vanishes and I exhale. Then, I look in my rear-view mirror and it's there, behind me, one car back. There must be hundreds of white vans on the motorway. No reason to panic. I speed up and see one ahead of me, a logo for a roofing company emblazoned on its side.

The van behind me seems to be unmarked and the windows are blacked out. I can't see the driver. I speed up again and pull into the middle lane. The van follows me, pulling almost level on my left.

My breath is coming in sharp pants and I'm gripping the wheel so tightly that my hands ache. My vision blurs and I ease off the accelerator. Grace is in the car; I have to be careful. It's probably nothing. The radio starts to play Ludovico Einaudi's *Due Tramonti*. It's a favourite of mine. I reach over and switch it off. I drive in a tense silence broken only by the swish of the windscreen wipers, the whistle of Grace's breathing and the whoosh of the traffic around me.

What is the van doing?

For a few miles I think the driver might be planning to run me off the road but they seem content to sit on my tail, either in the left- or right-hand lane. Every so often they change it up, forcing me to look for them. My hands start to shake. I keep glancing at my phone which I'm using as a sat nav. I wonder if I should call Naomi and tell her someone is after me. I wipe my hands on my trousers, one at a time. Sweat is making me lose my grip on the wheel.

Then I spot a police car. It's travelling at a steady seventy in the right-hand lane just ahead of me. With a rising heart, I speed up and pull in behind it. I don't care where he's going, I'm staying with him. I have one eye on the police car ahead and one on the van, which remains in the middle lane behind me. They won't try anything with the police here. They can't.

After another few miles, the van speeds up and sails past. I know what they're doing, trying to make me relax, to leave safety so they can pick me up again. I refuse to move. I remain behind the police car until it pulls into a service station. I debate following, desperate to keep close, but there is no sign of the van now and if I stop the car Grace will wake up and cry the rest of the way. I grit my teeth and drive on.

The van picks me up again when I leave the M6 and merge onto the A59. It's as if it's been waiting for me in a lay-by, as though it knew where I was going. But is it the same van? It's white, but how many white vans have I passed, my heart thumping each time? I think it is though: unmarked, blacked-out windows.

He stays on my tail until I turn onto Whalley Road, by which time tears are pouring down my cheeks and my breath is coming in short hitches. When I'm sure it's gone, I pull into the car park of a Booths supermarket and try to breathe.

The moment I slide to a stop, Grace stirs, but we're almost there: a few minutes from Neil and Sam's. I have to calm down before I see Tom. I can't tell him that I was followed, he'll say I'm crazy again. I pull out my make-up and retouch my eyes and lips. My face is pale so I add some blusher and fluff out my hair. Grace is wailing now but I can't take her out of her seat. I shush her and pat her red cheek. There's a dummy in the coin holder. I put it in her mouth and she sucks on it instantly, balefully.

'Nearly there, baby.' I look at my watch. We're only five minutes later than the arrival time I'd texted. Tom won't be worrying yet. I look at the supermarket, take a breath and get out of the car. I fetch Grace and balance her on my hip. I'll buy flowers and wine for Sam. I should have thought of that before setting off anyway. It'll give me time to recentre myself and I'd like to see the supermarket anyway, I've never been into a Booths.

Tom opens the door. For a suspended moment we stare at one another, half in shock, as though we're strangers. Then he realises my arms are full and, in the flurry of handing over Grace, flowers, wine and bags, suddenly I'm inside and we aren't alone any longer.

'All right, Fidget, how was the journey?' Neil gathers me into a hug, his big arms and huge chest enveloping me; he still has a rugby player's physique, not like Tom. Tom is much slimmer; he ran cross country and track at university and played football at the weekends. I manage not to answer him, swallowing the lie hovering on my lips: *fine, no problems*.

'You look really nice, Bridge.' Sam takes my bags. 'You remember which room you're in?'

I look over her shoulder at Tom. He's greeting Grace, rubbing his cheek against hers, like they're a pair of cats. She's still a bit groggy from the journey but she's babbling at him wildly and gripping his hair in her small fist. It's shorter than it was. He's made time for a haircut in the last couple of days. He's shaved too and I realise that he's made an effort. He's wearing a nice shirt and his chinos, almost as if he's dressed for an interview. I wonder if he's met with the recruitment agent today, or if he's dressed for me.

Self-consciously I touch my own hair. Has he noticed the effort *I* went to?

'Let me bring Grace to see India.' Sam wrestles Grace from Tom's reluctant arms. 'Why don't you take Bridge upstairs, Tom? She probably wants to decompress a bit.' She looks at me. 'Wine, beer, or soft?'

'I . . .' I look at Tom. 'What are you having?'

'I'll open some beers,' Neil says, without waiting for an answer. 'Moretti okay?' He heads for the kitchen, splitting off from Sam who is taking Grace into the living room. 'They'll be open and cold when you guys are ready.'

The hall is suddenly empty and quiet. I shuffle my feet and look at Tom's knees.

'Come on then.' He turns and starts upstairs.

I follow, watching his heels as he takes each stair.

'H-how have you been?' I speak to the back of his head. 'Have you . . . had a good couple of days?'

'Fine, yeah.' He opens the bedroom door and stands aside, waiting for me to walk past him. I look at his chest, then at the room beyond, unable to meet his eyes. What will I see there? The bed is made, and Tom's suitcase lies on the floor beside it. He hasn't bothered to unpack, which is very like him. His washbag is lying on top of the case, his trainers on the floor next to it. I fix my eyes on the dirty treads.

'Bridge, look at me.' His voice is by my ear, his breath on my face. I take a breath and raise my head. He seems stricken: lines are carved between his eyebrows and his cheeks are pale. His eyes are very blue. He rubs a hand through his hair. It's shaking. 'I'm sorry, OK.' He drops his hands. 'I shouldn't have walked out on you. That was shitty.'

'It was my fault,' I say. 'I should never have lied to you. I knew it was wrong.'

'You're not well.' Tom heads for the bed and sits down, his hands hanging between his knees as if they're too heavy to raise. 'I know you aren't yourself right now. I should be there, supporting you. It's just . . .' His eyes meet mine and they've darkened, the blue deepening so they're almost grey. 'It's not easy for me, watching you fall apart. And I thought . . .' He scrubs at his hair again. He'll be bald one of these days, like his father. 'I love Grace, don't get me wrong, but it's not easy to be the one who stays at home all day every day. It's not like I haven't tried joining a

195

group, Bridge, but they're almost all mums and I don't fit in. The only adult conversation I have is when your mum takes Grace and I go into college, but honestly, I'm the oldest on the course. What do I have to say to the rest of them? They're kids! Then, you're coming home later and later and . . . you could have been home but you *lied* so you could be off doing . . .' he tails off. 'I'm sorry.'

'No, *I'm* sorry.' I fall to my knees at his feet. 'I didn't realise.' I stutter a strange half-laugh. 'I've had Grace on my own for two days and it's been . . . I mean it's been wonderful . . . but it's been *hard*. She needs attention *all the time*. I don't get a moment to myself. I can't even pee. And . . .' I lower my voice. 'I love her but sometimes it was kind of . . . boring?'

It is Tom's turn to laugh. 'The key is to get out and about.'

'I know. But she has a cold.' I sit back on my heels. 'I wasn't sure if the cold air . . .'

'She's fine if you wrap her up.' Tom takes my hand. 'You should've called.'

'I didn't . . .' I bite my lip. 'I wasn't sure . . .'

'I know.' Tom sighs. 'My fault. I'm sorry. I should've called you, checked on you both.'

We sit, holding hands, staring at our conjoined fingers.

'Do you still want to do this?' Tom's voice trembles. 'Now you've had a taste of it. Do you want to give up work?'

'God, yes!' My head jerks up. 'It was hard, and sometimes boring, and she covered me in snot, and

I spilled Calpol on the sofa, but it was great too. She pulled herself up for almost a whole minute and stood there grinning at me. She was happy that I was with her, I could tell. I taught her to stick her tongue out *and* she stopped calling me Dada.'

'You taught her to stick out her tongue?'

'I thought she was a little young for rock-horns.'

Tom snorts. 'So, you still want to look at houses?'

I nod firmly. Ignoring the voice that is suddenly filling my head. *Happy where you are. Happy with what you have.*

He looks up, almost as if he's heard. 'How was therapy?'

'It was kind of weird.' I get to my feet and sit beside him on the bed. The springs creak. He takes my hand again. 'I don't remember much about the sessions after Dad died but it was like hearing a song you haven't thought about for years and suddenly finding you know all the words. You know what I mean?'

Tom nods.

'Gillian says I have to come off the antidepressants. And it isn't a talking thing, like we thought. She's doing hypnotherapy on me.'

'Hypnotherapy! Are you serious? Did she make you cluck like a chicken?' His eyes glimmer.

'It's not like that. It's more like you relax and she's saying stuff, and you know what's going on but you're so loose that you don't move. You just listen until she tells you to wake up.'

'And what did she tell you?'

'I . . .' I frown. 'I can't remember exactly. She told me to be happy.'

'Well . . . I suppose that's good enough advice.' Tom sighs and his thumb starts tracing little circles on my palm. I shiver. 'Are you going to do it, though? Give up the antidepressants I mean.'

'I . . .' I look towards the window. 'I don't know. I mean she was really insistent . . . but it's scary. What if things go back to the way they were?'

Tom's thumb stops moving, then starts again, circling in the opposite direction. My fingers curl around his, like the petals of a flower.

'Gillian says they're addictive and that I could have real problems coming off them if I'm on them for too long. And I *have* been having those nightmares. I want them to stop.' Tom moves closer to me. I don't look at him. 'I did some research last night and lots of people agree with her. There are stories about patients having to be on them for years and years because the withdrawal is so bad . . . but I can't go back!'

'Isn't the hypnotherapy meant to stop that from happening?'

'I suppose.'

'What do you want to do? I'll support you whatever you decide.' Tom puts an arm around my shoulders.

I meet his eyes. 'I want to know what *you* think?'

'I think . . .' He frowns. 'I think that the nightmares have been awful for you. For us. If there's a way to stop them without you getting ill again . . .'

'You think I should come off the Fluoxetine.'

198

'I think it's worth a try. But the minute you start feeling like you were, you should speak to Dr Lewis and start taking them again. Or maybe something else.'

'You're right.' I inhale, breathing in the scent of him.

'Can I kiss you?' He leans forward and I tilt my face up so that my lips meet his.

We have frantic sex on top of Sam's checked duvet cover, not even removing half of our clothes. Afterwards I lie on top of him, my face in his shoulder while he strokes my hair. We only go downstairs when it's almost time to meet the estate agent. Our beer is warm and flat.

The house is gorgeous; Tom has picked a good one. It's on the outskirts of town but closer to Neil and Sam than the one I liked on Rightmove. It's slightly more expensive but it has a garden plenty big enough to put in a swing for Grace, with room to spare for a table and chairs, the flowerbeds I dreamed of, and even a barbeque.

The kitchen is probably what would be described as modern country: wooden cabinets painted a gorgeous soft grey, against a cream work surface. I run my hand over the cold marble.

'It's lovely.'

'There's a utility room too,' Tom says, shuffling Grace from one arm to the other. 'We wouldn't have to do the laundry in the kitchen anymore.'

'And a downstairs loo.' I'm laughing. 'I can see us living here, can't you?'

Behind Tom, the estate agent is grinning. Tom shushes me. When we get to the master bedroom he leans close and lowers his voice. 'Play it cool, can't you? Or they'll raise the price!'

'Right, sorry.' The bedroom is twice the size of ours with huge windows that overlook a field and, not too far away, there's the glitter of a river winding towards hills. 'Oh my God.' I lean on the windowsill. 'I want this view.'

'Bridge!' Tom claps his hand on his forehead. 'We've got two more to see, you know.'

'But . . . this is *our* house. Can't you feel it?'

Tom nods. We go to look at the third bedroom. Grace's room. It's already painted a peaceful yellow with a bright white trim. It's a child's bedroom.

'What does Grace think?' I look at them and Tom puts her down. Immediately she starts commando crawling her way towards a box of toys in the corner.

'She seems happy.' Tom sweeps her back up before she can put a Lego brick in her mouth.

Tom turns to the estate agent who is still following us but has long ago stopped pointing out features, knowing he doesn't need to do a sales pitch. 'Has there been much interest?'

'Some,' he answers, adjusting his tie. 'There's another viewing this afternoon.'

My heart races. We're going to lose it. 'Tom!'

'We still have to sell ours,' he says, mournfully. 'We can only move as fast as ours goes.'

'Well . . .' the estate agent puts a hand on Tom's shoulder. He still has acne on his cheeks above a wisp of stubble. He can't be more than twenty. 'Have you considered let-to-buy?'

'You mean buy-to-let?' I frown. 'How would that help?'

'No,' the estate agent keeps talking to Tom, even though I was the one who answered him. 'Let-to-buy. Buy-to-let is where you buy a house so you can rent it out. Let-to-buy is where you rent out your own house so you can buy a new one. You could see what your own place is worth and talk to the bank. If you re-mortgage to release some equity, you can use that as a deposit on here. If you get an interest-only mortgage on your old place, you can use the rental income to cover it. You might even end up with some left over to contribute to the mortgage on here.'

'Are you serious?' Tom frowns. 'Is that a thing?'

'Oh, yes.' The estate agent pulls out a piece of paper and writes a number on it. 'If you want more information, call the office. But yeah, people do it all the time. You're near London, right? Commuter belt?'

Tom nods. 'Less than an hour overland into Euston.'

'Well then, you shouldn't have any problems renting yours. You just need a local agency to let you know what it's worth as a rental before you speak to the bank. You could be in a position to put an offer in on this place in a week or so.' He pushes a picture of the house into Tom's hands. 'If you like, I can let the owners know you're interested. If they get an offer while you're still working things out, they may wait for you to put in a counter.'

'We've got a couple more to see this weekend,'

Tom says, looking at the picture. I dig my nails into his arm, and he winces. 'Come on, Bridge. You literally can't buy the first thing you see. I've seen you take seven hours to pick a pair of shoes!'

'Yes . . .' I smile up at him. 'And how many times do I end up back in the very first shop at the end of it?'

'That's true.' Tom rolls his eyes at the estate agent. 'Take us to the next house. We'll let you know what to tell the owners after our third viewing tomorrow morning.' He looks at me. 'Is that fair, Bridge? You might love the next one even more.'

'I won't.'

Tom and the estate agent meet in a collusion of raised eyebrows. 'Well, keep an open mind.'

They're wrong, the next house is small and dark and nothing like as nice as the first. It hasn't even got a garden, just a flag-stoned courtyard.

I'm standing, arms folded, outside a dingy bathroom with black mould creeping around the silicone. 'What made you pick this place?'

'It's near the train station.' Tom points and, sure enough, I see a train going by. I shiver. 'I thought you might want fast access to civilisation.'

I think of the river meandering past the first house and compare it to the railway tracks. 'Nope.' I'm carrying Grace this time. She wailed when we tried to put her down as we had done in the last house. 'I'm done here.'

'But you haven't seen—' the estate agent starts.

'I'm done.' I head for the front door. 'It's a horror show.'

'It's not that bad, Bridge.' Tom is on my heels.

'I hate it!' I blow out of the front door and wait for Tom to join us. He is muttering to the estate agent who is nodding and smiling.

I turn to face the road and spot a white van heading into the railway station car park. Immediately I stiffen and Grace squeals. I loosen my grip on her. How did they find us?

Tom comes to stand on the pavement beside me. He puts an arm around my shoulder and blows a kiss to Grace. 'God, you're tense. I'm not going to force you to live here. I didn't like it either.'

'Can we just—'

'Head back? Okay.' He turns to the agent. '10.30 tomorrow morning, right? I've got the address.'

'See you then.' He heads to his little car and Tom smirks down at me.

'At least you liked *one* that I picked. We'll see yours tomorrow and make a decision over lunch, yeah?'

'Okay.' I'm still watching the car park, wondering if the van will emerge and follow us to Neil and Sam's. Am I putting India in danger? Oh God, what if the kidnappers decide to take Sam's India because I led them there?

'Come on.' Tom takes Grace and heads for our car. 'I've got that meeting with the recruitment agent in an hour. What are you going to do this afternoon?'

'I . . .' I tear my gaze from the car park. 'I'll probably drive around a bit, get to know the area, you know?'

'Good idea.' Tom finishes clipping a squirming Grace into her car seat, pops a dummy in her mouth and turns to kiss me. I lean against him, still wary. What if they're watching right now?

'Relax, Bridge.' Tom smiles down at me. 'This is going really well.'

I leave a full-stomached Grace fast asleep with Sam. I reckon I have at least an hour before she wakes up, so I get back into my car.

'Neil can go with you, if you like?' Sam leans into the window. 'He can show you the best places.'

'It's okay, I just want to drive around and get a feel for things.' The lie sticks in my throat.

'If you're sure?'

'I'm sure.' The book is beside me, under my coat. It feels like a decaying isotope releasing radiation. A ticking bomb. 'If Neil's with me we'll only end up down the pub.'

'True story.' Sam steps away from the car. 'Take your time. There'll be a glass of wine here with your name on it when you get back. If Grace wakes up, she can play with India.'

I give her an awkward thumbs-up and drive away.

I know what I'm about to do is wrong. It's not just that I'm betraying Tom and Grace by even considering it, but there's this new voice inside me, which says I shouldn't even be thinking about the kidnapped girl, that I should stop investigating. That I should focus on Tom and Grace, on Mum.

Happy with what I have.

I put my hand on my coat, feeling the shape of the book beneath. 'I have to do this.' I speak out loud because if I don't, I know I'll back out.

I believe that there is a kidnapping gang working in the North of England, focusing on train stations and now moving south. I believe that they're watching me. And I think there might be a clue here in Lancashire: Grant Dobson might know something. Perhaps something he doesn't even know he knows. He wasn't there that day but if his daughter was taken by a gang, the family must have been watched, perhaps even befriended.

The kidnapping of Frances Dobson couldn't have been spontaneous, it must have been planned, so what might Grant Dobson know that could help my missing girl?

In Sabden, I pull up opposite a terraced house that reminds me of the property I had such a visceral hatred for back in Clitheroe. It's the house from the photograph in the book. I'm so sure of it, I don't even need to compare it with the image. The number is the same, on the same door, although it's more weathered now and the paint is peeling. The garden has become overgrown and brambles cluster on the other side of the low wall; a few blackberries form an offering to the birds that sit cawing on the roof.

Worst of all are the remains of an old swing set, like the one I imagined installing in our new house for Grace. The frame lies on its side, legs pointing at the sky, the rope tangled among the brambles, the once red seat lying to one side. A little girl played on that swing. For a second, I imagine her: legs pumping, fingers gripping the rope. I find that my own hands have curled into fists. I open them.

I take a deep breath but, before I can get out of the car, my phone rings. The high-pitched buzz makes me jump and I stare at it for a moment. I don't recognise the number. It's probably a scammer so, eyes on the distant hill, I let it ring until it stops.

I reach for the car door and the phone starts to ring again, its buzzing somehow more insistent. I hesitate and then touch the screen, answering.

'Hello?'

I'm expecting that pause you get with cold callers. The moment before the machine realises you've answered, before a real person takes the call on: that click and whirr. But there's a human voice straight away. 'Bridget? It's Gillian.'

'Hello, Aunt Gillian.' I'm frowning at the screen. What could Gillian want? Does she need to rearrange my next appointment?

'I'm just calling to see how you're doing. The first day after hypnotherapy can be a little strange sometimes. How do you feel?'

'Oh.' I retreat from the door handle and lean into the car seat. 'I'm fine, thanks.'

'Did you reduce your dosage last night?'

'I . . . yes, I took a half dose.'

'And your nightmares?'

'A little better maybe?'

'Well, that's great. And what about this kidnapping you dreamed . . . are you still thinking about it?'

I pull the phone away from my ear, glare at it and bring it back into place. 'I'm trying not to.' The lie doesn't even taste sour going down. I didn't *dream* the kidnapping. It was real.

'And where are you now?' She's chirpy but there's something sharp behind her question and I don't want to tell her the truth.

Happy with what you have.

'I'm away with Tom and Grace. We're taking a couple of days.'

'That's lovely. Anywhere nice?' Again, that sharpness in her tone, as if I've done wrong by not asking her permission. Was I meant to run these things by her? I don't know the rules.

'We're just . . .' For a moment I can't remember my lie. What did I tell Mum? 'In a hotel in York. It's . . .' I think back to the work visit I made to the city a couple of years earlier. 'The Novotel. It has a pool. Grace is enjoying the winding streets and old buildings. I think . . .' I force a laugh. 'I mean as much as an eight-month-old can, I guess.'

'Of course.' There's a chilly silence. 'And you're feeling more positive. Happy with things?'

Happy with what you have.

'I suppose.' I laugh again, a brittle sound, and flick my gaze to the sky painting the windscreen. It's as grey as the bricks in the houses around me. 'Am I cured then?'

It's Gillian's turn to laugh; too high, too giddy. It's

odd. 'You'll need a few more sessions with me, I'm afraid.' There's a rustle. 'You're still happy to come in on Mondays and Thursdays?'

'Yes, I think so.'

'Well, I'll see you then. And remember, Bridget, happiness can be a decision you make.'

Happy with what you have.

I hang up and sit for a moment, staring at the phone. Could I be happy with what I have, living in the commuter belt? Already our flat feels tiny and dingy compared with the alternative. But a part of me feels pained, as if striving for change is wrong.

I'm not here to look at houses though, I'm here to talk to Grant Dobson. To find the people who kidnapped the little girl, who are following me, whose eyes I can *feel* crawling over Grace. That isn't something I can switch off or not think about.

LEAVE IT BITCH. I don't think so!

I open the car door and step out. It feels like rain. I pull my coat tighter around my neck.

The road has vicious potholes, as if the grief emanating from the Dobson house has torn into the land around it. I walk around them, heels clicking on tarmac. I climb onto the uneven pavement and shove my hands deep into my pockets. There is something familiar about this short journey to the front gate: a moment of vertiginous déjà vu. I think it must be the hill, familiar from all angles, its shape carved into the skyline. I take a hitching breath. The gate is hanging from its hinges, and splinters threaten my palm as I push it inwards. It squeaks loudly and I wince.

I edge onto the path, my soles making little noise on the mud that spatters the concrete. I swallow nervously, planning what I'm going to say, hoping that Grant Dobson will at least talk to me. Is he even in? The book said he still lived here but the house is silent and wears an air of abandonment. I look up. The guttering is only half attached, swinging loose in the rising wind and knocking against crumbling brick. The windowsills are rotting, the colour flaking off, the frames shedding shards of decomposed wood. I try to peer inside, but yellowing net hangs over each pane of filthy glass. The interior is impenetrable to prying eyes.

I take another step forward but as I lift my hands to press them against the glass my jacket is gripped by claws of thorn from the thicket beside me. I step back, tugging at my coat, and puffs of goose-down emerge from tiny rips and tears. 'Damn it.' I yank and come free, but the damage is done. I'll have to see if Sam has a needle and thread.

'Oi. Who're you? Get out of my garden!'

The voice comes from behind me and I turn. There's a man stumbling along the pavement, holding a bag that clanks as he hurtles towards me. His face is blooming with red patches, his hair nothing more than streaks of grease over a mottled skull. Full, almost girlish, lips are stretched in a mask of loathing.

He's wearing an old mac, dusted on the shoulders with dandruff, and a pair of sagging khaki pants that are too big for his skinny legs. I can smell him even from a distance, his stink crashing into me and making me retreat towards the brambles with my sleeve over my mouth, in a kind of awed shock.

'What're you doin'?' he warbles, lifting his bag as if to swing it at me.

I'm trapped. I can't go back the way I came with him standing in the way. I don't want to go further towards the house.

Then he drops his arms. 'Betsie?'

He's made the same mistake that Jack did; but surely Grant Dobson would know better? Betsie was his *wife*.

'N-no, I—'

He drops his bag and glass shatters. Brown liquid spills onto the pavement but he doesn't notice. 'Betsie, love. Why'd you do it?'

His breath is scorching, fumes strong enough to strip paint. He's drunk. Paralytic, my dad would have called it.

'I shouldn't have come here.' I look desperately for a way around his grasping hands, but he's on me before I can move. He's surprisingly fast and has a wiry strength. His fingers curl around my biceps, his face close to mine. My heart pounds as his rheumy eyes bore into mine. I let out a shriek as his ragged nails bite through my coat. 'Let me go!'

'You ain't Betsie!' He pulls his face back suddenly, his eyes sharper, more aware. 'You ain't Betsie. Who are ya? What're you doing on my land? Trespassin'!' He looks down abruptly, seeking his bag of booze and spots the spillage soaking into the soil. 'Fuck!' His scream of rage brings a neighbour to the window. 'You bitch. That was the last of my benefits. You owe me.' He shakes me again. This time his eyes fill with tears. 'I *needed* that. You made me drop it. It's broken. You owe me!'

A door slams to my right. 'Let her go, Grant.' I flick my eyes to see a middle-aged man in a vest and low-slung jeans. 'Let her go, man. You want her to call the police?'

'She's trespassin', Mick, an she's cost me my Jack.' He whimpers. 'You call the police, I'll tell 'em!'

'I'm so sorry.' I twist but he isn't letting go. There are points of pain where he's grasping me, mangling my arm.

'Come on, Grant. You don't need this kind of trouble.' The neighbour is coming closer now. He is talking to Grant but he's looking at me with uncomplicated disgust. His expression turns my heroic mission into something cruel and wrong. 'Thought we were done with the bleedin' crime tourists years ago. You got what you wanted, Miss?'

Grant looks again at his bag of booze and his face slackens, mourning the loss of the evening's oblivion. I yank my arm back. He lurches towards me, unbalanced by my movement and, desperate, I scratch the side of his face. Strands of his hair tangle between my fingers and I pull, trying to move him sideways. We do an ungainly dance, side-stepping, heads wobbling. His hair tears out and he yells. I scream, terrified at what is happening and how it's escalated. I shove him, hard and he releases me, falling towards the brambles with a cry. I run past him, boots hammering on damp pavement.

When the neighbour tries to catch me I kick him and run for the car. Once inside I slam the lock on the door. The neighbour follows me and knocks on the window as I'm fumbling with my keys. My breath comes in short sobs.

'Come on now, Miss. I just want to talk.' He puts his hands on the bonnet, looking as if he'll jump on the car if I try to drive away. His brown eyes bore an accusation into mine. 'You're not gonna call the police on 'im are you? This was your fault. You shouldn't have been in his garden. He's an old man, hurt, grieving. Why can't you people leave him alone?'

I bite my lip. I should never have come.

Happy where you are.

I grope for my purse and locate a £20 note. I slide the window down, just an inch, and poke the money out through the gap. 'What I owe him. To replace the broken bottle. I-I'm really sorry, I wasn't . . . I didn't intend . . .' I tail off and the man takes the money. 'I shouldn't have kicked you. Are you all right?'

'I've had worse. You won't call the cops?'

I shake my head. 'It's just . . .' Mesmerised by the attention in this stranger's eyes, and the fact that I'd never see him again, the words tumble out. 'I saw another kidnapping.' My words run into one another. 'A little girl taken from a train station. I think it could be the same people who took Frances. I–I thought maybe Mr Dobson might remember something that would help the girl I saw. I didn't realise . . . I shouldn't have come.'

'No, you shouldn't have.' The man glances back

towards Grant and then down at me. He leans over my car, lowers his voice. 'Look, I'm sorry. I shouldn't have called you a "crime tourist". But we've had a lot of them over the years. You really saw someone being taken? A little girl?'

I nod.

His plump cheeks wobble. 'There's been nothing on the news.'

I shake my head. 'She hasn't been reported missing. The police . . . they don't believe I really saw something. I don't know what to do. That's why I came here. I thought somehow it would help me to find her.'

The man sighs. 'Grant wouldn't be able to tell you anything anymore. Even if he did know something that would help this other little girl, look at him.' He points. Grant is on his hands and knees by the plastic bag, sobbing, slicing his fingers on shards of glass. 'His brain is pickled, love. There's nothing left in there but the route to the nearest boozer.'

Tears gather in my eyes as I nod. 'Will you help him?'

The man nods. 'I've been helping him for years.'

I hesitate with my fingers on my keys. 'Were you here when they lost Frances?'

'Not in that house.' The man tilts his chin. 'I lived in Whalley back then. Moved to Sabden about fifteen years ago. He's not a bad neighbour. Quiet mostly. He gets worse on the anniversary. Two anniversaries, now: Betsie and Frances.'

'I'm sorry.' I look at the old man scrabbling in the soil, pitiful now, rather than scary. Rags of hair dangle in his eyes and his fingers are blind crabs, dipping in moisture, then rising to his lips.

I can't help comparing him to my own dad, who'd been so healthy, so dignified. A flash of memory blinds me and, for a second, I see him hanging in the garage, shit staining his trousers and dropping in clumps from his loafers. I shake my head, frantically, as if I can dislodge the thought, like water.

I focus back on the man, my eyes prickling. 'Listen, if he says anything to you, anything that you think might help, will you call me?'

The man sighs. 'My phone's in the house. Text me your number.' He rattles off a mobile number and I enter it into my contacts so that I can send my own details.

The neighbour heads back towards the gate. 'I'll get him inside. You be careful. If you're right, these people could be dangerous, couldn't they?'

I think back to the van that follows me. If they think I'm getting close, what might they do to stop me? I nod and put unsteady hands on the steering wheel. Strands of Grant Dobson's hair remain tangled in my wedding ring. With a shudder I pull them out. It seems disrespectful to just throw them on the floor. I lay them in the coin tray: three hairs, coiled in the bottom. Then I drive away.

Tom's car is in the driveway when I get back and so I try to force what has happened to the back of my mind. For the sake of my marriage Grant Dobson is a secret I have to bury.

I pick up the book but instead of tossing it under the seat as I'd intended, I open it and stare at the picture. This time I see past my resemblance to Betsie to look at the man smiling at the camera. He's unrecognisable. His hair thick, dark and wavy, his skin unblemished. He stands up straight and his eyes sparkle off the page with good humour. Grant Dobson was once a good-looking man.

In fact, they're a handsome family. The girl, Frances, was going to grow up pretty, you can see that. She's a happy little thing, holding her mum's hand loosely as if she wants to go and investigate something but has been told to stand still for the camera. Betsie herself is slimmer than I am and, now that I look closer, I can see that her face is narrower, her brows thicker. She could be my sister though, or a close cousin. I touch her cheek, almost surprised to find the texture of paper under my finger.

Then I slam the book shut. This family is gone. Even the father is lost. There's no help here. It isn't worth dwelling on. I put the book on the floor and kick it under the seat, so Tom can't see it if he looks in the window. Then I get out of the car, straighten my coat and head inside.

Tom is in the kitchen with Sam and Neil; there's no sign of the babies. 'Still asleep,' Sam says on seeing my anxious expression. 'They must have been shattered, both of them.'

I turn my attention to Tom. 'How'd it go?'

'Good!' He's bright-eyed, excited. 'Sanjay – that's

his name – reckons he's got a few things that would suit me. He's sending my CV to a couple of places just to test the waters but he won't arrange any interviews till we've talked to the bank and organised things with the estate agent.'

'Interviews . . .' I hadn't thought. He'll be back and forth, leaving me and Grace alone. 'Of course.'

Sam hands me a glass of wine. 'Drink this. You look like you need it. Did you enjoy your drive around?'

I force a nod. 'It's a really pretty area.'

'Even better when it's sunny.' Sam gestures towards the leaden sky beyond the window and I nod as I hop onto a bar stool.

Tom leans on the breakfast bar beside me and puts his hand on mine. 'You look as tired as Grace was. It's been a long day for you, what with the drive up. Do you want a nap?'

I shake my head, knowing what I'll see when I close my eyes. I might not have dreamed about the little girl last night, but after today, the white van following us, my failure with Grant Dobson, she's going to haunt me. 'I'll be okay.'

'Are you still feeling up for this?' Tom looks concerned. 'You haven't changed your mind?'

'Honestly?' I put my wine glass down. 'This is all happening very fast and I'm worried about Mum, but . . .' I put my hand on his. 'That was our house, Tom. I want to live in it. I want to look at that view and have dinner in that kitchen and put Grace to bed in that yellow room. I want it so badly I can't bear it.'

'We might not get that house.' Tom's voice is a warning, but I ignore him. Sam is grinning over his shoulder.

'You should have come with us, Sam.' I lean closer to her. 'Tell Tom to stop raining on my parade.'

'When you move here we can go to all the toddler groups and slag off the other mums.' Sam knocks back the dregs of her wine and pours herself another glass. 'Tom can join Neil's football team. We can go drinking and shopping. It'll be like the old days.'

'Except we'll be shopping in Mamas & Papas instead of Topshop.' I look up as Grace's wail rips through the walls and straight into my heart. Two seconds later, India's less familiar cry joins her.

'Race you!' Sam rushes for the stairs. I'm on her heels. Tom and Neil watch us go.

On my way down, with Grace in my arms, I stop. There's a porthole in the hallway overlooking the driveway and my eye is caught by a white van parked on the road opposite. Then I spot the hooded figure standing beside my car. As I watch, a crowbar smashes the passenger window.

'Tom!' I scream his name and two seconds later he's in the hall, looking terrified. Neil is right behind him.

'What is it?'

I point towards the driveway. Neil doesn't hesitate, he races for the front door and pulls it open. He's too late though, the figure is already sprinting for the van. Neil runs from the house in his bare feet, yelling obscenities. Tom looks at me and then at the door, then he too runs outside.

'Be careful!' I intend to shout but my throat has closed on my terror and it's more of a whisper. The fleeing figure has a crowbar and Neil and Tom are defenceless. Vulnerable. What if they catch up?

Chapter 17

I clutch a crying Grace and stare through the window, unable to tear my eyes from Tom and Neil, even to comfort my daughter. Then the figure reaches the van and yanks the door open.

Tom has overtaken Neil and my heart pounds as if I'm running with him. I can picture exactly what the crowbar will look like embedded in his temple.

Before Tom can get closer, the van's door slams, and it peels away.

Neil and Tom run pointlessly after it for a few seconds, slowing to jogging speed, as it turns the corner. Then they turn back.

Neil is hobbling. Tom half carries him in. He leaves a trail of bloody footprints in the hall.

'Oh my God, Neil, your feet!' I rush down the remaining stairs. 'What do I do? Where's your medical stuff?'

Sam appears at the top of the stairs. 'What's going on?'

Neil spreads his hands. 'Some fucker just vandalised Fidget's car.'

'Oh no!' Sam is mortified. 'It's not like that around here, Bridget, honestly! We've never had this happen before. Never!'

I know she hasn't. I know the person who did this isn't local. This wasn't a random attack or some thug hoping to find an iPhone left on a car seat. But what do I say? Sorry, Sam, Neil, I led these kidnappers to your home.

And what if I tell them that I've been followed by the van? Tom might not believe me; Neil would go mental; Sam would insist I tell the police. I cling tighter to Grace. The whole idea exhausts me. Briefly, I consider speaking to Naomi Shaw, but there's no evidence that this was anything other than a motiveless piece of vandalism.

And what if I have to tell her my movements and Tom finds out where I've been?

I know it makes sense to tell Neil and Sam; I feel like a fool for deciding otherwise, but the words are stuck in my teeth like toffee. I can only nod as Sam insists that Clitheroe has a low crime rate, that these things don't happen, even as she uses tweezers to remove a shard of glass from the ball of Neil's bleeding foot.

'We'll have to speak to the police,' Tom says, taking Grace.

'What?' I stare at him, wild-eyed.

'Don't look so freaked, Bridge. We'll need a crime number for the insurance.' Tom groans. 'I'll take some photos, then we'll tape a bin bag over the window for tonight in case it rains. I'll call into the station in the morning. I passed it when I went to see the recruitment agent. I'm just annoyed we didn't get the number plate – you didn't, did you Neil?'

Neil shakes his head. 'Sorry, mate.'

'It's fine. The van was probably nicked anyway.' He kisses Grace's tears away then looks back at me. 'I'll take Grace's car seat for the drive home, she shouldn't be in a car without a window.'

I nod.

'I'll get Autoglass to come out when we're back.'

'What if it wasn't random?' I finally whisper.

Neil's head jerks up and Tom looks at me levelly. 'It *was* random, Bridge. Just joy-riding dickheads having a party. Truth or dare or some shit. Don't start spiralling.'

Truth or dare. It could almost be true. I feel around the edges of the idea as it takes shape.

'It wasn't a teenager,' I mutter.

Neil is pulling on a sock now. 'Adults can be dickheads too, Fidget,' he says.

I look at the Fluoxetine, rolling the pills between my fingers. I'm meant to be coming off them gradually, halving the dose, but I can't dream tonight; I just can't. In one swift movement, I toss the pills into Sam's toilet. They sink to the bottom and lie on the white ceramic, little green and yellow bullets turning amorphous as they dissolve in the water. I flush and watch them whirl away.

Tom is in bed waiting for me. He looks at my face. 'All right?'

221

I climb into bed beside him and twine my fingers with his. His hand is larger than mine. I love his big hands. I close my eyes.

I don't dream of the little girl this time. Instead, I am simply on a swing kicking my legs, leaning back and watching the clouds as the sky whips past, one way, then the other.

There are shapes in the clouds, broken up by the line that is the top of the swing and occasionally by my own feet when I swing too high and my heart thuds with the fear that I might go all the way over. Sometimes the whole swing wobbles, the legs moving in the soft earth and I think I might accidentally fling myself all the way over the wall. The thrill doesn't make me stop swinging. Up and down, up and down, up and down . . .

We drive home in our separate cars. As agreed, Tom takes Grace, leaving me to follow them as closely as I can, with the wind fluttering the duct-taped bin bag making a sound like a gunfire.

I didn't tell Tom that I was terrified to get going, or that I was certain a white van was going to appear in my mirror and stay there all the way home. That I thought someone might try to run me off the road or pull over and drag me out of the broken window.

I stay close to his Yaris, or I try to, but before long there's an impatient driver who shoves his way between us at a junction. Then another who separates us still further at a roundabout. Tom's car is faster than my Micra and soon he is gone.

There's nothing I can do but drive, with my heart pumping and my mouth dry and the sound of gunshots in my ears. Each time I see a van, my car wobbles, as if wanting to change lane. My breathing only comes easier when I see a logo, or the van speeds off ahead, uninterestedly.

My shoulders ache and my head pounds. I rub my head and eyes over and over again.

There's another problem too. I feel sick. I'm light-headed and dizzy and my stomach is in knots. I recognise the symptoms for what they are: with-drawal. I didn't take my tablets last night and my body is letting me know it needs them. This must be why I was told to come off them slowly. I consider stopping in a lay-by, finding my tablets in the boot and taking at least one just to feel better, but I'm afraid to stop and get out of the car. It will leave me vulnerable.

By the time I get home, I'm a wreck. I stumble through the front door and into Tom's arms with a sob.

'Bridget?' Alarm sharpens his tone.

'I'm fine. I just need to sit down.' I push past him and into the living room. The small living room, with its gas fire and low ceiling and Grace in her bouncer focused on *Paw Patrol*. It doesn't feel like home anymore.

'You're not okay.' Tom rubs my hands. 'Did something happen?'

'No.' I force a smile but I'm still shaking. I grope for the right story; this lying thing is getting easier each time. 'A near miss at a roundabout, that's all.'

Tom shuffles back onto his heels. 'You have to be more careful, Bridge.'

I wrap my arms around myself. 'I know.'

'Hey.' He sits beside me. 'I made a couple of calls. Autoglass will be here tomorrow.'

'Great.' I muster a smile.

'And I managed to get hold of the estate agent who sold us the flat. She's coming over on Tuesday, first thing, to give us a valuation for the bank.'

'That's good.' My hands won't stop shaking.

Tom frowns. 'Did something else happen?'

I wrap my arms around my stomach. 'Honestly? I feel sick. I think it's the withdrawal. I didn't take my pills last night.'

'Shit.' Tom looks quickly at Grace, but she hasn't heard him. 'How long will that go on for?'

'I don't know. I mean, I've only been on them a few months.'

'Go for a lie-down, I'll make you a cup of tea.' Tom pulls me to my feet and propels me towards the stairs.

'Okay.' I head upwards, my feet heavy, my body already leaning towards sleep.

I take my shoes off but leave my clothes on; then I lie on the bed, listening to the kettle boil and Tom murmuring to Grace. My eyes close but my mind stays open, racing.

Happy with what you have.

Betsie, why'd you do it?

Polly wants a cracker . . . let me take a ride, don't cut yourself

And then I fall asleep.

I wake up, automatically seeking the remains of the nightmare I'm certain must have visited, but I feel no vestiges of terror.

There are no lingering images, no dark claws in the back of my mind, no feeling of claustrophobia or vertigo. Is it possible that I *didn't* have a nightmare? That I haven't woken sweaty because I was afraid, but because I left all my clothes on?

For once, it isn't terror that wakes me but the sound of Tom and Grace laughing uproariously downstairs.

I sit up, fragile and groggy, as though a swift movement might shake a nightmare loose. But there's nothing. I probe my memory like a patient might touch a rotten tooth with their tongue, carefully, anticipating pain, but unable to stop. I've slept without dreams. I don't feel refreshed though, more like I've been woken from the start of a long slumber. I'm barely alert. There's a cold cup of tea on the bedside table beside me, congealing milk a white swirl on top of the brown. I look at the clock and frown. It says 10 o'clock, but then why is Grace up?

I tiptoe downstairs, almost as if I'm still in the dream I feared, worrying that a loud noise might bring monsters from the living room. Instead Tom appears. 'You're awake! Sorry, was it us?'

It's light outside, sunlight filters in through the hall

225

window and I rub my head, confused. 'I–I think so. What time is it?' I peer past him. Grace is lying on the floor surrounded by a whole phalanx of cuddly toys. There appears to have been a battle.

Tom checks his watch. 'It's just after ten, you've been out for over twelve hours. I thought about taking your clothes off, but honestly, I didn't dare move you. Luckily, there was enough milk in the freezer for Grace.'

'I'm so sorry, Tom.'

'It's fine. You obviously needed it. Do you feel a bit better?'

Automatically, I nod.

'The Autoglass guy just left. You've got a new window.'

'Okay.' I smile at Grace, feeling oddly detached.

'And your mum rang while we were away, she left a message on the house phone. You've got an appointment with Gillian at 1.30 p.m. Are you feeling up to it?'

I nod my head. 'I just slept without nightmares. Whatever she did, it's working.'

Gillian looks at me with her bird-like expression as I grope for the chair before sitting down. I'm afraid I might miss the seat and fall. Everything feels lopsided today, as if I'm leaning sideways, or everything else is. Mum is a little late and, honestly, I'm relieved. I didn't think I was going to talk about it but there's something in Gillian's face and I can't stop myself. 'I saw Dad.'

Gillian glances at the door, then calls the receptionist. 'Milo, give Mrs Monahan a cup of tea in the waiting room when she arrives.' She sits back down but doesn't pick up her notebook. 'You mean you thought about your dad. Remembered something?'

I nod. My head feels too heavy for my shoulders. 'I don't have many memories of him, and I never think about *that* . . . God, I sound awful.' I knot my fingers together, twisting them on my lap.

'You don't.' Gillian tilts her head at me. 'Finding your dad the way you did would have been a shock for anyone. You dealt with it – and I helped you deal with it – by forgetting.'

I peer at my reddening hands, nausea swirling, and I don't know if it's the Fluoxetine withdrawal or the fact that I'm talking about *him*. 'I hadn't really considered it before, but that must have been hard for Mum.'

'She agreed that I should help you block the whole thing from your mind.'

I look up at Gillian, quickly. 'Did you see her last week? After the session on Thursday, I mean. Was she all right?'

'You know your mum.' Gillian picks up the notebook. 'What triggered the memory, do you think?'

I consider telling her about Grant, about the fight. But I can't. 'I saw someone who reminded me of him.'

'And in combination with the anniversary . . .' Gillian nods. 'What was the memory?'

I flush, as if I'm admitting to wrongdoing. 'The day I found him. What he looked like.'

Gillian glances away as if she can't bear to meet my eyes. 'I'm sorry, Bridget,' she says eventually. 'That must have been awful.' She looks back up. 'I'll make

227

an amendment to today's hypnotherapy session; I'll make sure you don't have to think about that ag—'

A beep sounds from the speaker on her desk. 'Dr Thornhill, Mrs Monahan is here and doesn't want any tea. She'd like to know if she can come in.'

Gillian toys with her pen. 'Is there anything else you'd like to talk about, Bridget, before I let Alison through?'

I twist my hands tighter.

Yes, I want to say. Yes. I'm terrified of alienating Grace or losing Tom. I don't know how to help the little girl I saw. I don't know whether to take the map to the police, or not. I want to move, but I'm frightened of upsetting Mum. I'm being followed by a white van and I don't know how to make it stop. I feel sick and out of sync with the whole world.

I shake my head. 'No, I'm okay.'

'All right then,' Gillian rises and goes to her desk. 'Send her in, please.'

It isn't a proper film, not like The Little Mermaid, or Beauty and the Beast. *There's no story, there's just a man and a woman doing boring grown-up things: cooking and eating, hoovering and dusting, washing and ironing, talking, watching television.*

The lady is very pretty, she always wears her hair the same way and an apron over her skirt, like a mom in America. The man has a moustache. It makes him look funny. His hair is thick and brown, and he wears checked shirts. He smiles a lot. The lady looks at the camera when she smiles and then it's like she's smiling at her.

The little girl begins to watch the film all the time. Even when she's eating, even when the woman comes to check on her, or give her medicine, she doesn't take her eyes off the lady on her wall.

She begins to think that this woman, if she knew what was happening to her, might come to save her. She begins to think that this woman might be her hero, or her angel.

She begins to love her.

Chapter 18

We sit in Costa, the three of us, and stare at one another. Even Grace senses the mood and is quiet. I still feel groggy and displaced but this has brought me back into the moment. I pick up my napkin and tear it in half. My hands are shaking. 'Did they really say we could get £900 a month in rent?'

Tom nods, and his own face is pale.

'And the bank just offered us an interest-only mortgage for £450 a month? I'm not dreaming?'

Tom nods again.

'We're going to have an extra £450 a month to pay the new mortgage on the house in Clitheroe!'

Tom leans over the table and takes my hands. 'Are you sure you want to do this?' His face is half in shadow, one eye dark, the other light.

'We'd be mad not to, wouldn't we?'

'Excuse me?' There's a waitress standing by the table. 'It's Grace, isn't it? She was in here with her Grandma a week or so ago? I couldn't forget that gorgeous face.' She bends down beside her, long plait swinging over one shoulder. 'Do you remember me, Grace? Would you like another chocolate chip cookie?'

Tom stares at her. 'A what?'

'A chocolate chip cookie, that's what you had last time, isn't it, Grace? And you loved it, didn't you?' Grace grins at her and lifts up Frankie to show her. 'I remember him too.' She smiles at us. 'She's a lovely baby. So, would you like one?'

'A chocolate chip cookie,' I echo. 'You do dairy-free cookies here?'

'Well, no.' The waitress frowns. 'It's just the usual. Chocolate and butter, I guess.'

Tom puts his hand on Grace's hair, protective. 'And you say she had one last time? You couldn't be misremembering? I mean, you have lots of customers.'

The waitress takes a step backwards. 'I'm sorry if I—'

'It's okay.' I frown at Tom, then look back at the waitress. 'It's just that Grace has a dairy intolerance. Mum wouldn't have bought her a cookie.'

'You're right, sorry. I do have a lot of customers.' The waitress looks back at the counter. 'Can I get you anything else?'

'No, thanks, we're fine,' Tom says, without taking his palm from Grace's head. As the waitress retreats, he looks at me. 'She didn't make a mistake, did she? Grace was really off after your mum brought her back.'

My head is aching, I rub my eyes. 'It must have been an accident.'

'How?' Tom picks Frankie up off the floor where Grace has thrown him. 'Your mum knows Grace's needs. Why would she give her chocolate?'

'Maybe Aunt Gillian bought it and Mum didn't realise . . . or she didn't want to offend her.'

'Maybe.' Tom gives Frankie back to Grace and sighs. 'I know your mum helps out a lot, but . . . I don't think it'll be a bad thing to get a bit more distance from her. How are you going to tell her?'

I flick my eyes to Grace, picturing her eating that cookie. Picturing Mum *watching* her eat it, knowing how much it would hurt her. 'In our next therapy session. It might be good to have Aunt Gillian there.'

'You think she'll help your mum come to terms with things?'

'I hope so.'

Tom has brought the picture of the Clitheroe house out with us. I look at it again, yearning. 'So . . . shall we call the estate agent?'

'You're sure you don't want to talk to your mum first?'

'I don't want her to talk me out of this.' I grip his hand. 'You're right, it'll be good for us. We *need* this.'

Tom picks up his phone. 'Do you want to do it, or shall I?'

'You can.' I offer Grace a rusk but she pushes it away. She'd rather have a cookie.

I frown and take Dobbie from my bag. She smashes him against the table as Tom speaks. 'The bank has offered us a let-to-buy mortgage. . . . Yes, the rent will cover the mortgage and we'll have enough equity to cover the deposit on the new house. . . . Uh-huh. We'd like to make an offer. Five thousand below asking price.'

'Tom!' I sit up abruptly and the nausea bites again. My head swims. 'We didn't agree to that.'

He holds up a finger and keeps talking. 'I'll have my phone on me, let us know what they say. Thanks.' He hangs up.

'Five thousand below? They'll never go for it. We'll lose the house.'

'It's fine, Bridge. If they turn it down, I'll raise the offer. But they might not and then we've saved five grand. We can use it to buy furniture or get some stuff for the garden.'

My heart is pounding. 'But what if someone else has put in a higher offer?'

'The estate agent would have said so. Don't worry. They always put houses on for a bit more than they think they'll get. No-one expects full asking price, not really.'

I swallow. 'Do you think I should call Diane and tell her I'm handing in my notice?'

'Not until we've got a moving date. Wait a few weeks.' Tom's phone beeps and he frowns at it. A message has come in. He flicks it away with his fingertip before I can see what it says. He lowers his voice. 'When do you need to be back in work?'

'I said I'd go in this afternoon. My clients will be climbing the walls.'

'Even though you're still feeling sick from coming off the pills?'

'It's not so bad today.'

'I'll take Grace home then.' Tom gets to his feet. 'We can drop you off at the station.'

We're in my car but Tom is driving. I've been feeling too sick to risk it. As we move through the high street traffic I crane my neck, seeking the white van. What if, after I've gone to work, it follows Tom and Grace, thinking *I'm* in the car?

Tom needs to know. How can he protect Grace if he doesn't? I touch his hand, which is lax on the gear stick. My gut twists with fear and sickness. 'There's something I need to tell you.'

'What is it?' Tom changes gear and looks right as he turns into the station car park. I wait until he pulls up and bite my lip. The sky has clouded over and there's a heaviness in the air that matches the feeling in my stomach.

'Someone's been following me.'

Tom turns in his seat with his whole body, not just his head. He faces me. 'What do you mean, following you? Who?' Tension in his face, his brows pulled together in confusion and anger. 'For how long?'

'For a while now.' I exhale. 'Since I reported the kidnapping. It's a white van.' My words come out in a rush. 'Like the one in Clitheroe. It follows my car . . . so you need to know.'

'Are you serious?' Tom is clenching his fists. 'You've been thinking someone's following you and you haven't mentioned it?'

'I . . . I wasn't sure at first.'

'And now you are?'

'I think so. Especially after . . .' I gesture at the new window.

'A white van?' Tom leans his head back on the seat. There's a van a few spaces down from us. He points. 'Like that one?'

'I suppose.' It has a decal, advertising a painter and decorator on the front. 'But plain white, no logo.'

Tom's jaw tightens. 'And you haven't seen it today?'

'I don't think so.'

'Do you know how many plain white vans are on the roads, Bridge?' He keeps his voice calm, low, but his jaw tics. 'Maybe you're just seeing *different* white vans.'

'I'm not.'

'How do you know?' He takes my hand. The muscles in his arms are tight, his fingers stiff. 'You dreamed the kidnapping, so why would anyone be following you? I know this thing happened at Neil and Sam's, but honestly, it was a random act of stupid vandalism.'

'It wasn't!'

'Paranoia was part of your depression, Bridge. Don't you remember? This is because you've come off the Fluoxetine. There's no-one following you.'

'What if I'm right?' I pull my hand away. 'Just be careful driving with Grace, okay?'

'I'm always careful.' He sighs. 'I'm more concerned about you.'

'I don't know what time I'll be able to get away from work,' I tell him, as I open the door. 'It might be late.'

'Don't worry about it.' Tom glances at his phone and then back at me. 'It won't be for much longer.'

'You'll call me as soon as you've got news from the estate agent?'

'The minute I hang up.'

I open the back door and lean in to kiss Grace goodbye. She waves Dobbie at me and I give the bunny a kiss too. Then, regretfully, I shut her in the car.

I head into the station. Then I look back. Tom hasn't driven away, instead he's sitting with the phone to his ear. He is smiling.

I wait on the platform, phone in hand, ready for him to call me. If he was talking to the estate agent he'd be finished by now. But my phone doesn't ring. So, who was he speaking to?

Chapter 19

I get home early, sweat-soaked despite the afternoon downpour, nauseous and exhausted. Tom finds me standing in the hallway, swaying, staring at my coat, as if I'm not sure what to do with it. He takes it from me. 'Are you all right?'

'I spoke to Diane.' My mouth forms the words but they seem to come from a long way away. 'I said we were thinking about moving. She said they'd be sorry to see me go.' I rub my neck. I feel itchy all over. 'She didn't sound sorry. She asked if I was handing in my notice, so I told her I'd do it next week.'

'Well done.' Tom starts towards the kitchen. 'Let me just feed Grace and we can talk.'

'Let me do it.' I follow him into the kitchen. 'I should be able to pick up some freelancing work from them after the move.'

'Even with the last few weeks?' Tom doesn't look at me as he speaks.

I stiffen. 'I have a good track record, Tom. The last few weeks doesn't wipe all that out.' I slam Grace's bowl on the table and she jumps. She looks at me with wide eyes and a tremulous smile.

I try to smile back but there's something blocking it. A darkness around my edges. I can't raise a smile for her.

Tom puts a spoonful of mango chicken in her bowl. 'It's her favourite,' he says, as if I didn't know. As if I was a complete stranger. 'You shouldn't have any trouble.'

I pick up her purple spoon. But she presses her lips together and won't open her mouth. Instead she waves Dobbie at me.

I take Dobbie, put him out of reach and offer her the spoon again. She twists, trying to turn her back on me.

Tom is washing up at the sink. I can't bear for him to turn around and see me failing. 'Come on, Grace,' I whisper.

She spits the chicken out when I manage to get some in her mouth. Then she wails and reaches for Tom.

Tom turns. 'Do you want me to take over?'

'No, Tom, I don't want you to *take over*!' When Grace opens her mouth to shout again, I slide in another spoonful of chicken but she kicks me from her highchair and spits it over my blouse.

'Grace!' I pick up a cloth to dab at my top and she grabs hold of the bowl and hurls it on the floor where it splatters orange sauce up the cupboards.

'It's all right. If she won't eat it, she won't eat it.' Tom bends down with a tea towel but I dish up another portion, my movements jerky.

'She's eating it, Tom! If she doesn't, she won't sleep. Are *you* going to breastfeed her over and over again in the night? *Are you?*' I slam the fresh bowl down in front of Grace, take a breath and another spoonful. I'm so tired and the idea of being up all night nauseates me even more.

Grace manages to slap the spoon away. Some of the casserole splats on my face and I leap to my feet. 'Goddamn it, Grace! You are eating this!'

Tom looks up from the floor, alarmed. 'Bridge?'

'You've cooked it, she has to eat it. If she doesn't, *she won't sleep.*'

He jumps to his feet and tosses the tea towel in the sink. He's missed spots. I'll have to go over the whole thing again. I glare at him as he goes to Grace. 'I'll take her away. Maybe she'll be hungry later.'

'It's her bedtime later. Stop *interfering*, Tom. If I'm going to be at home with her, she has to learn to do what I say!'

Tom stares. 'She's eight months old, Bridge.'

'I don't care!' Rage rises like a chemistry experiment. Nothing there one second, foaming upwards in colourful, spewing, endless tentacles the next. Suddenly I'm shaking. I want to hurt him. Oh, God, I want to hurt *her*.

'She has to eat her dinner, or she won't sleep.' I say it again, as if it'll make a difference. As if she cares. 'Eat your dinner, Grace!' I grab her face, squeeze her cheeks until her mouth is forced wide and shove a loaded spoon into her mouth. She chokes and splutters. Tom yells and grabs my arm, pulling me backwards. I fight to escape from him, the rage is *everywhere*.

Grace makes a choking noise and suddenly there's

vomit all over her highchair, stinking of casserole and dripping from the tray onto the floor Tom has just cleaned. She looks at me and Tom in mute horror and then starts to scream, her face red and frightened.

'Jesus, Bridge.' Tom pushes me towards the sink and grabs our daughter, not caring that she's covered in sick or that her chest is hitching, her breath coming in shallow gasps.

'She's going to throw up again,' I whisper.

'Leave us alone.' Tom heads for the door. 'I'm going to clean her up in the bath. We'll talk about this when we're done.'

They leave and rage bleeds out of me like I've been stabbed. I stare at the spoon I'm still holding in disbelief. What did I just do? I throw it into the sink, where it lands with a soft thud on top of the tea towel. In a trance, I get a fresh towel and start to mop up Grace's vomit. It slides everywhere and I retch as the stink gets into my open mouth. I'm sobbing, my breath coming in great gulps. I'm the worst mum. The worst mum in the world.

I clean the vomit and get the Dettol spray. I spray it everywhere, then scrub as if I can clean away the evidence of what I just did to my little girl. I'm shaking so hard I can barely hold the cloth.

My phone beeps softly and I glance at the message: *India's just started throwing up! Hope Grace hasn't picked it up too. Nightmare!* ☹

She was feeling sick; that's why she didn't want her tea. I might not have made her vomit but I tried to make my sick baby eat by yelling at her, force-feeding her . . . I slump on the floor in a corner of the room, pulling my legs up. I duck into my elbows. My fingers curl into my hair and I sob, violently.

Tom comes back into the kitchen. Grace isn't with him.

'I'm giving Grace a bottle tonight.' He doesn't come to me. He goes to the fridge and I hear it open and close. I don't look up. I don't argue with him. 'This can't go on, Bridge.' His voice is expressionless. Hard. He microwaves the bottle. It pings. 'I can't go through this again.'

I wonder what it would feel like to take a kitchen knife into the bath, to cut the pain away. I am my father's daughter after all.

'I know.' I keep my face pressed into my own skin. My voice is hoarse from crying.

'You have to go back on the antidepressants.'

'I know.'

He retreats from the kitchen. I hear his feet on the stairs, a door closes. I don't move.

I wait until I'm sure he's feeding Grace before I drag myself up. Then I creep up the stairs and into the bathroom. I stare at the face in the mirror. It belongs to a stranger, the features of a woman who would hurt her baby. My skin is blotchy and my hair is wild. I pull strands through my fingers and stare at them as if I've never seen them before. Whose face is this? Is it my great-grandma's face, as Mum used to say? Is it Betsie Dobson's face? Who am I?

I pick up the packet of Fluoxetine. If I take the

pills, I'll have nightmares. If I don't, I might hurt Grace, or Tom, or myself. It isn't a dilemma. I pop two from the blisters and put them in my mouth.

I hesitate outside Grace's nursery door, listening to Tom's soft murmuring. It sounds as if he's telling her a story. Part of me wants to slink past but, instead, I steel myself and go inside. Tom frowns as the line of light slithers into the dim room with me. He's sitting on the rocking chair. Grace is in her sleeping bag, holding tightly to both Frankie and Dobbie. She looks pitiful. My heart stops beating as she peers at me. What if she turns away or cries at the sight of me? I'm not sure I could take it.

Then she reaches up for me. All is forgiven, apparently.

I drop to my knees in front of her. 'I'm so sorry, Grace. I won't ever do it again.' I stroke her hair and look up at Tom. 'India's sick apparently. She's caught a bug.'

Tom sighs. 'I was going to sleep in here tonight anyway.'

'Okay . . . unless you want me to?'

Tom shakes his head. 'Get some sleep, Bridget. I know you didn't mean it but you can't be on your own with her if you're going to snap like that. I'll have to stay at home.'

'I've taken my pills.'

'Good.' There's a heavy silence. 'I'm going to keep feeding her tonight. I know you'd rather do it but you need to rest.'

I don't argue. 'You're right.' I put my head on his knee, watching Grace. 'Has she been sick again?'

'Twice.' Tom gestures at the half-full bottle. 'It's going to a be a long night.'

Silently, I agree. For both of us. I wonder how quickly the girl will visit me after I close my eyes.

This time I'm in Sabden and the little girl is standing in front of the broken swing. She turns around and looks at me. The rose on her blazer is a Lancashire rose.

'You're not even *trying* to find me,' she says sadly. 'And look, it's all ruined,' Her voice is low and quiet with a northern burr. Blood drips from her fingers, splatting on the concrete path.

Then I'm standing beside her, both of us peering into the windows of the Dobson house. She steps towards the door, bends over and lifts a plant pot. There's a key underneath. She uses it to open the door and I follow her inside. The house is in good repair. I look at the windows, they are dust-free, sparkling clean. The net curtains are freshly washed: white not yellow. There are voices from the kitchen, laughter: a man and a woman. A room is visible to my right: a living room not much bigger than the one in my flat. The sofa is green velvet with brown cushions. The carpet is brown. There is a coffee table piled with children's books. I turn back to the girl. She is dripping blood on the clean floor. There are stairs ahead of us in a straight line from the front door. The kitchen is to the left. She stops outside the door and puts a finger to her lips. It leaves a smear of scarlet.

I want to ask her where she is and if she's all right,

but I can't make a sound. She leans against the door, listening. After a moment she pushes the door open and walks in. Grant and Betsie Dobson are standing in front of the sink. They look young and healthy. Happy. Betsie is showing Grant a letter. 'Look, it says she's won a prize. For writing a poem. Have you ever written a poem, Grant? Have you ever even *read* one? She's six!'

'A bleedin' genius.' Grant takes the letter and winks at his wife. 'She gets it from your side.'

They smile at one another. Then Betsie turns around. She looks past the little girl as if she can't see her, instead she sees me. Her face falls. Then, suddenly, she's gone.

The picture I'm looking at changes, as if it has shifted right into an 'after' version of this 'before'. The kitchen is dilapidated, cupboard doors hang from their frames, dishes are piled by the sink, unwashed. The bin is overflowing with bottles, the windows thick with grease. Grant is standing by the sink, bluebottles buzzing around his face. Filthy clothes hang off him. He is drinking vodka straight from the bottle: the cheap stuff. The little girl takes my hand, tears slide down her cheeks.

She pulls me towards the kitchen door and I follow her out and up the stairs. I don't want to, I have a horrible feeling that I know what we'll find. I want to scream, not again, not *again*, but my feet are not under my control. There are two bedrooms up here, and a single bathroom with a toilet and bath. *Not the bathroom.*

I pull back and it seems to work; the little girl stops outside the first bedroom door. She opens it with her bleeding hand, leaving a bloody print on the tarnished handle. It's a little girl's room and it hasn't been touched in two decades. Dust lies thick on a My Little Pony bedspread and a rug shaped like a flower. There is a poster of the Spice Girls peeling from the pink wall. The curtains are closed, the air musty and heavy. I struggle to breathe. There is a little desk in one corner, piled with more books. There are a few dolls on the floor. They look well-loved, secondhand maybe. There's a doll in a battered pram and a shelf of Beanie Babies. The little girl looks at the door opposite. It's the bathroom door.

No. I want to scream it. She shouldn't see this. *I* shouldn't see this. It's not the kind of thing a child should see; and I should know. But I can make no sound as the little girl steals across the hall and opens the door.

So much blood. The bath is full of it. It looks as if Betsie changed her mind at the last moment and tried to crawl out, perhaps to go for help. She's lying naked, half-in and half-out of the tub, her hair in a drying tangle, matted with more blood. The smashed vodka bottle is lying on the floor beside one curled hand. Bloody shards beside the other. I'd thought she'd done it with a razor blade, or a kitchen knife, but she'd downed the bottle and then smashed it, sliced her wrists with the broken glass. Her skin is open like a screaming mouth.

Perhaps she didn't plan to die like this: an act of impulse born from despair, and no-one to hear her cries for help.

My heart pounds and I look away from the body. There's a mirror right beside me. I stare into it and Betsie's face stares back. The little girl wraps her arms around me from behind, holds me still, won't let me leave.

'Why can't you find me?' she rasps. Her voice is filled with tears. 'Why can't you find me?'

I bolt awake, heart pounding, jaw aching. I put my hand to my face. I haven't been screaming; grinding my teeth perhaps. *Why can't I find her?*

I look at my clock. It's 5 a.m. I slip out of bed and stagger to the bathroom to splash water on my face. On my way back, I look in on Grace and Tom. He is lying on the floor beside her cot on our spare duvet, one arm thrown over his face, slack with exhaustion. By the door there's a pile of laundry covered in puke. Frankie is on top of it. Grace must have thrown up again, more than once by the look of it. I inch into the room and bend over beside him. I give his shoulder a gentle shake and he comes awake with a snort.

'Go to bed,' I murmur. 'I'll take over here.'

He doesn't argue. He is still mostly asleep. He rises, staggers to the door and vanishes into the hallway. Moments later I hear our bedroom door close and then the squeak of springs as he collapses. I lie down on the floor in his hollow of his warmth and stare at the ceiling.

Finally, listening to Grace's laboured breathing, I fall back to sleep.

Chapter 20

The next day, I'm outside Aunt Gillian's office about to go in, when my phone rings. It's Tom. 'They've gone for three under,' he crows. 'We've got the house.'

My knees turn to playdough and I grab hold of the balustrade beside the stone steps. 'Bloody hell!'

'I know!' I can hear him in the kitchen, the particular echo, the buzz of the dryer behind him. He's doing laundry.

'It wasn't real until just now.' I reach the wall and lean against it.

'Last chance to change your mind?' Tom's voice is quiet.

Happy with what you have.

'No. It's not that. I just . . . there's no getting out of it. I'll have to tell Mum today.' I look at the office door in front of me, painted a shiny dark blue. Silver letterbox and a sign saying, *Gillian Thornhill, Therapist.*

'All right then.' There's a thud from Tom's end and I wonder what he's doing. 'Let me know how it goes. We could go out tonight. Get a drink?'

'Who'll sit for Grace?' I sigh. 'I doubt Mum will be happy to do it once I've told her . . . I'll buy a bottle of Prosecco on the way home and we can order a Chinese from that place you like.'

'If you're sure.' Tom sounds a little out of breath.

'What are you doing?' I can't help asking.

'Just unloading the dishwasher while I have the chance.' Tom's voice remains happy. 'And a few million other things. She'll be awake in ten or fifteen minutes. Good luck with your mum.'

'Thanks.' I hang up and look at the stairs I have to climb. My knees feel unconnected to my legs. I stumble up the steps and into the waiting area.

The receptionist is a young black man, with nimble fingers and a skinny green tie over a white shirt. He raises his head as I stagger in. 'Mrs Carlson.' He leaps to his feet. 'Are you all right?'

'I'm fine.' I drop into the nearest chair. 'I'll just wait here for Mum.'

'You don't want to go straight in this time? You can; the doctor is free.'

'No, that's okay.'

He continues to watch me. 'Would you like a drink of water?'

I start to say no but, actually, I think I would. 'Yes, please.'

He's grateful to have some way of helping, I think. He practically races to the water cooler, fills a plastic cup and then puts it on the table in front of me. 'Something to read?'

I shake my head and look around, seeking something to focus my attention on, something calming. There are pictures on the walls: a seascape, a mountain scene,

248

and a single photograph of a woman staring into the distance, her pale hair whipping in the wind and half covering her face. There is something about her. I'm groping for the thought, trying to find her behind my racing anxiety. Where have I seen her before? For a moment, I wonder if it could be a young Aunt Gillian but they aren't that alike.

The door opens behind us and my breath catches as Mum walks in. Everything she's wearing is beautifully co-ordinated and it looks as if she's just been to the hairdressers. I'm struck for a second by how alien we are. How completely unlike one thing is to the other.

She looks at my feet. 'Trainers, darling?'

My shoes are in my bag. I should have changed them. I stand up, looking once more at the woman on the wall.

'Who is that?' I ask suddenly and the receptionist follows my gaze. 'Oh, yes, it's a lovely shot isn't it? Professional. It was taken a few years ago. That's Dr Thornhill's niece, Electra. She's like a daughter to her.' There's a faint beep from the receptionist's computer. 'Dr. Thornhill is ready when you are,' he says. Mum bustles past and I follow her inside.

Aunt Gillian is waiting for us, sitting at her desk with crossed legs. Today her hair is pulled back with an incongruous velvet head band, as if she's a cheerleader or something. It makes her look even more bird-like, her spike of a nose more prominent.

She gestures towards the chair that I'm coming to consider mine. I hesitate for a moment, then sit down. Mum takes the seat opposite.

'Lovely.' Gillian opens her notebook. 'Now, how have you been getting on without the antidepressants?'

I keep my eyes on my fingers. 'I'm afraid I'm taking them again.'

Mum frowns. 'I thought we'd agreed?'

'I came off them. It was awful.' I look up, nervously.

'That's to be expected.' Gillian waves a hand. 'Withdrawal. You have to push through it.'

'No, it wasn't that. I mean it was, but after a few days I went right back to where I started. It's not just unhappiness . . .' I look at Mum and quickly away again. 'It's like there's this rage inside me and without the pills, it's there, ready to explode and I can't control it. I almost hurt Grace. I force fed her casserole until she was sick. I can't go off the pills, Aunt Gillian. I don't know what I'll do.' Finally, I look at her. 'I tried.'

Gillian and Mum look at one another; it's as if I'm not in the room.

'All right,' Gillian says, eventually, and she makes a note with her gold pen. 'Stay on the pills for now.'

I relax back into my chair.

'Is there anything else you want to talk about before we start today's hypnosis?'

I tense up again. 'Actually yes, there is.' I look at Gillian. 'There's something you might be able to help us through.' I turn to Mum. 'I know you won't like this. You won't want to hear it but . . . we've made our decision and we're moving.'

'Moving?' Mum speaks carefully, as if I've uttered a foreign word and she isn't sure of the syllables. 'Mo-ving?'

'Yes. To Clitheroe . . . in Lancashire. There are jobs for Tom, a fantastic school for Grace, a lovely house. Honestly, you'd love it, Mum. I can work from home later . . .' I tail off.

Mum carefully places her hands on her knees, flat. Her knuckles are white. *Look how angry I am.*

'I specifically forbade this, Bridget,' she says eventually.

I laugh nervously and look at Gillian. 'You can't forbid us from moving, Mum,' I say. 'I'm almost twenty-eight years old.'

'You're an ungrateful little *bitch*.' The word is out there, a bite of sound, snapping at my skin.

I gasp. Gillian's head jerks up. She looks alarmed but she says nothing.

'We are grateful for everything you do, Mum. But we have to do what's right for us. What's right for *Grace*.'

'And it's better for *Grace* to live in the arse-end of nowhere, is it?' The words sound wrong coming from her carefully rouged lips. I try to think if I've ever heard her use the word 'arse' before. My mind stutters on the idea.

'It's a lovely place. There's plenty to do, a theatre, an art gallery . . . there's a train station. You can visit any time.'

'Why would I want to visit the end of the world?'

That sounds more like her.

'That's up to you, Mum, but this is happening.' My own fists are clenched.

Mum looks at Gillian and catches her breath. Tears appear on her cheeks. 'I know what this is really about. T–this is about money.' She sobs abruptly. 'Because I wouldn't lend you money!'

I take a shuddering breath. 'It *is* about money, yes. Not because you wouldn't lend us any. It's the only way we can afford for me to be a stay-at-home-mum. The new house is cheaper and bigger than the flat. If we let the flat out, we'll have a steady income. It makes sense.'

'Fine, you win.' Mum wipes her tears away. 'I'll *give* you the money. How much do you want?'

Am I blackmailing her? I didn't intend to . . . did I? But I am making her cry, so I must be in the wrong. 'I . . .' I look at Aunt Gillian. She has put her glasses on and is watching us in tense silence. I look back at Mum. 'We don't want your money, honestly. I told you, we've found a way to do what we need to.'

'I'll write a cheque. How much? Twenty thousand?' Mum reaches into her bag.

'Don't. Please. We don't want it.' I try to take her hand, but she flinches away from me.

'You want to take my grand-daughter away from me.' She stands up, she's shaking, tears filling her eyes again. 'I won't have it.'

'We'll be three hours up the motorway. It's not like we're moving to Spain.'

'Three hours.' She sneers it. 'I'm an old woman. You might as well move to Spain.'

'You're fifty-seven.' I sigh. 'You're not old.'

'Your father was the same age when he . . .' Mum falls silent and smooths down her dress. 'I can't believe you'd leave me . . . at this time of year.'

'Mum . . .'

'Maybe I should follow your father's example, is that what you want?'

'Oh my God.' Bile rises into my throat and I cover my mouth.

'Yes, maybe I should hang myself in the garage, just like he did. Wait and see who finds me. Maybe it'll be you again. Probably not though, it could be weeks before I'm found and you wouldn't care, would you? It's probably what you want anyway. Drive the old woman to her death and inherit all her money.'

'Jesus, Mum.'

Mum stumbles towards the door. Then she stops with one hand on the handle. 'I raised you better than this.' She leaves.

'What have you done?' I turn to see Gillian, her notebook forgotten on her lap, her face white, her fingers clenched on her pen. '*What have you done?*'

'What do you mean?'

Aunt Gillian rises to her feet, the notebook sliding onto the floor. 'I can't help you anymore, Bridget. Get out!'

Chapter 21

I'm sitting in the park, on a swing, toes embedded in grass, rocking back and forth without ever leaving the ground. The chain digs into my hips; I'm too big for the plastic seat and the chill of it has seeped into my bones. I've been here for hours and I'm so stiff I'm not sure I could stand if I tried. Tom rang a while ago, but I didn't answer, just sent him a text instead.

I need some time.

My mum called me an ungrateful bitch. She threatened to kill herself. What kind of daughter am I?

I bite my cheek, hurting myself and tasting blood, wondering what it would be like if I kept bleeding. It would stop me from hurting anyone ever again. I think of Dad: it's in me, that impulse towards destruction. Is it in Mum too?

I wonder when she will speak to me again.

A group of mums with toddlers has congregated at the other side of the park; they're glaring at me, trying to get me to relinquish the swing with the sheer force of their animosity. I don't.

Desperate to think of something other than Mum, and how I've hurt her, my thoughts veer back to the missing girl from the train station. It feels as if she's on the other swing, right next to me. I can almost see her: legs pumping, hair flying, fists curled around the chain. She isn't laughing though, how could she be?

Finally, the park empties, and I am alone. With some difficulty I uncurl my fingers from the iron links and touch the place where rust has turned my palms red. I can smell it: coppery, like blood.

I don't know what to do next to find her. Why couldn't someone more capable have seen her being taken? Why me? All I've done is create a map showing kidnappings, something that any half-decent analyst could have done, and probably has.

Suddenly I am desperate to speak to Naomi, the only person who thought, at least for a while, that I had genuinely witnessed a crime. The only person who hasn't labelled me paranoid, accused me of wasting police time, or called me a bitch.

I decide that I'm going to hand the map in to her and then let it go; focus on my family, on the move and on making Mum forgive me. If Naomi decides there's something in it, she'll be able to conduct an investigation and, if she doesn't, well, at least I've tried.

I wipe my stained hands on my coat, and, with cold fingers, I make the call.

'Patterson.'

'Oh.' I lick dry lips. 'I was hoping to speak to Sergeant Shaw.'

'Sorry, Sergeant Shaw is out on a call. Can I get her to ring you back?'

'If you can just let her know that Bridget Carlson rang, please?' I hang up after he agrees, unkink my limbs, climb off the swing and head back towards my car.

At the gate I look back. The swing I left is moving erratically, as if I'm still sitting there, pushing with my toes. Back and forth. Beside it the other hangs motionless.

When I get home, Grace is fast asleep and Tom is waiting for me. He leaps to his feet. 'Are you all right, Bridge? Jesus, you're chilled to the bone. Where've you been?'

'Nowhere. Just the park.' I freeze when I see a bandage on his hand. It's pink with blood that has soaked through. There's been too much blood recently. I sway, feeling sick. 'What have you done?'

'Cut myself chopping veg like an idiot. Don't worry, it's fine. Was therapy that bad?'

'Mum went mental. She tried to write a cheque for twenty grand to stop us from moving.' I wrap my arms around my chest, still shivering. 'She threatened to kill herself, Tom, it was beyond awful.'

'She threatened to *kill herself*?' He flushes, one slash of colour on each cheek. Is he angry or upset? I can't tell.

I swallow. 'Just like Dad.'

'I can't *believe* she'd threaten to do that. That's . . .' he frowns. 'Seems a bit odd that she wants to take Grace, then.'

'What?'

'She rang an hour ago. She wants to see Grace.'

I stare at him. 'You don't mean now?'

'In the morning. She says she'll be here at nine.'

'But . . . I didn't think we'd see her for weeks.' A sick feeling squirms around my gut. 'Don't let her take her.' I blurt the words.

Tom frowns. 'You think she might hurt Grace? She wouldn't, would she?'

'I . . .' I look at the picture of Grace that hangs on our wall. In it she's six months old and smiling. 'No, I just—'

'Then she isn't taking her.' Tom stands. 'If you think there's any chance at all . . .'

The snake wound in my guts loosens its bite. 'Okay.'

'She won't like it,' Tom warns.

'I know.'

'Don't worry, I'll deal with it.' Tom pulls me close and I inhale his scent. 'She already thinks this is all my fault anyway.'

I lean into him, feeling safe, feeling loved. And I stay there for a long time.

The next morning the doorbell rings at nine. I've been up and awake with Grace since six, checking the time every five minutes, tension making my muscles ache.

Tom takes a deep breath, then he goes to the door.

'I'm coming in.' I brace, but Mum walks gingerly into the kitchen, shoulders hunched like an old woman. 'I thought, seeing as you're going to be moving, you'll have a lot to do. Packing and what-not.'

I stare at her.

'So, it makes sense for me to take Grace for a few days.'

I open my mouth but Tom puts a hand on my shoulder. 'I'm sorry, Alison, Grace isn't well. Didn't Bridget tell you? She's been throwing up. A nasty sick bug. We wouldn't want you to catch it.'

Mum's eyes go from Tom's bandaged hand to Grace. 'She looks fine.'

'She is now.' Tom doesn't flinch. 'But the NHS website says she'll be contagious for another forty-eight hours.'

'Are you lying to me, Tom?' Mum says, her eyes narrowed in suspicion. 'After all the help I've given you, after everything I've done . . .'

I turn and open the washing machine. It is filled with Grace's clothes and bedding. I yank it all out and it slaps onto the tiles, sopping wet. Frankie-Lion topples from the pile and Grace squeals when she sees him.

I look from the pile of washing to Mum. She takes a step backwards. 'Forty-eight hours then? When will that be?'

'Let's leave it a couple of days, to be on the safe side.' Tom meets her gaze but I'm not looking at him. There's something else in the laundry: a woman's t-shirt. It isn't mine.

Mum leaves without saying another word. Tom sees her out but I don't watch them go. I bend down and pick up the green top. It's smaller than one I'd wear, expensive-looking, a silk blend. I hold it as Tom comes back in.

'What's this?'

'I don't know. Isn't it yours?' Tom asks, absently, as if I wouldn't know my own clothes.

'No.'

Tom picks Grace up and holds her tightly, a shield.

Water soaks from the t-shirt into my blouse. I feel the chill on my skin. 'How did it get into our wash load?'

'It must have been left in there from the last wash. Are you sure it isn't yours?' The voice isn't Tom's, it's a rough squeak, like a gear shift in a car gone wrong.

'Whose is it, Tom?'

He frowns at me. Then his expression clears. 'It'll be Sam's. Must have got swept up in our luggage when we were packing, then dumped in the laundry.' He relaxes visibly. 'Do you want me to call her and let her know we have it? She might want us to post it back.'

'Sam's?' I look at the shirt. It's possible. It's her style.

Tom laughs. 'What did you think, Bridge? That I had some woman round while you were at work, then offered to clean her clothes?'

'I . . . I don't . . .' I let the top fall back onto the pile of Grace's sheets.

Tom steps nearer and takes my arm. 'Don't!' I jerk my elbow back and my heel catches in the trailing end of a wet blanket. I topple over with a cry.

Grace screams as I hit my head on the breakfast bar with a solid thunk.

The sound of my head hitting wood keeps reverberating, as if it's going on and on and isn't just the work of half a second. Pain rattles through me and I curl up on the floor, elbows over my temples, my chest heaving.

'Oh my God, Bridge! Let me put Grace down. I'm coming.'

Tom tries to pull me up but I resist. He grips my arms and yanks, heaving them from my face. 'I need to *see*, Bridge.' My eyes remain closed, but I hear his gasp. 'You're going to have a hell of a bruise. Are you all right? Speak to me!'

I squeeze my eyes tightly shut and sob. It is all too much. Am I crying because of the pain? I don't think so. I'm crying because my dad killed himself when I was eleven, and because my mum threatened to follow him. I'm crying because there is a missing little girl that no-one cares for. I'm crying because Naomi hasn't called me back. I'm crying because my own head is a mess, filled with nightmares and darkness and holes where happy memories ought to be. I am crying because I think Tom just lied to me.

'You'll be okay.' Tom is beside me again. I hadn't noticed him go. 'Here, take some Nurofen, quick.' He presses a glass of water and two tablets into my nerveless fingers. 'Sit up.' He hauls me into a sitting position and wraps his arms around me from behind, holding me upright. My bones have vanished, I am only blood and flesh: human gelatine.

With a hand that shakes so hard I splash water on the tiles, I take the tablets, even though I can't see what difference they'll make. The throb in my head is nothing. In fact, it's a blessed distraction.

Tom is making shushing noises, rocking me, but Grace will need dealing with soon. I choke back my tears.

I don't know how much time passes before I calm down enough to get to my feet.

Tom installs me on the sofa in the living toom, with Grace and a cup of tea. Then he perches in front of me, leaning forward in the easy chair, resisting its comfort. 'We should get you to hospital, you might have a concussion.'

I start to shake my head but when the movement sends spikes down my neck, I stop. 'I'll be all right.'

He exhales shakily. 'You really scared me. What was that abou—'

My phone beeps, the sound echoing between us. Without thought, I twist and pull it from my pocket. Pavlovian training. I shouldn't have, my eyes are too blurry to read the display. Tom reaches over and takes it from me, automatically glancing at the message as he slips it into his own pocket. 'You don't need to look at this now, do y—' He stops and frowns, takes the phone back out and re-reads the message more carefully. Then he lays it on the coffee table between us. The case clicks on the wood like a closing door. 'Who the hell is Grant Dobson?'

'Grant Dobson?' I lean towards the phone. The message sits there, longer than my usual texts, practically an email. I squint until the font begins to make sense.

* * *

This is Grant Dobson's neighbour. You asked me to let you know if he said anything that might help you. We walked to the shop together this morning and there was a van parked on the corner. He lost his shit – thought it was after him. Said Betsie had been seeing a white van before the kidnapping. He went on a bit. Forgot when and where he was. He wanted me to put his posters back up. Said people kept taking them down. Of course, he also claims that demons drink his whiskey while he's asleep, so . . . good luck. Mick.

Tom points at the screen. 'What's going on, Bridge?'

I can't think straight. There is only one way to explain. I stand carefully, like an invalid, holding my head. Then I take my keys from the table and slip into the hallway. Tom follows. I leave the house and go to the car.

'What are you doing? You can't drive anywhere, not like this!' Tom's demands grow more strident, but he stops when I go to the passenger seat and feel on the floor for the book. My head throbs as I bend over and pull it out. I hold it to my chest. When I show him this, he'll go mad, he might even leave me and go to stay with Neil again.

I hand the book over.

'*Kidnapped!*' Tom reads the cover. 'I don't understand. I thought you'd stopped thinking about this stuff.'

'Page twenty-six,' I rasp, and head back into the house.

Tom doesn't follow. He remains standing in the driveway. I can't watch him read the chapter. I go back inside, sit on the sofa to watch Grace, and wait for my world to implode.

Footsteps in the hallway and then Tom is standing in front of me, staring as if I'm a stranger. 'I don't understand,' he says eventually. He tosses the book on the sofa next to me and sits on the other side of it. It lies between us, the spine bent, the pages creased.

'What?' I ask him. 'What don't you understand?'

'A lot of things.' Tom rubs his face. Stubble rasps against the heel of his hand. 'I thought you'd agreed to drop all of this.'

'I know. I just . . . couldn't.'

'But when did you get in touch with Grant Dobson? And why him? Why not one of these other families?' He pushes the book towards me. 'Why not Mr Barraclough or Mr Scott?'

I touch my forehead gingerly; I can't help it. I wince at the swelling under my fingers, it feels alien. I drop my hand. 'There are similarities between his daughter's kidnapping and the one I saw. And . . . he lives near Clitheroe. I–I don't know how to say this. I went to see him when you were at your meeting.'

'What the *fuck*, Bridge?' Tom spits. Grace looks up sharply. She's found Dobbie and is gripping him with both hands.

'Tom!' I hiss.

He gets up and switches on the television. *Mister Tumble* comes on. Grace is immediately absorbed in the colours and sounds.

He doesn't sit back down. Instead he begins to pace, his hands restless too, as if he doesn't know what to do with them. He pulls his hair, turning the curls into spikes. 'What the *fudge*, Bridge?' he hisses. 'You lied to me before and now you've lied *again*. You said you were checking out the area while I was job-hunting, and instead you go and look into more of this kidnapping crap. It didn't happen, Bridget. It was a *dream*.' He looks sad. 'What's wrong with you? Don't you care about us at all?'

'It *wasn't* a dream.' I close my eyes against his expression. 'I saw a girl being taken, Tom. Why won't you believe me?'

The doorbell rings.

Tom frowns. 'Who the hell is that?'

I touch the book beside me, like it's a talisman. 'Are you expecting anything, anyone?'

Tom shakes his head.

'Ignore it then.'

The doorbell rings again and this time there's an additional hammering, as if the person on the other side is impatient or doesn't believe the bell is working.

'Open up, please, Mrs Carlson.'

'The police?' I look at Tom.

'Why would it be?' Tom rises. 'I'll go. You stay here. We still have a lot to talk about.'

I don't stay in place. I follow him as far as the living room door. He goes into the hall and opens the front door.

'Mr Carlson?' There is a woman in a suit at the door. Behind her, a policeman I don't recognise. The

264

woman lifts her hand and shows Tom something that I can't quite see. I can hear her though. 'My name is Moira Johnson. I'm from Social Services. Can I come in?'

Tom hesitates for a second, as if he's going to slam the door, then he stands to one side. The two visitors crowd into the hallway and the policeman closes the door behind them.

'Tom?' My voice is a quiver. The woman takes in my bruised temple and moves closer, blocking my sight of him. The policeman shifts with her. Now they're both between us.

The woman is comfortable-looking, as if she's been upholstered, but she looks tired; a tiredness that goes to the bone and deforms the shape of her face. There are smile lines beside her eyes, but unused, forgotten. She reminds me of a once enthusiastic teacher worn down by decades dealing with uncaring teenagers. 'Are you all right, Mrs Carlson?' She glances back at Tom, as though she knows what's happened and that it is an old story she is sick of hearing.

He flinches. He knows what she's seeing. 'She hit her head—' he starts.

'Let your wife answer, please.' The policeman lays a hand on Tom's arm. They're the same build, the same height; but Tom falls silent.

The social worker moves closer to me. 'My name is Moira. Can you tell me what happened,' she gestures, 'to your face?'

'I did hit my head.' I touch my temple and flinch. 'We were in the kitchen and I tripped . . . on some

265

laundry. You can still see it in there. I hit my head on the way down.'

Moira lowers her voice. 'We can take him out of the room if you'd like. You can talk to us alone.'

'No. Honestly, that's what happened. Tell them, Tom.'

He nods but his eyes are on the policeman in front of him. He doesn't speak. Suddenly the policeman lifts Tom's hand, like he's at show and tell. His bandage has slipped overnight and the cut on his palm gapes. He should have had it stitched.

'Oh, Tom,' I whisper.

'How did *this* happen, sir?' The policeman has altered his stance. He looks now as if he's protecting Tom.

Moira straightens. 'Where is Grace?' she asks.

'I don't understand.' I lean on the wall; my arms are jelly. 'Why are you here? It can't be for this.' I point to my head.

Moira shakes her head. 'Can you fetch Grace, please?'

Instinctively I move to block the living room door, but she pushes past me. Grace is sitting in her bouncer. When Moira bends down to look at her, Grace grins and holds Dobbie up for review. Moira takes him, makes a cooing sound, then hands him back. 'She looks like a healthy little girl. Why don't we all sit down and talk?'

Tom walks around the policeman, takes my hand and leads me into the living room. We both sit on the sofa. The social worker takes the chair, by Grace. The policeman remains standing.

'This is just an initial visit,' she is speaking but I can hardly hear her. My head hurts too much. I try to concentrate but all I can do is feel Tom's hand in mine, see Grace in the bouncer. Social Services; they must be here to take my baby.

'Multiple credible reports . . . professional opinion . . . rage issues . . . believes Grace is in danger . . .' Slowly Moira's voice gains clarity, like a radio being tuned into the right station. '. . . hallucinating, is that right? Seeing things that aren't there. After I received the initial report, I spoke to a Sergeant Ward, who told me your wife reported a crime that never happened.' She is speaking to Tom. 'According to the reports we've received, Bridget is dangerously depressed, she has spoken about experiencing rage in reference to the baby and, more recently, she has hurt Grace. Force feeding, from what I understand. That's abuse.'

'But—' I look at Tom, the blood draining from my face. 'Did you . . .?'

'Of course not!' Tom puts his arm all the way around me, as though I might fly away, but he looks at the social worker. 'Bridget is on antidepressants. There was an incident the other day, after her therapist told her to come off them. As soon as we realised what a bad idea that was, she started taking them again. It'll never happen again. You can talk to her doctor. Dr Lewis . . .'

'Tom looks after Grace.' I rush to fill in the silence. 'He's the primary carer, not me. I'm at work most of the time. I won't risk changing my medication again. I'm fine now.'

267

'But when you made up a crime for the police, you were on the medication, Mrs Carlson?'

'Yes, but . . .'

'Your mental health isn't for me to assess. Today, I'm here to ensure that we have a sensible plan going forward, one that ensures that Grace is safe and—'

'You're here to take her away!' I twist out of Tom's arms and lurch to my feet. Tom stays sitting, his face like paper.

Moira lifts her hands, placating, and the policeman takes a step towards me. *Rage*, she'd said. 'Multiple. *Credible*,' I mutter. Who knew about my rage? Whose report would be so 'credible' that a woman from social services would race to the house and bring police support?

'. . . goal is always to keep children with their families. . . . set up a child protection plan . . .'

I can barely hear her. I lift Grace out of her bouncer and hold her tightly. Too tightly. She starts to squirm and cry. 'Grace, stop it. *Grace*!' She cries harder, reaching for Tom. 'Grace isn't in any danger, I swear!' I whirl to face the woman sitting on our chair. Grace screams in my ear. I wince as the sound rips through my head like a saw. 'I'd never hurt her, neither would Tom.' I hold Grace even more tightly and she wails. Moira glances at the policeman and suddenly he is right in front of me.

'Hand Grace to me, please, Mrs Carlson. You're upsetting her.'

'No!' My head pounds and all I can think is that they're going to take her away. And it was all I'd ever feared: that I wouldn't be a good enough mum and I'd lose her. I back towards the corner and look at Tom. His face is bloodless and he's half standing, as if he wants to come to me but doesn't dare move.

Moira gestures and he rises. 'Can you calm your wife down, Mr Carlson, is that possible?'

The policeman steps to one side and suddenly I can breathe a little easier. 'Tom?'

When he reaches us, he holds his arms out for Grace. 'It's all right, Bridge, I'll take her.'

'No!' I look at the door. There's a clear path down the hall. I can take Grace and run. I hear a car outside. The world is still turning, unbelievable as it seems. The policeman sees the direction of my gaze and side-steps into my line of sight.

'Multiple credible reports,' I say again. 'Tom! More than one report. It *was* you, wasn't it?'

'Of course not, you think I'd risk our family—'

'Then who? Who was it?'

'What's going on?' Mum's voice. She's standing by the open front door, her back straight as if she's bracing for battle. 'I came back to discuss . . . never mind. I can hear Grace screaming all the way down the road.' We all fall silent, except Grace who continues to howl: a long, terrified wail that makes my heart pound. She has dropped Dobbie and is now gripping my hair so tightly that I think they'll have to cut it off to take her away from me.

Mum scuttles down the hall, so quickly I barely see her feet move. She looks at Tom, at the policeman, at the social worker who is now standing beside the sofa. Our tiny living room is so crowded, there's no air.

'Bridget, give Grace to me, darling.' I start to turn towards Tom but Mum takes my chin and holds my eyes. 'Darling, listen to Mummy. Let me take her. Then we can sort all this out.'

My fingers loosen and then Grace is out of my arms and into Mum's. Almost immediately she starts to whimper instead of wail, gripping Mum as if she's a lifeline. My own arms feel empty.

Moira turns to her. 'You're Mrs Carlson's mother?'

'Yes, I'm Mrs Monahan.' She strokes Grace's hair. 'I called you.'

Tom's head turns like he's a bird of prey, sharp and fast. 'You what?'

Mum's was one of the credible reports. Crimson covers my vision and I lunge. Strong arms wrap around me and yank me backwards. The policeman. I'm spun around, my wrist and elbow are grabbed and suddenly I'm bent over, facing the floor with my arm twisted behind my back.

'You need to take a deep breath, Mrs Carlson.' His voice in my ear is deep and low. It reminds me of Dad's. I have no choice but to stop, to dangle in his grip like a doll. The position makes the blood rush to my aching head. I strain to look up at Mum.

'What choice did I have?' She runs her palm over Grace's hair again, her attention on Tom. 'Bridget has been *hallucinating*. Obsessed with kidnappings. I had thought that, between the two of us, Grace would be all right. But then she's admitting to hurting Grace and telling me that you're moving away, that you're going back to work, leaving her in charge . . .'

I'm gaping, opening and closing my mouth like a carp in a bucket.

Tom turns to Moira. 'This is nothing but vindictiveness.' He says it as calmly as he can but his face is bruised with colour. I've never seen him so furious. 'Bridget's mum doesn't want us to move.'

'That's ridiculous.' Mum smiles. 'All I want is what's best for Grace. And leaving her alone with my sick daughter . . . is that what's best for her?'

I'm shaking so hard I can barely see. Tom's fists are clenched. Grace buries her face in Mum's shoulder.

'You said *multiple* reports?' I twist to look at Moira. 'Mum's wasn't the only . . .'

Moira shakes her head.

'Aunt Gillian . . .' I struggle, but the policeman's grip is unrelenting. 'You got Aunt Gillian to call them too. When? After we first told you we were thinking of moving?'

Mum looks at Moira. 'I know you aren't here to take Grace away; I confirmed that already. But how about if I take her anyway, just for a few days? It'll give everyone a break, a chance to calm down. She'll be perfectly safe with me. I've got a nursery all set up.'

Tom's head snaps up at this. 'How long have you been planning this, Alison?'

She ignores him as if he hasn't spoken. 'I think if my daughter were to get a break, things might improve. She's just so exhausted, you see, trying to do everything. You can sort out your protection order, or whatever it is you need to do. Grace will be safe.'

'Grace is safe *here*.' I squirm again but still can't straighten. I find myself staring at the policeman's boots. Black and shiny. I can almost see my face in them.

'All right, Sergeant,' Moira says. 'Let her go.'

'Are you sure?' There's a pause, in which I assume Moira nods, then his hold on me relaxes. I straighten, rubbing my wrist. I don't look at him.

Moira is taking something out of her bag. Paperwork. 'Mrs Carlson, come and sit down.' She gestures and I walk to the sofa like a marionette. 'Listen to me very carefully. When you see the social services on the news, you are seeing the absolute worst situations. Children are very rarely removed from their homes. We are here to support families, not break them up.' She is keeping her voice steady, she thinks I won't listen otherwise, but I'm watching Mum and Grace. Mum is humming in Grace's ear, soothing her. All I did was make her cry. Moira takes my hand, drawing my attention again. 'I am *not* here to take Grace away, Bridget. I am here to make sure that she is safe.'

'From me?' I shudder and look at her. Her eyes are kind.

'What your mum says makes sense. I'm not telling you what to do at this point but it seems to me that you could use a break. Babies are exhausting. I'm guessing you haven't had a day off since the day she was born?'

I shake my head.

'You need a rest, Bridget.' She looks at Tom. 'You too, Mr Carlson. If you're the primary carer, you need a break too.'

'I don't need a break from my daughter!' Tom snaps.

Moira touches my arm. 'Your mum's offer is a good one. Now, according to Section Twenty of the Children's Act, you can volunteer to have her go with your mum for a set period of time but, honestly, I'm not sure we need to formalise anything right now. Just let your mum take Grace for a few days, so that you can both have a rest. When you're feeling better, we can have a meeting and put a plan in place going forward, that will enable us to help you as a family.' She puts her card on the table and turns to Tom. 'I'm not saying you have to agree to this, Mr Carlson, but I do strongly recommend it.'

Tom nods, curtly.

'I'll get a few of Grace's things.' Mum heads for the stairs with Grace and the policeman follows her up.

Tom staggers to the chair as if he's been punched in the stomach, then he sits, his fists pressed against his knees.

After a while Mum comes down. She's carrying Grace and the policeman has one of our suitcases. It bulges.

'You don't have to do this.' I say, hopelessly. 'You don't have to take her.'

Moira squeezes my hand and stands up. 'You're doing the right thing, Bridget. Let your family help you. And get some sleep, you look exhausted.'

I follow the social worker into the hall. Mum says something to the policeman and he takes Grace's pram from the cupboard, her car seat. They all leave the house: the policeman, the social worker, Mum and Grace.

'I don't want this,' I say, but it's as if I've made no sound. For a moment I wonder if it's possible that I haven't. That I'm making no impression on the world at all. Perhaps I've disappeared.

I follow Mum onto the steps. She stops, makes Grace wave bye-bye and then goes to her car. The policeman helps put Grace in the car seat.

I watch until both vehicles have vanished around the corner. Then I watch some more. A bird alights on the fence and cocks its head at me, perhaps wondering why I'm just standing, frozen. What would be the point of going back inside? Grace isn't there.

Eventually, I realise that I'm getting cold, the autumn air biting through my long-sleeved t-shirt. My breasts too, are hurting; Grace's screaming triggered my let-down. I wrap my arms around my chest and stumble back into the house. I don't want to. It'll be a strange and empty place without Grace, an alien planet, but what choice do I have? Tom is still sitting in the living room exactly where I left him. He hasn't moved an inch.

He looks up when he hears me and I reel back as if I've been slapped. His face is stricken. He looks destroyed.

'T–Tom?' I edge into the room and realise that he must have moved since I'd left. His hands aren't empty anymore. He is crushing a damp Frankie-Lion in one fist.

'Your mum forgot Frankie.' His voice isn't his. Again, I get that sensation of having entered an alien world or a different dimension. 'Your mum did this. Because we said we were moving. And she was able to get Social Services on her side because you couldn't stop obsessing about that kidnapping.' His voice is emotionless, as if he's just learning to speak but hasn't worked out how to do it properly.

'I . . . yes, I suppose.'

Tom looks back down at Frankie. 'I'll call the estate agent and withdraw our offer on the house.' Suddenly his gaze flutters to the sideboard where the map I'd made is still lying face down, its creases rendering it topological.

Tom stands, picks it up, stares at it. Then, with a flash of fury, he tears the page in half. It's as if all the energy he wants to spend getting Grace back is going into tearing the paper again and again until it is confetti on the carpet.

I can do nothing but watch.

'This is your fault,' he mutters. 'I can't even look at you.' He reels past me. 'I'm going to stay with my parents until Grace comes home. That'll give you a rest, won't it?' He looks back at me and a stranger is behind his eyes. 'You speak to the social worker and find out what you have to do to make them trust us with Grace. Go and see a court-appointed psychiatrist, whatever it takes.' Then he is gone and I am alone.

Sometimes the film follows the woman into a room that makes her jealous. It's a little girl's room and it's lovely. There are toys in there. Toys that she has always wanted but never had, like a Barbie Dreamhouse and a giant rocking horse that looks like it would carry her away on exciting adventures. Its mane is long and silky and it has a real leather saddle.

There's a bookcase in one corner with lots of books she knows she would love. Sometimes the woman takes the books out and looks at them, just flicks through the pages, and she can see lots of pictures and big writing. She knows if she had the chance, she'd be able to read them.

The bedding is white and pink, and the walls are mostly white with pink trim. The window has long white curtains and there is a pink rug on the floor that looks very soft. The bed has actual posts, like it belongs to a princess and there's a big, almost life-size dolly that sits on the bed. She has brown hair like hers and a pretty checked dress. She wishes she could play with that doll.

She longs to be in that room, and that longing is so strong that it is an almost physical ache.

She dreams about that room.

She dreams about the man and lady now, too. She is finding it hard to remember her mummy's face but she can picture the lady very clearly.

The funny thing is, they have a little girl's room but she never sees a little girl.

When the woman goes into that room, she smiles at her through the camera.

Chapter 22

I don't sleep. I lie there all day and night, head pounding, staring at the ceiling, with my breasts bleeding impotent milk, certain that Grace is crying for me. Mum didn't take my supply from the freezer which means she's feeding Grace cow's milk. My baby will be in pain. Part of me hopes that if Grace keeps her up, Mum will return her in the morning.

I roll onto my side and stare at the clock as it ticks the hours away, my breasts turning to rock. I should express, but I can't get out of bed. I don't see the point. So what if I do get mastitis? I deserve it.

When images of Grace become too torturous, my thoughts veer towards the missing girl. My mind has become Scylla and Charybdis. On one side, too painful to contemplate for long, the unnamed, uncared for kidnap victim, whose own mother hasn't even reported her missing, and on the other Tom and Grace. Either way is a maelstrom.

Beyond the clock, the wardrobe hangs ajar. Tom's side is empty. Everything went into his case. I want to reach out to him, to find out if he's got to Chesterfield okay, to see if he's awake too, thinking of Grace, or of me. But I am afraid that he'll ignore my call and my heart can't take it.

So, I turn my back on the wardrobe and pretend that he is in the other room with Grace.

I don't leave the house the next day. What would be the point? I call work and let them know that I can't come in. They suggest a meeting with HR when I get back. I can't bring myself to care.

I can't bring myself to eat either. Or move from the bed. Or call Moira to 'set up a plan'.

I keep watching the phone, expecting Mum to call and ask what to do about a screaming Grace. The phone never rings.

My limbs ache from inaction. My breasts have almost stopped releasing milk. When I'm not thinking about Grace, I'm looking at the message from Mr Dobson's neighbour.

Grant was frightened by a white van. A white van had been following his family before his daughter was taken. It *has to be* the same people.

If I speak to Naomi and tell her what I've found in the data, I really can let it all go, and focus on making sure that the social worker knows I'm a good enough mother for Grace.

Naomi hasn't called back since I left my message. I have to go and see her in person.

It takes me an hour to muster the willpower to get out of bed and then I throw on whatever clothes I find on the floor. I gaze at myself in the bathroom mirror before I leave. Both eyes are sunken into bruised flesh. The contusion on my forehead is a livid green and purple, the swelling deforming the shape of my skull. My cheeks are pinched, my lips chapped, my hair a greasy tangle. I don't recognise myself.

I leave the house in a daze but I immediately see the white van parked opposite the driveway. I freeze on the steps, my heart pounding. Watching them, watching me. There is no way to know how many people are inside; sunlight glints from blacked-out windows. The engine revs as if to warn me to go back in.

I hurry to my car. What are they going to do, follow me to the police station? I feel oddly reckless. I have nothing to lose.

They do follow me, tailing me almost all the way, twitching close to my bumper, trying to force me to stop, to pull in. White paintwork fills my rear-view, but my eyes are blurry anyway, from no sleep and unshed tears. I ignore them.

I almost miss the turning to the station, despite the sat nav warning me in its strident tones. I've tuned out, head nodding, eyes heavy. I whip the wheel around at the last moment and the van passes me, too close to follow the turn. I watch it heading into the flow of traffic and jump as a Subaru beeps at me. I veer back into my own lane and look for somewhere to park.

I've never been into a police station before. I've never been in trouble and Tom reported the broken car window. I stand in the doorway, confused and disoriented. Rows of plastic chairs sit between me and the front desk, a bit like a doctor's waiting room, many of them filled with people who look bored, or desperate, or angry. I'll have to walk past them all. I wrap my arms around my chest and stare at the posters on the walls: *Be Safe; Cycle Security; Handling Stolen Property is a Crime*. And then the other posters, the ones that break my battered heart: *Police Appeal for Assistance*. These show pictures of missing children. The most recent has a familiar name: Vihaan Sharma. In his picture, black eyes peer out from under a long fringe.

'Are you all right, love?' It's a middle-aged woman, wearing a beige raincoat over a thick jumper. Her eyes are brown and kind. She's looking at me with a blend of compassion and horror.

I nod, but she leaps to her feet anyway. 'Here, let me help you.'

As her arms go around me my knees weaken and I have to force myself not to collapse into her. She reminds me of Althea, Sam's mum. She leads me towards the front desk, chattering away, as if sensing that I need to hear her voice to keep going. Vaguely I think that I'm being treated like a stray dog or skittish horse, but it's working.

'It isn't the cost of it, I mean the bikes were expensive, of course, but we are insured. It's the violation, isn't it? The fact that these people just came onto our property and took what they wanted, like they deserved it, like they're owed it. They just picked through our belongings.' She sniffs and I realise that she's not at the police station to help anxious women coming in from the street, she's here to report a crime herself.

'Some people,' I whisper. 'If they want something, they just take it.'

She nods and squeezes me tightly. Then we're at the desk and she's knocking on the glass partition. A young officer is looking at me, his eyes widening when he sees my bruised face. 'Ma'am? How can I help you?' He's half out of his chair as he's speaking. 'Do you need medical attention?'

'No, I'm fine.' I reach up as if to touch my head, but then my hand drops. The other lady is still holding me up. 'I just . . . I need to speak to Sergeant Shaw. Is she here?'

The officer taps at his keyboard and is about to answer when the door behind us opens again and I turn. Sergeant Shaw strides in. She isn't alone; there are three of them, all women, perhaps starting their shift or returning from a call. Her blue-grey eyes flicker over me and she returns to her conversation.

Then, suddenly, it's as if her brain has caught up with her quick scan of the room and she does a double take. 'Mrs Carlson?' She rushes towards me. 'Is that you?'

'Naomi.' The relief is immediate. This time my legs do give out. But Naomi is there to help the older woman take my weight and they help me to a chair. I grip Naomi's hands and the whole world regains its edges, as if I've just received a television channel that has been out of service. 'Thank God.'

Naomi says thank you to the other woman, who

understands she has been dismissed, then she helps me to my feet again. 'Let's talk in an interview room, you'll be more comfortable.' She leads me deeper into the police station and I don't dare look up at all the other people, still sitting on chairs, still waiting for attention. Instead I stare at my moving feet.

The room is small: grey walls, one desk, three padded chairs. I sit on one and Naomi pulls another around so she's sitting next to me rather than across from me. She takes my hands again. 'You're freezing. Can I get you a cup of tea?'

'No, thank you. All I've had for the last twenty-four hours is water, I can't stomach the idea of anything else.'

'What's happened, Mrs Carlson?'

'Social Services came.'

Sergeant Shaw rubs my hands, as if to warm them. 'I know. Ward told me they'd been in touch. They take a multi-agency approach when there is a credible concern. Is that why you're here?' She looks at my forehead.

'No. No . . . I just . . . I'm sorry. Grace has gone to stay with Mum for a bit and Tom . . . he's gone to his parents.'

She nods, still watching me in her quiet, intelligent way. 'So, you're on your own?'

She's struggling to understand why I'm here.

'They said I hallucinated the kidnapping, but I didn't.'

'Do you want me to speak to someone, is that it?'

'Yes! No. I'm not explaining myself very well. I tried to call you a couple of days ago. I left a message.'

283

Naomi frowns, indenting her smooth freckled skin. 'I haven't picked up a message, I'm sorry. What did you need?'

'It's hard to get it all organised in my head. I haven't had much sleep. Any sleep. Not since Mum took Grace.' I clench my fists. 'I went to Lancashire, to visit friends, we all did. And this man saw me and thought I was someone else, a woman called Betsie Dobson. He was confused, but then I saw a picture and I'm the image of her.'

'All right.' She's listening at least.

'And then I found out her story. She's dead. She killed herself because her daughter was kidnapped. And it was the same sort of thing that I saw. I mean, she was taken from a train station and I thought . . . I thought it could be the same people. I thought that maybe Grant Dobson, that's Betsie's husband, he might have seen something that could help me find the girl I saw.'

'So, you went to see him?' Sergeant Shaw fills in the quiet that falls after my confession.

I nod. 'It was awful, he's an alcoholic . . . but his neighbour, Mick, he told me that the Dobsons had been seeing a white van before Frances was taken. The same one that's been following me.'

'You're being followed?' Naomi straightens. 'Have you reported that?'

I shake my head. 'Tom said . . . never mind. That's not why I . . .' I shake my head again. 'I'm a mathematician,' I say. 'Statistics: probabilities, correlations, patterns. That's my job.'

Naomi frowns.

'I made a database of kidnappings and abductions and I found a pattern. I should have brought my laptop. I–I can bring it in and show you.'

'All right.'

'There's a gang. I'm sure of it. They take kids from train stations, or near to them. They were in the North of England, but now I think they're moving south.'

Naomi is silent.

'It's the same people, I know it is.'

'Okay.' Naomi stands up. 'Stay right here, I'm going to make a couple of calls. I'll be back as soon as I can. Are you sure you don't want a cup of tea while you wait? It looks like you need it.'

I shake my head and she marches out of the door. It closes behind her with a click. The relief is immense. I close my eyes.

The door opens. I raise my head, trying to see through sticky eyes. It isn't Sergeant Shaw, it's the young officer from the front desk. He's holding a cup of tea and a sandwich. 'Sergeant Shaw says to get stuck into this.' He puts it down in front of me. 'It's cheese. Is that okay?'

He looks almost pathetically eager to please, so I nod.

'There's milk in the tea and one sugar.' He backs towards the doorway. 'Sergeant Shaw says she won't be much longer.' He vanishes and the door closes once more. I stare at the food. I haven't a clue what to do with it. But steam rises from the polystyrene cup and I pull it towards me, inhaling the warmth. I hadn't realised I was cold until I wrapped my palms around the heat. I don't drink but I let the steam bathe my face.

When Naomi Shaw comes back, the tea is tepid, the sandwich stale. 'I'm sorry that took so long.' She's frowning. Something isn't right. I sit up straighter.

'What is it?'

Naomi looks at the uneaten sandwich and full cup of tea and sighs. 'I've spoken to Moira over at Social Services. I've told her that I believe you did see something. That you weren't making up the kidnapping.' She sits back down. 'She's been expecting your call and she's a little concerned that she hasn't heard from you. She was about to ask us, in point of fact, to check on you.'

'I'm going to speak to her after this . . .'

Naomi nods. 'I've also opened a file. I want you to officially report that you're being followed. That way, if something happens, we've got a record, a history.'

I nod.

'It's only been since you reported the kidnapping?'

'Yes.'

'If you *are* being followed, have you considered the possibility that it's someone messing with you? One of the other passengers from the train perhaps. Someone who resented being held up?'

I stare at her. 'I hadn't even thought . . .'

'Well, it's something to look into.' She makes a note. 'So, it's a white van, no markings, like the one you think you saw before?'

'The same.' I straighten. 'There *is* a police report, a record. My car window was smashed. Tom saw it, and our friends. It was the person driving the white van.'

'I'll look into that as well.' She folds her arms. 'Bridget, in the meantime, go home, get some rest. If you see the van again, call us.'

'And you'll look into the kidnappings? The gang?'

Naomi hesitates.

'I'll send my database over.'

'I'm not the one who would look at something like that, Bridget, but I'll forward it to the relevant team.' She helps me stand up, leads me to the door. 'Did you drive yourself here?'

I nod.

'Do you think you can drive home?'

'I'll be fine.'

I've done all I can. I've told the police all I know. The little girl is in their hands now.

Chapter 23

Mum rings just as I am about to call Moira. In the background, Grace is screaming.

'Darling,' she sounds brittle. 'Would you like to come and visit for an hour or so? I think Grace would like to see you.'

I'm moving before the echoes of her voice have fallen silent. I pack a bag of expressed milk from the freezer, grab Frankie-Lion, shove my phone into my pocket, and race to the car.

I drive like a maniac to Mum's house, a property far too big for one person, on the outskirts of the next village. I pull into the drive, leap from the driver's seat, grab the bag and slam the car door. Then, I race breathlessly down the long path towards the front door, towards Grace.

On either side of me is a manicured lawn, but the main garden is out of sight, surrounded by a six-foot wall. When I used to play outside, I would pretend that it was the secret garden. No ivy is permitted to grow, the brickwork pristine as if it was laid yesterday. The only thing that breaks the expanse of brick is the coal chute which, as far I know, has never been used. It's the same on the other side: featureless bricks all the way around.

The house itself looks like it should have wisteria or climbing roses on the front, but it doesn't. It's a severe septuagenarian: clean lines, not permitted to lose its edges. I hammer on the door, making it shake. Mum's had it painted recently; I can smell it. I almost expect my fist to leave a mark on the scarlet but there's nothing to show that I'm here, not even a fading handprint.

I can hear Grace wailing; the thick wood is not enough to contain her cries. My stomach knots and I bang harder until Mum opens the door.

She raises an eyebrow. 'Bridget. Are you all right? You look awful.'

I try to push past her. 'Does it matter what I look like? I'm here to see Grace.'

Mum blocks my entry. 'Of course it matters. You'll terrify her looking like that. And she's fine; she's learning to self-soothe.'

I force my fists to open. 'You mean you're leaving her crying on purpose?'

'It's not as if I can't hear her, darling. I have a lot of damage to undo.'

'Damage?' I lower my voice so that I don't scream.

'Yes, Grace is very manipulative.' I see now that Mum looks tired, her eyes more deeply sunken, her make-up less carefully applied. 'She has to learn that crying doesn't mean she gets her own way.'

'She's a *baby*, Mum.' I grit my teeth. 'She isn't crying to manipulate you; she's crying because she

289

needs you.' I force another step forward. Now I'm in the hallway, my voice echoing. 'You said I could see her for a couple of hours.'

Mum sighs. 'I know.' She looks at me regretfully. 'But what kind of mum would I be if I allowed her to see you with a face like that? Go to your room and get cleaned up. I've still got your old clothes. Some of them might even fit you.' Even though my stomach feels hollow and hunger is a distant ache, I glance at my waistline. 'Once you've freshened up and put some make-up on that bruise, *then* come down and see Grace.'

There's a mirror on the wall beside me. I catch my reflection and my objections die on my tongue. I look like death warmed up, like I've been beaten and then 'dragged through a hedge backwards', as Mum used to say. She's right. I can't see Grace looking like this.

'Fine, I'll clean up. But she needs this.' I push the bag towards Mum. 'It's her milk, and Frankie-Lion.'

Mum removes Frankie, then hands the bag back to me. 'I've got milk.'

'What sort? She needs special—'

'It's SMA.' Mum tosses her head. 'The man in the chemist said it was a good brand.'

'But is it dairy-free?' I try to give the bag back to her. 'She has to have dairy-free.'

'There's no such thing as food intolerance,' Mum says. 'No-one had it when *I* was a girl. She's just seeking attention.'

I tighten my grip on the bag. 'You *did* give her a chocolate chip cookie in Costa!'

Mum tilts her head, she doesn't even look guilty. 'She loved it, Bridget. There was nothing wrong with her afterwards.'

'It takes a little while. She was up half the night in agony. That's why she's crying now. She's hurting.'

'Don't be silly,' Mum snaps. 'It's not the first time I've sat for Grace, Bridget. And she's hardly the first baby I've raised. I'll let her have her cuddly toy when she calms down. That way she'll learn that it is *not* crying that gets her rewarded.' She sighs. 'Honestly, Tom's spoiled her.' She steps to the side and, automatically, I walk forward. The air in her house is cool; she keeps it at seventeen degrees. I always need a jumper when I visit and I take a moment to wish I'd remembered to grab one when I left.

Behind me Mum closes the door and throws the bolt. Then she latches a padlock over it. She's been terrified of burglars since Dad died but her paranoia seems to have worsened.

'Is that really necessary?'

She looks at me as she pockets the key. 'You want someone to come in and take Grace?' she says and suddenly I'm grateful for her fears. Whoever is shadowing me in the van will never be able to get into Mum's house, it's a fortress. Grace is safe from them here.

She gestures to the stairs. 'Go on. Your room is just the way you left it.'

'All right.' I can still hear Grace's sobs, although she seems to have quietened a little. 'If you use this milk from now on, she'll be happier; it's my breast milk.' I try once more to give her the bag.

'You should certainly be weaning her off that.' Mum gives me a tight-lipped smile. 'I can't imagine how hard it must be for you, working and breast-feeding at the same time. I'm surprised Tom hasn't said something.'

From deep inside the house, Grace's wails ramp up a notch, as though she can hear my voice. My chest aches. The faster I can clean up, the faster I can see her. With each step in what my heart tells me is the wrong direction I feel a terrible wrench. But I clench my fists and head up the stairs.

The carpet is thick. A spongy lawn which absorbs my footsteps, turning them silent as though I'm not even here. The bannister gleams. I reach out a fingertip. There, on the woodwork under the rail above the sixth tread, where no-one can see them, are my initials: BM. I etched them into the wood with the tip of Dad's screwdriver one day. At the time I wondered how long it would be before Mum found them but I don't think she ever did. Or perhaps she has, and she's left them here on purpose. That would be like her too. I run my skin over the roughness and almost smile. Then Grace's crying reaches a crescendo and I hurry upwards, leaving them behind.

Every few treads there is a sampler above my head: *Home is where the heart is; Honour thy father and thy mother; Manners cost nothing; A job worth doing is worth doing well; A lie hurts forever; When you love what you have, you have all you need.*

Most of these are old, some yellowing behind their frames. I know them by memory, when so many other moments from my childhood have been buried behind the grief of Dad's death. There are newer ones on the landing though; Mum is always adding: *Family is everything; A child is an uncut diamond; There is no substitute for hard work.*

There are five rooms upstairs. My old room, the master where Mum sleeps, her sewing room, the bathroom and the study, where Dad used to work but which, I assume, is now Grace's nursery. I want to see where she is sleeping so, instead of going straight to my room, I head for Dad's old study and open the door.

To my surprise, this is not the nursery. In fact, the study has hardly changed. There's a heavy desk in front of the window and shelves filled with books and boxes neatly labelled by year. A green rug forms a splash of colour on top of the carpet and there are pictures on the walls, photographs: one of the three of us, several of me.

I touch the shot of the three of us. There are no photos of Dad elsewhere in the house. Mum removed them after he died, perhaps following Aunt Gillian's advice. I'd forgotten the exact cut of his hair and the way he wore his moustache. I run my finger over his face. His eyes are blue and smiling.

But the smile is a lie, I think. He killed himself. Hung himself in the garage using rope that he must have bought from a garden store. Wearing his good suit, with shit on his shoes, and his nails torn where he must have fought for breath, and his eyes bulging from his head.

I jerk away from the photo and, needing to cleanse the image from my mind, I peer at the one hanging beneath. In it I'm a baby, and there's a pink bear lying beside me in the cot. I don't own this bear anymore. I wonder if it was a favourite. I can't imagine Grace ever losing Frankie-Lion or Dobbie. When she grows out of them, I'll keep them on a shelf with whatever other precious things she accumulates. Mum isn't so sentimental.

I lean closer, hoping to see similarities between my past self and Grace, but the baby could be anyone. The eyes are still dark blue and unsettled. There's nothing of Grace in there, I think suddenly, nothing of me.

In the next image I'm maybe three years old, wearing a pink dress with so many frills that I am almost buried under them and shiny patent shoes. I am looking at the shoes with what can only be described as unmitigated loathing. I know it's me but I don't feel any jolt of recognition.

Under this is one in a more ornate frame. I'm a little older and wearing yet another frilly dress. My eyes are narrowed at the camera and my curls are teased into ringlets. My hands have formed angry little fists.

I sidestep to the right, fascinated. Now I'm perhaps four, or five. I'm playing on the patio, bending over a cluster of Barbies. I remember the Barbies but still feel no connection to the girl in the picture. To myself.

Dad is in this photo, bent over a flower bed, his back to the camera.

Then, finally, a picture I connect to. I'm seem to be about nine years old and I'm lying in the garden, reading, with the sun behind me. There I am: the expression is mine, the absorption in the book. I wonder if this is the age that people turn into themselves. I wonder how much Grace will change between now and nine.

I turn from the photos to see that there are more samplers in here: *Do the hard jobs first; Blessed is he who has found his work*.

Although my need to see Grace burns, I haven't been in Dad's study since he killed himself, and I move towards his desk, inhaling, wondering if some part of him remains.

Aunt Gillian did a good job of helping me wipe him from my mind but a few memories remain: the sound of him yelling that we're making too much noise in the hallway while he's working, the buzz of his shaver in the bathroom, his cheers when the cricket was on, the fizz of beer in a glass.

Like the bulky computer on the desk, which has been replaced by a laptop, the scent in the office is no longer his. I stumble backwards with unexpected tears in my eyes and my shoulder knocks one of the samplers from the wall. I fumble and catch it before it can hit the floor and break. *Do the hard jobs first* it says. I turn it to check where the hook is and there, scrawled on the back of the frame, in Dad's spiky, distinct capitals are the words *NOBODY'S PERFECT*.

'Now *that* I can agree with,' I whisper. I rehang the sampler and turn to leave. Mum must have turned her sewing room into Grace's nursery. I hurry towards it and pause with my fingers on the handle when I hear Mum calling. 'Bridget, what are you doing up there?'

'Nothing.' I lurch away and into the room opposite: my room.

Once inside I freeze. I haven't been in here since I moved in with Tom, it never seemed important, but now here I am, as I once was. I almost expect a younger version of myself to look up at me from the bed.

The room is spotlessly tidy. There is no dust, not a single cobweb or item out of place. I walk forward. Under the window sits the desk where I did my homework. The bed is made with pink sheets. Nothing in my own house is pink but here the colour reigns supreme: pink curtains, a darker pink rug. I drift to the bookcase in a trance. It is filled with school text-books, but behind those, peeking out are some of my old favourites: *Malory Towers*, *Howl's Moving Castle*, *The Weirdstone of Brisingamen*.

There are more samplers in here too: *Tidy room, tidy mind*; *Be better today than yesterday*; *A smile is the best make-up*; *A well-behaved child is a gift*.

There's an old CD player by the bed and I know there will be CDs in the drawer beneath it. I used to listen to them to help me get to sleep. But I'm not here to listen to music. I can still hear Grace crying, although she seems to be calming down. Has Mum finally seen to her?

I head to the dresser and open the drawers. My old clothes, the ones I didn't take with me, are still here. Long skirts, which never suited me, blouses with delicate lace trim, and high-necked tops with long sleeves.

They're all too small, of course. I've put on weight in the last ten years, changed shape. I'm not the same person. Still, I manage to find a wrap-around skirt that reaches all the way around, a pair of black leggings with accommodating lycra, and a shirt that I can wear unbuttoned over my own.

The clothes smell fresh, as though they haven't been hanging here for years. It's as if Mum still washes them, irons them and returns them to their hangers. I feel in the back of the underwear drawer, looking for an old diary, suddenly wanting to hear my own voice, the sound of who I was before Tom, before Grace. The notebook isn't there. I wonder what she's done with it.

I strip, dropping my jeans on the rug. They land with a thump, my mobile phone still in the back pocket. I leave it where it is and quickly dress.

My old make-up bag slouches in front of the mirror beside my hairbrush. I open the zip. Inside, ten-year-old lipsticks are jumbled among almost empty pots of shadow, cracking face powder and dried up cream blush. The foundation is the wrong colour now. I've become more tan; my skin less delicate. Still, it'll cover the worst of the bruise. I wipe it on with my fingers, wincing at the discomfort. The make-up has clotted and feels like glue, but it still stains my skin and, to my relief, the bruise starts to vanish beneath it.

I pat some more foundation on the bags under my eyes, then, using a clean finger, try to brighten them with a smudge of pale brown eyeshadow. I pick up a pinkish lipstick, but I don't put it on. I think of how I'll be kissing Grace in a minute and drop it back in the bag. But my lips are visibly chapped. I find a lip balm at the bottom of the bag and smear some on.

Now that my face is less of a horror show, my hair appears even worse. I pick up the hairbrush and try to drag it through the knots. I haven't washed it for days: it's heavy with grease and salty around my face where I've cried into the curls.

There is nothing I can do with it unless I take a shower but there isn't time for that.

I find a scrunchie and tie it into a ponytail but it only reveals more of my swollen face. I almost scream my frustration. Mum will *not* be satisfied.

Then I remember that I had a drawer of scarves and hats. I can't wear a hat indoors but I can leave my hair down, wrap a scarf around my head and pull it to cover at least some of my forehead. The scarf I find is pink and white. I hate it. I put it on.

I don't look like me anymore. I'm a weird amalgam of a friendless teenager who never knew how to fit in and an overweight mum whose skirt is cutting into her stomach. I adjust the itchy lace around my collar and sigh. Tom would laugh if he saw me. The pink scarf alone would have him in fits.

I touch the skirt, which flounces as I move. I feel like a snake trying to slip back into a skin I've long ago sloughed off.

Grace's cries penetrate my thoughts and I jerk away from the mirror, the seam of the leggings twisting uncomfortably as I move. Then I race downstairs: *When you love what you have, you have all you need; A lie hurts forever; A job worth doing is worth doing well; Manners cost nothing; Honour thy father and thy mother; Home is where the heart is.*

I stop in the hallway. The kitchen is to my right, Grace is in the living room at the other end of the house. I head left, my feet once more soundless on the carpet, the skirt swishing around my shins.

As I enter the living room, Mum looks up. She is holding Grace, thank God, and Grace has Frankie, but her face is bloated from crying, at least as puffy as mine. She's wearing a mauve dress that I don't recognise. It has frills and flounces all the way from her chest to her knees. She's obviously thrown up on the bib and the dress has ruched up in Mum's arms, showing that she has matching frilly knickers on, over her nappy.

She looks ridiculous and my arms ache with how desperately I want to hold her.

She sees me and instantly reaches out, wailing. Frankie is hurled to the floor. I lunge forward, but Mum holds her back. 'You're teaching her that crying is a good thing.' She shakes her head at Grace. 'You can go to Mummy when you calm down.'

'Give her to me, please.'

'Not until she stops.' Mum turns so Grace can't see me anymore and she shrieks.

'Mum!' My rage is blistering hot but I force it to a smoulder.

'I mean it, darling. A little pain now will save you a whole lot of agony later. Grace won't even remember this. But she'll learn and then things will be much easier for you.' I stare at her. Mum's face is tight and for a moment her eyes are pools of pain. I blink and the expression is gone.

'You're doing this for *me*?' I whisper.

Mum flinches. 'You think I enjoy hearing her cry like this?' There's hurt in her voice. 'Grace is still at an age where she can learn, as long as you don't give in to her. I'm not *making* her cry, I'm *letting* her cry. If you carry on giving in to her every whim when you have her back, you won't be able to cope. You might . . .' She swallows. 'You might snap again. You might . . .'

'Oh my God.' I collapse into a chair. 'You really think I'll hurt her.'

In Mum's arms, Grace has stopped fighting. Her cries begin to tail off. 'That's better.' Mum says, speaking to her. 'That's how we behave, Grace. *Now*, we can reward her.' She drops her into my lap.

Grace is still crying with little hiccoughing sobs. As soon as I put my arms around her she clings with feral strength, as if she'll never let me go.

I pat her back, trying to suppress my own tears. I can't scare her. 'It's okay, I'm here now. I won't leave you again. I'm here. Mummy's here.'

'Let's give you an hour.' Mum says and I look up to see her setting a kitchen timer.

300

'Are you serious? A timer?'

'One hour, Bridget. We all need a bit more discipline.' Mum turns away. 'By the way,' she turns back to me, 'you look very nice.'

For half an hour I don't move from the chair. Grace won't let me. Every time I shift position her arms tighten and her little fingers dig into my sides. She smells of baby shampoo, tears and sick. She's hot against my body and the ruffles on her dress tickle my arms. After a while, I think she is going to fall asleep and my own eyes start to sag but then I look at the timer. I don't want to miss a moment with her so I force them to stay open.

Mum stands up. 'I'm going to make us a cup of tea.'

I don't look up. 'Okay. Thanks, Mum.'

She leaves the room.

By the time she comes back Grace has started to move. In fact, she's wriggling to be let down. I don't want to let her go but I think about the timer and about how awful it would be, for all of us, if Mum is forced to drag her from my arms, so I release her. She thumps to the floor and I realise that we are surrounded by toys. They're scattered all around us: building blocks, dolls, a shape sorter. I don't recognise any of them. Mum has been shopping.

Grace picks up a square brick and holds it out to me. I slide to my knees beside her and drop it into the sorter which offers an electronic fanfare as it lands inside. Grace hands me a triangle.

Mum puts the tea on the coffee table. 'Drink this, you need it.'

I nod but ignore the cup, focused wholly on Grace. 'I'll let it cool down a bit.' I drop the triangle in and Grace crawls towards the circle.

'It'll be better for you hot.' She pushes it closer to me.

My eyes are drawn past her, to the timer; precious minutes are ticking away. I blink back tears and move to help Grace pick up the round block but it rolls away from my clumsy fingers.

How long has it been since I've slept?

It takes me two tries to get it into the shape sorter. Grace moves onto the dolls and I pick up the tea. It's pale with too much milk and it won't be dairy-free. I hesitate but then I remember that there's a bag of breast milk in the kitchen. One milky tea now won't hurt. I lift it to my lips.

I've been drinking almond milk for three months now and I've had nothing but water for two days, so the tea is cloying on my tongue. I swallow and put it down.

'You should drink more,' Mum says. 'I'm worried. Have you been eating at all?'

I shake my head.

'You'll be no use to Grace if you pass out.' Mum puts the cup back in my hands; I hadn't even seen her move. 'Have this, then take a nap. I'll make something easy to digest for dinner. Chicken soup?'

'Dinner?' My head feels heavy but I take another

sip of the tea. It doesn't taste so bad second time around. 'I thought I was going home?'

'You're in no state to drive.' Mum jerks her head towards my car, which sits outside the window. 'You'd crash if I let you. I can either call you a taxi or you can stay here. Of course, I don't know what Social Services will think about—'

'I'll stay.' I don't mean to interrupt, she hates that, but I don't want her to talk herself out of the offer.

'All right,' Mum says as the timer starts to beep. She bends down and picks up Grace. 'Take your tea, go to your room and have a rest. I'll call you for dinner.'

I stand on shaking legs, holding the warm tea when I should be holding Grace. She realises that I'm moving and her face fills with terror.

'I won't be far away. I love you, baby.'

'Go quickly,' Mum says, 'Like tearing off a sticking plaster.'

I stumble away, spilling tea onto my fingers. 'Would it really matter if I had longer?' I beg at the doorway.

Mum sighs and looks disappointed. 'Remember, Bridget, good discipline is a—'

'Sign of dignity.' I finish. That one is in the kitchen.

Grace starts to scream again and with tears burning my eyes, I stagger towards the stairs. My legs feel like rubber. Mum is right, I'm going to faint if I don't rest. Grace is safe, nothing will hurt her. We're *letting* her cry, not *making* her cry.

I grip the bannister as I climb and don't even try to find my initials underneath.

The little girl is woken up by a new voice. She thinks, for a second, that someone has come to save her, then she realises that the lady in the film is speaking. She is telling her how much she is looking forward to meeting her, how much she loves her already and what a wonderful family they will be.

The little girl cries until she is hoarse but she isn't sure why. Is it because she wants to go home to her real mummy, or is it because the beautiful lady says she wants her?

Chapter 24

I wake with a head full of wisps that I can't catch: the sound of a girl's cries, the look in Tom's eyes when Mum took Grace, the growl of a van.

My curtains are open and starlight turns my window to silver. I've slept for hours. Automatically, I reach for my phone to check the time but it isn't there. I sit and massage my temples. I feel almost hungover, very sick, and I realise that I haven't taken my Fluoxetine.

Tense, I test my emotions, as if pressing on a bruise, terrified that the rage which has been bubbling under the surface is going to erupt, but mainly what I feel is weak and hungry. Still, if I'm staying for a while, I should go and fetch my medication. It isn't safe for me to be in the house with Grace otherwise.

The thought of Grace makes me realise that I can't hear her. I strain my ears but she isn't making a sound. She must be asleep. Again, I wonder what the time is and how long before she's likely to wake. Between my inability to eat and failure to express, my milk has all but dried up but there are bottles downstairs. If I get to her before Mum, I can do the night feed.

My legs are tangled in the crumpled skirt; I swing them over the edge of the bed and pull it off. It'll be all right to go downstairs in just the leggings; it's the middle of the night, or at least, I think it is.

My bare feet are silent on the carpet and my door swings open with barely a sound. The only light in the hallway comes from the window at the end of the landing; the moon is shining through it, casting long shadows. I pause, then, instead of heading for the stairs, I go to Mum's sewing room, or what once was.

The room has been repurposed. The curtains are closed, but there's a little night light: a pink bulb that makes it feel like sunset in here. The room is full of sudden, sharp memories. A rocking horse in one corner, a pile of books beside a chair under the window. My old things. The cot though, is new. Its slats are painted white and it's one of those that will turn into a bed once she's old enough. How long does Mum think she'll be here?

Grace is passed out in the very centre of the mattress, as though she hadn't wanted to touch the bars. Her arms and legs are spread wide, reminding me of a sleeping Tom. She is completely unmoving. The old terror of SIDS grips me and, although I know it's because I went to bed without my pills, I step nearer on shaky legs. Grace's cheeks are flushed, her eyes sticky, her mouth slightly open. She snuffles slightly, then resettles and my heartrate slows. She's fine. She's sleeping with no sign of waking. I can go and get something to eat.

At the bottom of the stairs I turn towards the kitchen, passing the coat cupboard and the locked cellar door which I'm not allowed to touch. It's dangerous down there. Dad used it to store his tools and other rubbish, and it floods.

Hanging in an alcove, just before the entrance to the kitchen, is a large family portrait, almost life-size, of Mum and her parents. It was painted in the sixties when Mum was a young teen, perhaps the same age as she was in the photograph in Gillian's office. It's creepy as hell and I wait for the frisson of fear that always had me hurrying past when I lived here, but it isn't there anymore. It's only an old painting of mostly dead people.

I lean closer, looking for the source of the terror that had always gripped me at the sight of it. The man, Mum's father, is tall and stern; she gets her looks from him. He has one hand on her shoulder, proprietary. Her own mum is shorter, and a stranger glancing at the portrait might think she appears frail, but there's a look in her eyes, a viciousness that reaches out of the picture and grips you by the throat. She's standing in an odd way, almost half turned and, with a moment of shocking clarity, I realise why. There's someone missing. Mesmerised, I touch the paintwork. There was once a fourth person in the picture but they've been brushed out. It was a good job, professional, but you can just make out the outline of the figure where the new paint was applied. There's a ghost standing beside my grandma. Was that what had always scared me, the ghost? Or was

307

it the idea that someone could be brushed out of existence so easily?

I wonder briefly what caused this black sheep to be erased from history, then I step away from the picture. It's nothing but an old family mystery. There's probably a good story here but it doesn't seem important now, with everything else going on.

I turn and open the kitchen door; heavy dark wood that I have to lean on. The kitchen is large and echoing, the range is spotless, and the stainless-steel fridge echoes the orange streetlight on the other side of the garden wall. There are two doors to my left: one to the laundry room, one to the pantry. An oak table dominates the centre of the room, it has four chairs, even though there were only ever three people here. I was home-schooled right there, beneath the samplers, next to the fireplace which smoked in winter and stank in summer. There's something new here too: a highchair at one end of the table.

I reach out and click on the light switch.

'Hello, darling,' Mum says.

My hand flies to my chest. 'Mum?' There's a high-backed chair beside the fire, facing the window. She stands up from it. 'Why were you sitting here in the dark?' I step forward, dizzy.

'I'm finding it hard to sleep these days.' Mum is wearing a nightdress with a large collar, which makes her look like an ageing virgin sacrifice. The belt of her dressing gown is undone. She ties it swiftly and pulls it tight. 'What are you doing out of bed?'

I glance at the fridge and then away. I won't be

able to feed Grace now. 'I was hungry,' I say. It isn't a lie but my eyes slide from her face to the new sampler above the range: *Kitchens bring families together*.

I feel a sudden pang, picturing Mum all alone, stitching the message and hanging it up.

'You slept right through dinner.' Mum moves to the fridge. 'I'll reheat your soup.'

'I can do it, if you want to go to bed.' I try to keep the hope from my voice but Mum gestures to the table. 'Sit.'

I sit at the same chair I always use, facing the sink, and watch as she pours soup from a Tupperware into a pan. Blue light from the gas hob plays on her throat and chin. I realise that the draining board next to the sink isn't empty like the rest of the kitchen. There's a line of empty bottles, upside down, recently cleaned. I lurch to my feet.

'Are those Grace's bottles?'

Mum doesn't look at me; she keeps stirring the soup.

'Mum, did you get rid of my breast milk?' My heart pounds and rage twists like an eel at the bottom of a river, disturbed by the wake of a boat. It slithers.

Mum doesn't answer. She's emptied every bottle, washed them and left them to dry. My fingers ache and I realise I'm pressing my hands on the table, flat. I whip them up and pull them to my chest.

'How could you?' I snap. 'I told you Grace needs it.'

Mum keeps on stirring, the spoon making little scraping sounds as it circles the pan.

'Mum?'

She removes the spoon from the pan and switches off the hob. Moving stiffly, she dispenses the steaming liquid into a bowl.

'I told you,' she says as she places the bowl in front of me, 'there's no such thing as food intolerance. You're pandering to Grace and making a rod for your own back. Working and expressing, it's ridiculous.' She fetches a spoon from the drawer, puts that next to the bowl, and switches the kettle on. 'Eat your soup.' The kettle starts to rumble as I stare at her.

'*I'm* her mother, it's *my* decision.' I half stand, leaning on the table. 'She's been to the hospital, she's been tested, she's got a dairy intolerance. She doesn't like the milk she was prescribed, so it has to be breast milk.' I touch my right breast. 'How am I going to express all that again?' I almost sob at the thought.

Mum takes two cups from the cupboard, adds teabags, milk, pours on the water.

'Mum, are you even listening to me?'

She puts a cup of tea beside my bowl and wraps her hands around her own mug. I stare at her knuckles, the road map of wrinkles on the back of her hand. I've upset her and now she's not talking to me. 'Mum?'

She looks at me, pointedly, until I sit, dip the spoon into the bowl and eat.

For a moment my throat rebels, closing and refusing to swallow. The soup pools in my mouth, hot and salty. Shreds of chicken stick to my tongue. I taste cream, pepper and some bitter herb. Mum watches in silence until I force it down. As soon as the warmth hits my stomach, I shake, as if my body is only now allowing me to feel that I'm starving. Mum was right, I needed this. I eat faster. She pushes my tea towards me too, more warmth. I gulp it down and think of Tom. Has he eaten since Grace has left? Is June looking after him? Then I think of the missing little girl. Is she hungry too?

I put my spoon down before I finish the bowl. 'I can't eat any more.'

'Your stomach has shrunk,' Mum says, with a chill in her voice. She's still upset. 'You'll have to eat little and often for a couple of days.'

I nod. The food in my belly has made me shockingly sleepy.

'Are you happy to be here?' Mum asks, suddenly with her head on one side.

There's an echo in my mind. *Happy . . . happy with what you have.*

I nod, tiredly.

'Then say thank you for your dinner and go back to bed.' Her voice has the snap of command and I'm standing before I can consider whether or not I should.

'Thank you, Mum.'

'Good girl.'

Mum remains in the kitchen as I leave. I look back to see her staring at a photo on the mantel, her back straight, her face in shadow.

The painted eyes of her parents bore into my back as I stumble into the hall, as tired as if I haven't just slept for who knows how long. I still don't know the time and there are no clocks.

I reach the stairs. *Home is where the heart is; Honour thy father and thy mother; Manners cost nothing; A job worth doing is worth doing well; A lie hurts forever; When you love what you have, you have all you need.*

I stop outside Grace's room. She is completely silent. I peer around her door, she hasn't moved. It isn't like her; she usually throws herself around, twitching, curling and uncurling in her dreams. She's never slept so soundly.

I stand there, watching her, until my chin knocks into my chest, jolting me. Then I stagger into my room and collapse onto the bed. I was lucky to at least be in the same house as Grace. Tom wasn't.

Chapter 25

I open my eyes and the room reels. I'm dizzy and sick from Fluoxetine withdrawal. I *must* go home today and pick up my medication. I lie still for a long time; there's no reason to get up, not until I hear Grace. I wonder if it was her crying that woke me and listen, but there's no sound. Not even the growl of traffic breaks the quiet, the windows are triple glazed. The outside world is a perfect child: seen, but not heard.

My door opens. 'I've brought you a cup of tea.'

'How did you know I was awake?' I struggle to sit up as sickness washes over me.

'I didn't.' Mum puts the tea on my bedside table. 'I was going to leave it here for you.' She looks at me. 'You didn't sleep well?'

I frown, trying to remember, as though sleep, only moments old, was actually a long-distant memory. No Fluoxetine, no terrible dreams, but I still feel rotten. My stomach growls and I reach for the mug.

'I'll bring up some breakfast,' Mum says. 'You'll be better for something to eat.'

Nausea makes the idea awful but I wonder how

much of my dizziness is withdrawal and how much is simple hunger. I force the tea down. 'Is Grace okay? I haven't heard her.'

'She's fine. She's in the kitchen chewing on a piece of toast.'

'I should go and see her.'

'Stay here and drink your tea, she's happy enough.' Mum glances around my room. 'You've left things in a bit of state, haven't you?'

Dazedly, I look around. Make-up is scattered over the dresser, drawers are haphazardly open, and piles of discarded clothes lie on the floor. Strangely, there is no sign of my own jeans and top.

'I've washed your clothes,' Mum says, as if she can read my mind. 'They were filthy. Now drink your tea and tidy this mess. Tidy house . . .'

'Tidy mind.'

I finish my tea as Mum watches. Then she takes the mug and leaves.

I remain sitting as my stomach starts to settle. My room faces the garden and I can see the top of the oak from my bed. Its leaves have fallen but it's sunny outside and birds have settled in its branches. Suddenly the muffled quiet in the house is suffocating. I have to open the window, hear the birds, gulp in fresh air. I drag myself out of bed and stagger to the casement but the key is missing. It was always sticking out of the little lock when I lived here. I pull at the steel handle and the sash creaks but doesn't move. I slump onto the wide sill, defeated, and it moves under my weight.

I shift and it creaks again. Curious, I get to my knees and see hinges, painted white and hidden from the casual gaze by the sill's overhang. I don't remember the sill being a storage bench. I wonder if this is where Mum keeps the key to the window. I reach across to the other side of the seat and lift.

As I do, something tickles the back of my mind. An old memory, long dormant. I've done this before. But I don't *remember* doing it.

Then I hear his voice:

'It's our secret, Bridgie.' Dad is putting his tools back in his box. 'Somewhere for you to hide your treasures. Don't tell your mum.' His eyes flicker. 'Everyone needs a little privacy.'

Dad made this for me? A little privacy. What had I hidden inside the little alcove under the sill? What secrets could I have wanted to keep from Mum? Fascinated, I reach inside.

There is a stone in there, quartz I think. I pull it out and look at it, searching for the memory it will bring, but there is nothing. Where had I found it? Or had someone given it to me? I shrug and put it on the carpet.

Under that is a small square of cloth. It's soft; is that why I'd kept it? I smile to myself, thinking of Grace and what she might consider worth hiding in a treasure trove as she gets older.

Under the cloth, laid as if it is sleeping, I find a teddy bear. I pick it up and stare at it. It's pink and soft and someone has torn into it: dug out its eyes, slashed a hole in its belly and ripped out its stuffing, pulled off one ear, shredded an arm. There's a lot of rage here. A lot. My hands start to tremble. Was it me? Did I do this? Then why settle it under a piece of cloth? Was I just hiding it in case I got into trouble? Was I trying to make it all better? How old had I been?

I hesitate before I lay the teddy down beside the lump of quartz, then I cover it up again with the cloth. I can't stand its empty eyes staring at me. I reach back into the box with a trembling hand. I find some dried flowers that fall apart in my fingers and, lastly, sprinkled with their mummified petals, there's a notebook.

I frown as I turn it around. It's just an old school notebook like the ones I used to fill in for maths. But there's no name or date on it: the cover is blank. Had I stolen it? A small rebellion to prove that I could. It's dusty and the pages crinkle, yellow around the edges and slightly damp. It's probably empty but I open it anyway.

The handwriting inside is big and loopy, that of a child who has recently learned joined-up and is still forming the shapes of the letters quite carefully. It scrawls into bad spelling and almost illegible scruffiness near the bottom of each page.

What it says though; that has spikes.

All the stories tell me I'm meant to write Dear Diary. But I won't. This book is about me not doing what I'm meant to. I've got a diary anyway, it's in my underwear drawer. I know She reads that one. But it's

*not real. In that one I write things like 'I love Mummy'
and 'today we had sausages for tea'. I know when
She's read it because she's extra nice to me afterwards.*

This are my real thoughts.

Sometimes they scare me.

*I'm writing by the windowsill, using the light from
the streetlamp. I'm scared She might wake up and
check in on me.*

*I stayed up the last few nights, not writing, just to
see if She does check on me after She thinks I've gone
to sleep. She hasn't done at all this week, so now I'm
risking it. I'm writing. This is me, Bridget Monahan,
aged eight and a half.*

I stare at the writing, my eyes blurring. I have no
memory of this. No memory of a diary kept in a
secret alcove under my windowsill. I know I've
blanked out a lot, but this must have meant a lot to
me once. Still, maybe I grew out of it, lost it, like the
names of favourite dolls.

I turn a page.

*She hasn't spoken to me for two days. I broke a plate
while I was washing up. She said I did it on purpose
to get out of my chores but I didn't. I hate her.*

This was a funfair mirror, but instead of making me
look fatter, or taller, it showed me younger. Another.

*Dad was going to take me fishing but she says he
can't. She says I have to stay home because I didn't*

get all my maths right. I wish I could be with Dad all the time. I wish she'd just LEAVE ME ALONE.

There's a lot like this. A child venting about her mum. I want to smile as I turn another page but I can't. There's so much anger on these pages, so much rage.

I'm not allowed to write poems anymore. She says they're for babies and they're not very good anyway. She says I have to do maths and science because I can get a good job with maths but not by writing poems. She says she doesn't want to see them anymore. She burned my poetry book. Burned it. In the fire in the kitchen. I hate her, I hate her.

This makes me hesitate. Why would any mum burn her child's book? Burn the work they put into something they loved. What had I done to warrant such a punishment? I probe my memory like it's a sofa and I'm reaching under with a long stick, trying to prise out a lost object. But there's nothing. I don't even remember *liking* poetry, let alone writing it. I don't own a single poetry book. The idea has no appeal. Who is this child?

I broke a vase while I was playing Barbies and lied about it. She caught me. She always knows. Today I found a new piece of material on my bed. I know what it means – she'll start speaking to me again when I've finished the sampler. The note with it says A Lie Hurts Forever. *That's what I have to sew. I hate sewing, I always prick myself with the needle and I'm not even allowed to use a thimble. But if I sew quickly, then she'll talk to me again and I won't be so alone. Dad's away for work, but Aunt Gillian is coming on Friday. At least she'll speak to me.*

That sampler is hanging on the stairs. Part of me wants to go out and look at it. I don't remember sewing it, but I must have. I stare at my fingers. I loathe sewing. I never sew. Not even to fix loose buttons. But I must have been able to do it once.

The next entry is frightening in its familiarity and I touch the written words, as if I can reach back through the years and touch the little girl herself.

I can't sleep because I'm having bad dreams. In the dream I'm sitting on a swing but then I swing too high and fly off and I'm flying away from my parents, and I know I'll never see them again. It's horrible, I don't like it. I won't close my eyes. I don't want to dream again. Aunt Gillian is coming tomorrow. She says she can help.

After that entry there's a gap. I know there's a gap because the next piece of writing is in a different pen and the handwriting has changed, grown neater. It reminds me of the time I tried to keep a diary at university. I did it religiously for a few weeks, then the entries tailed off; once a week, once every few weeks, until I forgot about it. I must have been the same as a child. I'd lost interest.

I told her I want to go to boarding school, like the girls in Malory Towers. Now She's taken my books away. Dad says I'll be going to high school when I'm eleven. She says only if I've learned enough by then. I have to learn enough by then.

I flick through, realising that there are other gaps in the diary, chunks of time unaccounted for. There are no dates but I can see when I stopped writing for a while and started up again. There is always a blank page and then the handwriting matures, or the pen alters from blue to black, or, once, to purple.

Then I spot a pattern. I'm good at spotting patterns after all. There are two things that get repeated before a lot of the time gaps. Not every time, but often enough so that I know it's related.

. . . *I'm having bad dreams.*

. . . *She says Aunt Gillian is coming over tomorrow.*

. . . *Aunt Gillian is coming tomorrow.*

. . . *She says I have to be good, because we're seeing Aunt Gillian tomorrow.*

I stop reading every entry. Now I'm looking for something specific. I don't want to, not really, but I know it must be in here. And, near the end, I find it.

Dad is dead. I don't know how She did it, but She did it. It's because he loved me.

I found him. It was the most awful thing I've ever seen. I keep throwing up and I keep crying but that's not the worst thing. The worst is that he'll never come home. I'm on my own with her now.

When the ambulance came and took him away, the paramedics wanted to take me to hospital too. They said I was in shock but she said she'd deal with me, that she knew what to do. The paramedics told her to make sure I was kept warm and to keep my blood sugar up. Then they left. I wanted to go with him, but they wouldn't let me.

I WANT MY DADDY.

I almost drop the book from nerveless fingers. That child's scream. So much pain: *I want my daddy.* Tears gather in my eyes but they don't fall. I don't feel that pain any longer. I hardly remember him. But the little girl did. She'd only just lost him. My unshed tears are for *her*, not him. How could he leave her like that?

It was the funeral today. I wasn't allowed to go. She said it would be too hard for me but I should have been there. She went and Aunt Gillian stayed with me. Aunt Gillian says she's going to give me some more therapy, she's going to help me forget. But I'll never forget my Daddy, never!

I turn the page; my hands are shaking now.

Aunt Gillian made me go to sleep again today. She says it's hypnosis but it's not like on the telly. She told me I had to think of a happy place but it was hard, I don't know anywhere except this house.

321

There's a corner of the garden where I sit and read. I told her that was my happy place but it's not. My real happy place is anywhere but here.

After, I felt weird, like something had gone out of my head. But I felt better too. Mum made me my favourite dinner. I felt sick afterwards though, so I had to lie down.

I read on, mesmerised. These aren't the words of a child who was desperate to forget their father, a child whose instincts to block him from her memory were being facilitated. These are the thoughts of a child who is having something taken from her against her will.

I told Aunt Gillian that I'm forgetting things. Dad's face, the sound of his voice, his smell, his favourite foods. She says it's normal, but is it? I don't know. I want to remember everything about him but it all seems to be going. It's just like last time. And I feel so ill.

I hesitate on this page. What did I mean by 'just like last time'? I try to think but there's nothing there, I have no idea what I was writing about.

Another session with Aunt Gillian. Mum tried to watch this time but Aunt Gillian said she was making me too tense, so she went away. She wasn't happy about it. Afterwards though, she let me have ice cream. She was very nice all evening. I was allowed to watch

Kim Possible and read till nine and it wasn't even a homework book, because I felt sick again.

After that the pages are filled with what I ate, what the weather was like, what I watched on TV, what schoolwork I was doing, and how nice Mum was being. I was ill a lot. There was nothing more about Dad's death.

Then the entries just . . . stop. It's as if I've forgotten that the diary even exists.

I start to put the collection of treasures and hidden crimes back in the hole but then I spot two photographs lying flat against the wooden board, almost hidden under a layer of dust. I lift them both using my nails and hold them by the edges.

One is of Mum. She's only nine or ten, but she hasn't changed enough that she's unrecognisable. It's the eyes. Next to her is the girl from the picture in Gillian's office. They're wearing matching dresses and smiling stiffly into the camera. Their dimples are the same and knowledge sinks into my heart: they were sisters. This has to be the figure who was painted out of the family portrait downstairs.

The other image, I think, tells me why. It's Mum's sister. Now her hair is as short as it was in the photograph Gillian has of them in her office. She's sitting with a lover. You can tell they're lovers; they're both so relaxed. It reminds me of shots of me and Tom from the early days. Their arms are intertwined and they gaze into each other's eyes with complete devotion. Their bare legs touch, even their toes. The sun plays on their skin. It's a beautiful shot. Both are women.

Not just any woman. I recognise her just as easily as I recognised Mum. It's Aunt Gillian.

Gently I slip the photos into the diary, put it back where I found it and shut the sill.

I don't know why I had the photographs, or why I'd hidden them. Perhaps they were just family photos that I'd liked: a picture of Mum at around the same age I'd been, a picture of my only friend, Aunt Gillian.

I sit back on my heels and blink at the room. I haven't tidied and Mum will be up any moment with breakfast. I scoot around, sickness swooping and diving within me, sweeping up clothes and shoving them into drawers.

As I'm wiping a smear of foundation from the outside of my make-up bag, the door opens.

Mum looks around the room with a slight frown. 'You missed the bed,' she says, and I turn, too fast. Dizziness makes me wobble. She's right though, I haven't made the bed.

'I'll help you.' She slides a plate of toast and jam onto the dresser and tugs at my duvet. I take the other side and pull it straight. She adjusts the pillow.

'Thank you.' I look at the window again. 'Do you know where the key to my window is?' I gesture. 'I wanted some fresh air.'

Mum laughs. 'I collected all the keys up after you moved out. I didn't want to encourage burglars. I mislaid them years ago, I'm afraid.'

'You lost the keys to the windows?' I shake my head. 'You know you can call the double-glazing company and have more sent over?'

'I didn't think of that.' Mum walks to the dresser. 'I don't think there's any need though. I never open them. I like to keep the house at a certain temperature, it's best for my health.' She picks up my hairbrush. 'Sit down and I'll brush your hair.'

Automatically I sit on the bed. She sits behind me, making the springs creak. Then I feel the bristles in my hair and sigh.

'If you want fresh air,' she says, 'there's always the garden. It's a nice day, we can sit out there with Grace before lunch.'

I nod as the brush moves through my curls, tugging at the knots, and I feel something inside me loosen. I think again of Tom who must be missing Grace like a limb.

'I should call Tom.' I look at the floor. 'Where's my phone? I left it in my jeans . . . didn't I?'

'I didn't see it.' Mum puts the brush down and stands. 'I'm going to check on Grace.'

'But you washed them. You're sure you didn't see my phone?'

'Sorry, darling. Maybe you didn't bring it with you.'

I think back, struggling to remember. I *thought* I'd slipped the iPhone into my jeans, or had I believed I'd done it because it was what I always did? Mum had called the house phone, so it wouldn't have been in my hand. Had I actually left it on the charger in my hurry to get to Grace?

'I'd better use the house phone.' I start towards the door but Mum blocks me.

'Eat your breakfast first. You really don't look well.'

I can smell the toast. Hunger digs into me. 'I guess I'd better.' I head back to the plate.

'Bring it to the kitchen once you're finished.' Mum smiles. 'Then we can take Grace outside.'

I nod, already eating. There's no emergency. No reason for calling Tom right now. In fact, if I'm popping home later, I can pick up my iPhone and call him then.

My thoughts fill with Grace. It'll be nice to show her the garden.

The little girl has started to look forward to seeing the woman. Now, when she behaves, the woman hugs her tightly. The little girl has begun to hug her back.

When she comes in and asks her to lie down, she does so right away.

The woman tells her about a lovely beach and asks her to picture herself on a boat. It's hard. The little girl has never been on a boat before but soon she can feel herself rocking as the woman talks to her. It's like magic.

The woman tells her that soon she'll forget her old life and all the bad things that have happened to her. The little girl can't remember why that would be wrong. She wants to forget. It's easier and it makes the woman happy.

She wants to make the woman happy.

Chapter 26

As I emerge onto the landing wearing my old dressing gown and carrying my empty plate and mug, the doorbell rings.

There's a beat of inattention, and then Mum emerges from the kitchen with Grace in her arms. Grace is almost unnaturally still but she's awake. I start for the stairs and both of them see me. Grace cries out and reaches upwards and Mum's eyes widen.

'Stay up there,' she snaps.

But—'

'Out of sight! I mean it.' I stop moving, caught on the edges of Mum's tone. She looks at me and I realise that she won't open the door while I'm standing there. Why not? Is she trying to hide *me* or hide the person at the door *from* me? Is she ashamed of me? Ashamed of the way I am now?

As I step backwards she puts Grace down at her feet, takes a key from her pocket and turns it in the padlock. The doorbell rings again as she's undoing the bolt.

She slides the key back into her pocket, picks Grace up and looks meaningfully up at me. I retreat towards my bedroom. Then I stop. My room overlooks the garden but the study is at the front of the house, right above the hall.

I open and shut my bedroom door loudly, then I tiptoe back along the carpet to slip into the study. I hear Mum open the door and race to the window, where I look out to see a car that I last saw driving away from my house. It's the social worker, Moira.

Is this something to do with Grace?

I open the door so that I can hear.

'Mrs Monahan.' Moira's voice drifts up the stairs and suddenly I'm terrified. What if she finds out I'm here and haven't taken my pills?

My nails dig into my palms, I am barely able to hear above the roaring of blood in my ears. '. . . just a routine call to see how Grace is doing. May I come in?'

'Of course,' Mum replies and I hear footsteps in the hall.

If they go into the living room, I won't be able to hear them. 'Stay in the hall,' I whisper. But then I wonder if Moira will want to see Grace's bedroom; if she'll spot me standing up here, by the open door. I look wildly around the study for a hiding place and end up standing by the desk, thinking that I can duck behind it if I hear footsteps on the stairs. Then I hear them go towards the kitchen with Mum offering a cup of tea.

Weak with relief, I thump into the desk chair which spins as I collapse, leaving me facing the bookshelves and boxes of Dad's paperwork. The boxes are organised by year and I don't know why – perhaps because I'm stuck in here until Moira leaves and I've been craving more connection with Dad – but I decide to get one of them down. The box for 1998 has an unevenness in the tape holding it closed and a rip in the cardboard, as if it's been opened and closed more than once. That one then.

I use my nail to break the seal on the box and open it.

I find financial records. Kept because the taxman might one day request back-dated evidence. Invoices, receipts and, on top, a folder, with all the transactions laid out: incoming, outgoing, totals.

I flick through the folder, not because I expect to find anything, but because I can picture Dad typing all of this into an Excel spreadsheet, his spiky signature on each page and it feels, somehow, comforting. Then I spot an inconsistency.

Even with my mind on the distant sound of my daughter crying in the kitchen, once I find the first anomaly, I am on the lookout for more. The incoming and outgoing columns don't make sense. They look like they should but they don't. Expenses claims are doubled up, floats go out and never come back in, money is paid into operations that appear to have no equivalent entry for services rendered.

Was Dad a *crook*?

Before my world can crash around my ears, I open a drawer to find a notebook, with Mum's passwords carefully listed inside the front cover. There's a pencil beside it and I tear out a blank page to go over the figures again, fingers flying.

Twenty thousand pounds. In 1998, Dad took twenty thousand pounds from the business and hid it. It wasn't difficult to find once you knew where to look, but if you were honest every other year and you were willing to take the risk, it might well slide past the inland revenue.

Desperate to know the extent of his criminality, I take down the boxes for 1997 and 1999. There are no irregularities. What would Dad have needed twenty thousand pounds for in 1998?

I try to think back, but I was six in that year and my memory is full of holes. There was no way I'd be able to remember a financial problem from back then, even if Mum and Dad had talked about it in front of me.

I go back to the box and search for a missing receipt or invoice. Anything to account for the twenty thousand.

Instead of an invoice, at the bottom of the box I find a book: it's thin, only thirty or so pages long. There's a picture of a flower on the front, in primary red and green and the title is *I am the Seed*. I slip it into the pocket of my dressing gown and forget about it immediately at the sight of an unsealed envelope tucked into the bottom flap. Is this the answer?

The envelope contains pictures.

At first, I simply don't understand. The first one in the stack is a picture of a child sitting on a swing in the front garden of a house. It isn't our house, but it *is* familiar. Then I realise why; I've been there. This is Grant Dobson's garden. Grant Dobson's house. This is a photograph of Frances Dobson.

I gasp and drop the pictures onto the desk.

I can't take my eyes from hers. The little girl is obviously happy. Her face is turned towards the sun and her legs are straight out in front of her, hair fluttering out of its band. The photo has been taken from a distance, zoomed in, a little blurry.

I reach out with nerveless fingers, fanning out the haphazard heap to find more photographs of Frances. In one she's walking down the street, holding Betsie Dobson's hand. I know it's her because she looks like me.

In another, taken through the window of the kitchen, Grant Dobson is obviously yelling. I pick through them, shock making me slow. There's a picture of a lorry: Grant Dobson climbing out of the cab. A shot of Betsie weeding the front garden. Frances is colouring in beside her.

In some of the shots the weather is sunny, in others it's overcast, gloomy. Frances is wearing a different outfit in each image. These photos weren't taken in a single day but over days, weeks even. This family was *watched*.

I don't know why Dad has these photos. What could he possibly have to do with Frances Dobson?

A tiny part of me screams that I know the answer but I thrust it away; make it howl into a void. With fingers that shake, I tuck the photos back in the envelope and put it into the pocket of my dressing gown with the book.

Moments later I hear voices in the hall and pad towards the door.

'Grace seems to be doing well, Mrs Monahan. I am concerned about Bridget though. There is no answer at the flat and our office hasn't been able to get in touch with her or Tom. We need to set up a child protection plan and ensure that the family is supported going forward.' She sounds exasperated. She should be. Naomi had told me to call and I hadn't.

'I'll let her know.' Mum's voice is tight.

'Thank you very much. Goodbye, Mrs Monahan. I'm sure I'll see you again soon.'

The door closes and my heart pounds. I dump the financial records back into the box and shut the lid. Then I shove it back into its place on the shelf.

I'm not ready to confront Mum, not until I've had time to think about what this all means. I flee to my room, grateful for the muffling effect of the deep carpet. Then I stand in the doorway, waiting.

Chapter 27

When Mum comes up, she doesn't have Grace with her. She's left her in the kitchen again. She does have a cup of tea though.

'You didn't want me to see the social worker.'

Mum hands me a cup of tea. 'Honestly, darling, I was worried. I wasn't sure if you were meant to be here or not. I didn't want to get in trouble.' She walks past me and sits on my bed. 'Drink your tea.'

I take a sip, then put the mug on the dresser and turn to her. 'I want to see Grace.' I lurch for the door but I move too fast and have to hold my head until it stops spinning. When I look back up Mum is blocking my exit.

She folds her arms. 'I'm trying to sort out Grace's behaviour for *your* benefit, you know. You're acting like I'm some kind of . . . wicked witch.' She looks hurt and I flinch. 'She's already sleeping better, haven't you noticed? We need to limit her time with you until she's learned how to conduct herself.'

'I—'

'You're not good for her at the moment.' Mum looks at me sympathetically. 'And you're still not well.

Why don't you have your tea and a nap? I'm about to put Grace down anyway.'

'I c-can't.' My voice quivers. How can I be bad for Grace? 'I have to go home and fetch some things; my medication and my phone. And I need to call Tom.'

Mum glances at me and then away. 'I don't think that's a good idea.'

'What? Going home?'

'Speaking to Tom.' Mum's eyes slide away again. 'I didn't want to tell you this right now, I didn't think you were up to knowing.'

'Tell me what?'

Mum gives a kind of huff, still blocking my way out of the door. 'You should sit down.'

'I don't want to sit down.'

'Don't be difficult.' She taps her fingers against the doorframe.

Grace has been quiet for a long time now. I ache to go and see her but my heart bangs against my chest. I've got a lot to think about, my head is spinning. Maybe it isn't the right time. I remember holding her so tightly that she cried, and I sit.

The mattress creaks as Mum sits beside me. 'There's no easy way to tell you this,' she says. 'Tom is having an affair.'

I jerk. 'What?'

'An affair.' Mum says as if I'm slow. 'He's seeing another woman.'

'No! I mean . . . he wouldn't do that.'

But then I start thinking. I think about how I've been hardly letting him touch me for months, how

335

dreadful I look now, how terrible it must be to be married to someone as miserable as I've been, and how he has endless hours alone at home. So much time to do his own thing. And then there're the phone calls I've seen him make. The paper that fell out of the pram. The top in the laundry that isn't mine.

Mum is still talking. 'I tried to warn you, Bridget. I encouraged you to spend time with him.'

'Y-you did.' My mind is racing. She was right to make me sit down. Then I blink. 'But . . . how do you . . .?'

'How do I know?' Mum shakes her head. 'It's embarrassing to say. But I followed him.'

'You what?' I stare at her.

'As soon as you started to let yourself go, I knew. A man like that won't hang around for long.'

'A man like that . . .' Again, I think of Tom and try to fit my head around the idea of him betraying me. It's a shirt that doesn't fit, I can't make it go over all of his edges. 'He loves me.'

'Maybe.' Mum shrugs. 'But men have needs.'

'I think . . . no. You must be wrong.'

'You want the evidence?' Mum tilts her head.

'Evid—'

'Photographs.' She stands. 'I can fetch them for you.'

More photographs. There are photographs in my pocket heavy as death, two under the windowsill, more in Gillian's office. I feel as if I might vanish under the weight of old images and their secrets.

I nod my head.

'Don't move.' She stands, takes the mug from the dresser and presses it into my cold hands. 'Drink your tea.'

I sit there and then I drink my tea, because otherwise I'll think and I can't bear it.

When she comes back in, I'm holding the empty mug, letting the heated ceramic warm my hands. She takes it from me and replaces it with two pictures. One is recent, the other is not. I can't bear to look at the recent one yet, so I focus on the other.

I can date it almost exactly. It can't have been taken long after we first met. Tom is wearing a running jersey that was ruined during a pub crawl on our third date. He's looking sideways, laughing at something someone is saying, and his arm is around a girl I recognise. Tom's ex-girlfriend. Trisha, that was her name.

'That's the girl he was with when he started going out with you,' Mum says.

I can't take my eyes from Tom. He looks so young and happy. Where was I when this was taken?

'After you told me about him, I had him checked out.'

'You didn't tell me.'

'You wouldn't listen.' Mum sighs. 'You'd left home and wanted to make your own mistakes. You told me to leave you alone.'

'I . . .' My fingers flex as if to crumple the picture, but Mum takes it from me before I can ruin it.

'Once a cheater . . .'

'Always a cheater,' I whisper. The second photo shows Tom in a park. For a moment I don't recognise the person he is with and then . . . I do. I take back the first photo and hold them together.

Mum nods. 'It's the same girl.'

In the picture they're intimate. They aren't kissing, but it's like the photo of Gillian and Mum's sister, you can just tell. They hold their heads together, his arm is on her back, her hand delicate on Grace's pram. Anyone walking past would have thought she was the mum.

A scream builds in my throat.

'Don't. You'll upset Grace.' Mum takes the pictures from me and tucks them into the pocket of her skirt.

I taste salt. I don't know if I'm grieving or furious.

Mum lifts my feet and pushes me back against my bed. She pulls the duvet over me, tucking me in as if I'm nine again. She kisses my forehead. 'Sleep it off, Bridget. We'll be here when you wake up.'

I close my eyes so that I don't have to look at her and find that sleep is lingering beneath the surface of my heartache, as if I'm too weak to sustain the anguish for long. It overtakes me like a wave and I pass out, sobbing into my pillow.

Frances Dobson is sitting on her swing: back and forth, back and forth. Her legs pump, making her fly higher and higher. She watches me as she swings, never taking her eyes from my face. Then there's a crack as the rope snaps and she's flying. I reach out to catch her but I'm too slow. She smashes into the

338

ground behind me, or I think she does, but she doesn't make a sound. I whip around, scared of what I might see. She isn't alone. She's standing to the left of a row of girls, all holding hands. There's Frances, then the missing girl from the station, then Mum's sister. All girls who have vanished.

'*Wake up!*'

Frances says it first, then the missing girl, Mum's sister and little Bridget.

'*Wake up!*'

It becomes a kind of chorus. All of them chanting it at me.

'I don't know what you mean.'

'Wake up!' I have no idea how long the words have been hissed at me. I try to open my eyes but they're coffin lids and I struggle to pry them open. Eventually I manage to blink some light in and stare. Aunt Gillian perches on the end of my bed.

Through blurred vision I can tell that she's frantic, her head jerking as she turns to check the door, then back to me, then back to the door again.

'Wake—'

'I–I'm awake.' I struggle to sit, pillows against my back.

Gillian's face is pale under her make-up, her eyes unnaturally bright. She looks almost feverish. Her lips are wet and a little chapped, as if she's been repeatedly licking them. Her glasses gleam gold.

'Gillian . . . are you all right?'

She shakes her head and grips my arm. 'I haven't

much time before Alison realises where I am. Why couldn't you just leave it?' Sharp nails dig into my skin and I try to pull away. 'I tried to help you, to make you forget. I even tried to scare you straight. I had my niece follow you in the van, threaten you, but you wouldn't stop, would you?' She takes off her glasses and rubs her eyes. Then she puts them back on. 'There isn't time to explain but you have to drop all this stuff about kidnappings. And you have to get out of here. Take Grace and get out.'

'What do you—?'

'Gillian, are you up there?'

Gillian's hand hits my chest as she shoves me back down, my dressing gown pocket crumples beneath me and I remember the book and envelope. I'm crushing them. 'You're asleep,' she hisses. Then she leaps to her feet and goes to the door.

She takes a breath, opens it and calls out. 'I was just checking on Bridget, Alison. She's fast asleep.'

'Still?' Mum's voice comes closer.

'Well, you gave her quite a shock, and in combination with—'

'Yes, all right.' Mum is in the room now and I can't lie still. I don't know what's going on, but I blink my eyes open as if I'm just waking.

'Mum?'

'Hello, dear. How are you feeling?'

'Aunt Gillian?'

Mum stands by the bed, her shadow lying over me. 'After what I told you about Tom, I thought a therapy session might help. What do you say?'

'Thank you.' I frown at Gillian. 'I think that would be a good idea.'

'We'll let you get up and dressed.' Mum gestures to my dressing gown and I nod. When I glance up again, they're leaving.

For a long time I just sit there, trying to make sense of what I just heard. *Had* I heard it, or had I been dreaming still?

I even had my niece follow you in the van. That's what Gillian said: her *niece*. I think back to the portrait in her office and my fuzzy mind finally makes the connection that I'd been struggling for. The woman on the train, the blonde woman. She was Gillian's niece. How long had she been following me? And why would she do it? Why would either of them do it? *Get out*, she'd said. *Take Grace and get out.*

Why? I clutch my temples, a headache forming.

Slowly I move around the room, looking for something to wear. There's a long, loose dress in the wardrobe with large pockets. It stretches around me, then clings. I catch sight of myself in the mirror and quickly look away. It's as if the old version of myself is trying to suffocate me, overlaying her appearance on mine, her behaviour. I slide the book and envelope into my left-hand pocket.

Mum will expect hair and make-up and so I go to the dresser. It takes a few minutes before I'm presentable. The bruise is fading now and I hardly need any foundation to cover it. I desperately need to wash my hair. Perhaps a shower after I've seen Grace again.

341

Finally, I hang the dressing gown on the back of the door and head to the stairs, my footsteps swallowed by silence.

As I descend: *When you love what you have, you have all you need; A lie hurts forever; A job worth doing is worth doing well; Manners cost nothing; Honour thy father and thy mother; Home is where the heart is.* I hear voices, edged with argument. They're in the living room, so I creep to the alcove outside and listen.

'You have to stop, Alison!'

'You don't know what you're talking about.'

'It isn't healthy.' Gillian is pleading. I press my hands under my armpits, abruptly afraid.

'You can't do it again. Grace is a baby. Do you even know how much you've given her? It's not for long-term use. Look at Bridget's hallucinations, her memory problems.'

I straighten. What is Mum giving to Grace?

'That was dissociative amnesia,' Mum snaps. 'She had a trauma.'

'At first. But later?'

'It was good that she forgot where she came from,' Mum's voice is a low hiss. 'I was helping her.'

'And now?'

'She remembered the kidnapping!' Mum's voice rises again. 'She has to forget it. She has to learn how to behave again. She was going to leave me, Gillian, take Grace and move away. Letting her go to university . . . that was my mistake, allowing all those outside influences. That medication she was taking. I won't make the same mistake with Grace. I'll home-school her all the way through this time and I won't allow univer—'

'You can't expect her to stay here forever, Alison.' Gillian's voice is calm, reasonable.

'Why not?' Mum again. 'Grace will have everything she could possibly want. I've learned from my mistakes. She'll be the perfect daughter.'

'But she isn't *your* daughter,' I whisper.

'There isn't such a thing,' Gillian says.

Mum does not reply.

'I understand.' Gillian says. 'I know why you crave perfection, after what happened to Abigail—'

'We don't *know* what happened to Abigail.' Mum's voice is oddly small and I lean closer. *Who is Abigail?*

'Yes. We do. It's why I've always done my best to help you. Abi wanted me to look after you. And you and I . . . you know how I feel. But Abi wouldn't want this.'

'So, you won't refill the ketamine?'

'Not if you're giving it to the baby. I can't.'

Ketamine? My head reels. ketamine. Isn't that a date rape drug? Is that why Grace has been so quiet, sleeping so well? And me? I thought my tiredness, my dizziness was withdrawal from the Fluoxetine but have I been taking *ketamine*? How? When? Gillian is right, I have to get Grace and go.

Then I hear Grace cry and I realise that she's in the living room with Mum and Gillian.

'Aren't you going to pick her up?' Gillian asks.

'You sound like Bridget! She's learning to self-soothe.'

Mum is moving across the room. 'Look at the dolly,' she says. 'Isn't she a nice dolly?'

I clench my fists.

'Alison, I've said it before but now I really must insist. You need therapy. You have to deal with what happened to Abi . . . and Bridget.'

'Bridget is fine.' Mum's voice gets fainter; she's moved across the room. I step closer.

'Bridget is dead.' Gillian says gently. 'She's dead, Alison and you have to deal with that.'

I reel. What Gillian is saying doesn't make any sense. I touch my face, part of me wondering if she's right, wondering if I'm dead. If I've always been dead. I want to scream but I bite my lip until I taste blood.

'Shut up!' Mum is vicious now. 'You're in this as deep as I am. You want to stop *now*?'

'Yes.' Gillian half-sobs. 'We have to stop some time, Alison. Be sensible. You're too old to start again with a baby—'

'Don't be ridiculous.'

'Grace's sleeping patterns are normal for a child her age,' Gillian says.

'No! All that crying, it's bad behaviour. Attention seeking.' Mum raises her voice again and I start to back away. 'Look, she's stopped already and she's falling asleep. It's working. Let me get you a drink, Gillian. Then we can talk this through sensibly.'

I have to call someone: it's the only way I can see out of this. I want to speak to Naomi Shaw but I can't recall her details. Without my mobile, the only number I know for sure is Tom's. Fury unfurls at the thought of him. But, if nothing else, Tom loves Grace. He'd go out of his mind if he knew that Mum was drugging her.

There's a landline in the hallway. I race for the handset and pick it up. There's no dial tone. I stare at it, follow it to the wall The cable is plugged in, so why isn't it working?

I consider getting in my car and seeking help that way. But I don't want to leave Grace.

I stand there, phone in hand, I don't know how long for. I blank out. When I open my eyes again at the sound of a closing door, the shadows in the hallway have moved. Mum stands in front of me, rubbing her hands on her slacks. She looks at the phone in my hand. 'What are you doing, Bridget?'

'I–I thought I'd ring Tom.' I grip the handset more tightly.

Mum shakes her head. 'You should have asked; the line is out. An engineer will be coming in a few days.'

I clear my throat. My instinct to confront her is at war with fear of what she'll do if I say anything. She has Grace. 'What's wrong with it?'

'If I knew that, I wouldn't need an engineer.' Mum takes the phone from me and puts it carefully back in place.

'Is . . .' I blink heavily. 'Is Aunt Gillian ready for our therapy session?'

Mum frowns at me. 'Aunt Gillian?'

'Yes, you said . . .'

She tilts her head at me. 'We aren't seeing Aunt

Gillian today. Your sessions are Mondays and Thursdays, remember?'

'But . . . she was here. You said—'

'*I* said?' Mum laughs. 'You've been asleep all afternoon, darling, this is the first time I've seen you since I popped you into bed. It isn't a bad idea though, after what I told you about Tom.'

'But . . . she was here.'

'Who? Gillian?' Mum touches my arm. 'Darling, I'm worried about you. I think you must have had a bad dream. Is that what you think has happened – you've had a bad dream?'

'But . . . I thought I heard . . . weren't you in the living room?' My head hurts.

'That medication must still be affecting you, I told you not to take it. Grace and I have been watching some television. Now she's fast asleep.' Mum takes my arm. 'Are you all right? You don't look very well.'

'Can I see Grace?'

'You've had a nasty shock and you don't look very well. How about after tea?'

'After tea?'

'Yes, in a couple of hours. You could go and lie back down or you could stitch a new sampler. Remember how you used to enjoy those?'

I look at the frames on the walls: *A Lie Hurts Forever.*

Suddenly I think of Dad's study. There's a laptop on the desk. I can email Tom. He'll know what to do.

'Maybe I'll do some work,' I say, backing towards the stairs.

'Work?' Mum blinks. 'You're in no condition to work. I have plenty of money, Bridget. Your father's life insurance . . . you don't need to worry about work. It's not like it was when you were living with Tom.'

'Right.' I clear my dry throat. 'I'll lie down then. I don't feel well.' I put a hand on the bannister and start upwards. 'Where will you and Grace be?'

'In the garden.' Mum smiles. 'I have a flower bed to dig. She can watch me.'

I feel for my initials with shaking fingers and press the pad of my thumb into the roughened wood, as if trying to remind myself who I am. Had I really dreamed everything? I must have. Aunt Gillian saying I was dead. That was the stuff of nightmares, wasn't it?

'You *are* going to behave, aren't you?' Mum says. 'You know how I feel about bad behaviour in my house.'

Chapter 28

I head back up the stairs, legs trembling. Again, I go to my room and open and close the door. Then I stand on the landing, listening. After a few minutes, I hear the kitchen door open and close. Mum has taken Grace into the garden.

I slip inside the study.

The laptop starts quickly. I remove the notebook containing Mum's passwords from the top drawer. I hesitate when I see that she uses Grace's birthday, then I type it in.

The screen opens onto the last thing Mum was working on: a Word document. I stare at with a complete lack of comprehension. It's a letter to Tom.

Tom,
I'm leaving you. It isn't you, it's me.

Grace is better with Mum. She raised me right and she'll raise her right too. Leave her where she is and move on. I'll fight you if you try to get her back.

I know you can meet someone else and be

348

happy. By the time you read this I'll have left the country. Don't try to find me.

I'll always love you but we aren't meant to be together.
Bridget

I stare at my name at the bottom and for a moment I wonder if wrote it and forgot, like I've been forgetting other things, but I wouldn't have; I'd *never* have said Mum could keep Grace.

I don't know if she's already sent this. I have to contact Tom. I launch Internet Explorer, planning to use my Gmail but there's no connection. The line really is down.

I want to cry but what would be the point?

I lean back in the chair trying to think clearly. The mist over my brain is terrifying and I want, almost as much as anything else, to find out the side-effects of taking ketamine. When did she dose me? And why? I can't get on the Internet so there's no way to find out.

There's nothing else I can do here. My eye falls on the still open notebook and the list of passwords. The oldest is at the top titled: *Government Gateway*.

A sudden thought surprises me. This is Mum's notebook. Why would she need a *Government Gateway* password? The obvious answer is for filing tax returns, but she closed the business just after Dad died.

A sudden memory surprises me. I'm standing in the study doorway and I'm holding a Barbie, I'm looking in, watching Mum work. Dad grips my shoulder and I look up.

'Don't disturb your mum while she's doing the finances.'

'Finances?' I frown.

'Money stuff.' Dad tickles me. 'Boring money stuff.'

Mum barely looks up. 'Take her away, Edward. I need to finish this.'

The book in my pocket is digging into my thigh and I pull it out. It's bent now, a crease through the centre of the bright cover. I open it to the first page.

I am the Seed:
poems by children aged five to thirteen.

These are the winning entrants of the national poetry competition run by Faber and Faber Books on behalf of Greenways Garden Centres.

I find the contents page with trembling hands and, before I even locate the name, I know what I'm going to see: *You Found Me*, by Frances Dobson, Age 6.

Her poem is on page twelve.

Deep in the earth you dig.
You make a hole with strong fingers. You drop me in.
You give me water and sunlight
Then I grow. I show you my petals.
How did you do it?
You found me.

'You found me,' I whisper. Beside the poem is a picture of a smiling Frances Dobson. And beside the image clearly written in Mum's neat copperplate writing, which is nothing like Dad's spiky scrawl, two words:

This one.

Something clicks in my mind like a light has gone on. I blink in its illumination and it's lucky I'm sitting down. *Mum picked Frances out.* From a book. Like it was a goddamn catalogue.

I look at the boxes of invoices and receipts. The ones that *Mum* had filled. Dad hated doing the finances. It wasn't him who had taken twenty thousand, it was *Mum*. She had Frances Dobson watched. Then she had her taken. But why?

I look at the year on the box: 1998. I was six then, the same age that Frances was when she vanished. I look like Betsie Dobson, I . . .

'I'm Frances Dobson,' I whisper. The sound of the name strikes something inside me. '*Frankie and Dobbie.*' I clench my fists. 'I never forgot. It was always there!'

Bile leaps into my throat and I swallow it back. I can't throw up in here, or she'll know where I've been. I wrap my arms around my chest, suddenly freezing, and the serpent in my belly uncoils. It rises, showing its teeth and this time I don't know if I can stop the rage from taking me over.

The poetry book goes back in my pocket with the photographs. I'll need them to show Naomi Shaw. Now I have to get Grace; we're leaving.

Footsteps stifled by the carpet, I stamp downstairs: *When you love what you have, you have all you need; A lie hurts forever.* I hesitate at that one. Then I take it from the wall. Now it is in my hands I can feel the ghost of the needle, the way I frantically stabbed the material desperately trying to get it finished, hurting myself over and over again so that she would speak to me. She has lied to me my whole life. I hurl it away from me and the frame hits the bannister. Glass smashes and I keep going. *A job worth doing is worth doing well; Manners cost nothing; Honour thy father and thy mother; Home is where the heart is.*

I stumble past the painting of Mum and her parents and into the kitchen. Then I pause. Mum keeps her keys on hooks in the pantry and I'll need the key to the padlock on the front door. I open the pantry door. There are two keys hanging there. One is my car key, and I snatch it gratefully. I grab the other and put both in my pocket. We're getting out.

I burst into the garden. Autumn sun shines on the patio flagstones and the lawn is perfectly green. Flowers are regimented into beds: one of roses, smelling of Turkish Delight, one of azalea, one of fuchsias just in flower, their pink and purple heads nodding at me as if to say 'where have you been?'

Grace is asleep on a large cushion with a blanket over her. The shadow of the house falls over her face and there's a half empty bottle of milk beside her. There's no way she should be asleep at this time of day, no way.

Gillian said that Grace was being drugged. But Mum said Gillian wasn't there and there's no sign of her now so how could I have heard her say so? Dizzily, I run to Grace and pick her up. She flops loosely in my arms. That's wrong: she should have stirred, made a sound, resettled. In my head I start to scream.

'Grace!' I want to shake her awake but you can't shake a baby. I don't know what to do. Cold water maybe. I'll need to take her to the kitchen.

'What do you think you're doing? You'll wake her.' Mum turns around. She's digging a flower bed on the other side of the garden and the spade in her hands is heavy with mud.

'Wake Grace?' I cry. 'Wake Grace? Look at her. She's not asleep, she's unconscious! What have you done?' Drool slips from my daughter's open lips.

'Don't be ridiculous, she's just very tired. It's the fresh air.' Mum walks towards me, holding the spade. 'You shouldn't be here, I sent you to your room.'

'I'm not a child.' I carry Grace towards the kitchen, deeper into the shadow cast by the house. 'You can't just send me to my room.'

'My house, my rules,' Mum says. She hefts the spade.

'I know what you did.' The door is right behind me but I don't go through it, not yet. Grace is hot against me, her breath wet on my collarbone, her limbs limp. 'I've got proof. You took me from the Dobsons. *I'm* Frances Dobson!'

'Don't be absurd, Bridget.' Mum tilts her head to one side. 'You're being very badly behaved. Good behaviour . . .'

'Is a sign of dignity.' My response is automatic and I shake my head to clear it. 'Fuck good behaviour.'

Mum gasps. '*Bridget!*'

'I've got proof. I'm taking Grace and going to the police.'

'Take her from here and social services may never let you see her again.' Mum looks almost sorry.

'You're drugging her!' I sob. 'I heard Aunt Gillian – ketamine.'

'Hallucinations.' Mum says calmly. 'You can't have heard Gillian saying anything because she was never here. It's just like when you were on the train. You're hearing things as well as seeing things.'

'I didn't—' I bite back my denial, shift Grace so I'm holding her with one arm, and pull the poetry book from my pocket. 'I'm not hallucinating *this*.'

Mum freezes. 'Where did you get that? Give it to me.'

I slip it back in my pocket. '*This one*, it says. In *your* handwriting. You *chose* me.'

'You think the police will believe anything you say? After lying about the kidnapped girl.'

'I wasn't lying, Mum!' To my relief, Grace stirs slightly in my arms.

Mum sighs and smooths one hand over her slacks. There's a smudge on one knee, red in the sunlight, and she frowns at it. Then she meets my gaze again and leans on her spade. 'You didn't *see* a kidnapping, Bridget.'

As I open my mouth to object, she keeps speaking.

'You *remembered* one.' She shakes her head. 'It was those drugs you were on, the anti-depressants, they started to bring it all back.'

'I . . .' I stop, I think, picturing the girl being taken

354

from the station, wearing her blazer and her lace-trimmed socks. All the little details I couldn't have seen. I think of her face, there and gone in a moment. The same face as the one in the photograph: *this one*.

'Frances Dobson,' I whisper.

You found me.

There *was* no little girl to find. I'd almost lost my daughter, all for a child who didn't even exist.

'Oh God,' I whisper. 'Grace!'

'Stop being melodramatic.' Mum rolls her eyes. 'Growing up, you had everything you wanted. You think you'd have had the same if I'd left you with the Dobsons?' She laughed. 'I doubt you'd have even been able to go to university.'

'You don't know that.'

'You're the statistician. Think about it: poor, northern, female. Rising tuition fees.' Mum waves her hand airily. 'You'd have been pregnant at sixteen.'

'You really believe that.' I stare. 'You honestly think the remote possibility of being a teen mum is worse than being *kidnapped*?'

Mum sighs. 'The Dobsons were hardly parents of the year, Bridget. Look what happened to them, alcoholics both. You'd rather you'd had alcoholics for parents?'

'They only drank because they *lost me*.'

Mum snorted. 'I was there, Bridget. I watched. Grant drank a lot even then. Betsie forgot you twice, did you know that? She left you outside a post office one day and in a supermarket another. I only didn't take you home with me then because it was so busy.'

She leans closer. 'Think! Would we have been able to take you if she hadn't left you alone? What kind of mother forgets her own child?'

'What kind of mother *drugs* her own child?' I grip Grace tighter, trying to warm myself as chill frosts my heart. She genuinely believes she saved me, gave me a better life. 'How much did Dad know?'

Mum looks at me for a long time and then she shakes her head. 'I told him it was a private adoption.'

'And the twenty thousand?'

'I couldn't do the job alone. I had to pay someone. He worked for your dad, needed the money.'

'Then . . . there's no kidnapping ring. It was all *you*.'

'Kidnapping ring?' Mum's laugh pierces my ears. 'You really have been fantasising, haven't you, Bridget. Did you tell *that* to the police too?' She carries on laughing, pulls the blade of the spade out of the grass and steps nearer. 'Now, put Grace down before you hurt her. You aren't well.'

I shake my head.

Mum is still talking. 'You were a good daughter, Bridget, until you went to university. Until you left me. But it's all right, we're together again now, the three of us. Life is hard, you've learned that now. But I can protect you from it. You don't have to be hurt by Tom anymore. He won't come looking for you, I've fixed that. You don't have to commute and miss Grace. Or work so hard that you're so exhausted you start seeing things. I can look after Grace for you. All you have to do is focus on being the perfect daughter. Once I get rid of your car, no-one will even know you're here. Can't you be *happy with what you have?*'

I sway: her suggestion is hypnotic. Would it be so bad to live in my childhood home, to let myself be looked after, to have no worries? There's a voice inside me saying that I should be grateful, I should be happy, *happy with what I have*. My hold on Grace starts to loosen.

Then another voice:

Deep in the earth you dig.

You make a hole with strong fingers. You drop me in.

'Frances?' I whisper.

You give me water and sunlight

Then I grow. I show you my petals.

Grace stirs again, and I shake my head. 'I'm sorry, Mum. Grace and I are leaving.'

'You can't.' She glides nearer and I see, with a jolt, that she is in striking distance with the spade. I put my hand in my pocket and touch the keys. One for the door, one for the car. It's time to go.

I turn and race for the kitchen. Mum walks slowly behind me, shoes ticking on the patio. She doesn't seem in any hurry to stop me. Relief straightens my shoulders and I reach the front door. The key is in my hand before she's reached the hallway. I look at her standing in front of the picture of her parents. She's still holding the spade in front of her. All four watch me, unmoving, eyes glittering.

I shift Grace again and tilt the padlock, trying to

slide the key in, but it doesn't go. I try again. Then I rattle it desperately. Why won't it *fit*? My knees tremble, I don't feel well, not at all. I can't get us out.

'Bridget, darling!' Mum calls. 'Are you looking for this?'

I turn. The key for the front door is between her fingers.

'Give it to me!' I meant to sound threatening but I'm pleading. Mum laughs without humour.

I look again at the key I'm holding. It's old. I should have known the second I saw it that it isn't for the front door but, then, what *is* it for?

'Give Grace to me.' The spade swings at Mum's side, almost idly. I look around, frantic. How do we get out? The door is locked, the windows are locked and triple glazed, I can't smash them. There's a wall around the back garden that I have no way of climbing. I need space to think, somewhere Mum can't reach me.

There's a door under the stairs: the cellar door. I look at the key in my hand . This has to be the cellar key; it can't be anything else. I can lock the door behind me, wake Grace, take some time to *plan*.

But I'm not allowed in the cellar.

You make a hole with strong fingers.

'All right,' I whisper. I'm speaking to Frances, but Mum doesn't know that.

'Good girl,' she says, leaning the spade on the wall beside her, holding her arms out for Grace.

I walk towards her, Grace sagging over one arm. The cellar door is halfway between us. I grip the key.

When I reach the door, I stop and Mum sighs. 'Faster, Bridget, don't be difficult.'

Moving fast, just as ordered, I whip around and slide the key into the lock. It turns smoothly and the door opens.

'*You bad girl* – don't you dare!' Mum shrieks. The tone in her voice terrifies me and I look up. She's grabbing the spade again. I gasp and leap through the door. There is a short staircase in front of me. I hold onto Grace tightly, snatch the key from the lock and slam the door behind me, as fast I can. The door shudders as Mum hits the other side. Gasping I turn the key and stumble backwards, leaving it in the lock.

'Come out of there, Bridget,' Mum screams. 'You aren't permitted. It's forbidden. You come out of there, *right now*!'

My heels rock on the top stair and I grab the rail just in time to arrest our fall. There's a light switch beside me. I flick it on and the cellar floods with light.

Chapter 29

I walk down the stairs on shaking legs, holding Grace tightly. She's still frightening me with her limp stillness. At the bottom of the steps there's an open space containing a desk and two doors on either side. There is no sign of dangerous work tools, or damp: this isn't the place I'd always pictured.

It seems strange that there're rooms in Mum's house that I didn't know existed, like I've wandered into an M. C. Escher drawing; everything feels surreal. Of course, that might be the fluoxetine withdrawal or the effects of the ketamine.

Behind me there's a crash, as Mum hits the door with the spade. 'Come out of there, Bridget.' Mum yells. 'Come out, right now!'

I run to the desk, wobbling under Grace's weight, which seems to be increasing, wondering if there might be something in there that can help us. The top drawer is slightly open and there, lying on top of a pile of old letters, next to a jiffy bag of window keys, is my mobile phone. For a few beats I just stare at it, barely able to believe it's here. Then I snatch it up.

There's only two per cent battery but there are

bars; I have a signal. I turn and sit on the desk, balancing Grace on my knee, and without even thinking, I call Tom.

As the phone starts to ring, I realise I should have rung Naomi Shaw. I pull the phone from my ear and check, but even just making the call has used up precious battery life: one per cent left.

With every trill, I'm terrified that the battery will die. 'Answer it. Answer it.' I chant. If Tom has received a copy of Mum's letter he may not. I look at Grace, her face unnaturally pale under the fluorescent light. 'God, baby, what if Daddy doesn't answer?'

'Bridget?' His voice comes through muted, as though the cellar walls are muffling the signal.

'Tom!' I sob into the handset. 'Tom, you have to listen.'

'Where are you? The woman from Social Services says you haven't called her – what's—'

'Shut *up*, Tom,' I scream. 'You have to help us. She's out of control, she's drugging me. Grace too. I'm not me, Tom, I'm Frances Dobson. You have to call the police, call Naomi Shaw. She's . . . are you listening to me?' I pull the phone from my ear. It's dead. I don't know how much he heard, if anything. '*Shit!*'

Grace opens her eyes, then they drop closed again as if they're too heavy for her.

The cellar door shudders and wood splinters. I run for the nearest room.

The door has a simple slide bolt on the outside, as if it was used to keep someone or something in. It isn't locked. I step inside and freeze.

I've never been in the cellar and yet I know this room. There's a bed in one corner, a simple frame with a mattress, and there's an old-fashioned projector facing one wall. It's linked up to an old video player. I stagger across the room, head pounding. Outside Mum is still hammering on the door. I don't know how long we have before it breaks.

I know I should be trying to get us out but it's as if I'm hypnotised. I turn on the projector and press play.

A picture appears on the wall in front of me: it's the kitchen upstairs but the walls are a different colour. This is an old film. After a moment, Mum walks into view. She is younger here, but just as well put together as always. She goes to the oven and removes a roast chicken. Then she turns and talks to someone out of shot. There is no sound, only picture. I find myself unable to tear my eyes away as she puts the roast on the side and starts to carve.

Over the roaring in my ears, I realise that I'm hearing a soft voice, a woman's voice: Aunt Gillian. She is telling me about this wonderful woman, how delicious her cooking is, how clean she keeps her house, what an excellent wife she is, how much she wants me to come and live with her.

The movie keeps going and so does the insidious voice. My heart skips as Dad appears, sits down and eats. The voice doesn't mention him and he seems unaware of the camera. The two of them are talking but I can't tell what they're saying. I find myself leaning forward, trying to lip-read.

In the movie they clear the table as Aunt Gillian's low voice, just on the cusp of hearing, talks about what wonderful people they are.

I don't know how much time has gone by. My eyes are dry, as if I haven't blinked for a long time. A loud crash sounds from the door at the top of the stairs and Grace wakes, screaming. I grab her, remembering the lock on the outside of this door. We can't be trapped in here.

'*Bridget!*'

Grace wails, a thin and reedy sound, and clutches at me. I rush from the room and look up. The door above us has a hole in it, large enough for Mum to slip her hand through. I shouldn't have left the key in the lock. She puts her face against the gap and I freeze.

'You're being *very* badly behaved, Bridget! And you're upsetting Grace, I can hear her crying.'

And then I hear something else. Under Mum's fury is the sound of someone pounding on the front door. A voice yells for an answer. It sounds like Tom, but he's in Chesterfield, so I know I must be hallucinating again. I look at the door to the other room at the same time Mum does.

'Don't you *dare.*' Her face vanishes and her hand appears, groping for the lock. 'You stay right there and wait for your punishment, you *bad girl.*'

I plunge through the other door and slam it behind us, leaning against it with all my weight.

It's dark in here, so I reach sideways with one hand, looking for a light switch. I don't find it with my left, so I switch Grace to my other side. 'It's all right, I'm going to get us out of here. Everything's okay, Mummy loves you,' I'm murmuring desperately, trying to keep my baby focused on my words rather than the cold terror that is streaming from me. I find the panel and turn on the light.

There are two things in the room: a cupboard and the end of the coal chute.

'We have a coal chute.' I tell Grace. 'Hang on.' I'd like to put her down at my feet so I can open it up, but she clutches at me with hysterical strength and I can't let her go. I let her cling to my neck as I unlatch the wide door and look up. My heart sinks. I can't climb up the chute. It's too high, too steep.

But there's a cupboard in the room. If I drag it over here, I could climb on it, maybe get high enough to reach the other end. 'Grace, I have to put you down, just for a second.' She snuffles miserably into my ear and then her body jerks. Her legs curl and I stiffen as she vomits over my shoulder, then releases an ear-piercing shriek.

Warm sick trickles down my spine and spatters on the floor behind me. I rub her back. I have to get her to a hospital. Then I hear it again: Tom's voice. This time it's coming from the other end of the coal chute. 'Bridget! Are you down there? I can hear Grace. Can you hear me?'

'Tom!' I scream his name and the top end of the coal chute slams open, letting in a shaft of dusty light.

'I can't get to you.' Tom looks desperate. 'It's too small. Can you climb to me?' I shake my head. Now that light is flooding the shaft I can see that there's no way I can get up there. But I *might* be able to pass Grace up to him.

I'll have to put her down. I harden my heart and place her protesting little body on the floor where Tom can see her. 'There's Daddy, look.' I take her chin and turn her face so that she can see him, and, for a blessed moment, she falls silent.

But that means I can hear Mum. She's on the stairs, shoes clattering on the treads.

I run to the cupboard and tilt it sideways. It's heavy, there's something in it. I groan as I drag it, creaking across the floor.

The door to the room bursts open. 'Bridget, no.' Mum lunges for me, spade raised. I leap backwards and the spade hits the floor where I'd been standing. At the same time, the cupboard hits the ground. The door bursts open and Mum screams as if she's been stabbed.

Something falls out of the cupboard and Mum staggers backwards. At first, I don't get it. What has scared her so badly?

It's a life-size doll of some sort, wearing a frilly mauve dress, identical to the one Grace is wearing. Perhaps it's a dressmaker's dummy. I tilt my head, trying to understand. And then I see it. This is not a doll.

'Bridget,' Mum gasps and I realise that she isn't speaking to *me*.

'What's your name?'

'F–Frances.'

'No. That's not your name.'

'It is!'

The woman pulls the little girl over her knee and pushes her new frilly dress to one side. She slaps the back of her legs. The little girl is shocked. The woman hasn't smacked her for a long time. She's been good.

'What's your name?'

'I–it's Frances.' Tears pour down her face as the woman hits her again and she struggles not to cry out.

'What's your name.'

'F . . .' She stops and raises her tear-stained face. 'I don't know what you want me to say.' She sobs out loud this time.

To her relief, the woman lifts her off her knee, adjusts her gold-rimmed glasses and looks into her face. 'Well, why didn't you just tell me so? What a silly girl, to not know your own name.' The woman strokes her hair and she leans into her touch, grateful that she isn't hitting her anymore.

'Would you like to know your name?'

'Y . . . yes?'

'Well, do you, or don't you?'

'Yes, please.'

'Better.' The woman smiles at her and she blinks. 'Your real name is Bridget. Bridget Monahan. Isn't that nice?'

The girl hesitates. She doesn't really like this new name. 'I . . .'

'Yes?' The woman tilts her head.

'Y–yes.'

'So, what's your name?'

'It's Bridget,' the little girl gasps. 'M–my name is Bridget.'

'Good girl.' The woman sighs. 'Don't worry, Bridget, you won't remember any of this.' She looks away. 'Only in your nightmares, perhaps.'

Chapter 30

Mum is no longer paying me any attention. I check on Grace who hasn't moved, then I edge closer. Mum is flat against the back wall, her eyes pinned to the tiny corpse. I look between them. The mummified child has fallen from the cupboard onto her side. Before she was placed inside, her hair was carefully twisted into ringlets. She is wearing white tights and gloves. Her feet are in shiny black shoes. Her skin is dust, peeling from her skull, her eyes sunken, her teeth bare. A small pink teddy has fallen out of the cupboard as well. It lies beside her on the flagstones.

'*Oh God,*' I whisper.

'Are you all right, Bridge?' Tom shouts. 'What's going on?'

I can't see what killed the little girl. Apart from being horrifyingly desiccated, she looks perfect. 'Who is she? What did you *do*?'

Mum answers without taking her eyes from the dead child. 'That's my daughter. That's Bridget.' Mum still doesn't look at me. 'You don't understand. How could you? You were raised by a good mum, a *perfect* mum, one who loved you.'

I don't dare release the words that swirl on my tongue but the serpent in me slithers. Instead I say. 'And you weren't?'

'We had to behave *perfectly*.' Mum says and now she's walking towards the body. She kneels and I swallow a wave of sickness as she tenderly sits the girl up and rearranges her dress. Her knees are bent. She must have been sitting upright in the cupboard for over twenty years. 'My sister, Abigail . . . Abi, she *never* behaved. They told her she was bringing shame on the family. But she wouldn't listen.'

'By having a relationship with Gillian?' I say softly.

'How do you . . .? Never mind.' Mum neatens Bridget's hair. 'That's better. Yes. She was a . . . a *lesbian*. I heard them fighting. Father wanted her to go on a date with a man he approved of from his work and she refused. They got angry. So angry. They didn't realise I was there. They didn't know I was watching.'

'What did they do to her?' I whisper.

Mum jolts and her eyes meet mine for the briefest of moments before she looks away. She rights the cupboard, lifts Bridget up and places her back inside.

'Father was building the patio,' she says, as she closes the door.

'Your sister is under the patio? You never had her . . . dug up?'

'Now what kind of behaviour would that be?' Mum turns to face me. 'You see, it's important that people behave *right*. It's the only way to be *safe*.'

'And what about Bridget?'

369

'A proper little Madam,' Mum sneers. 'I was only trying to make her behave.'

'You killed her.'

'It was an accident!' Mum jerks. 'Bridget was always talking back, always misbehaving, and she was a liar. Never told the truth if a lie would do. One day she ran off, into the road . . .'

I look at the girl in the cupboard. The life-size doll. 'She was hit by a car?'

Mum shakes her head. 'But I knew then that I'd spoiled her, like you're spoiling Grace.' She looks at me sidelong. 'I knew that if I didn't make her behave, then she would die.'

'Because that's what happened to Abi?'

'I had to make her *behave*,' Mum says. 'And next time she told a lie I shook her. I shook her and . . . I know you don't shake babies, but she was almost five. She had a seizure and then . . .'

'She died.' I swallow.

'Gillian knew it was an accident. So did Edward. It's why he never called the police – he knew it wouldn't be right if I went to prison.' She sniffed. 'Then I found you, and you looked so much like her, but you were a *good girl*. You were the daughter I was *meant* to have. No-one needed to know that Bridget was gone.'

'But didn't she have friends . . . teachers?'

Mum shrugs. 'We told them she was sick. Too sick to play or go to school. Then I home-schooled you until you were old enough that no-one who ever knew you would be able to tell the difference.'

'And Dad went along with all of this?'

Mum hunches her shoulders. 'I told Edward it was a private adoption. That's what he believed. But when you were eleven, he went away on business and saw one of the posters that Dobson man kept leaving all over the place. One that Gillian had missed. And he worked out what we'd done.'

I want to collapse but there is nothing to lean on. I sway. 'He couldn't live with it.'

The sharp wail of a siren shatters the peace and the truce between us. Grace starts to cry again and, as I run to her, Mum's head snaps up. She raises the spade. 'I hate to have to do this, Bridget.' she says, and she brings the blade down. Blood splashes and I scream.

Mum leaves me in the room, standing alone with Grace, both of us muzzy with shock. She limps for the stairs, leaving bloody prints on each tread. There's a gash in her head that probably looks worse than it is.

I hear her open the door and the voices of the police as she tells them that I turned up, tried to take Grace, and attacked her with a spade.

I start to shake. 'Tom,' I call, weakly. 'Tom?' He doesn't answer. He *had* been there . . . hadn't he?

James Ward comes down the steps first. He looks at me holding Grace, then at the bloodied spade on the floor and he pulls out his cuffs.

'You're under arrest, Mrs Carlson,' he says. 'I don't know what you were thinking.'

'This isn't what it looks like.' I retreat, hugging Grace tightly. 'It didn't happen the way she said.' But my head is spinning. Tom *had* been here . . . hadn't he? But then, where was he? And Gillian Thornhill had been here too . . . hadn't she? But then, where was *she*? Mum *had* chased me . . . hadn't she? *She'd* had the spade . . . hadn't she? Or . . . had I chased her?

'Hand me the baby,' Ward says. Naomi is behind him. Mum stands at the top of the stairs, watching. There's a white towel pressed to her temple. It's already tie-dyed with crimson splotches.

'I–I didn't . . .'

Naomi side-steps around Ward. 'Hello, Bridget.'

I dig my face into Grace's curls.

'Bridget, you need to give Grace to me. You don't want to hurt her.'

'She needs a hospital.' I'm shivering now. 'She's been drugging her.'

Hasn't she?

'Who has?' Naomi says softly. She's reached me now and her hands are rising. She's touching Grace, carefully detaching her from me.

'Mum. She's been feeding us ketamine.'

Mum snorts loudly but Naomi doesn't turn around. 'Ketamine, is that right?'

'Where would I ever get such a thing?' Mum says. 'See what I mean? She's not sane.'

'From Gillian.' I stand very still as Naomi takes Grace. 'Dr Thornhill – she's a therapist.'

Naomi turns and hands Grace to Ward. He takes

her and his gaunt face sags with relief. He really thought I was going to hurt her and that he is saving the day.

'*I'll* take Grace,' Mum says as Naomi takes Ward's cuffs from him. 'We can continue this upstairs, in the kitchen. I can make tea.'

'Raise your hands, please,' Naomi says to me and she clicks the manacles around my wrists. I don't even watch her. I can't take my eyes from my daughter. She's curled up, quite still, in Ward's arms, as if she knows she's safe there. She's not even crying anymore.

'Don't let Mum take her,' I beg. 'I'm telling the truth.'

'Come along, Bridget. It'll be all right.' Naomi tugs me towards the door. My head pounds. If only there was a way to prove my story, to find out what is real?

My eyes fall on the cupboard. It's upright now and closed, as if it's never moved. I yank my arms from Naomi's hold.

Ward shouts and Naomi reaches for me but I lunge to the right and kick the door open. Nothing happens. I did hallucinate it, all of it. I touch my pocket and feel a small book.

You found me.

Then from the darkness in the back of the cupboard, the child Bridget topples into the light. She lands with her desiccated face towards Ward.

He half turns, protecting Grace from the sight with his body. 'What the *bloody shitting hell* is that?'

'Found you,' I say.

Chapter 31

Mum does not go quietly into custody. I watch with Ward as Naomi marches her away from us. He continues to hug Grace. The handcuffs still hold my wrists together.

'I'm sorry,' he says eventually, as Mum's shrieks fade from hearing. 'But I *am* going to have to take Grace to Social Services until this is all sorted out.'

'What about Tom's parents?' I ask, my eyes fixed on Bridget's small body. 'Can't they look after her?'

Ward sighs. 'I honestly don't know, Mrs Carlson. CPS may want to place her with a family they've used before. But first, if she really has been given ketamine, she'll have to go to hospital.'

I nod, tiredly, then I look at him. 'There's another body, under the patio. Mum's sister.'

Ward stares at me and Naomi returns. 'Let's get those cuffs off.' She unlocks the bracelets and I rub my wrist, the scar I'd received when fighting my kidnappers so long ago. I hit it on the side of the van when they pushed me into it. 'You'll have to come to the station and make a statement, I'm afraid. Your husband is waiting for you outside. He wanted to come in but, as this is a crime scene, we made him stay with his vehicle.'

'Wait . . . Tom *is* here?

'Weren't you talking to him?' Ward asks. 'He told us where you were.'

'Yes, but . . .' I'm shaking again but this time it isn't with fear. 'I thought I'd dreamed him. I thought . . . it's so hard to tell what's real.'

Naomi looks at Ward. 'You say your mum had you on ketamine too?'

I nod.

Naomi touches my shoulder. 'In the short term it can make you feel chilled, relaxed, compliant; that's why criminals use it as a date-rape drug. But it also alters your perceptions, makes you hallucinate, causes agitation, panic attacks, damage to short and long-term memory and depression.'

'Memory damage and . . . depression,' I echo. 'She's had me on it for half of my life.'

'I'm sorry, Bridget.' Naomi takes my arm. 'Let's get you out of here.'

'But how did you know where I was? How did Tom . . .?'

Ward steps around us and carries Grace up the stairs. Naomi leads me after him, careful to guide me around the bloody spade and withered corpse.

'You *called* Tom, do you remember that?'

'Yes. But my phone died.'

'The handset might have been dead, but *Find My iPhone* shows the last location.'

'It does?'

'As soon as he knew where you were, he called us.'

We're in the hallway now and I feel the painted eyes of Mum's parents on us as we walk towards the open front door. *They* started this, by murdering Mum's sister in front of her, by making her obsessed with perfection.

Tom is standing in the driveway, fidgeting anxiously. It's as if he's on starting blocks, desperate to run. As soon as he sees Grace in Ward's arms, it's like the shot he's been waiting for has been fired. He lunges and Ward lets him take Grace. The moment I see them together, the world falls back into place.

Then Ward takes Grace back. 'I'm sorry, Mr Carlson,' he says. His hooded eyes flick between us. 'CPS are on their way. We'll get everything sorted out as fast as we can, but honestly,' he looks at me, 'your wife needs you more than your daughter does right now.'

Tom turns to me but I can't shift the pictures from my mind: Tom was with Trisha. He betrayed me.

When I stumble, Naomi takes my elbow and holds me upright.

'I thought you were in Chesterfield,' I rasp.

Tom shakes his head. 'I came home when I got your letter. I hoped you might go back to the flat to pick up your things or come to talk things through . . .'

'The letter wasn't from me.'

He pauses. Then he jerks his chin towards the police car. '*Her*?'

I follow his gesture. Mum is sitting in the back of the vehicle, her head hanging, her shoulders hunched. She looks old. 'Yes.'

Naomi helps me towards Tom's car. 'Can the two of you meet us at the police station?'

Tom nods. 'I'll drive us.'

I lean my head against the passenger window, tired, watching the world flash by. It's not as fast as a train but everything's just as blurred. My arms are empty, my chest hollow. Grace is in the car in front of us but it feels as though she's a hundred miles away.

I know that Tom wants to know what went on in that house but talking feels like so much effort. I'm going to have to tell the whole story at the station anyway.

'I know you're having an affair,' I mutter eventually.

Tom turns to stare at me and then back to watch the traffic. 'Where did you get that from? Your mum?'

'There are photos,' I rasp. Terror has acted like sandpaper on my vocal cords. 'You and Trisha. You were together at university and you're together now.'

'Jesus.' Tom takes his eyes from the road again, 'I didn't think . . . I don't know what you've seen, Bridge, but it isn't an affair. I would never cheat. Not . . . now.'

'But you did at uni?'

He focuses back on the traffic as we turn left. 'You overlapped by a few weeks, that's all. As soon as I started falling in love with you, I ended it with Trish. Honestly.'

'And now?' I think of the photo, of his arm on her back.

Tom sighs. 'Trish got in touch via Facebook a

couple of months ago. She's just had a baby, Bridge, and she's moved into the area. She saw that I was staying at home with Grace, so she suggested we meet up. You know I've been lonely, I told you that. We're just friends. We meet up every week or so for a walk in the park or a coffee. She works in publishing. We talk about my writing.'

Again, I think of the picture. There was no other pram in shot but it could have been taken at an angle that cut it out.

'You promise, you haven't . . .?'

'No!' Tom punches the steering wheel. 'Your mum was just trying to force us apart! I love *you*, Bridge. I fancy *you*. I don't even *see* other women.'

'*That's* not true!'

'They aren't invisible.' He laughs shortly. 'But they might as well be. No other woman turns me on like you do, challenges me, makes me think like you do. There's no other woman like you, Bridget.' He shakes his head as we turn into the police station car park. 'I know these last few months have been hard but . . . we'll be all right, won't we?'

His cheeks glisten and I realise with a shock that he's crying.

There's been so much tragedy. Two families shattered now: the Monahans and the Dobsons. I want to protect the Carlsons. I want to find out what fighting for our marriage looks like.

I touch his hand, where he is clutching the gear stick as if it's a lifebelt. 'Can you call the estate agent and ask if that house in Clitheroe is still available?'

Chapter 32

I spend a week in the hospital. Ketamine withdrawal is brutal, and I need professional supervision. I think back to the first month in university, when I'd felt like my world was falling apart, and realise that this is not the first time it's happened.

I think about the diary I found hidden under my windowsill. About the times I said I felt sick. It isn't even the *second* time it's happened.

It's *lucky* that Grace isn't with me as I vacillate between shakes, rage, fatigue and nausea. I can't sleep and, as I prowl the ward at night, I constantly hear things. The growl of a white van, a baby crying and Gillian's fading voice: *happy with what you have.*

Eventually, I even out and my doctor prescribes me some sleeping pills to help with the insomnia. I refuse more therapy.

I'm trying to shake my obsession with the news. I don't want to see my story on the Internet or hear it on the BBC, but I'm walking past a screen when a headline catches my eye: *Kidnap Victim Found.*

The story is about Vihaan Sharma, the little boy who vanished from Peterborough. His mum sobs as she tells the interviewer that he is back home. Some part of me is still convinced that there *was* a kidnapping ring, numbers don't lie, but when the reporter reveals that he had been taken by a family friend, I'm nothing but relieved.

When Tom brings me home we find a police car parked in front of the flat.

Naomi Shaw gets out. 'Sorry I didn't call ahead, and I don't like to interrupt your homecoming.' She slams her car door. 'But I thought you might want an update.'

'Come in.' Tom unlocks the flat and gestures for her to go in ahead of us.

I hesitate. It feels like forever since I've been home. Our stuff is in the hallway, familiar things, family pictures. But it all feels strange, alien. Grace isn't there. She's staying with Charlie and June right now. It isn't home without her.

I take the final step inside and run my fingers over the wallpaper and the handle of the cupboard where Grace's pram should be. The living room door is closed but the kitchen is open. Tom and Naomi are inside waiting for me.

'Can I sit?' Naomi asks. 'I've been on my feet all day.'

'Sure.' Tom gestures and we all take a stool.

'Right, well.' She removes her hat and puts it on the breakfast bar. Her hair is looser than I've seen it. She looks tired, her freckles standing out like pen marks. 'First of all, we've been keeping the press away from this but we can't hold them off forever. You'll be getting calls from reporters soon. Especially now that . . .' She shakes her head. 'Sorry, this is a *lot*.' She opens a notebook filled with her tiny neat hand-writing. 'Right, first of all, your mum has been charged with your original kidnapping, as well as unlawfully imprisoning you more recently. Her defence will argue that you went to stay with her voluntarily but don't worry about that right now. She's also been charged with the death of her natural daughter, Bridget Monahan. The coroner says the cause of death was abusive head trauma, so it seems likely that the story she told you was the truth, or a version of it.'

I slump on the stool. I want to hate her for what she's done, but . . . she's my mum.

Naomi looks at Tom. 'Can I get a glass of water?'

Tom leaps up and pours her a drink. She sips and looks at me.

'You were right about the patio. There was a body – a nineteen-year-old female. We're still waiting on the results but the victim was found with a belt still looped around her neck, so we're operating on the assumption that she was strangled.'

'It's Abigail.' I take Tom's hand. 'Abigail Monahan. Her parents did it. If you speak to Gillian Thornhill, she'll tell you—'

Naomi bites her lip and looks from Tom back to me. 'Abigail's wasn't the only body in the garden, Bridget.' She picks up her pen, then puts it down. 'Gillian Thornhill was buried in a flowerbed near the oak tree.'

Tom squeezes my hand as I start to shiver. Mum

killed her. Gave her a spiked drink, waited until I went upstairs. Did she do it in front of Grace or did she take her outside first? I hope she took her outside. I hope she thought of what Grace might see.

'Her niece, Electra Olsen, was next of kin.' Naomi gives me a moment to recover, then keeps on talking. 'She's told us that her aunt asked her to follow you, to try to scare you, to stop you talking about kidnappings. She told her you were in danger and so she went along with it. Electra says she tried to talk her aunt into speaking to us, but Gillian Thornhill was totally devoted to your mother and, we believe, she was afraid we'd find out about her role in your kidnapping. She was trapped.' She looks at me. 'We aren't charging Electra with anything at this juncture.' She looks at me. 'Unless you want to . . .'

'No.' I shake my head. 'She was trying to help by making sure I didn't trigger Mum.'

'Perhaps.' Naomi closes her notebook. 'We're going to be sorting this mess out for a while.'

'And my DNA results?' I lean forward. 'Are they back yet?'

Naomi reaches into her pocket and removes two envelopes. 'They're back and I think you know what they say.'

'I'm Frances Dobson.'

Naomi hands me the first envelope and I open it. Tom reads over my shoulder.

Based on the analysis of fifteen independent DNA markers, the donor of Sample A has been confirmed as the biological father of the donor of Sample B because three or more of the DNA components from Sample A are present in the DNA profile of Sample B.

Naomi nods. 'Grant Dobson is your father. He wanted to see you, but honestly, he's ashamed of your last encounter; of his drinking, of what he's become, I suppose. He sent you this instead.' She gives me the second envelope.

Dear Frances

I keep thinking that this is a dream and I'm going to wake up but Mick tells me the police have spoken to him too and that you're alive. If only you'd found out the truth earlier. Your mum is dead now but she never stopped loving you. Neither did I. I'm sorry that I'm a useless drunk. I'm sorry I can't be the father I'm sure you were hoping to find. I hope you've had a good life.

Tom looks at me and his eyes are full of tears.

The police say I've got a granddaughter. If it's okay, I'd like to meet her. But not like this, not with my liver pickled and my brains gone to mush. Mick's going to help me. I'm going to try and stop the drinking, if I can. I want to get to know you, who you became. I want to know my grandbaby. Someone took my chance to be a father to you but if I can be a grandfather, that'll do me fine.

There's no signature, as if he didn't know how to sign off.

I take Tom's hand and he squeezes mine, while looking at Naomi. 'Do you have his phone number?'

Naomi hands over a final piece of paper.

I smile. 'Let's send him a picture of Grace,' I say.

Chapter 33

Moira is sitting in our living room. Her briefcase is by her feet and she has Grace on her knee. We've signed a bunch of paperwork. Grace is under a child protection order but Moira says it's a formality at this point. She trusts us.

Charlie and June are in the kitchen. Moira has asked Tom and me to sit on chairs by the window. Grace watches me, and her eyes are filled with suspicion. She is clinging onto Moira and glaring out from under her lashes. Dobbie is clutched in one fist, Frankie in the other.

'Why won't she come to us?' I'm trying not to cry. I don't want to scare her.

Moira looks apologetic. 'It can take them that way. What she's been through . . .' She swallows. 'I wish I'd seen it when I dropped by your mum's. I should have realised that Grace was more docile than she should have been. I'm sorry.' Moira puts Grace down on the floor. Grace tries to hide behind her long skirt.

I get down on my knees and start to crawl. I take it slowly, moving across the room, past Grace's empty bouncer, until I reach her. I don't make any sudden moves. I don't grab her, although I want to. 'Grace, it's Mummy.' She presses her face into Moira's calf. 'Grace, I'm so sorry.'

She glowers out at me.

'You're home now.'

She still refuses to come near.

'Are you playing hide and seek?' I put my hands over my face; she used to love *Peepo*. 'Where's Grace?' I lower my hands. She scowls. I cover my face again. 'Where's Grace?' I lower my hands. 'There she is!'

She is looking with interest now.

'Where's Grace?' I cover my face.

'Don't move, Bridge,' Tom whispers. So, I don't. A moment later hot little hands cover my trembling ones and tug them away from my face. Grace is smiling now.

'Found you,' I whisper.

And she crawls into my arms.

Acknowledgements

When I was nine years old, my French teacher gave everyone in the class a French name; the one closest to their own. John became Jean, Michael became Michel, Sophie became Sophie, Angela became Angela, Bryony became Brigitte.

This is a novel with an unreliable narrator who has mental health issues. She isn't me any more than my name is Brigitte, but she is close to me, close enough for me to decide to name her Bridget.

I myself have long suffered from anxiety and depression, for which I now take medication, having resisted doing so for many years.

In particular, after having my daughter in 2005 (and suffering from osteoarthritis that resulted in a total hip replacement in 2007), I was one of the ten per cent of recently delivered women who go on to develop postnatal depression. To avoid medication I tried counselling, CBT, hypnotherapy, reflexology, acupuncture, all of which helped, but none of which worked in isolation. I had this notion that taking drugs would represent a failure, would mean I'd given in, would twist me into someone barely recognisable.

389

But refusing to take anything while attempting to deal with two young children, one of whom had a dairy allergy, lactose intolerance, silent reflux and literally slept for no more than two hours a night, while depressed, anxious, insomniac and in pain and also working on my burgeoning YA writing career, was retrospectively the most foolish thing I've ever done.

It wasn't until three years later that I finally admitted that, without drugs, I was likely to lose my battle with the illness.

I was lucky – I didn't do it alone. Andy and his family (Pat and Charles, Gill and Ros) were always there on the occasions when I admitted that I needed them. I had an excellent health visitor, Rosie Gay (now retired, sadly), who diagnosed and supported me. I had a brilliant doctor, Tom Lösel (now at the Middlewood Partnership), who literally turned up on my doorstep after I had a breakdown and marched me to his surgery so that he could prescribe the magic bullets that saved me. I am so grateful to these medical practitioners.

I know that many people, especially new mothers, are not as lucky as I was. Just before I had my son, a new mother of twins in my local area jumped from a motorway bridge, and every so often I see a news story which breaks my heart: a new mother whose depression and fear has seen her take her own life. And it isn't just mothers; fathers too can suffer from postnatal depression. We have a way to go yet to make sure that signs of depression in new parents are caught early enough and treated appropriately. Budget cuts don't help.

So, this is to acknowledge the help that I had, the

support that I had and the measures that were in place to help me. This is to acknowledge that some mothers (and fathers) aren't as lucky as I am. This is to acknowledge that I got through a hard time and came out of it with an amazing family. This is to acknowledge that I am lucky.

While I have you here, I would also like to thank my incredibly kind sources: Jon Wilkie (social services) and Joseph Fourie (police) – thank you for your time, patience and expertise; my agent, Catherine Pellegrino, for believing in me and my writing; my excellent and incisive editor, Molly Walker-Sharp, for taking me on, and the rest of the awesome team at Avon, whose work has put this novel into your hands. It's great to be a part of team Avon.

And thank you, reader for getting this far. Do follow me on Twitter if you'd like to keep up with my news: @BryonyPearce. And if you ever feel that you yourself need extra help, or you know someone who you suspect might be struggling with their mental health, there are numbers you can call:

APNI (Association for Post Natal Illness): apni.org/ 0207 386 0868

Samaritans: 116 123

NHS Mental Health Crisis Team: 0800 169 0398
NHS Let's Talk: 0800 073 2200

Baby Buddy App (NHS approved, 24-hour text support)

DadPad app

Stay safe and well.